T0026653

Also by Juliet Marillier

The Warrior Bards Novels

THE HARP OF KINGS
A DANCE WITH FATE

The Blackthorn & Grim Novels

DREAMER'S POOL
TOWER OF THORNS
DEN OF WOLVES

The Sevenwaters Novels

DAUGHTER OF THE FOREST
SON OF THE SHADOWS
CHILD OF THE PROPHECY

HEIR TO SEVENWATERS
SEER OF SEVENWATERS
FLAME OF SEVENWATERS

The Light Isles Novels

WOLFSKIN
FOXMASK

The Bridei Chronicles

THE DARK MIRROR
BLADE OF FORTRIU
THE WELL OF SHADES

HEART'S BLOOD

PRICKLE MOON

MOTHER THORN

For Young Adults
The Wildwood Novels

WILDWOOD DANCING
CYBELE'S SECRET

The Shadowfell Novels

SHADOWFELL
RAVEN FLIGHT
THE CALLER

BEAUTIFUL

A
SONG
of FLIGHT

—◦◦◦◦◦—

Juliet Marillier

ACE
New York

ACE

Published by Berkley

An imprint of Penguin Random House LLC

penguinrandomhouse.com

Copyright © 2021 by Juliet Marillier

Penguin Random House supports copyright. Copyright fuels creativity, encourages diverse voices, promotes free speech, and creates a vibrant culture. Thank you for buying an authorized edition of this book and for complying with copyright laws by not reproducing, scanning, or distributing any part of it in any form without permission. You are supporting writers and allowing Penguin Random House to continue to publish books for every reader.

ACE is a registered trademark and the A colophon is a trademark of Penguin Random House LLC.

Library of Congress Cataloging-in-Publication Data

Names: Marillier, Juliet, author.
Title: A song of flight / Juliet Marillier.
Description: First edition. | New York : Ace, 2021. | Series: Warrior bards
Identifiers: LCCN 2021010459 (print) | LCCN 2021010460 (ebook) |
ISBN 9780451492821 (trade paperback) | ISBN 9780451492838 (ebook)
Subjects: GSAFD: Fantasy fiction.
Classification: LCC PR9619.3.M26755 S67 2021 (print) |
LCC PR9619.3.M26755 (ebook) | DDC 823/.914—dc23
LC record available at https://lccn.loc.gov/2021010459
LC ebook record available at https://lccn.loc.gov/2021010460

First Edition: September 2021

Printed in the United States of America
2nd Printing

Book design by Tiffany Estreicher

In memoriam
Aiki Flinthart
1969–2021
Writer, editor, warrior, bard, most generous of souls

CHARACTER LIST

Pronunciations are given for the more difficult names. *Kh* is a soft guttural sound, as in the Scottish *loch*.

COURT OF DALRIADA
Oran: king of Dalriada
Flidais: his wife, queen of Dalriada
Donagan: Oran's adviser and friend
Saran: lawman
Frassach: physician

WINTERFALLS
Aolu (*eh*-loo): prince of Dalriada
Galen: his bodyguard and companion; brother to Liobhan and Brocc
Baodán (*beh*-dahn): master-at-arms
Finnian: steward
Fraoch (frehkh): man-at-arms
Grian (*gree*-an): seamstress
Oisín (uh-*sheen*): a wandering druid
Blackthorn: healer and wisewoman; mother of Galen, Liobhan, and Brocc

Grim: her husband, a master thatcher; father of Galen, Liobhan, and Brocc
Trusty: family dog

SWAN ISLAND

Liobhan (*lee*-von)
Dau (rhymes with *now*)
Illann
Archu (*ar*-khoo)
Brigid (breed)
Hrothgar
Elka
Haki
Cionnaola (kin-*eh*-la): leader of the Swan Island community
Cuan
Garbh (gorv)
Yann
Eimear (*ee*-mer)
Conor
Criodan: island druid
Guss: his helper
Odar: boatbuilder
Cairenn: boatbuilder
Deirdre: herbalist
Justice: Dau's dog

DARKWATER

Almha (*al*-va): chieftain
Sciath (*skee*-a): her adviser
Fursa: steward

ELDERBROOK

Ferchar: saddler
Colm
Morna
Cian (*kee*-an): traveling musician

BROTHERHOOD OF THE DOBHAR-CHÚ (*DOOWAR-KHOO*)

Scoithín (sku-*heen*)
Ruairi
Sealbhach (sal-vakh)
Muna
Finchán

OTHERWORLD

Brocc
Eirne (*ehr*-nyeh)
Niamh (*nee*-av)
Rowan
True
Nightshade
Moon-Fleet
Nimble-Swift
Thistle-Coat
Gentle-Foot
Moth-Weed
Dandelion
Shadow
Watcher
Storyteller
Mother Ash
Robin
Hazel

Thorny
Conmael

AND ALSO

Íobhar: a Christian monk; Dau's second brother
Seanan: Dau's eldest brother
Lord Scannal: Dau's father
Dáire: a farmer

1

AOLU

I want to talk to the druid. Brother Oisín is an old man, but age hasn't slowed him much. He walks long distances and doesn't always keep to the roads. He is solitary by choice, loving wild places, praying alone, meeting with other folk from time to time to offer teaching or advice or help. At such meetings, if one is lucky, Oisín will tell tales of long ago, stories of wonder and terror, of joy and heartbreak. His tales are magical. They challenge the mind and refresh the spirit.

We are fortunate. Every spring, the druid spends time at Winterfalls, in a hut deep in the forest, not far from my holding. I have offered him one of the cottages that lie within my outer wall—we generally keep one available for visitors—but he prefers to be out in the woods, where birds and creatures and the ever-changing trees are all the companions he needs. My household provides him with supplies, and every so often he walks down to visit us, for he knows I am fond of poetry, philosophy, and the like.

This spring there has been no sign of him. No word. As time passes my concern grows. So, on a particularly fine day, I suggest to Galen that we should ride out as far as the druid's hut to discover if Oisín has been there.

Galen reacts in keeping with his official role as my bodyguard. "What about the Crow Folk?" he asks. "You know they've been spotted in that part of the forest."

"All the more reason to check if all's well with him."

"You could send Baodán with some guards. No need to risk your own safety."

Baodán is my master-at-arms. We both know he won't relish being given such a job. Everyone fears the Crow Folk with their random attacks, their wildness. For a long while this area was free of them, but of recent times they have appeared in our northern forests, and we must be careful. "No need for Baodán's men to risk themselves simply because the prince happens to care about a druid's welfare," I reply, catching the hint of a smile on Galen's face. He's been my companion and dearest friend since we were twelve years old, and we know each other very well. "Just you and me, a leisurely ride, a stop for refreshments somewhere. The weather's beautiful. Come on, Galen. I'll teach you a song on the way."

He lifts his brows, twists his mouth into a grimace. My friend lacks the remarkable musical talent of his siblings, though he can, in fact, hold a tune passably well.

"What if I promise to turn back if the Crow Folk appear particularly menacing?" I ask. "Not that they will, my friend. You're fearsome enough to frighten away dragons." Galen's a very tall man, strongly built, with a shaven head and a luxuriant, fiery red beard. He doesn't simply guard me. Over the years he's made sure I can defend myself, handle a horse capably, and generally get myself out of trouble. If not for him, I'd have spent most of my time in my library reading old tales and writing poetry, and I'd be far more of a weakling than any prince should be. One day I'll be king of Dalriada. A king must be a man of many parts, even if his bent is more toward scholarship than action.

"All right," Galen says, grinning. "But keep to your word. If I say we should turn back, we turn back."

The day is indeed warm. When we've covered a fair distance, we stop in a clearing among birches to let our horses rest awhile and drink from a stream. No Crow Folk here; they'll be in the upper reaches of the forest, and we have not yet climbed far. It's good to be alone, just the two of us without the bustle of a royal household around us. I have a council tomorrow with the local landholders, at which I must listen to their grievances and arbitrate in any disagreements. I suppose it is good practice for the time when I become king, though I fervently hope my father has many long years of healthy life ahead of him. I love the quiet of Winterfalls; I love being my own master, with my own household where we lack the formalities and protocols of court. But I love still more the times when Galen and I can get away on our own.

We eat a little of the food we brought with us, then pack up the rest for later. If Oisín is indeed at the hut, he may appreciate a share. We sit on the rocks in the sun, and I teach Galen a song about a man who got three wishes from a clurichaun and squandered them all on silly things. The moral of the story being, when dealing with uncanny folk, think before you speak. There's a chorus all made up of nonsense words, a tongue twister, and we're in fits of laughter trying to sing this when Galen goes suddenly still.

"Wha—" is all I have time for. He's on his feet, drawing his weapon. Men are moving in from under the trees, men with cloths tied over their faces and weapons in their hands.

"Run!" shouts Galen. I obey, sprinting across the clearing, diving into the cover of the forest. We've rehearsed this kind of thing over and over. He's drummed it into me that I must obey him instantly, no questions asked. Shouting breaks out behind me, the clash of metal, the thud of blows, and a scream. Something huge and shadowy flies over my head. Crow Folk. They're here, too. Galen. Oh, Galen. My heart pounding in fright, I risk one look back.

He's surrounded, slashing, kicking, getting his shoulder in, woefully outnumbered. And as I stare, my heart doing a wild dance in my chest, two Crow Folk join the melee, diving, pecking. It's a bloody maelstrom in which I cannot tell attacker from victim, bird from human. Blinded by tears, I slip my talisman from my neck and drop it on the forest floor. "Be safe, dear heart," I whisper, and take to my heels. I cannot save him. I can only do as I know he would wish, and try to save myself. I run, I run, dodging trees and bushes, slipping in mud, stumbling over rocks and fallen branches. When my breath is almost gone, when my head starts to spin, someone—some*thing*—is beside me, a presence felt rather than seen. Something touches my arm, but when I look, there is only shadow. My breath fails. I fall. Down, down, too far down. I land with a jolt. Pain spears through my ankle, then all is dark.

2
LIOBHAN

W e're halfway up the cliff when Elka spots a boat coming in and casually lifts a hand to point it out. "Ours, yes?" she asks.

"Both hands on!" My heart's thumping. I take a slow breath in and out. "Remember the rule: two hands, one foot. Or two feet, one hand. Keep your attention on what you're doing. Now move your left foot. That's it." I'm watching as closely as I can while maintaining my own position. It's Elka's first climb without ropes and, for a little, her life is in my hands.

Being a trainer is harder than I expected. Since Elka arrived on Swan Island I've worked with her on a wide range of physical skills. I've taught her quite a few unarmed combat moves. She's good; she wouldn't be here if she wasn't. But I'm learning how hard it is to put a trainee in a situation of risk. It's not at all the same as taking a risk myself.

"Now we're moving up and to the right. Long stretch with the right arm—don't move your foot, make sure of your hand grip first. Good. Now the right foot up to that crack, toes in, check it's secure. And left foot up." Elka is shortish for a Swan Island warrior, barely up to my shoulder, but muscular and sturdy, and what she lacks in reach she makes up for in strength. I have to admire her calm confidence.

"Right, you're coming up to the crevice. Ease in as far as you can. Good. Now work your way slowly up. You're on your own for a bit. Call when you get to the ledge, then I'll follow. Don't do anything stupid."

Elka pauses half-in and half-out of the narrow split in the cliff face. Birds are passing very close to us, another distraction, though we've been careful not to climb near any roosting sites. "You are never stupid, Liobhan?"

"Focus!" I've done so many stupid things I've lost count. Things that were risky not just for myself but for people I care about. I've spoken out when silence would be far wiser. During my training to join the Swan Island community, I stretched the rules as far as they could possibly go. Sometimes I did things my own way when we were supposed to work as a team. There was that time when I leaped out of a tree and over a wall of spikes. Probably best forgotten, though I made it in one piece. And without that crazy episode we might not have succeeded in our mission. "Up you go," I tell her. "Don't rush it, it's not a race. If this were a real mission, there might be a big man with an ax waiting to meet you at the top."

"Or a big woman." Elka's voice is almost drowned by the screaming of the gulls.

"Either way, you want to be ready. Ignore the birds. They're helpful. Their racket stops your enemy from hearing you coming."

I wait for her call—"Clear!"—then I follow. I wonder again why Archu, who's our chief combat trainer, has given me the job of training Elka. Not solely because she's a woman, I'm sure. We're all treated as equals here, that's part of the code. And it's not as if there's a lack of older, more experienced tutors on Swan Island, where we teach not only the art of fighting but also strategy, mapmaking and path-finding, and a number of special skills required for covert missions. Who knows when we might be required to scale a cliff in a hurry, or make a quick escape in a leaking boat, or get through a series of locked doors with armed opponents on our tail? This sort of training keeps our bodies and minds ready. We're called upon by leaders from all over Erin to undertake missions their regular household men-at-arms can't perform for them. Covert missions. Perilous missions. Often, missions that step nimbly past the rules of law. There's a reason our community is housed in a place that's hard to reach. There's a reason we're trained to keep secrets under extreme pressure.

"Right," I say, reaching the narrow ledge where Elka stands, her pose entirely relaxed as she rests her back against the cliff face and gazes out northward over the sea. She has both hands touching the rock, but that's not a lot of help when you're facing outward. I bet she had her arms folded just before I came into view. One step forward and she'd plunge to her death. "Turn carefully, then head up and to your left. The overhang is about one body length above us. Ready?"

"Ready."

She's been up this pitch before, with ropes. She knows her way. But I give the instructions anyway, because people can freeze partway through a climb. Their minds can go suddenly blank. I don't think that will happen with Elka.

"Go, then."

We haven't come out on our own, of course. Hrothgar is at the top of the cliff, picked not only because I trust him, but also because he speaks Elka's native tongue. She's not entirely fluent in Irish yet, though she gets by, thanks to the somewhat hybrid version of our language that is spoken on the island. The school of warcraft has existed here for a long time now, and we draw in recruits from far beyond the shores of Erin. Over the years the languages brought by new arrivals have added words and expressions to our daily speech, and that has made life both easier and richer for the inhabitants of the island and the smaller group in our mainland settlement, a short but often turbulent distance away by boat.

I watch Elka as she climbs to the overhang; as she hesitates briefly, craning her neck. I don't call out a reminder to go around, not over. This wouldn't be a good time to startle her.

She inches across, flawless in her adherence to my instructions. When she's almost around the overhang and moving out of sight again, I follow. The gulls pass above me, screeching. I ignore them. I move one hand, one foot. One foot, one hand. Balance and flow. Breathe. Wait. Move again. When I'm past the overhang I hear Hrothgar's voice from above, greeting Elka, helping her up the very last bit. Good. She's done it. There's a satisfaction in seeing her succeed. Men outnumber women greatly in the Swan Island community, and among the warriors the disparity is even more striking. So I welcomed her arrival, though I've failed to have much conversation with her beyond what's necessary for training. In fact, I've hardly seen her talking to anyone except Hrothgar, and she does need to practice her Irish. Perhaps, as trainer, I'm supposed to work on that as well.

I'm about two body lengths from the top of the cliff when my right foot misses its target. I curse as a cascade of small rock fragments rattles down. With my heart pounding to an annoying degree, I tighten my hand grip.

Hrothgar calls, "All right, Liobhan?"

I'm scrabbling for a fresh foothold. I swear again, loudly.

The rope Hrothgar's fastened at the top snakes down beside me, not quite close enough to reach without taking a leap of faith. I'm still trying to find a spot for my right foot. I can hear my own breathing, and it's not the steady, controlled sound it should be. A moment later Elka appears, climbing down carefully if a little more quickly than is wise.

"Hold still," she says. "Here." She edges toward me sideways, and with her comes the rope. She's managed to get her shoulder underneath it, perhaps with some assistance from Hrothgar up above.

I allow my right foot to find the purchase I've known was there all the time. "Thanks," I say. I take a few breaths. What just happened was planned, but that didn't make it any less frightening. "You go on up, I'll be fine."

"First you, Liobhan," says Elka.

I don't point out which of us is the trainer and which the trainee. That's for later, when we debrief. I climb the rest of the way, not using the rope, and wait with Hrothgar.

"Next time we try that, you can do the climbing part," I murmur.

My comrade doesn't reply, because Elka is at the top now, and I'm helping her over the edge. But perhaps she heard me, because once she's on level ground she turns her gaze on me—she has startling, ice-blue eyes—and says, "You scare me for nothing? Is all a play?"

"It doesn't matter whether it was a play or a real slip," I tell her. "Either way, it was a test of how you respond to an emergency. You did well. You showed courage, you made a decision quickly—there wasn't time for you and Hrothgar to debate who should do what, because in those few moments I could have fallen—and you kept your control and focus right through."

Hrothgar is coiling up the rope. He makes no comment.

"But . . ." Elka wears a small frown. "No need for this. You tell me, be careful. I am careful. What if you fall, doing this?"

"I've been up and down this cliff a hundred times, Elka. Yes, there's always a chance of messing it up, and if you do, you're dead. But this is Swan Island, and when we go out into the world on a mission, the risks we take are entirely real. Our training methods reflect that." When she stares at me, her brows up, I add, "I needed to know how you would respond in that situation—a comrade in danger, only a moment to act. If you'd been aware it was only an exercise you might have acted quite differently. Told me to stop play-acting and treat you like a grown woman, maybe."

Hrothgar says something to Elka in Norse, perhaps a translation of what I just told her. She nods, looks at me again with grudging respect.

"We're done for now," I say. "Before we go back, think over the whole exercise. Tell me what you got right and what you could have improved." I take a long drink from the waterskin Hrothgar offers.

"Two hands, one foot," Elka says, flipping her wheaten-fair plait back over her shoulder. "One hand, two feets. At all times, yes?"

"Except when you can't. Sometimes you have to make that leap of faith. You need to know your body well and trust your instincts. But avoid that leap if you can. I'd rather not have to explain your sudden demise to your family. Any further comments on your performance?"

"I do again tomorrow, I make perfect, yes?"

Hrothgar's bearded features crease into a grin. He sees me looking and rapidly assumes a deadly serious expression. I suppress a smile. "Each time you do this, aim to improve on the last time," I tell my trainee. "Nobody gets perfect just like *that."* I snap my fingers. "You do it in small steps. Not that anyone's ever quite perfect at anything. There's always more to learn. By the way, don't turn to face the sea when you're on a narrow ledge, unless there's a better justification than admiring the view."

Elka clears her throat.

"Anything else?" I ask.

She starts to say something, then thinks better of it and shakes her head. She looks crestfallen; disappointed.

"You did well today, Elka. Strength excellent, control very good. Your fast response when you thought I was in trouble was impressive, and I did notice that when you came down with the rope you followed all the climbing rules. If I'd thought you lacked the skill for that exercise, I wouldn't have tried it."

She dips her head in awkward recognition, then we head on back to the settlement. Where it seems a boat has arrived from the mainland, because I'm greeted by a familiar friend who runs to me with tail wagging and fearsome mouth open in a slobbery grin. The big brindled dog sits in front of me without any command—he wants to jump up, but he's been trained not to. Every inch of him is quivering.

"Good boy, Justice. Who's my best boy, then?" Justice does not live on Swan Island, though he's allowed to visit—both he and Dau live in the mainland settlement. When Dau and I returned from our extraordinary stay in his father's home, we brought the dog with us. Justice had been used for fighting and when we first saw him he was a cowering mess. Dau bought him for the princely sum of five coppers. He put remarkable patience and skill into rehabilitating the terrified animal—you'd never know, watching Justice close his eyes in bliss as I scratch behind his ears, how shut-down he was back then.

If Justice is on the island now, Dau must be here, too. I wasn't expecting that. Dau works mostly on the mainland, helping Brigid with spy training. Handy for Dau and me, now we're a couple. It's understood on Swan Island that intimate relationships between members of the warrior band don't happen, or shouldn't happen, the main reason being that they can create problems when you're out on a mission. If you're attached to someone in that way you're not going to be able to make cool-headed decisions when that person is at risk. Some of the warriors are married to nonfighting members of the community—the people who provide all the services that keep a place like this going. Dau and I broke the rules not once, with Justice, but twice. There was no way we could hide how we felt about each other. People could see it as soon as we came back from that grueling time at Oakhill. Our relationship meant sacrificing the opportunity to work together on future missions. In my heart of hearts, I suspect we will be sent on the same team again at some point. Though relatively new to the warrior band, we're both good at what we do.

For now, Dau shares one of the cottages in the mainland settlement with Illann, who works with the horses. I live and work mostly on the island, reporting to Archu. But when I'm over on the mainland, Illann tactfully takes himself away to the sleeping quarters in the Barn, the place where spy training happens, and Dau and I have the cottage to ourselves. Archu finds reasons to send me over there quite often, and is generally happy to let me stay more than one night. It's enough, barely. Dau and I never saw ourselves settling down together in domestic bliss and raising a brood of children. We love our work too much for that. But when we're apart we miss each other with an ache that's not just of the body, but heart-deep.

"Who'd have thought it, Justice?" I murmur to the dog. "Him and me. Took against each other the moment we met. Fierce rivals all through the training. And now look at us." I straighten, seeing figures walking up the path from Swan Island's small jetty, where one of the ferries is moored. Inevitably, my eye is drawn first to Dau: a tall, straight-backed man of my own age, with golden hair. He's been described more than once as resembling a handsome prince from an old tale. With him is an older, leaner man: Illann. Justice runs back toward them, but I wait. Two others are coming behind them. There's Brigid, who's in charge of activities at the Barn, and walking beside her is a middle-aged man in plain, good riding clothes. I recognize him as King Oran's adviser and friend, Master Donagan. We seldom allow outsiders onto Swan Island, but as a trusted member of the king's household, Donagan is an exception to the rule. If he's here in person something significant must have happened. I give Dau a wave and a smile, then whistle for Justice to come back to me.

I greet them as they walk past. Illann nods acknowledgment. Dau stops for long enough to grasp my hand and give me a chaste kiss on the cheek—we've learned to keep our feelings under tight control in public—then the four of them head on toward the community buildings. Might be a while before I find out what's happening.

Elka's still close by, and so is Hrothgar; they're conversing in their own tongue, and I understand only a word or two.

"Bathhouse first, then you can take a break," I tell my trainee. Unlike me and Dau, Elka didn't come here as part of a group of aspiring fighters competing for places. She arrived on her own, recommended by some fellow who knows Haki, our trainer in maritime combat. The elders don't often run the competitive training that weeds out the less able. Places on the island are seldom available, and it's more usual for aspiring fighters to make their own way here, and to be taken on if they can show they have the right skills and attitude, and if there's room. Some of the new fighters are folk of mature age, and they haven't all led lives of honor and virtue in the past. But the code we live by, a code established by the outlawed warrior who set up the place, means a person can be accepted provided they set their past behind them and start again in a spirit of honesty, respect for others, and readiness to put their whole energy into the work of the island. That code keeps the community strong. It unites us as comrades for life.

When Elka and I emerge from the bathhouse, Illann is waiting for me outside.

"Cionnaola wants you," he says. Cionnaola is head of the island community, a much-respected elder. "There's news from court."

The look on Illann's face worries me, and so does his tone. "Can you tell me more?" I ask.

"We'll talk behind closed doors."

Quite a formidable group is gathered in the room used for private discussions: Cionnaola with three other island elders—Archu, Brigid, Cuan—along with Master Donagan and Dau. Illann ushers me in and Cionnaola gestures for both of us to sit down. All eyes are on me. I'm suddenly cold. I hadn't considered that whatever's happened might affect me personally. My parents live very close to one of the royal residences.

"Liobhan," says Archu, "we have some news for you. It concerns your brother Galen. He's been injured."

"Go on," I say into the silence that follows. I feel my nails digging into my palms, and with some effort relax my hands. I catch Dau's eye, see his nod of reassurance, and make myself breathe slowly. Galen, my big brother. Bodyguard, companion, and close personal friend to the prince of Dalriada. I worry a lot about my other brother, Brocc, who chose to live in the realm of the uncanny. But Galen? He's never in trouble. He held my hand as I learned to walk. He taught me to stand up for myself. Galen's invincible.

Master Donagan clears his throat. "Liobhan, I have to tell you that Prince Aolu and Galen were attacked while out riding in the forest south of Winterfalls. They were on their own, so the household was not alerted to a problem until late afternoon, when they did not return as expected. A search party was dispatched straightaway. Just before nightfall they stumbled upon the bodies of two men unknown to them, lying in a clearing. One had a deep knife wound; it seemed likely he had died from loss of blood. The other was mutilated, very likely by Crow Folk, since one of the creatures also lay dead nearby. Someone put up a good fight."

Galen, my mind says. *Galen, be all right.* I relax my jaw and count silently to five.

"They found Galen a short distance away, lying unconscious, with some injuries. There was no sign of Prince Aolu. Your brother is at the prince's house, Liobhan. Your mother is looking after him, along with one of the court physicians."

I swallow hard, not sure what to ask first. "How long ago did this happen? Has the prince been found?"

"This is the third day." Master Donagan's voice is well under control, but his eyes tell a different story. "A wider search began at dawn the day after they brought Galen home. They found the horses wandering, frightened but unharmed. Prince Aolu remains missing."

"Where were Galen and the prince riding to?" I ask.

The look on Donagan's face suggests more bad news is coming. "I'm told Aolu wanted to visit a druid, Brother

Oisín, who sometimes resides deeper into that forest. The druid had not been seen recently, and Aolu was concerned." Another pause. My heart is thudding now, and my skin is clammy. I refrain from snarling *Get on with it*. "It wasn't possible to search as far as the druid's hut. The Crow Folk were present in numbers."

I force myself to ask the next question. "Was Galen attacked by the Crow Folk, Master Donagan? How serious are his injuries?" The Crow Folk are far bigger than ordinary birds, and have formidable beaks and claws, along with a tendency to attack fiercely and at random. The wounds they inflict don't heal easily.

"It would seem so. He suffered defensive wounds, as one might expect. A gash to the cheek and ear, claw marks on the arm and shoulder. And a bad knock to the head, enough to render him insensible for some time; that, we believe to have been inflicted by human hand."

"Has Galen said what happened?"

"His memory of the events is hazy, but he confirmed there were both human attackers and Crow Folk. He couldn't tell us what happened to the prince."

A chill is creeping through my bones. I work on my breathing. I've seen what damage the Crow Folk can inflict. I've had a scratch from a claw myself, as has Dau, and I count both of us extremely fortunate that our injuries healed without much trouble. One thing I do know—even if he's on his deathbed, my brother will see it as his personal duty to find the prince. He's not only responsible for Aolu's safety; he loves the man with all his heart.

"The king needs Swan Island's assistance to find his son," Donagan says. "I'm hoping you can put a team together and be ready to ride to Winterfalls with me in the morning. King Oran will meet us there. We have no idea who the human assailants were or where the prince might be now. We're faced with the task of searching that entire tract of forest, with the Crow Folk more or less everywhere." He leans forward, his elbows on the table. "The searchers did find an item belonging to Prince Aolu in the forest, in the general direction of the druid's hut. The king believes this was an abduction."

"King Oran's only son would certainly be a tempting target for an unscrupulous person looking to enrich himself," says Illann. "But how could anyone harness the Crow Folk to assist such a move?"

"They couldn't, surely," I say. "I mean . . . there are ways to deter them. But using them in an attack? You'd need to be a mage. A sorcerer. And a powerful one at that."

"I know you've had some dealings with the Crow Folk," Cionnaola says, looking from me to Dau. "Anything you have to contribute to the discussion will be welcome. This may simply be the work of some opportunistic individual who happened to be close by. Or it may be something more calculated. But there's no doubt the prince is in danger. Crow Folk or no Crow Folk, the next step must be a more thorough search. If that proves fruitless, we'll need plans put in place with speed."

If Crow Folk were there, fighting alongside human attackers, something extremely odd is going on. I wish we had Brocc here. When we saw him at Oakhill, he seemed on the brink of some great discovery about the Crow Folk. It was clear he'd begun to see them as lost souls needing their own rescue. If only we could get a message to him . . .

"We'll certainly meet the king's request," Cionnaola says. "The initial team will be Dau, Illann, and Garbh, led by Archu. I'll give Garbh the details later; he's out on the boat with Haki at present. His experience as bodyguard to a prince could prove useful. We might add to that group, but we'll wait to consult with the king before making that decision."

A protest springs to my lips. I bite it back. The elders will expect me to act with restraint, even though my big brother is hurt, perhaps dying. With the Crow Folk involved, they need someone with knowledge of the uncanny on the team, and since Brocc is no longer part of the Swan Island community, I'm their best bet.

"Liobhan," says Archu quietly, "you know why you can't be sent on this mission." I see on his broad features a look of real understanding. Our combat leader knows me very well.

"But I could—"

"I know you could. But you're too close to this. Your family's involved. Your parents are friends of both the king and Prince Aolu. Not to mention that we're sending Dau. I'm afraid I can't even release you to visit your brother. Not until we find the prince." Unspoken, but understood by every one of us—our faces show it—are the words he doesn't say. *Dead or alive.*

Through a churning mix of feelings I manage a courteous tone. "Who else will you send, if it comes to that?"

"As yet undecided." That's Cionnaola. "We'll choose someone with skills complementary to those of the others."

It occurs to me that I have another skill that could come in useful. I'm not just a warrior, I'm a musician. Before we came to Swan Island Brocc and I used to play in a band for weddings and village celebrations. I still sing and play in the evenings after supper. There are other musicians in our community, including Archu, who is expert on the bodhrán. Though it's Brocc who is a true bard. When folk say someone's singing could coax the birds down from the trees, they might be speaking of him. What Archu and the others perhaps don't understand is the power of music when dealing

with the Crow Folk, and not only to deflect an attack. Brocc
has used it to reassure them. He even got me to sing when
he set some captive birds free, and it kept them calm. But if
I say this, it's going to sound as if I'm pleading for them to
send me on the mission, and I know perfectly well that Archu's word is final.

While I've been pondering this, the others have been suggesting possible team members, all seasoned Swan Island
warriors, all suitable. Except for one thing.

"May I make a suggestion?" Dau's been quiet up until
now; I can't guess what he's about to say.

"Go ahead, Dau," says Cionnaola.

"If there's even a hint that the Crow Folk's involvement
was part of a plot, we need a team member who's experienced in dealing with the uncanny. I understand your reasons for not choosing Liobhan. But to the best of my
knowledge, she's had more experience of such things than
anyone else on the island. Crossed a certain threshold. Spoken to beings that don't belong in our world. And . . . while
she and I have battled Crow Folk, Liobhan has also dealt with
them in a . . . in a more benign way." He glances at me as if
asking whether he should tell the full tale of our strange
experience with the creatures at Oakhill. To do so would
mean revealing a very unsavory story about Dau's family, a
story known to some of the elders, but perhaps best not
spread more widely.

"Brocc can reach the Crow Folk through music," I say.
"He thinks they're misunderstood. That's hard to believe, I
know. But when we last saw him, he did seem to be making
some progress with them. The same principle applies with
other uncanny beings. Music touches them. It unlocks doors.
It's a way of proving you're a friend and can be trusted, or at
least that you're prepared to negotiate."

"Dau." Cionnaola's tone is level. "Were you suggesting Liobhan should go in your place?"

I save Dau from having to respond to this impossible question by saying, "I've been ruled out, haven't I? But if you call in more team members later, especially if King Oran believes the search might go beyond the human world, you might consider who would be best for that side of things."

Master Donagan gives a polite little cough, then speaks. "I will say that with Galen hurt, the king will not want any other member of Mistress Blackthorn's family put at unnecessary risk. But it is a fair point."

"We'll consider some strategies and meet again later," says Archu. "Master Donagan, you must be tired after the ride. We'll provide you with food and drink, and give ourselves some time to think and plan." He looks at me. The man is expert at reading my thoughts. "You have work to do on the island, Liobhan," he says. "Your trainee is just finding her feet in our community. Besides, if both you and Dau went off as well as Illann, who would look after the dog?"

3

DAU

There's one night on the island before the team leaves. Liobhan and I won't be sharing a bed, since apart from some modest huts already occupied by married couples, everyone sleeps in communal men's or women's quarters. There's not much level ground here and most of it's taken up by our training facilities, the living quarters, and a few outbuildings. The rest is crags, cliffs, sea-birds, seals, and long-haired island sheep.

I find Liobhan out on a cliff path with Justice, who spots me from a distance and comes running. He's happy in the straightforward way of a dog—how can he know I'm leaving tomorrow? It's clear Liobhan doesn't share his mood. She's sitting on a rock, knees up, arms around them, staring out over a sea whose choppy restlessness is reflected in her expression. Gulls scream overhead; the west wind whips Liobhan's red-gold hair into a coronet of flame. I move to sit beside her. Justice settles by my feet, still alert. It's his self-appointed job to keep both of us safe.

"Cionnaola still believes it was a kidnapping," I say, "and that the Crow Folk just happened to be close by. He's expecting a demand for ransom, which should give us an idea of who's responsible."

"Why would someone kidnap the prince?" asks Liobhan, sounding as fierce as she looks. "That would be crazy. King Oran has a firm hold on power. He's on good terms with his local chieftains. And Aolu is well-liked. Who'd want to stir up conflict? If it was a personal thing, someone at court with a grudge, Donagan would have suspicions, surely. He knows pretty much everything that goes on there. And Illann's idea of someone doing it solely for a ransom payment is not convincing."

"Maybe they'll have found Aolu by the time we get to Winterfalls. He might limp out of the forest with a broken ankle, after tripping and falling down a hole."

Liobhan gives me a look. "About as likely as someone using the Crow Folk as their personal strike force. But, Dau . . . what if Aolu wasn't taken at all? What if he escaped?"

"If he escaped, why didn't he come straight home as soon as the way was clear?" I imagine our team searching that tract of forest—it would be a massive task—and Aolu waiting day by endless day, held somewhere by his captors, helpless and perhaps hurt. A dark memory visits me, of the day and night when Liobhan was snatched away to be bound, drugged, and tortured by my brother Seanan. When I think of that time, I feel something sharp and cruel inside me, a thing that stabs at my vitals, wounds my heart, drives me half-crazy. That was the worst time of my life. I reach out and take Liobhan's hand.

"Are you all right?" She's looking at me now, her expression softer. It's as if a cloud has lifted and she finally sees me.

"Mm. Bad memories. You don't think . . ." I can't say it.

"That Seanan could be embroiled in this? I doubt it. Your brother was banished with almost no resources. And this would be a pretty roundabout way to get back at us. Why Prince Aolu?"

"Because the prince's close friend happens to be your brother?"

"How could Seanan make that connection unless he came here and observed it all and asked questions? A man with no friends and no money is hardly in a position to do that. Besides, although he knew I trained with you here, he was given no information about my life before that. I was simply referred to as Liobhan of Dalriada."

"Don't dismiss the idea. There's been no word of Seanan since he left Oakhill. That doesn't mean he's gone far away and settled down quietly. You know him. You know what he's capable of. He'll be full of resentment, convinced the world has treated him unjustly. Eager for vengeance."

"You should mention that to Archu, then," Liobhan says. "We should consider everything. Including Seanan. And the Crow Folk, of course. Though how we get any further with *them*, I have no idea. Brocc might know. But he's too far away. And he can't be reached by the ordinary kind of messenger."

"A pity we don't have those strange little birds, the ones that go between worlds," I say. "We could send one to ask for Brocc's advice."

"Hardly worth discussing that, since even if we had one, we wouldn't know how to use it." Liobhan sounds sharp. She's wound up tight.

For a bit I say nothing, just lean over to give Justice a scratch behind the ears. It's always good to be chosen for a mission. But it means I won't be seeing Justice or Liobhan again for who knows how long.

"Sorry," Liobhan says. "I sound like a thwarted child. I understand why he's not sending me. It's just—oh, never mind."

"Archu did ask for suggestions," I point out. "You have time to talk to him again."

"He told me I needed to work with Elka. How can that be more important than a mission?"

"Archu knows what he's doing, even when he seems to be making odd decisions. In that, he's very like you."

Liobhan lets out a frustrated growl. "They should be investigating the uncanny side of this as well as the kidnapping theory. That's my opinion, anyway. Give me a hug, will you? Sounds like you're definitely going, which is a good thing. Only I'll miss you. More than I can put into words, Dau."

We stand, wrap our arms around each other, and hold on while our hearts beat together. We're in a place where anyone might see us, so we keep our embrace seemly, for all the tide of desire that runs through our bodies. It's a new part of our warrior discipline, and a difficult one to master. Made still more difficult, at this moment, by the knowledge that we won't be spending the night together. There may be various bolt-holes across the island, caves and so on, but they're not the most comfortable spots for making love, and there's always the possibility someone will walk in.

"What about Justice?" murmurs Liobhan. "I can't live on the mainland with him and train Elka at the same time."

"They'll tolerate Justice over here, given the circumstances. Talk to Archu. See him on his own, if that's easier. Suggest he take the bodhrán with him. And . . ." I'm not sure how she'll take the next suggestion.

"And what?" Liobhan may be snuggled up against me, but her tone is combative.

"Couldn't your mother provide the kind of guidance the team needs, about the involvement of Crow Folk and anything else uncanny?"

Liobhan steps back and releases me. "Up to a point, yes. She'll be able to advise the team before you head out. She knows about the Fair Folk, she can do a little hearth magic, she has a practical attitude to such matters. And . . ." She hesitates.

I wait. If she doesn't trust me with some piece of information, I'm not going to demand that she divulge it.

"This is between you and me," Liobhan says. "A lot of really strange stuff went on when my mother was younger. You've heard the tale of Dreamer's Pool, how the water can change people. And there are some odd stories about the forest beyond Dreamer's Wood. I think there might be portals in that area. Leading to somewhere a person might not want to go. A place not as benign as Eirne's realm. You could talk to Mother about that possibility. Perhaps those men Galen saw were not actually men." She pauses, then adds, "That's confidential. Not to be shared with the team. Or with anyone, apart from Mother. And Galen. And my father, if he's there."

For a while I say nothing. But I have to ask. "Then why tell me?"

"They're my family. And although we're not husband and wife, you're my family, too, now."

Sudden tears prick my eyes. Close as we are, forever bound by love and comradeship and understanding, she's never said this to me before. I've turned my back on my blood family. Their cruelty, their blindness, their weakness came close to destroying me. When I left that place for the last time, I had made my peace with the brother next to me in age, who is now Brother Íobhar, a Christian monk. But I'll never go back. My family came close to destroying me.

A tear rolls down my cheek; Liobhan reaches a gentle finger to wipe it away. "Mother has a friend in the Otherworld," she says. "A powerful friend. That's just something to bear in mind. If all else fails, perhaps she could call on him for help."

"Chances are we'll be too far from Winterfalls to ask her,

if there's a crisis. If you were in the team, would you be able to summon this person?"

Her brows go up. "Me? Hardly. Not a scrap of magical ability in me."

"What about when you were searching for Brocc? Your voice got you through that portal and into the Otherworld."

"That isn't magic. It's just the Fair Folk liking music and using it as a key into their world. Same as they use riddles."

"And when you let those Crow Folk out of the cage? You sang to them and they flew away without attacking us. Surely that was magic."

"I sang because Brocc couldn't. If there was magic in my voice that day, it was his magic, not mine."

I have long believed Liobhan's voice has a special power. I, who never believed in the uncanny, was captivated by that rich sound long before she and I became friends. But she's probably right about Brocc. On that day, he couldn't use his voice to keep the Crow Folk calm because he was under a curse of silence, and he asked her to sing instead. Brocc was brought up as brother to both Liobhan and Galen, but he is part fey. I suspect the person who delivered a newborn infant of mixed blood into the care of Mistress Blackthorn and Master Grim might be the same family friend Liobhan just spoke of. I can't see myself asking Mistress Blackthorn about such a personal matter. But then, I never imagined myself confiding in a wisewoman at all, yet it was just such a person who set me on my pathway out from the shadows of the past.

Liobhan shivers suddenly, wrapping her arms around herself. "This whole thing feels wrong to me. Strange. Do talk to Mother, please. Not about her friend, unless you think it could be useful. But about dealing with the Otherworld and what it might mean. You and Archu could talk to her together."

"You say you're not like him." I put my arm around her shoulders as we walk back toward the community buildings with Justice running ahead, confident on the cliff path. "And here you are planning the mission for us."

"I wish I could. I hope Galen is better by the time you get to Winterfalls. I hope he can tell you more clearly what he saw."

"He's as strong as an ox." I remember the time I met Liobhan's elder brother. Galen is a man who would stand out in any group. He's tall and powerfully built like his father, with the features of some mythic god of battle. His head is shaven, his beard is of the same striking red as Liobhan's hair. Galen is a giant alongside Prince Aolu, who has the build of a poet or scribe, and a quiet, scholarly manner. The two have been fast friends since they were boys, despite their differences. I met them when I was at Winterfalls. I wondered then if they might be more than friends.

"That makes this all the odder," Liobhan says grimly. "Galen would die before he let anyone hurt Aolu. But he's alive, and Aolu is gone."

It's evening, and the island community is gathered for supper and entertainment. I've packed my bag, readied my weapons, made sure the elders will accept Justice's presence on the island until I return from the mission—he is trained to stay away from the sheep. I've spoken again with the rest of the team. Now, as people wipe the last of the sauce from their platters and refill their ale cups, Archu and Liobhan head for the raised area at one end of the hall, along with Eimear, to play and sing for us.

Justice has picked up my unease now. He sits quiet by my side, showing no interest in my food and making no move to greet other folk he knows. I feel his warm body against my leg, and alongside anticipation of the mission I am filled with sadness to be leaving him. Before our paths crossed, his life was not a happy one and he bears the scars of that. As for Liobhan, our parting will feel like wrenching out our hearts. But we are Swan Island warriors, and the mission, the team, the work must come first. We know what a privilege it is to be part of this community; we both fought hard to win our places. The way we live sometimes hurts. But that is the choice we made.

The band launches into a lively reel. The two whistles dance around each other, while Archu's drumming sets feet tapping all over the hall. His strong arm can coax all sorts of sounds from the bodhrán. Often the beat is curious to me, seeming at first uneven, then making sense all of a sudden as the whistle tune seems to glide into place. I am no musician; I wish I were. Sometimes Liobhan persuades me to sing with her and seems pleased by my efforts, but my voice is nothing beside hers. Archu also sings, in the deep, resonant tone one might expect from a person built like a one-man fortress. Eimear is capable on the whistle, while Liobhan is a shining star, her nimble fingers adding new flourishes and decorations every time the refrain comes around. In the slow tunes, her playing is full of feeling. I see sorrow and joy on the faces of her audience, the awakening of memories, hopes and dreams. I never thought of music this way until I heard her and Brocc perform. It's surely a kind of magic.

The band plays several dances. Liobhan sings a song called "The Farewell," which is all too apt tonight, though a shiver runs through me to hear it, since it ends up with lovers parted by death. When it's done, and the listeners have given the players the respect of a few moments' complete silence before they burst into applause, she addresses them, standing tall in her russet gown with her lovely hair loose on her shoulders and her cheeks a little flushed from her efforts. I store up the memory for when I am gone. Justice lays his muzzle on my knee. I stroke his head.

"Any requests?" Liobhan asks, smiling as she looks around the hall. "Nothing sad, please. We're going to end this on a cheerful note. Garbh?"

Garbh, a very big man who retains a particular admiration for Liobhan despite her attachment to me, asks for the song about the fisherman and the mermaid. It has a sad ending for the fisherman, who has to relinquish his scaly sweetheart, but a better one for her, because she gets to swim free.

"Good choice," says Liobhan, grinning at Garbh. "I need some of you singing the chorus so Eimear and I can both play—volunteers?" She's looking at me, and I feel obliged to put my hand up. She motions me forward, along with Garbh and our Armorican fighter, Yann, who can hold a tune with confidence. All we need to do is sing a fishermen's chorus— *ay-oh, way-oh, waves of the sea*. With Liobhan singing the verses in her strong, rich voice, accompanied by Eimear's whistle and the bodhrán, and the three of us, with Archu, singing the refrains while the two whistles play together, the performance fills the hall. The audience claps in time. Even Master Donagan is joining in. I'm proud to be part of this. It tells me I'm home.

Right at the end, Justice lifts his voice in a howl and the place dissolves into laughter. Illann moves to reassure the dog. I return to my spot and listen while the band plays the ridiculously quick "Artagan's Leap" at Haki's request, and then a slower dance to finish the evening's entertainment. Nobody gets up to dance tonight. Everyone knows a team is leaving in the morning.

"That's it, friends," Liobhan says, as the band members bow and return the audience's applause. "Time for bed, early start tomorrow for some."

The hall empties. The folk on kitchen duty clear away the last of the cups and platters; the musicians pack up their things. I have a word with Illann about the arrangements for tomorrow, and then Liobhan makes her way over to me. She waits until Illann has said good night and headed off to the men's quarters, then slips her hand through my arm and says quietly, "Eimear says we can have her and Conor's place for the night; they'll sleep in the quarters."

And so, after all, we have our night together. That we know each other's bodies well by now does not lessen the sweet pleasure of touch, the strong tide of desire, the ecstasy of fulfillment. Nor does it alter the delight of the aftermath, when we lie close and breathe as one. From beyond the shutters of this modest hut comes the changing music of wind and waves, lulling us to sleep. Tomorrow we will say good-bye.

4

BROCC

Our daughter can sit up on her own. She reaches out for whatever takes her interest—a feather caught by the breeze, a leaf, a beetle crawling by. If captured, such items go straight to her mouth. This makes it necessary to watch her constantly, and my wife finds the duty wearisome. Fortunately there are many willing helpers, particularly the smaller beings of our clan, such as Thistle-Coat, who despite her resemblance to a hedgehog has hands like a human's, though diminutive in size. Gentle-Foot and Moth-Weed, who have a child of their own, are particularly helpful—their infant can safely scamper about while one of them watches over our larger but more vulnerable child.

We have named her Niamh, after a goddess from the ancient tales. Our Niamh does not much resemble a goddess as she plunges her hands in mud or tries to feed herself the mash of stewed roots she increasingly prefers over her mother's milk. Generally more of this ends up pasted across her face than in her mouth. But I suppose even a goddess starts life as an infant. Our girl has hair like mine—dark and irrepressibly curly—and eyes like Eirne's, wide, gray, very direct in their gaze, as if she would see inside a person and judge them. Though small, Niamh has the look of a queen.

I do not say this to Eirne, I cannot, but the thought that
Niamh may someday become queen here in her mother's
place sets deep unease in me. The folk of our clan are good
folk, from our huge stony man, True, to the tiniest of the
birds that act as Eirne's messengers. We have among us
the brave, the wise, the courteous, the joyful. We have the
sage and the healer, the stalwart warrior and the fleet messenger. My wife is the queen. I am the bard. But we are few.
So very few.

Despite my efforts and those of True and Rowan, who aid
me in patrolling our gathering place and the wider woodland
around it, the Crow Folk remain in our forest. They stay a
certain distance from the area where our clan lives. We
judge their number increases, though since the death of a
young creature while in my care, we have seen no fledglings
among them. Whether they are indeed breeding and hatch-
ing young, or whether other adults are flying in from elsewhere, there is no telling. Sometimes they swoop low as we
perform our daily check of the boundaries. Often they perch
high in the trees, watching us and exchanging harsh cries.

Not long ago one of Eirne's messengers was killed. There
was little left of the tiny bird when Rowan and I found it on
a pathway, but the bright, broken feathers, the splinters of
bone and shreds of flesh left me in no doubt as to what had
happened. The Crow Folk strike without reason, or so it
seems. They neither eat their prey nor carry it away to feed
others. One day they will leave a flock of sheep in a field or a
party of travelers on a road to carry on their lives. The next
day they will swoop and kill.

I wondered if they believed the messenger to be a young
one of our clan. They might have taken its life as retribution
for the death of their own small one, which was killed on my

wife's orders while I slept unawares not two strides away. That sad passing was many moons ago. Do they remember as human folk would? Does their grief grow in their hearts over seasons, over years, until finally it drives them to violent action? I fear for the child of Gentle-Foot and Moth-Weed, which I could hold in the palm of my hand. I fear for Niamh, so fearless in her curiosity yet so helpless still. I wonder anew at Conmael's motives when he brought me to my adoptive parents, long ago when I was a newborn babe. What would he think now, that Otherworld lord who may or may not have fathered me? I met him last year when spring was turning to summer, before I knew my wife was with child. I spoke to him. He called me *my boy*. Had I known I would soon become a father, would I have had the courage to ask him about his choice? I cannot imagine giving up my precious daughter. That would surely kill me.

Now it is spring again and the Crow Folk are restless. We hear from our messengers that the creatures are still venturing out into the human world, terrifying farmers, menacing travelers. Should I, too, venture out, perhaps to meet with King Faelan and lay before him my theory about the Crow Folk? The more they are seen, the more they attack, the less likely that even he, who was once a druid, will believe we can make our peace with them if only we understand what drives them to such savagery. They respond to music. Music must be the key. But to what, exactly? What is it the Crow Folk want? I am working on this. I will find out. If Eirne does not stop me. Such work must be carried out in secret, and secrets are not easily held in such a small community.

Today True and Rowan are out on patrol, while I stay at the gathering place to guard the clan and to watch over my daughter. Eirne is resting. Feeding Niamh exhausts her, and she is often out of sorts. She will be glad when our girl no longer needs to drink her mother's milk, though it seems to me there is more to that than the simple nourishment of the body. I have seen how the small one presses her fist into the soft flesh of Eirne's breast as she feeds. I have seen how she snuggles in her mother's arms, soft, safe, her face rosy with satisfaction when she has drunk her fill, and I believe there is a natural magic in the bond. When Conmael passed me, a babe newborn, over to my adoptive mother, she was only a moon or two from giving birth to Liobhan. Perhaps our mother fed both of us at her breast. The bond between me and my sister suggests it may have been so. I have never asked.

Moon-Fleet, our healer, is showing Niamh a little figure she has made with twigs and leaves and vine tendrils. Moon-Fleet builds a tiny path with pebbles and makes the poppet walk along it. Niamh gurgles and waves her hands about. I wonder when they learn words? Niamh has many sounds. And she loves music—that I can tell already. Because of a curse, for a whole year I could not use my singing voice; if I attempted even the simplest lullaby, all that came from my mouth was a rasping, tuneless whisper. Some bard! But the others sang for me. Eirne has a lovely voice, and when Niamh was tiny she would sing her to sleep, though my wife seldom sings now, and it saddens me. I played my harp—the curse did not forbid that—and I saw from the start how that music soothed my daughter, lulling her to rest; how it entertained her when she was wakeful. She would lie beside me on her little blanket, watching the movement of my fingers on the strings, her great eyes solemn as an owl's. How vividly I recall the day the curse reached its end, and I could sing again. It was like the return of my soul, profound and healing. I stood under the great oaks with my arms outstretched, while joy and hope spread through me. The folk of Eirne's clan came running in from far and wide to listen, bright-eyed with wonder.

I do not sing now, but play a piece I have made for Niamh especially. When she is bigger and has learned to be steady on her legs she can dance to this. The tune came to me after a vivid dream in which my daughter had gossamer wings and danced not on the forest floor but high in the air, borne on friendly breezes. I call the piece "Flight of the Fair One."

Moon-Fleet makes her twiggy poppet prance along the little path, and Niamh lets out a squeal of delight. The small ones of our clan dance, too, for music excites them and they cannot keep still. Moon-Fleet, who is sitting on the ground, lifts Niamh onto her knee and helps her to join in, jigging her up and down. Soon enough my daughter will be too big for the more delicate members of our clan to lift. Silver-haired Moon-Fleet is no taller than a human girl of eight or nine; Eirne's devoted adviser, Nightshade, is not much bigger. Even my right-hand man Rowan, Eirne's long-term protector, who has characteristics of both man and fox, is only as tall as a lad of twelve or so. True is big and broad, a giant of a being. And I? Although I have a blend of fey and human blood, I will be able to lift my daughter even when she is grown; I was a Swan Island warrior.

The clan is far from strong. That has troubled me from the first. Now that I am a father, it weighs heavily on me. But I play my harp and smile at my daughter as she waves her arms more or less in time. I want her to dance one day. I want her to chatter and sing and be joyful. I would teach her to play the harp. I would teach her to make songs. I would teach her hope. I want her to live her life in peace and gladness. I want it so much I could weep, even as I pluck the strings with a bard's confidence and send the tune ringing out through the forest, and the small folk twirl and leap and collapse in gales of laughter. "Flight of the Fair One" is a favorite. As I draw the tune to its close then set my instrument aside, I consider that the title I chose might be taken to mean not a flight on wings, but a flight away from something—a shadow, a menace, a trap. A dream may have a surface meaning and also a hidden one, deep down. I would talk to Eirne about this if I could. I cannot speak to my wife as I would to my sister, frankly, in full truth, holding nothing back. Is this as it should be? I do not know. Thinking of my parents, who share a remarkable understanding that often needs no words, I suspect it is not.

There is a time every day when Niamh sleeps soundly. Eirne often rests then also, while Nightshade stays by them. It has become a quiet time, for every being in our clan respects the need for a babe to sleep undisturbed. Rowan, True, and I take turns to keep watch over the gathering place. And on the days when I am free of this duty, I do my secret work. My two comrades have not asked me why I head off into the forest alone while they stay with the clan. They have not asked if I want a companion. Perhaps they can guess what I am doing and why I never speak of it before others. If so, their loyalty warms my heart, for they have been Eirne's folk since she was deposited in the Otherworld at the age of five, a child of mixed blood brought up in a human family only to be returned unceremoniously to a place where someone thought she belonged. Rowan, True, and the others became her family, and that child grew up to be their queen. A queen who, if she knew how I was spending my quiet time, would turn on me in fury. She would never understand the nature of what I am doing, nor the profound need for it. She must not know of it. I tread a perilous path, a path that puts my little family, my strange clan, and perhaps the Crow Folk themselves at great risk. But I must do it. Is not this the higher purpose of a bard—to heal the wounded spirit, to spread hope and understanding, to mend what is broken? I am called to this task.

I walk softly, humming under my breath as I make my way to a certain spot in the woods, some distance south of our clan's dwellings. I remain within the Otherworld; what I do, what we do, is safer here than in the human world, where we might be spied on and misunderstood. I enter a clearing between tall beeches. There is a patch of light here, an opening to the sky, and a flat rock patterned strangely with lichens and mosses. Here I sit cross-legged, and my hum grows into a song. The same tune every time, slow, soothing, nothing threatening in it. The words differ each time, but are always an invitation. I have no language to use but the one I speak daily. I must reach the ears and the understanding of one who does not, cannot, speak that tongue. But I have learned to fix my whole being on the message as I sing; to make the music more than tune and verse. I started that journey some time ago, when I played a certain ancient harp at a king's coronation. A simple tune can possess great power. A simple verse can contain generations of meaning. A song can bring folk together. Yes, even Crow Folk and humankind. Eirne would scoff at that. But Eirne does not know what I know.

> *Three truths from the lips of a bard:*
> *The truth of oak and ash*
> *The truth of earth and sky*
> *The truth of the ancestors.*
> *Three wishes from the lips of a bard:*
> *A trusting heart*

An open mind
A fearless spirit.

If I had my harp with me, I would draw my fingers across the strings in a flourish, to mark the turning point of the song. Today that is not needed, for in the pause a bird somewhere high above me lets out a cascade of notes. The beauty of it, the liquid, perfect sound in the deep silence, brings a smile to my lips and tears to my eyes. The bird's voice stills, and I finish my own song.

I come in peace.
I come in trust.
I come in friendship.
I am here.

And I wait, silent on my stone, earth holding me safe, sun lighting my pathway, the trees my guardians and companions on the journey. I open my mind to possibility. Perhaps he will come today, perhaps not. I do not summon. I invite.

And he is here, winging down to perch on a fallen branch some ten paces away. A huge crow, but not a crow. A bird-shaped being whose glossy plumage is spoiled here and there by scars, a creature that has been ill-treated, a survivor. I know what torment this being suffered. I saw what was done to the creatures by Dau's brother with his foul experiments. This one and another, we managed to free: Liobhan, True, and myself. This one is recovered. He is strong. He has a companion, but that being does not come down from the trees; I think of her as the Watcher.

I bow my head in greeting, laying an open hand over my heart. I keep my movements slow, as if I were in deep water. The bird—in my mind, I call him Shadow, and I believe he understands that name—dips his own head and moves his feet on the branch. He perches awkwardly. His claws have damage that cannot be repaired. We regard each other. I do not see enmity in Shadow's gaze. I do not see fear, although I am of the same kind as those who tormented him. I see strength and a willingness to listen.

What he sees in me, I cannot judge. We found each other in the forest by chance, when I was alone. Or maybe not by chance, who knows? I knew him by his scars, and by the other being that accompanied him at a distance, also a survivor of torture. Shadow could have attacked me with beak and claws. He could have inflicted deadly injuries. I could have used my bone knife to slash and stab, to wound, perhaps to kill. Instead we settled at a short distance from each other. I sang quietly, Shadow listened, and although, back then, I had no window into his thoughts, it was plain that each of us had a wish to understand the other better. To heal wounds. To set a sad situation right, if we could. After some time we exchanged nods again and went our own ways. But the next day, at the same time, we met again. And so it began. A friendship between human and Crow Folk. A thing nobody would have believed possible, least of all my wife.

Each time we meet I edge closer to understanding Shadow's thoughts. It is a challenge to communicate without a shared language. Now, at this moment, his mind is full of restless movement, though his body is still. Is this the turmoil one feels when everything is going wrong, when friends become foes, when trust begins to fail? I think not, or he would show his unease as a bird does, by shifting from one foot to the other, or turning his head sharply, or shaking his feathers. Or he would fly away. Shadow holds himself as calm as a meditating druid. But that storm within . . . Perhaps it is an image from memory. From the time *before*. I still believe this tribe of strange, disturbed beings has flown here from some distant place. If so, they have not found a home on this shore. Neither the Otherworld nor the human realm accepts them. If they could fly back, why do they not attempt that?

When Liobhan sang for Shadow and his companion, that day when we released them from captivity, she chose to sing of cliffs and crashing waves, of islands and surging seas. She sang of a flight to freedom. Did she discern the same thing in Shadow's mind as I think I do? Crows are not seabirds. But then, these remarkable creatures are not, in fact, crows.

I glance quickly around the clearing. I must not be found here so close to Shadow, whom Eirne and the clan believe to be our enemy. I must ensure nothing severs the delicate bond between us, so carefully nurtured. I look into his eyes, not wild and mad now, but steady despite the churning thoughts. He gazes straight back at me. Perhaps he *is* a druid. Perhaps this extraordinary being is the wise man of his clan.

I don't speak. Instead, I mirror in my own mind what I believe may be in his. A vast ocean, whitecapped waves. A wild sky full of heavy clouds and a chill wind blowing. An island. An island all steep slopes, with no discernible landing place for a vessel such as men might sail. Above the rocky peaks, a great bird flying, a creature that would dwarf Shadow. Its feathers are not crow-black; it is pale gold against the lowering clouds. It moves effortlessly on that mad wind, as if no storm can trouble it. No other birds in sight; only the one. Its strength has a haunting beauty. Its solitude hurts my heart. What are these feelings? Are they mine or Shadow's?

As I look across at my companion, he lifts his wings a little and sways from side to side, with his gaze still fixed on me. I raise my arms—poor substitutes—and copy his movement. *Yes, the great bird. Yes, the storm. Yes, the lonely island. Your home?*

Shadow ceases his dance. He tucks his head under one wing to mimic sleep. *Home. Rest. At last, rest.* And for a moment I see them, like nesting gannets on the cliffs of that lonely isle, dark figures in small groups, huddled along the ledges. Only, these are not gannets. They are not Crow Folk. They are not birds at all, but something else.

5

LIOBHAN

I throw myself into activity, whether it's running, climbing, fighting, or perfecting a challenging piece on the whistle. And, of course, I have Elka to train.

We go through the exercises every morning, often with a bunch of other fighters. We need to keep our bodies strong. Mission-ready, I heard someone call it. Today I'm with my friends Hrothgar and Yann as well as Elka. She's working hard. I wish I knew more about her past, but it's not the Swan Island way to ask personal questions. If a newcomer wants to tell their story we listen with interest, and if they don't—Dau was a perfect example of that—we respect their silence. Elka might have built those muscles laboring hard on a farm or on a fishing boat. She might have learned to climb by taking cliff-dwelling birds or their eggs for food. As for the reserve that often holds her still and quiet, I wonder about that. There could be all sorts of reasons for it. But unless she decides I can be a friend as well as a trainer, those reasons will remain a mystery.

We complete the exercises, all but the last part, which is to jog around the edge of the training area a few times and then stretch. Justice has been hunkered down on the sidelines watching us, but now he gets up and shakes himself, ready for the run.

"Beautiful day," observes Hrothgar as we drink from our waterskins before starting off. "Why don't we change this for once, run down to the west point and back instead? Brigid's going to show Yann and me some tricks with the bow later, but we have time."

It is indeed a fair day, with tiny clouds scudding across a perfect blue sky. There's enough of a breeze to keep us cool and we do have plenty of time. But there could be a problem. People have been reporting odd things about the west point—the birds that nest in that area in springtime have been unsettled, and there's been some talk of Crow Folk. "The elders won't want people wandering around there," I say, knowing I want to go, but aware that as Elka's trainer I should set a good example. "We can go as far as Brother Criodan's hut and consult him. If he says no, we'll turn back. Yann, you lead. Elka next, then me, and Hrothgar last. Keep the pace steady and be watchful." When we're doing circuits of the training ground we do get rather competitive. But on the cliff paths only a complete fool would try to push the pace.

We've run a fair distance from the community buildings when Yann spots the island druid, Brother Criodan, out in his vegetable patch, which is bordered by a sturdy drystone wall. The winds are fierce in these parts and the island is almost treeless as a result. This small sheltered garden to the south of the druid's hut is all the more remarkable for that. Criodan was a gardener before he was a druid, and we all benefit from his skill; the vegetables and herbs he grows are a welcome addition to the fish that forms a major part of our diet. We work our bodies hard. We get hungry. The island can't produce all the food we eat. Over in the mainland settlement there are chickens, a beehive, goats and cows, looked after by the folk who live there. Some of those who work over there, or here on the island, are ex-fighters, now retired from active duty because of illness or injury. Guss is one of those, and he's out helping Criodan in the garden now, doing some heavy digging. The druid himself is standing by the wall, waiting to speak with us.

Yann halts; the rest of us gather behind him. Justice takes the opportunity to relieve himself against the wall. "Good day to you, brother," says the Armorican. "And to you, Guss. Hard at work, hm?"

Guss mumbles a greeting, offers a grin. His head injury was quite severe, but he seems happy as Criodan's helper, doing genuinely useful work and sleeping in the lean-to at the back of the druid's hut.

"Good morning to you all," says Criodan. Usually the most serene of men, today he wears a small frown. "Are you going all the way to the west point?"

"We'd like to do that, but we can turn back. I know there have been some concerns."

"I saw something earlier today. Down on the rocks near the cave entrance. Something moving about. From a distance it looked almost like one of *them*. But I could not be certain it was a bird at all. It was moving oddly. It seemed wiser not to go too close."

"Should we take a look?" asks Hrothgar.

"Thank you, yes," the druid says. "I intended to report this to Master Cionnaola later. But look now, if you can. Keep your distance from the cavern. The creature may have taken shelter there."

"We'll take a quick look from the path and let you know if we see anything," I tell him. On my own, I'd be tempted to go as far as the cavern entrance. But I'd better not risk Elka's safety. "And we'll pass this on to Cionnaola, save you the walk."

The druid smiles acknowledgment and goes back to his gardening.

"Run again?" queries Yann.

"No, walk. If the Crow Folk really are here, we don't want to attract their attention." I hesitate. "Elka, perhaps you should go back. Yann, you go with her. Two of us will be less obtrusive than four."

Elka seems about to say something, but thinks better of it. Yann looks somewhat put out; she may be answerable to me, but he is not.

"There might be more than one of them," Hrothgar points out. "Safety in numbers, don't they say?"

"We're unarmed." Actually, that's not quite true; I have a small knife in my boot, though it wouldn't be much use against the Crow Folk. From the looks on the others' faces, I'm guessing they're also carrying concealed weaponry. Even Elka.

"Good practice for Elka," says Yann. "Approaching with stealth in difficult territory."

"You're crazy." However, the idea has some appeal, and Criodan did say there was only one creature. "All right, we'll do it. Elka, follow my instructions."

"Yes, Liobhan."

We proceed at a slower pace, eyes out for trouble, feet careful when the path takes us close to the cliff edge. When Justice gets too far ahead I call him back. It may be springtime but the sea is all over whitecaps, and waves break on the rocks below us in extravagant plumes. Beyond the cliff face, gannets wheel and glide on the currents of air. I see no Crow Folk among them. Where the path branches, one track going down to the cavern entry and the other looping around and back to the settlement, we pause in the partial cover of a strange rock formation—a larger boulder sits on a smaller, looking as if it might topple at the touch of a finger. It's known as the Dragon's Egg, and folk say it's been there for generations, maintaining its precarious balance through the fierce storms that lash the island every winter. I lay my hand gently against it, just for a moment. Sometimes I'm more my mother's daughter than feels quite comfortable. She would certainly believe in honoring such a survivor.

"Stop here," I say, just loud enough to be heard. "Keep still and keep quiet. Use your eyes. Justice, sit."

I wish I could go down to the cavern, just to take a look. Mostly we stay away from there. The place is so ancient and solemn, so filled with presences unseen—memories, ghosts, something else—that a person shouldn't simply wander in out of curiosity. Brocc used to go there and play the harp sometimes. I think the spirits, or whatever they are, might have appreciated that, though my brother always came back in a somber mood. There's a freshwater pool in the cave, and natural light spilling down from an opening in the rocks above, though nobody has ever found that window from the outside. Brother Criodan goes to the sheltered place occasionally to meditate. It would make a safe bolt-hole for a fugitive, at least for a short time. A hiding place. I wonder if Dau ever went there? *Don't think of him, Liobhan. Concentrate on the job.* I scan the area below us, where the terrain allows a possible descent to the water, being more tumble of assorted boulders than steep cliff. A fit person could pick their way down without much trouble, provided they took care not to twist an ankle. To one side there are sloping rocky shelves where, in calmer weather, seals come up to bask. Closer at hand are rock pools, pebbly stretches, tangles of seaweed, scuttling crabs and clinging shellfish. I don't see anything unusual. It's the absence of something that strikes me. There'd usually be a crowd of birds busy on the shore, picking over the tide's offerings. Today, there's not a single one.

"We go down?" asks Elka. She keeps her voice low, but there's an intensity in it that I can't miss.

"No. The tide's turning and the waves are unpredictable here. Just observe."

We stand quiet a long while, the four of us, but I see nothing but clouds drifting across the sky and the waves washing over the rocks. I'm about to suggest we head back, when Justice growls deep in his throat, his hackles rising. Elka utters a soft exclamation in her own tongue. Her hands and Hrothgar's go up in the same gesture, something too quick to interpret.

"Walking shadow," translates Hrothgar in a murmur. "I don't see it."

Elka points in the general direction of the cave entrance. "There!" she says. "Oh. Gone now."

This is not the time to ask questions. I can't see anything in the area Elka indicated, but she saw something, and so did Justice. We must stay quiet. We wait a little longer, then I gesture to the others that we're heading back. Justice walks uneasily, tail down, body tense. Once we're a safe distance away I call a halt. "What is a walking shadow?" I ask.

Hrothgar and Elka look at each other. "A wandering spirit," Hrothgar says. "A walker between worlds."

"A—a guide," says Elka. "Is the right word?"

Hrothgar nods.

This is so startling that I can't think what to say.

"This thing, this shadow—I think it is like a soul fallen from the Ankou's cart," Yann says. "Lost before it could be delivered to the Afterlife."

I've heard him speak of the Ankou before. It's a guardian of graveyards and a collector of souls, and is in many tales from Yann's homeland. An old man in black, driving a rattling cart. Death's assistant. Galen returns to my mind, Galen lying insensible in the forest, balanced between this world and the next. An icy finger touches my heart.

"Not dead," Elka says. "Waiting. There is old tale . . ." She falls abruptly silent.

This day is full of surprises. "Tell us more as we walk," I say, heading off in the lead. But Elka hangs back, letting Yann go ahead of her. It's plain she doesn't want to elaborate, and I can't push her. Seems she may have hidden depths, but she's not going to let me know about them yet. And perhaps never. I mustn't be quick to judge her. I did that with Dau in his early days on Swan Island. When I found out the reasons for his distant, superior manner back then, I knew how wrong I'd been, and was ashamed.

We pause by the druid's garden again. Yann and Hrothgar use the stone wall for support as they stretch. Elka folds her arms and gazes out over the sea as if the rest of us weren't there. Brother Criodan is planting out seedlings in the area Guss dug over earlier. "We didn't see Crow Folk," I tell the druid. "There were no birds on the shore at all, though some gannets were flying near the cliffs. But . . . Elka saw something."

Elka's features are closed-up now; she doesn't want to share this. But she's a Swan Island warrior in training. A member of the team. And at the moment, my responsibility. "Elka, can you tell Brother Criodan what you saw?"

She turns those remarkable eyes on me. It's like looking into the depths of winter. She shakes her head. Mutters something under her breath, in her own tongue.

"It will help if you can tell us." I'm keeping my tone level. Trying to do as Archu would.

"He is a . . . a priest. He would judge."

I glance at Brother Criodan, who has been following this

interchange with interest. "I am not a priest in the way you imagine, Elka," he says. The druid knows the name of every person on the island. He makes no distinction between those who follow the old ways, those who practice the Christian faith, and those who have brought other beliefs from far-flung places. He is a friend to all, always happy to engage in civil conversation or lively debate on points of philosophy, human behavior, gardening, and anything else of interest. "I enact rituals to celebrate the turning of the year; I conduct ceremonies to mark the turning points of our lives. I tend my garden with the help of my strong friend here." He bestows a gentle smile on Guss, who is leaning over the wall to pat the dog. "I listen. I meditate. I consider the wonders of this earth we live on, and all things that grow here, ourselves included. I make no judgments."

Hrothgar is translating for Elka, quietly; this is a lot for her to take in, though I'm starting to think she understands more than she lets on.

"This island is remote," says the druid. "Its shores are a safe haven for creatures and humankind alike. If an unusual visitor reaches Swan Island we share that information. We tell what we know so all may better understand it. And take action, if action is needed."

Elka's silence is becoming unsettling. She's holding fast to whatever it is. Hrothgar speaks to her again, and she answers him with a few words in a tense undertone. Then she says, "Something there, yes. Not Crow Folk. A shadow. A spirit. Or maybe nothing."

"It may have been just a trick of the light." Hrothgar sounds awkward.

Clearly there's no more to be got from either. "I'll pass this on to Cionnaola, Brother Criodan. Not that it's much help. It does sound as if there may be something in or near the cavern, and we probably should remind folk again to keep away. We'll bid you good day now; time we got on with our work."

"Good day and blessings to you all."

Elka and I practice unarmed combat moves. Then we go and watch while Brigid takes Hrothgar and Yann through an archery session full of surprises—she teaches them some tricks a person would never use in a real situation, only to show off for their friends, and I realize there's a lighter side to our tough trainer. I've always admired Brigid. When I first came to Swan Island, that admiration was mainly because she's a woman and an elder and a respected fighter, and she takes no nonsense from anyone. Hard as nails. Tough as boot leather. She set up the training I went through at the Barn with Dau and Brocc before heading out on my first undercover mission, and it was pretty confronting. When I first heard the rumor that she and Archu had once been lovers, I found it hard to believe. But I know her better now. I've seen her drinking and laughing with her friends in the hall at suppertime. I've noticed how she listens when we're making music and I've heard her wholehearted applause. I saw how kind she was to Archu after Dau's terrible accident last spring, an occurrence for which Archu believed he bore a share of the blame. Brigid is a woman of many parts. One of them is most certainly cheeky humor. After showing Yann and Hrothgar how to shoot three arrows in rapid succession by holding the spares in the draw hand while releasing, she puts them through an increasingly difficult set of exercises, calling me and Elka in to throw up straw-packed cloth balls as moving targets. I'm itching to have a turn at shooting, but I don't have my bow with me. Elka seems happy; she's busy running around following Brigid's instructions and doesn't need to talk.

Hrothgar manages to hit two targets immediately after executing a leap and twirl. Yann hits a difficult target while jumping down from a wall. Brigid declares herself satisfied and tells them to pack up. She thanks me and Elka, and I let her know that if she's doing this again sometime, I'd like a chance to participate.

"Of course, Liobhan. And you?" Brigid glances at Elka, eyes shrewd, brows up. With only one trainee on the island at present it's inevitable that all the elders will be watching Elka's progress.

"Thank you," Elka says politely, dipping her head. "At home, learn to shoot on ice. Slide, shoot. But only one arrow each time. I try, yes."

Hmm. I've heard she's competent with the bow, but I haven't seen her in action; generally that training is done by Brigid or Archu. Sounds as if she may be a whole lot better than competent.

When we're back at the bathhouse it occurs to me that there may be a subtler way of asking her to explain this morning's episode. I do need to know, not only because of Galen and the prince and the mission, but also because the presence of Crow Folk would endanger our whole community. If I ask her outright, I'm pretty sure she'll tell me it was all a mistake.

"Good work today," I say as she stands in the shallow tub washing her hair. I finish drying myself and get into a clean shirt, tunic, and trousers.

"Thank you, Liobhan." She speaks through a cascade of water; she's trying to rinse off her hair with a scoop and managing to create a small flood on the floor.

"Here, let me do that. Bend over a bit more, that's it." I scoop clean water from the rinsing bucket until I'm sure there's no soap left in Elka's hair, which is as long as mine and much thicker. "Ever thought of cutting it short?" I ask. "Makes wearing a helmet a lot more comfortable. And it's much easier to keep clean."

"You not cut yours?" Elka wrings out her dripping hair as best she can, steps out of the tub and wraps herself in a cloth.

"If I weren't a musician I would hack it all off, believe me." If I want to know more about her, perhaps I need to share more about myself. "Before I came to Swan Island my brother and I traveled about with a band—he's a singer and plays the harp. The gown and the long hair feel right for the performance. Also, it's handy if I need to go undercover." I thrust a hand through my damp locks. "Traveling minstrels are readily admitted to the halls of the highborn and power-ful. And they tend to have good ears." I wait a little then ask, offhand, "Do you sing, Elka? It's just that with Brocc—my brother—no longer here, we're in need of a replacement. And now Archu will be away for a while, too."

"Where this brother go?"

I should have expected this question, but she catches me unprepared. "Away," I say. "He chose to leave Swan Island. He's a married man and will be a father by now. It's not easy for him to send news." It's odd to think of that. The child of Brocc and Eirne will be a couple of seasons old, by my calcu-lations. I can hardly imagine what it would be like to bring up an infant in that place. It's just as weird to realize I'm an aunt. "What do you think?" I ask. "Would you consider sing-ing with us?" Elka's speaking voice, when she's not stifling it for one reason or another, is strong and resonant, and she has the right sort of face for a singer, the cheekbones prominent and the jaw strong. And powerful lungs. She can shout when she needs to—you can't do combat training without learning how to let out a challenge or a curse.

"I come here to fight, not sing." She turns away and starts to brush her damp hair, a monumental task with such a luxuriant mane.

I can hardly argue with that. And I'm not going to press her about the walking shadow, either. Push too hard and I risk making an enemy of her. "Ah, well," I say as I start plaiting my own hair, "never mind. Maybe later, when you're more settled here."

The brush moves through Elka's hair like a hard wind through a wheat field. She says nothing at all.

6

DAU

I t's a tradition in the royal line of Dalriada that the heir lives on his own holding, not at the king's court, which lies on the coast twenty miles or so to the north. Prince Aolu's residence is at Winterfalls, where Liobhan and her brothers grew up. Her parents still live in a rambling cottage on the edge of Dreamer's Wood, a smallish patch of forest containing a certain pool of which the local folk are extremely wary. You wouldn't want to take a summer swim, or even a wade, in that spot.

The arrangements at Prince Aolu's home are seamless. They know Master Donagan, of course, and they've been expecting our party. Our horses are led away to be stabled and we are taken to a comfortable chamber in the main house, where we're given refreshments. We have time to rest a little before our meeting with the king. But soon after I've finished eating, the household steward, Finnian, comes in to say Mistress Blackthorn has asked to speak with me in private, while Galen is resting. I glance at Archu; I'll need his permission for this.

"Go, then. But be back for the council." He doesn't need to remind me that I must act as a member of the team, not as a friend of Liobhan's family. Ears open for anything useful; be ready to share that information with him later.

"Dau!" exclaims Mistress Blackthorn, rising to her feet as I enter the chamber. She's a woman of slight build, not tall, and it's clear her hair was once of the same vibrant hue as her daughter's, though it's now streaked with gray. Perhaps it's the fact that she is a healer, a wisewoman, or maybe it's something in her character, but although she must be over fifty now, she doesn't seem old. Her features are full of life, and she smiles warmly as she reaches up to put her hands on my shoulders. "How good to see you! I'm glad the team could come so quickly."

Galen is lying on a pallet. Mistress Blackthorn has been sitting by his side, and now moves back there. Her son is a fine figure of a man by any measure, but now he looks diminished, the bones of his face stark beneath the sickly pale skin, his eyes shadowed, his breathing shallow. A bandage is wrapped around his head, coming down over his left ear. I assume he is asleep, but he seems remote, as if the world he inhabits is not the one in which we stand.

"How is he?" I ask.

"The wounds are staying clean so far. His main need is rest." Mistress Blackthorn falls silent for a little, gazing at her son. "It's hard to keep him quiet, Dau. I'm dosing him with soporifics, but there are limits to what is safe. He took a heavy blow to the head as well as the other injuries. When he's awake he's all for leaping out of bed, getting straight onto a horse and riding out on a heroic one-man rescue, with no real idea of where to start. And my son is exceptionally strong. He feels responsible for the prince's disappearance. He's weighed down by guilt, unreasonable as that is. It sounds as if the two of them were very much outnumbered. Both men and Crow Folk. Odd."

I feel for Galen. I know exactly what must be going through his mind. "Has he been able to explain more clearly what happened that day?"

"His memory is vague. One thing is plain to me. A bird, even an unusually large bird, doesn't deliver a blow to the head hard enough to render a man unconscious. Galen has wounds made by beak and claw. But the knock that felled him was delivered by human hand, or to be more precise, by a blunt weapon in a human hand. So at least one of the attackers survived and got away, taking that weapon with him. Why did they leave Galen alive to bring the tale back home?"

I recall that Mistress Blackthorn has a reputation for solving mysteries. Her mind will go down each and every pathway necessary to get to the truth. This is no ordinary herbwoman.

"As for what might have befallen Aolu . . . who knows? To me, the pieces don't add up." She rises, letting go of her son's hand. "We won't wake him. Sit there awhile, keep your eye on him while I mix his next draft."

There's a long table at one end of this quite capacious chamber, and on it are vessels and jars and other paraphernalia of an herbalist's craft. This household must have a stillroom, but I understand why Mistress Blackthorn would want to stay close to her son while she attends to his needs. "Dau," she says over her shoulder, her hands already busy on the worktable, "how is my daughter?"

"Liobhan's very well, Mistress Blackthorn. She sends her best regards to all the family, and wishes very much that she could be here."

"Mm-hm."

I hear in this muted response that there's no need for me

to explain that Liobhan was desperate to be part of the mission, and that if the elders hadn't barred her from being here she'd have rushed straight to the rescue, proving that she's not only her mother's daughter, but also Galen's sister.

"Liobhan could most certainly have made herself useful," Mistress Blackthorn says. "But I understand why she didn't come with you. And in a way I'm glad of it."

I remember at this point that Liobhan has not been home to see her family since she and I came to Winterfalls to give them the news about Brocc. That means they know nothing of the trials their daughter endured at Oakhill. It's for Liobhan to tell them that story if and when she chooses, though opportunities are scarce—members of the Swan Island team only get leave to visit family under exceptional circumstances, because of the need to keep ourselves and our activities out of the public eye.

Mistress Blackthorn is stirring something in a jar. The spoon clinks against the vessel, and Galen wakes with a shout, startling us. He sits bolt upright and tries to get out of bed. "I have to go! Now!"

I move fast, restraining him, while Mistress Blackthorn speaks with measured calm. "Galen. Breathe slowly. Take your time."

"Time? There is no time!" He struggles to shake off my grip; the man is indeed strong, but I am a Swan Island warrior and I can match him. A door opens, someone looks in, but Mistress Blackthorn shakes her head and the person retreats.

Galen is not breathing slowly. He's not calming himself. This takes me straight back to a time when I woke from unconsciousness to find that I had lost my sight. A nightmare, during which I recall behaving with less than perfect self-discipline. Thank the gods that's behind us now. "We'll help you, Galen," I say. "That's why our team is here. To do that, we need you to talk to us. We need to know everything you can tell us."

"And for that to happen," puts in Galen's mother, "you must first calm yourself. Breathe with me. In, two, three, four; out, two, three, four. And again, two, three, four . . ."

"Let go," Galen mutters. "I'm not some wild animal." I release my hold, staying close enough to stop him if he tries to bolt. He swings his legs over the side of the pallet. "Privy," he says.

"I'll take you," I offer, then realize I don't know where it is.

Galen squints at me. "Dau," he says, taking a moment or two to recognize me. We've only met a couple of times. "Is Liobhan here, too?"

"Sadly, no."

A grunt from him. I take it to mean, *That's a pity, because she'd certainly be getting things done, not sitting around talking about it.*

"All right to go?" I ask Mistress Blackthorn.

"I don't need a nursemaid," snaps Galen.

"Indeed not," says his mother. "But that draft makes folk weak in the legs, and I don't want you falling down any steps and adding a new collection of injuries." A tactful lie, at least in part. She doesn't want him making a run for it. Not that he'd get far; there'll be guards on the gate. "Let Dau help you, and come straight back here."

Galen gives me directions to the privy, which is not far away. He is unsteady on his feet and curses under his breath. We pause on the way back. Galen looks from one side to the other, as if for spies, then says, "Dau, you've got to help me. We've got to find him. Aolu's no fighter. They'll hurt him. We have to act quickly. Say you'll help me, please."

"We will, Galen. And we know time may be short."

"I don't know who took him," he says, putting a hand up to his face, where the bandage obscures the marks made by his attackers. "I don't know where he is. We were just sitting there, Dau. Talking, joking. Laughing over his attempt to teach me a song. And now Aolu's gone. What sort of protector am I? What sort of friend?"

"I'm sure you did your best," I tell him. "But sometimes even your best isn't enough. I know what a Crow Folk attack is like; I've survived one myself. Come, we'll go back in." My attempt at a casual tone is not entirely successful. "We have a meeting with the king soon, and we'll make a plan."

Back in the sickroom Galen refuses to return to his bed, instead sitting awkwardly on a chair with a blanket around his shoulders. Mistress Blackthorn gives him a cup of something that smells of honey and berries and he drinks it without protest. The short trip to the privy has exhausted him; a sheen of cold sweat coats his skin. But he wants to talk now, and since nobody has called me to the meeting, I sit and listen.

He tells a tale of how an innocent ride out into the forest ended in a sudden fierce attack by both Crow Folk and masked men. "I jumped to my feet." His eyes are dark with the memory. "I grabbed my knife, shouted, *Run!* And before I could draw breath, almost, there were Crow Folk above me, two at least, maybe three. Claws and beaks and beating wings everywhere, and I was hacking, slashing, fending them off . . . both men and birds . . . I was hurt—my face, my shoulder—and then . . . there was a moment, one clear moment . . ." Galen sets down the cup. Falls silent.

"Shall we leave it until later, Galen?" asks Mistress Blackthorn.

"No. I want to tell it now." Galen goes on, his voice unsteady. "I glanced over toward the path to the druid's hut, and I caught a glimpse of Aolu, looking back over his shoulder as he moved away. His face was ghostly pale. And . . . and something else beside him. Perhaps someone. Hardly more than a shadow, then I was struck on the head and it all turned dark. I knew nothing more until I came to, close to dusk, with Baodán's men crouched over me." A shudder runs through him. "I was dizzy, confused. My head was throbbing. I couldn't get my story straight. Baodán's men searched while there was still light. They found my knife, smeared with blood. Dead Crow Folk. And two dead men, one of whom it seems I killed. And Aolu was gone."

This would be devastating for a trusted bodyguard. How much worse when a man was as close to his charge as Galen is to the prince? "Donagan told us the searchers found an item belonging to Prince Aolu. Where was that found, and what was it?"

Galen's jaw tightens. After a moment, he looks at Mistress Blackthorn.

"We have it here," she says, rising and going to a small chest on a shelf. "May I . . . ?" she asks her son, brows up.

Galen gives a curt nod. His mother retrieves an object and brings it to him. The hand he reaches out is visibly shaking. With a jerk of the head he indicates that Blackthorn should pass the thing to me. It's a good luck charm, small enough to be threaded on a cord; there's a hole for that purpose. I'm impressed the searchers found something so unobtrusive on the forest floor. Perhaps the dogs sniffed it out. It's a shaped piece of wood, a perfect oval, and on it is carved what looks like an ogham sign: one upright, two branches.

"*Luis,*" says Mistress Blackthorn. "Rowan. A powerful charm of protection. It helps a person stay on their true path and not be swayed by false guidance. The prince would have had this around his neck; he wore it all the time."

"It was found like this? Still threaded on its cord?"

"It was. Not far from where the attack occurred, but in the general direction of the druid's hut."

A silence. An image is in my mind of someone wrenching the thing off the prince's neck by force. Unpleasant. And almost as unlikely as the amulet falling off by accident. "He must have slipped it over his head and dropped it as a clue." I wonder how he had time if someone was dragging him away. But I don't say that aloud.

"Yes," says Galen, turning a look of such gratitude on me that I can hardly bear it. My guess is that this good luck charm was a special gift of Galen's own making. Master Grim can turn his hand to fine wood-carving as well as expert thatching; he's a man of many parts. I expect he taught his children whatever they were keen to learn. I can't see Liobhan having the patience for carving. She does know how to mend thatch and dig drains, in addition to her other skills.

There's a tap on the door. It's Finnian, come to fetch me. I rise to my feet. "I'd best go. Thank you for telling me the story, Galen. We'll do our best, I promise."

"Just find Aolu," Galen says. "Find him quickly. I'll be on my feet soon, tomorrow most likely, I can go with you—"

"You know that's not going to happen." For all her stern words, Mistress Blackthorn finds a smile for her son. "I may be a capable healer, but I'm no miracle worker. Those wounds need time to mend." There's an authority in her voice that nobody could deny. Then she turns away, and I wonder if she's hiding sudden tears.

"Dau," says Galen quietly.

I stop and turn.

"Come and talk to me later. When you have a plan. Promise."

"I promise. Rest well, Galen."

As I leave the room, I realize I almost called him brother.

* * *

The arrangements have changed. The king is delayed and may not be here until tomorrow. There's enough time to get out to the druid's hut and back before full dark, barring disasters on the way, so we decide to do just that. Archu falls short of criticizing the prince's master-at-arms, Baodán, and his household guards for their limited searches thus far, though a wide search should have been the first priority, Crow Folk or not. We need Baodán's cooperation.

Someone brings a tracking dog and an item of the prince's clothing. We ride to the place where Galen was attacked and leave our horses tied up there. The hound then leads our party of four—Baodán and one of his men, Fraoch, along with me and Illann—to the druid's hut, which is closed up, with no sign of recent occupation. The dog makes it clear the scent does not end there. We consult, and decide to move on. The woods are quiet. We're armed, but although we spot Crow Folk once or twice high in the trees, they make no move to attack. Not ignoring us; watching and waiting.

At first the dog goes forward eagerly, nose to the ground, and we stride after him. Then he slows, as if the scent is less certain here. He's not ranging from side to side as if trying to get back on track, but walking with tail down and shoulders tight. Uneasy. Disturbed. I glance upward, my hand on the weapon at my belt; Illann does the same. But the dog has not been spooked by Crow Folk. As we go slowly forward, a smell reaches us, sweet, nauseating, unmistakable. The stench of death. Illann mutters under his breath; Baodán curses. If we've found the prince, we've found him too late.

"Move on," says Baodán. "Slowly."

"Watch your step," Illann adds. Meaning, don't trample all over possible evidence.

First, gouges in the soil. Then, undergrowth trampled or

torn. Dark patches that might be dried blood. And always the smell. The dog halts, holding his stance but shivering hard. Baodán calls the animal back, bids him sit, praises him for good work. Before us, on what might or might not be a track through the forest, there's a body. A cloud of buzzing flies surrounds the still form. Even without moving closer, I can see that someone has been done to death with extreme violence. And I can see the person has—had—fair hair. It's not the prince.

"Stay here, keep guard," says Illann to the master-at-arms and his man. "Dau, we'll go in closer."

The smell is enough to turn your stomach. The sight is worse.

"Crow Folk," I say. The damage is such that it's hard to tell which wound killed this man, but one thing I can see. The pitiful corpse, now bloated and discolored, was wearing a garment with a hood. And if I'm guessing right, the stained expanse of cloth that lies across his neck was a facial covering, worn to disguise his identity. This may be one of the men who crept up on Galen and Aolu.

"Dau," says Illann, who has moved away ten paces or so while I examine the dead man. I don't like the note in his voice.

There's a second man, killed with the same extreme brutality. Eyes gone. Gashes to the neck, tunic ripped open, a massive wound to the chest. Like the other, this man was wearing a hood and a face covering. He, too, is not Prince Aolu.

Illann calls Baodán over. Shows him one corpse, then the other. My eyes fall on something out of place, a little further off. Something hanging from a tree. Weapon in hand and skin crawling, I approach.

This victim was not killed by Crow Folk. Crow Folk are

untidy in their attacks; they rip and slash as if crazed, and they leave their victims where they lie. There is no sign of triumph in their killings. They do not cut off the head of their prey, fasten a strap around it, and hang it from a branch in macabre display, while the headless corpse lies on the ground below, blanketed by crawling insects. With my gorge rising anew, I force myself to look at this more closely. Creatures have been busy here, but the only way this head could have been severed was by a very sharp weapon in a human hand.

"Illann? Baodán?"

This head—this *man*—has dark hair. His clothing, like that of the other two, is quite plain; he could be any ordinary traveler. Like the others, this body bears no visible weapons. I shudder at the thought of searching all three of them, though we must do that. And then, gods help us, we'll have to carry them back to Winterfalls. I make myself ask the question. "Could this be the prince?" For although I did meet Aolu, I don't know him well. And this man's face is so disfigured he might be almost anyone.

Baodán drags his horrified gaze from the dangling head and squats down to examine the body. "Not him, thank the gods. Morrigan's curse, strung up by his own belt! Who would do such a thing? If only we'd searched up here sooner . . ."

We stand quiet for a bit, then Illann says, "The other two were killed by Crow Folk, Baodán. Your instinct to hold back was sound. To move earlier would have been to put your own men at greater risk."

My mind is racing now, trying to put the pieces together. This was an execution. A punishment. And whether it happened after the other two were attacked or before, whoever decapitated this man could still be out there. I consider and dismiss the idea that the prince might have done this. "Surely nobody deserves such a death. And . . . we must face the fact that whoever did this may still have Aolu captive."

"We must attempt to track them beyond this point." Illann sounds remarkably calm, though like Baodán he is rather pale. "You won't be wanting to send the same dog on further right now."

"You're right, I wouldn't ask it of him. He needs to go back to the kennel and rest. And we can't risk being caught out here after dark. We'll have to come back in the morning to retrieve the bodies. Might just about manage it with the four of us, but not with Crow Folk around."

"Mm." Illann's looking at the head more closely. "Dau, look at this belt. What's that marking on the buckle?"

The head moves oddly in the stirring air as I peer at the blood-smeared buckle. We can get a good look later, when the head's been laid next to its body. Gods, who'd want to be the one carrying *that* home? "Some kind of creature. A dog? A snake?" Every part of me wants out of this accursed place. I want the stink out of my nostrils, I want the wretched corpses out of my sight, I want the sounds of the forest, which include the occasional harsh calls of the Crow Folk, out of my ears. But I know what a Swan Island man should do under these circumstances. "Someone should stay here and keep guard," I say. "It feels wrong to walk away and leave these poor wretches, even if they were up to no good. I'll do it."

Illann and Baodán look at me in silence. Further away, Fraoch is still on watch, with the dog by his side. "All night?" Illann says eventually. "Hardly."

There's another possibility. But I shrink from it; it would be worse than waiting alone.

"We can't carry them all the way back," says Illann. "But we might manage as far as the druid's hut."

"Dagda's bollocks," mutters Baodán. "This makes my flesh creep. But better than one man, or even two, staying out here for so long. Wouldn't wish that on my worst enemy. And I won't leave these fellows lying, miscreants as they may have been. They're sons or fathers or husbands like the rest of us. I'll go and have a word with Fraoch. No need for him to see the worst of it."

And so I undertake what is a hard duty, even for a Swan Island man: carrying the body of a man over my shoulder, with his severed head in an improvised sling around my neck. Gods help me if the Crow Folk attack. Illann, too, carries a corpse, while Baodán and an ashen-faced Fraoch bear the heaviest of the bodies between them. The dog walks beside us, head down, tail tucked in, its unease plain in every part of its body. To stop myself from spewing up my guts or collapsing in a dead faint, I ponder the possibilities as I walk. Number one: the kidnap was bungled, the men fled, they were set upon by Crow Folk for a second time. All right as far as it goes, but where is Aolu? And who decapitated this poor sod? Number two: they made it this far with the prince in custody, then Crow Folk attacked again, killing two more. One of the survivors—we don't know how many men there were to start with—killed another and displayed his head as a warning, then the remaining men went on their way with Aolu still a captive. Number three: Aolu is dead like the others, out there somewhere. Number four: some unknown hand is moving all the pieces in this bloody game, and it's part of something else, something much bigger. I struggle down a steep decline, a cloud of insects buzzing around me and my evil-smelling burden. Number five contains my brother Seanan, whose current whereabouts are unknown. Seanan has always enjoyed bizarre acts of cruelty. As a child, I was often the victim. I have no reason at all to suspect he was involved in this, though he does know where I live. He does despise me to the depths of his soul, or would if he possessed such a thing. He does dispense punishment to those who offend him.

"Wait a bit," I grunt, working on my balance. I have to do this. I can't be weak. Fraoch's looking as if he might pass out, and even Baodán's breathing hard. Got to stop thinking about Seanan. Got to keep walking. Set this burden down and I may never pick it up again.

"All right?" That's Illann's voice, steady as ever. "Not so far now."

"Good work, lads," says Baodán. "We'll give these fellows back a bit of dignity, hm?"

I'm impressed. Surprised. Maybe I shouldn't be. Prince Aolu is a good man, wise and balanced like his father. He's considered an excellent candidate to be king when his time comes. He seemed to me respectful of other folk, no matter what their position in society. Never more so than in the way he dealt with Liobhan's parents at that difficult time. Perhaps every person in his household has learned that same way of looking at others. The sorry remnants of men that we're carrying were almost certainly up to no good. Another prince, another master-at-arms might have treated them very differently. Liobhan would find this interesting. Not the stench, the flies, the ache that goes from neck to shoulders to spine like a curse deep in the bone. But the moral questions. Which of my possibilities would she think most likely? Oh, she'd have a number six. Something involving a portal to another realm. I wonder if a new dog will pick up Aolu's scent again, over the vile stink of the recently dead. I wonder if that might lead both dog and searchers into a different world.

Finally, after what seems an age, we reach the druid's hut once more and lay our pathetic burdens inside the modest shelter. My clothing is soaked with a foul mixture of my own sweat and the effluvia of the decapitated man. I'm shaking with exhaustion, but I volunteer to stay. Someone should. Fraoch is clearly too distressed to be here on his own, and it's more appropriate for Illann and Baodán, my seniors in age and authority, to take this news back to Winterfalls. Whether this find will change our plans remains to be seen. Maybe someone there will know these men. They must have homes and families. Someone must have sent them here.

"No," says Illann. "We secure the door as best we can, and we all return to Winterfalls. Baodán?"

"I'm in agreement. Let's get ourselves and this hound back there and leave the task of retrieving these"—he waves a hand toward the corpses—"until the morning. We can bring horses as far as the path allows. Drink some water, men, take a little time to rest, then we'll seal this place up and head back as quick as we can."

I don't press the point. I want to be strong. But I'm aching all over, the stench is terrible, the insects are still hanging about, driving me crazy with their buzzing and whining. I'm not sure exactly what the stuff is that's soaked through my tunic to my bare skin and I don't want to know. I long to get into a hot bath and set this whole disgusting experience behind me. The bath will surely happen, since we smell so bad nobody will want us to set foot inside the prince's door. Forgetting won't be so easy.

7

AOLU

Am I dreaming? The sharp pain in my ankle tells me no. The strange whispering voices and a star-sprinkled night sky suggest otherwise.

I try to sit up, and a little voice says, "No, no! Lie still!" The voice is clue enough. Someone reaches to put a blanket back over me, and I look into a face that is child-sized, round-eyed, and decidedly nonhuman. Pain or no pain, I am lost in a dream. But . . . fragments of memory stir. The forest . . . the Crow Folk . . . running, running, falling . . . And after that what? Something evil, something that filled me with terror . . . clutching hands, scratching claws, ominous voices . . . Something kicking at my damaged ankle, an agony near unbearable . . .

But this voice is different. I dare to think it is kinder. "Where am I?" I croak. "Galen . . . Where's Galen?" My hand goes to my neck, feeling for the familiar shape, the comfort of my amulet. It's not there. How can that be? I would never let it go, never . . .

"Hush," the owner of the voice says. Not a child. A thing from an ancient tale; a being from a different world. "Lie still, you are hurt. Make no sound. Bad folk all around."

"But—"

"Shh! We must carry you to safety. Keep still or you may fall."

The surface on which I'm lying wobbles and lifts. In the velvet sky a crescent moon appears and disappears between treetops. It's cold. My ankle screams with pain. I am a prince, and I do not cry out.

Slowly my eyes adjust to the darkness. I am lying low to the ground; if I reached an arm down, my fingers might brush earth, stones, grass. I'm on a stretcher of some kind. And now, in the dimness, I can see the stretcher-bearers. The tallest of them might come almost to my waist, the smallest to my knee. Five or six of them on one side, the same on the other. My weight must surely be too much for such diminutive folk, but they trot along at a good pace, confident in the poor light.

I try to spot the one who spoke to me before, but I cannot tell which it is. Not that one, who looks a little like a rat. Or that one, with a mask over its face that glints silver in the moonlight. Nor yet that one, with its pelt of soft green fur. What are they? Where have I strayed? "Where are you taking me?" I ask in a hoarse whisper.

"Shh! Not safe yet!"

"You fell." It is that first being, the round-eyed one, its voice a murmur in my ear. "Fell between worlds. Fell into a dark place. Long time there. Quiet now."

They walk and walk. After a while I have to close my eyes, for the movement of the stretcher is making me nauseous. A fierce pain throbs right up and down my leg. Are they taking me home? My injury needs attention or I will be unfit for anything . . . A meeting. With councilors and landholders. Tomorrow. Or . . . perhaps tomorrow is long past.

"I need to—"

"Shh!"

"I am the prince of Dalriada, and—"

"Shh!"

I want to sleep. My body denies me, responding to each jolt or stumble with a fresh stab of pain. A meeting . . . a council . . . How far are they taking me? Did that being really say *between worlds*? "Galen." I form his name with my lips, but make no sound. "Galen, where are you?" And I see it, a flash of memory, the woodland clearing, the armed attackers with their faces masked, the Crow Folk. Galen fighting for survival. I hear him shout, *Run!*

I groan aloud, and my small captors hush me once more. "Quiet! Not a sound!"

I lie back, knowing myself too weak to do anything but comply. The stretcher moves on, bearing me I know not where. And as we move, the soft footfalls of the bearers are joined by other sounds: insidious whispers, echoing hoots, mocking laughter. *Come, come this way . . . oh, come this way . . . Small ones, set your burden down. Rest now, all will be well. We will take care of it . . .* A cackle. A strange drumming sound. *Trespasser! Spy! Give him to us! Ours! Ours by ancient right!*

"Steady," murmurs the big-eyed being to the others, and they walk on. I make myself lie still, though every instinct pulls me to leap off the stretcher, draw my weapon and stand ready. These small folk are in charge, and I must do as they tell me. Besides, I have no weapon; it is gone from my belt. As for standing, that will be out of the question.

A long, long time later, when the sky is beginning to lighten and the voices have died away, we walk along a pathway between silver-leaved birches and across a meadow. At last the bearers set the stretcher down.

"Safe now," says the big-eyed being. "Rest. Breathe. Well done. Hazel, go fetch Mother Ash. And watch out for the stranger."

One of the others—Hazel, I assume—goes ahead, and the rest of them sit in a circle around the stretcher, easing their tired limbs, rubbing their necks, and universally staring with curiosity at me.

"I am Robin," says the big-eyed being. "Prince of Dalriada, will you help us?"

8

DAU

Morning, and I'm in the garden of the prince's house. Some of Baodán's men have gone up to the druid's hut to remove its grisly contents. Baodán would have led them himself—I admire him for that—but Archu, as mission leader, overruled him. Once we'd passed on a brief account of what had happened, our entire filthy, exhausted party went straight to the bathhouse, on Donagan's orders. Our clothes were taken away, some to be laundered, some to be burned. We scrubbed and lathered and rinsed ourselves to within an inch of our lives. But I'm not sure I'll ever feel clean again.

I couldn't sleep. I've been up since first light. Someone offered food, but I can't eat. My stomach is still roiling. The smell of death lingers in my nostrils.

I wander about for a while, hoping to regain my composure before this meeting with King Oran. Baodán and Illann have passed the sorry tale on to those who'll be attending. Our arrival was such that almost everyone in the household must soon know what happened. Will they bring the bodies right into Aolu's holding for burial? I suppose there's no other choice.

I walk into a walled garden and see Mistress Blackthorn

alone, sitting on a bench. She looks distant, thoughtful. And exhausted—the sharpness of her features is more marked than usual, and I hesitate to disturb her. But she spots me in the garden entry and gestures me forward, summoning a smile.

"Dau. Come and sit down for a while, you don't look well. The royal physician, Master Frassach, is with Galen. Any news?"

She hasn't heard. I'll have to tell her. "There's news, yes. We haven't found the prince, but . . ." I lay it out, not insulting her by attempting to make the story kinder, cleaner, less violent. But not going into unnecessary detail either. Mistress Blackthorn is a good listener. When she asks a question, it's always to the point, but there's a gentleness in her tone, a kindness on her face that tells me she knows my insides are still knotted up with the horror of what happened earlier. I tell her what I had to carry back from that wretched scene. I recall the belt, which was taken away to be cleaned up. From time to time I need to stop talking and just breathe. The wisewoman sits and waits until I'm ready to go on.

"That's all," I say when my account is done. "We have to meet with King Oran soon. I don't know how this will change the plan. Perhaps someone here will recognize these men, although they were . . . they had been dead a while. Since the day of the prince's disappearance, I would guess. And their clothing was plain, apart from the . . . the belt. The one that . . . The buckle had a pattern on it. Mistress Blackthorn, I . . ."

She waits again. When I find I cannot say the words, she asks quietly, "You have a suspicion? A hunch?"

I can't tell her everything that happened when Liobhan and I were at Oakhill. Not on top of today's wretched tale. "A suspicion based on nothing more than my knowledge of a certain individual and what he is capable of," I say. "A . . . a style of cruelty that I've seen before, over and over. But there would be no reason for him to abduct the prince, unless it was simply because he wanted a nice bag of silver. No reason for him to be in these parts . . . I speak of my own brother, Mistress Blackthorn. Estranged brother. Banished from the family home. Whereabouts unknown to me."

She nods, asking no questions.

"There's a whole story attached, and it needs to wait until Liobhan is here to tell it. I'm probably wrong. No doubt there's more than one person in this world who enjoys inflicting terror on others."

"Indeed. I've learned that lesson for myself several times over. Dau, I should take this news to Galen. Best if I tell him myself. Can it be shared with Master Frassach as well?"

"He'll hear it soon enough; better coming from you than from household gossip. Our arrival caused something of a stir. A party's gone out to bring back the bodies." I hesitate, a question on my lips but unspoken.

"And the king will want both Master Frassach and me to examine them, in case our expertise allows us to uncover useful information. I see from the look on your face that you know that task will be neither easy nor pleasant. But I've seen a lot of death. I've seen some things that would curdle your blood, Dau. I try to remember that the dead deserve respect, and I just get on with the job. What else can a person do?"

I nod, but I can't find words. I wish I could be as strong as she is. I wish I didn't still feel shivery and sick. I remind myself of how stoical Liobhan was when we found her after my brother had tortured her and locked her up, bound, overnight. Soon after, she picked herself up and fought like a true warrior. "I see where Liobhan got her strength of purpose," I say, attempting a smile.

"Don't forget her father. He's like an oak. Strong, steady, and wise. He worries about her, Dau, though he'd never say so. He worries about all three of them."

"Please give Galen my apology. I'd promised to speak to him last night, but when we got back in I was fit for nothing." Morrigan's curse, Galen had been so close to meeting the same miserable fate as those men, ripped to death out in the forest. Why would the Crow Folk spare him? Why would they spare some of the masked men at first, only to kill them further into the woods? And what in the name of the gods has happened to the prince?

"I'll pass that on, Dau. Now go and have something to eat and maybe a restorative drink of mead before you attend your meeting."

I grimace. "I'd rather not distinguish myself by vomiting in public, Mistress Blackthorn." I've done that before. I don't plan to repeat the experience.

"I'm a healer, son. I know what I'm talking about. Something plain. A bannock. Stewed apple. Go and find Finnian, explain. That's part of being strong, Dau. Asking for help when you need it. Comes easier to some than others. Off you go, then."

The king has two advisers with him, one of whom is familiar: the lawman, Master Saran, whom I have met before under somewhat fraught circumstances. He and I exchange polite nods. Each of us is aware, no doubt, that the hearing at which we first encountered one another is best put behind us. I find a seat on a bench next to Illann and settle as best I can.

King Oran, pale but composed, greets us all and thanks us for our efforts. He makes special mention of yesterday's discovery. "I hope your retrieval party is well armed, Master

Baodán," he says. "There's no predicting the actions of the Crow Folk."

"My men are well prepared, my lord. As well as they can be."

"Good. The involvement of the Crow Folk confuses the situation greatly. For my son to be abducted by a hostile force or an aggrieved individual would be hard enough. But at least we'd have an idea of what to expect: a demand of some kind in return for his release. The Crow Folk muddy the waters. There are many questions to be answered. We'll need our healers to examine these bodies as soon as they arrive and report back quickly. Unfortunately, it seems the chances of identifying the victims are slim. We could spend a great deal of time trying to work out their origins, and meanwhile Aolu"—he falters a little on his son's name— "might be taken further and further away."

Master Saran speaks, perhaps to allow the king some breathing time. "My lord, it may be helpful if I provide the team with a summary of our action to this point. With your leave?"

"Yes, go ahead, Master Saran."

The lawman proceeds to advise us that various councilors and advisers from the court of Dalriada have been dispatched, appropriately escorted, to the most trusted leaders not only in Dalriada itself but also in the neighboring territories of Tirconnell to the west and Ulaid to the south. King Oran has decided this open approach is best. Nothing accusatory about it; it will be a request for whatever information may come to light, and perhaps assistance with searching.

"But of course," Master Saran adds, "no mention will be made of the involvement of the Swan Island team. Those to whom we have sent these emissaries are all personally known to the king and viewed as friends. The likelihood of any of those parties being involved in the prince's disappearance is next to none."

"What about the southwest?" Archu asks. "Northern Argialla? Breifne? If we're looking at a kidnapping, both should surely be included."

Now we're on uncomfortable ground. I hold myself silent, biting my lip.

"For now, we've ruled out Breifne as too distant, Master Archu," says Master Saran. "As for Argialla—the northernmost holding, Darkwater, shares borders both with ourselves and with Ulaid, so must be considered possible. But we are not familiar with the chieftain there, so we will make no direct approach. The same goes for the holding of Lakelands, in southern Ulaid, where there has recently been a challenge to the chieftaincy, with some hostilities as a result. Donagan tells me it would be awkward to send an official representative, since it is currently unclear to whom that person should be dispatched."

Garbh surprises me by putting up a tentative hand. "May I speak?"

"Go ahead, Garbh," says Archu.

"When I was working for the prince of Breifne, he traveled to visit the chieftain of Darkwater a couple of times. The old chieftain, that was, Lord Cernach. I heard his widow is chieftain now. Odd place. Strange feeling about it. Hard to put a finger on it. Everything looked all right, people going about their business and so on. But it was . . . edgy. Had the sense I was being watched all the time. And I wasn't the only one. Folk always looking over their shoulders, like they expected a nasty surprise."

Garbh has all our attention.

"If you were there as bodyguard to a visiting prince, I

suppose you were able to observe the chieftain and his wife. What was your impression?" asks Archu.

"He was a lot older than her. Seemed in good health for his age. Nothing remarkable about him that I could see. Lady Almha was very quiet. Almost timid in company. Makes it hard to think of her as chieftain. One of her advisers took against Prince Rodan. That caused a bit of a scene."

Those of us who were on the mission to Breifne exchange glances. It was all too easy to take against Prince Rodan, who was a singularly unlikeable person. His decision to relieve Garbh of his duties as bodyguard had been Swan Island's gain.

"Do you recall that adviser's name?" asks Archu.

Garbh shakes his head. "Sorry, no. A woman, it was. Very high in that household."

"If you think of anything further, Garbh, please let us know," says Archu. "And thank you." He looks at the king. "Darkwater should be one of our priorities. It's plausible that the attackers could have taken the prince back there. It sounds as if there may be a certain unrest in those parts. That, of course, is hardly sufficient reason for such an act."

"As for Lakelands, that's quite a distance to travel with a captive," Illann puts in. "They'd need to have been well organized, with good horses and perhaps some kind of conveyance. Therefore, not an opportunistic job, but a plan put in place by someone with funds. How this would link into a conflict over the chieftaincy I can't understand, unless one party intends a false accusation against the other to discredit him. A trumped-up charge of kidnapping."

"Of course," puts in Master Saran, "we anticipate some kind of ransom demand. Once that arrives the situation will become clearer."

"And if no such demand is received?" There's an edge to Archu's voice now.

There's a silence, then King Oran says, "You must act as you think fit." He's working hard to keep his voice steady, with some success. "I cannot hope for miracles. But I know your team is expert. And I trust you to take swift action."

"We will, my lord. The examination of these bodies may provide useful clues; we will at least wait to hear what Mistress Blackthorn and Master Frassach have to tell us. We'll work out a plan for Lakelands. As for an approach to the young widow at Darkwater, we have two men here who will be ideal for that."

I hold myself still. I put on a calm face.

"Dau will have no trouble passing for a visiting nobleman. It's plausible he'd be traveling with just one guard. If he makes himself pleasant to the ladies of the household he may uncover secrets quite readily. That's unless you're already known at the residence of this Lady Almha, Dau." He turns his head. "The same goes for you, Garbh. If there's any chance you might encounter someone you know from your former life, you're not sent on that part of the mission."

"Long while since I went there," says Garbh. "And if someone does know me, I can just say I lost one job and gained another. Simple truth. That's if I'm using my real name."

"Lady Almha wouldn't know me," I say. "I left those parts over eight years ago and I have no memory of visiting Darkwater as a child. Only . . . My lord king, you may not be aware that my father is Lord Scannal, one of the southern chieftains in Argialla. We have been estranged for some years. I have two brothers, and I resemble them quite closely. Both would have traveled, the elder perhaps widely. He is now gone permanently from home, his location unknown.

I must be honest. He and I are very alike. The brother next to me in age is a monk. He, too, has traveled. And . . . as Master Saran knows, I did pay a visit to my father's household in more recent times. A somewhat fraught visit."

"There's an obvious solution," says Archu. "But you won't care for it, Dau."

I hope he's not going to say what I think he's going to say.

"You go under your own name, quite openly. You have a cover story for why you're traveling in that part of Argialla. The most effective form of disguise is one that's close to the truth. As your bodyguard, Garbh will be well placed to pick up information from men-at-arms, serving folk, and the like."

The idea appalls me. But this is a mission; my personal feelings don't come into it. "While I attempt to gain Lady Almha's confidence? If we were to discover she was implicated in the prince's disappearance, what action could we take, just the two of us?"

"None. You'd be there solely to gather information, and to get out swiftly if you find any suggestion they're involved. You'd make your way to a safe house and get a message to Master Donagan or to me. We'd then act in whatever way was appropriate, and you'd be provided with whatever backup was required."

"The smaller the team, the less likely it is to attract notice," comments Illann. "But it might be helpful to have folk you can call in more quickly than that, if you do discover these people are implicated."

"You and I could tackle Lakelands, Illann," Archu says. "That's if we all agree it's worth investigating. A long ride, and a tricky situation at the other end. Staying in contact will be difficult under the circumstances. Master Donagan, I may ask you to send another message to the island before we depart. I believe Illann is right about backup. We could do with a couple of people at a midpoint, to be called in as required. Somewhere they can receive messages. But . . . numbers are already stretched. I don't know if Cionnaola would be able to accommodate that request."

We're all silent for a while. I feel I must speak up. "We haven't discussed the involvement of the Crow Folk and what that might mean. I know how unlikely it is that they were part of an organized attack. More likely their presence was mere coincidence. But . . . I have heard that in that forest there may be portals, entrances to another world. Places guarded by magic. Some folk would dismiss that as superstition; I would have done so myself not long ago, but I know now that such phenomena do exist. Prince Aolu disappeared, leaving no trace but the talisman he dropped on the way to the druid's hut. We should at least entertain the possibility that he has gone beyond the human world."

There's another charged silence. Nobody looks scornful or disbelieving, though Master Saran raises his brows.

King Oran sighs. He's not an old man, but there's a heavy weight on his shoulders, and it shows. "Such portals reveal themselves in their own time," he says. "I have considered this possibility. I have no idea how one might go about pursuing a search beyond this world. I imagine it would be fraught with peril, and I hesitate to suggest that your team should try such a thing. It seems to me wiser to act first on the assumption that this is a political kidnapping and that the presence of the Crow Folk was coincidental. It is early days yet; the ransom demand may come soon."

I can't say I think he's wrong. I can't put forward an argument based on gut feeling. I want to tell them about how

Liobhan got herself into the Otherworld by singing, and how Brocc calmed the Crow Folk, and various other strange things I've seen. But there's a plan, we have to move on, and the king is probably right—we could spend a long time hunting for portals to the Otherworld while the prince is locked up somewhere, or being taken ever further away.

There's a knock at the door. A man-at-arms stands there, with something in his hands. He passes it to Baodán.

"This is the belt I mentioned, my lord king. Cleaned up now."

The buckle catches the light; that looks like silver. Not the possession of a man-at-arms, and most certainly not that of some wayside ne'er-do-well. Now that the encrustation has been cleaned off, the pattern is striking.

"Not sure what that creature is," the master-at-arms says, passing the thing up the long council table to King Oran. "Look at it one way, you see a hound. Turn it a bit and there's a serpent. Something from an old tale, maybe. Who'd wear that?"

The king turns the belt in his hands, examining the buckle. "Dobhar-chú," he says. "A creature somewhere between dog and otter, or dog and fish. You have it correct, Baodán. The dobhar-chú appears occasionally in the ancient lore. I've never heard of it associated with a particular household or holding. Yet wearing it on the clothing does suggest a clan allegiance, an identity of some sort. A pity Brother Oisín is not in these parts; he'd have been sure to know more."

The king is a scholar and poet, like his son. One look is enough to identify him as Aolu's father. A strange thought comes to me. Liobhan's brother Brocc was adopted into a family whose members he resembles not at all, save for his and Liobhan's shared talent at music. But Brocc would fit right into this family. The king and his son are both men of middle height with a slender build and curling hair—Aolu's dark, Oran's iron-gray. If Brocc were introduced as Aolu's long-lost brother, folk would believe it. That's a notion I won't be sharing, knowing how unlikely it is. King Oran is known to be a man of flawless character and devoted to his wife and family. Besides, even if it were true, it would bear no relevance to this discussion.

I ask to see the buckle more closely, though when I take the belt in my hands, my stomach protests. I'm in danger of spewing up the very small meal I consumed on Mistress Blackthorn's orders, but I manage to keep it down. "The belt itself looks quite old," I say. "It shows signs of wear and tear beyond the foul use it was put to recently. But the buckle is in excellent condition, almost new. Recently purchased? A gift from a patron?"

"Could have been a bribe," suggests Garbh. "There's some kinds of men would do whatever a person wanted in return for a fine trinket like that. Pure silver and skillfully crafted. Worth a fair bit, I'm guessing."

"Surprising the man wore it openly," Archu puts in. "It would surely have been a covert mission, if Prince Aolu was the intended target. I'd have expected the plainest of clothing in the drabbest colors. They wore hoods and face coverings. A silver buckle seems distinctly out of place."

"None of the local families has this as an emblem?" I ask.

"None within Dalriada," says Master Saran. "And none of the most prominent clans in our neighboring territories."

"My lord," puts in Archu, "in the lore you spoke of, are there any places within Dalriada or the bordering kingdoms where this dobhar-chú is reputed to have been seen? It would be a water-beast, I imagine, if it's half otter or fish. Lakes, streams? Such tales are often connected with a particular spot, aren't they?"

"Indeed." The king manages a smile. "A very good point, Master Archu, and one we should pursue before we determine our course. Lacking Brother Oisín, we need someone who can look through the prince's library for pertinent information and locate it quickly. Today if possible."

"If I might have the assistance of the household scribe," says Master Saran, "I will undertake that task. Old tales do not fall within my field of expertise, but I can read quickly in both Irish and Latin, and I know how to find what I am seeking. Provided it is there to be found, of course."

"We might also ask Mistress Blackthorn about the dobharchú," I venture. "As a wisewoman, she may be better acquainted with this kind of tale than any of us."

"Good," says the king. "Both of those things should be done without delay; we may be able to narrow down the search. Though Mistress Blackthorn's other task must take precedence. We ask a great deal of that woman."

The meeting is adjourned until the bodies have been examined. Master Saran heads off to the library to begin his research. Garbh and I spend some time talking about our visit to Darkwater and planning our cover stories. We may be acting as ourselves, in name at least, but that doesn't mean we'll be sharing our true personal histories.

Archu comes to tell us that we'll need more appropriate clothing. I can't borrow Galen's clothes; he is taller than me and more solidly built, close to his father's size. But those garments are, of course, well suited to a nobleman's bodyguard, and they fit Garbh quite well. He accepts the offer of a tunic, two shirts, and some trousers. I can't borrow Prince Aolu's things either. They're too small for me, and besides, wearing them would feel wrong.

"I don't need to look like a nobleman," I tell Archu, who's frowning over a selection of not-quite-right garments found for us by Finnian. "If I'd stayed at Oakhill as my father wanted me to, I'd have chosen to wear the plainest garb I could find. Even if I'd eventually ended up as chieftain."

"You may be using your real name and identity for this," Archu says, "but you'll be playing a part from the moment you ride out. You wear what Lady Almha and her household will expect the son of a chieftain—even the estranged son—to wear. Plain is fine. Nobody's insisting on silver and gold and fancy hats. But it needs to be of good fabric and an excellent fit."

Finnian's hovering, looking anxious. "We have a capable seamstress here," he says. "If there's something that's a near fit, Grian should be able to adjust it for you in time. Try this one again, Master Dau."

Oh gods, he's already talking as if I'm the highborn individual who has to weasel his way into Lady Almha's confidences. I am not looking forward to this at all.

I put on the tunic over one of Galen's shirts. "It's not too bad. Those gray trousers were the best fit. The shirt shouldn't need altering." The tunic that nearly fits me is blue. When I left my father's house for the last time I swore I'd never wear blue again. His serving folk and men-at-arms wear the color, and the family tunics have a silver emblem embroidered on the breast, a sword and dagger crossed. My brother burned that emblem onto Liobhan's arm; he carved it onto the bodies of captive Crow Folk. Let me not encounter Seanan on this mission. If I do, it will be hard not to kill him.

"Excellent, Master Dau. I'll call Grian now and she can work out what alterations are required. She's very quick."

I stand still, turn, and move various parts of my body on

request while Grian the seamstress takes measurements and puts in little tacking stitches here and there. She tells me one set of good clothing won't be enough, and makes me try various other garments until we find a second almost-fitting outfit. She says the shirts can't be worn without what she calls *some tidying up*. Grian is efficient and decisive—she'd be an asset on Swan Island—but I'm glad when it's over. Both outfits should be ready to try on later in the evening, the seamstress says, and if finishing touches are required she'll have them done by morning. I'm so grateful she doesn't call me Master Dau that I give her a big smile and my heartfelt thanks. She grins back, eyes bright, then heads out with the garments over her arm. I wonder if she'll need to work all night. She looks fifteen at most. I think of an even younger girl who narrowly escaped marrying my brother. I thought I'd banished those memories during the healing time back on Swan Island. Liobhan and I have been content in each other's company, training hard and working hard. We've been busy. We've been happy. Justice has helped, too. He's been a good companion; a reminder that even the gravest of wounds can heal with time and love. Now it's all crowding back, just when I don't want it.

I can't go and unburden myself to Mistress Blackthorn. She's got the bodies to deal with today. I don't want to talk to anyone in the team. They might decide not to send me after all. I must set aside my personal difficulties. They're irrelevant. As a child I learned how to lock my feelings away. I can do that again. A Swan Island warrior strives to be the best of the best. Where others fail we succeed. Even if the task seems impossible.

This is my first mission since I was sent home to Oak-hill. It's a test. I will excel. Even if I come face-to-face with my brother. Even if he's played a part in this. Even if acting like a nobleman sickens me. There's a job to be done, and I'll do it.

Later in the day we're called back in. Everyone who was there earlier is present, with the exception of the lawman. We're joined by Mistress Blackthorn, pale but calm, and a grim-faced Master Frassach, who confirms our assumptions about the deaths of those three men we found. Two perished from Crow Folk wounds. The third died by human hand, the weapon most likely a sword. His head was not severed as cleanly as I thought; Frassach estimated the assailant delivered two strikes, possibly three, before the man was decapitated. By this point, even the seasoned Swan Island men at the table are looking a little green in the face.

"And something further," says Mistress Blackthorn. "That man had a crippling injury to his legs, most likely inflicted while he was still alive. It would have prevented him from standing. From walking. He could not have fled from his attacker."

We're all silent for a moment. "Crow Folk?" asks Illann eventually.

"Crow Folk don't smash people's bones. This was the work of humankind. Done with a club, or similar."

"Troubling," says King Oran. "It seems probable this man was killed, viciously killed and made an example of, by one of his own party. Why? Did he fail to show courage against the Crow Folk? Did he refuse to follow orders? We could go on guessing forever, and meanwhile . . ."

Meanwhile Aolu could be moving further and further from our reach. There's no need to put that into words. But there is one possibility I think needs mentioning. "By the time those men reached that spot and were attacked, it's possible Prince Aolu was no longer with them," I venture. "The killing of that man might have been a punishment. For letting their captive escape. For a failed mission."

"The dog followed the prince's track all the way to that place," points out Baodán. "He must have been there."

"He might have passed that spot before his pursuers reached it," suggests Illann. "Passed it and moved on."

"Not the right direction for home," someone says.

"He was hardly going to turn back and walk straight into his pursuers' arms," says Mistress Blackthorn. "When a man's in fear for his life he may make foolish decisions, and we must allow for that. But this is Prince Aolu. If your son was alone, running from his would-be captors, Oran, what would you expect him to do?"

I note her casual use of the king's first name, and the little smile he offers with his reply.

"He'd stay calm and use his wits. He'd hide somewhere until he judged it safe, then return home. We will all rejoice if that does occur, my friend. But days have passed since he went missing, and we need to act on the other possibility: that he is still in the custody of a person angry enough to sever a man's head from his shoulders, and warped enough in his thinking to put it on display. Not to speak of crippling the poor wretch first." The king draws breath; for a moment he puts a hand to his face, as if to shield his eyes from a vision we can see only in our minds. "Dau and Illann are right. That the dogs could not find a trail beyond the place of that killing does not mean Aolu was never there. Baodán?"

"My lord, as I said earlier, it's now been some days since the prince went missing, and a trail does eventually go cold. Our dogs are good. If there's anything to be found, nine times out of ten they'll find it. I can't offer any explanations. The prince can't have vanished into thin air. Either he's gone off on his own, or he's still with whoever survived the Crow Folk attack."

Or he's dead, I think. Lying alone and cold out in the woods. Or he's gone where we can't reach him.

"Any further observations, Mistress Blackthorn?" asks the king.

"At this point, no. I'll think on this further, as will Master Frassach, and I'll have a word with Grim. If we come up with any more ideas we'll inform you at once. Right now, if you'll excuse me, I'd best get back to my son."

"Of course," says Oran, and stands courteously as she leaves. I did know they were old friends, but this level of respect from the king of Dalriada to a local wisewoman is quite startling. Maybe one day I'll hear the story behind it.

Donagan begins to talk about exchanging messages by pigeon, but he's interrupted by the entrance of Master Saran, holding a bound book and looking as excited as a skilled man of the law can look—that is, marginally less grave and controlled than usual. "I have a reference," he says as all eyes turn to him. "No exact location, and the place-name is an old one, I believe, perhaps no longer in use. There's an extraordinary illustration, done in colored inks with gold leaf. Let me show you. But don't touch the page; the book is precious."

The image depicts what must be a dobhar-chú. If that's a full-sized man it's got in its teeth, then it's a lot bigger than an otter, and would dwarf Justice, who is a big, solid hound. This thing is a monster, and the beautifully painted illustration makes that clear: blood pours from the victim's throat, around which the dobhar-chú's jaws are clamped, and the man's face is one great scream of terror. The two appear to be in the shallows of a river or pond; on the bank are an overturned cup and a leather bag such as a traveler might wear on his back. A shoe lies abandoned. In the distance, dark forested hills.

"There's a whole story in this picture," Archu says as we take it in turn to look. "A man sits by the river to bathe tired feet and have a drink and a bite to eat. Up comes the monster and takes its own bite, and the fellow's journey—to find better employment, to attend his sister's wedding, to be reunited with his sweetheart—is over in the blink of an eye. To the dobhar-chú, the story is briefer: a satisfying dinner is had. A person could make a song about that. A warning to travelers. What kind of book is this, Master Saran?"

"A bestiary, full of creatures that may or may not exist in this world, Master Archu. Such a project allows the creator to exercise his imagination fully, and this one certainly has, though there is a discipline and method to his approach that pleases me greatly. Each entry includes a short tale—this one runs much along the lines of your interpretation—and some details about the nature of the animal. So, the dobhar-chú is rarely found, it haunts waterways and feeds mostly on fish. But it will also take sheep, goats, or cattle that stray too close to its haunt; young deer, foxes, whatever it can catch. Including humankind."

"Cattle?" Illann's brows rise. "How big is this thing?"

"Its dimensions are not provided. Big enough to set its jaws around a man's neck. Big enough to take down a cow. This part is interesting." He reads aloud: "'The dobhar-chú fills its belly, then retreats to its riverside hollow to sleep. Its howl is greatly feared, for the shrill sound is an assault on the ears. Should three or four of these creatures congregate to make music together by night, the sound of it can drive folk out of their wits and cause cattle to drop dead in the fields. Fortunately, such a gathering is rare. It is thought to occur only under the first full moon of springtime, if the sky is free of cloud. In places where the dobhar-chú is known to dwell, folk lock their animals in the barn on such nights. They bar their doors and close their shutters, block their ears with wads of wool, and stay indoors until morning.'"

"Where was this man supposed to have been attacked by a dobhar-chú?" I ask. "Judging by the painting he didn't live to tell the tale."

"In the story it simply says the traveler was in the north," Master Saran says. "That could mean anything. North of where? But the writer has made a note at the end. 'The last known sighting of a dobhar-chú was recounted to me by an old woman from the settlement of Illady Falls in the north, and occurred in the hills above her home. When gathering lichens for dyeing, she spotted one of the creatures swimming in a remotely situated lake. The dobhar-chú lifted its great head from the water, fixed its hideous eyes on her, and let out a piercing cry. The woman laid an offering on the shore. At this, the creature allowed her to go on her way unharmed.'"

"That woman showed some presence of mind," comments Archu. "What was the offering?"

"That information is not provided. Food, maybe."

"With a lake full of fish ready for the catching?"

"Such details are hardly important," says Baodán, failing to mask his impatience. "The location of this settlement is all we need to know. Anyone heard of Illady Falls?"

Nobody has. "There are clues," I point out. "Hills, lichens, a remotely situated lake. But there must be many places matching that description."

"Dau, talk to Mistress Blackthorn about this when she's free," Archu says. "Ask if she knows of the place and whether she thinks it's worth pursuing the dobhar-chú link, bearing in mind that we must now move with speed. I'll speak to you again later."

"One question," I say. "What is the emblem of Lady Almha's clan?"

"It's a kind of twig with leaves on it." That's from Garbh. I'm surprised that he knows this. But he did visit that household as a bodyguard, and he wouldn't have been accepted as a Swan Island warrior if he didn't have good powers of observation.

"What plant?" asks Archu.

"Not being knowledgeable on such matters, I can't tell you."

Master Saran fishes a stub of charcoal from his pouch and hands it to Garbh. "Draw it for us." He indicates the tabletop. "It will brush off."

Considering the materials, Garbh's drawing is quite good. The stem is long and narrow, and carries pointed leaves in neat pairs. "On the household tunics this is upright, embroidered in cream on a green background. I never asked anyone what plant it was. That's from Lord Cernach's time, of course, when I went there."

Master Saran glances around the table. The first to reply—no surprise—is King Oran. "Elder," he says. "Without a doubt. Note that elders love water, and the dobhar-chú lives in or near lakes and streams. But it's a tenuous connection. I don't know what the emblem of Lakelands might be. We can find out, but perhaps not before you need to be on your way."

"Leaping to conclusions on the basis of one man's belt buckle wouldn't be wise," says Archu. "We will listen to Mistress Blackthorn's opinion, if she wishes to offer one. But since we're leaving in the morning, we'd best concentrate on the strictly practical."

★ ★ ★

After supper, I seek out Mistress Blackthorn again. The wise-woman seems pleased to see me, late as it is. And not only because I've brought a flask of mead. Galen is asleep.

"How is he?" I ask when I've settled myself and poured a drink for her.

"Much the same, Dau. He can't sleep without the drafts. But I believe he's a little better each day."

"I'm glad of that. How soon do you think he'll be up and about again?"

"We'll get him moving in gradual stages. You've seen how he is. How furiously he wants to be his old, strong self again. The challenge will be persuading him not to rush things. I'm forever grateful to Donagan, and to the king, for trusting me to look after him and letting me make use of the facilities here. It's not common for men of power to trust village healers."

"I believe you're a great deal more than that," I say, surprising myself. I've thought so since the day I first met Liobhan's mother. But I seldom put such thoughts into words.

"Not in some folk's eyes. But we landed in a place where we were appreciated, Grim and I, and I never cease to be thankful for that."

I ask her about the dobhar-chú, and am unsurprised that she knows what the creature is and has heard quite a few tales about it. She's not familiar with either Lakelands or Darkwater, and she's never heard of Illady Falls.

"I've heard a story about a traveler being bitten in half, but it was supposed to have happened somewhere in Connacht," she says. "And there are tales in the south, too, where I lived as a child. Many of the lakes were supposed to have a resident dobhar-chú. I wondered if those tales were invented to warn children off entering deep water and coming to grief." She takes a sip of mead. "It's not the sort of thing you choose as a family emblem, Dau. Too easy for folk to interpret it as ill luck, a curse. The usual choice is something like a crown, a sword, a brave steed, a sun or moon."

I think of my family's emblem, a sword and dagger crossed, and feel suddenly sick again.

"Dau?" Her tone is all concern.

I shake my head, as if that might rid it of the vile memory. "Nothing," I mumble, and recover myself as best I can. "So the belt buckle is not going to help us?"

"That kind of sign might be worn by someone other than a chieftain or a chieftain's retainer. Someone with a link to the uncanny. A wisewoman or druid, possibly, though I would never choose such a token. A practitioner of magic. Or, perhaps, an artisan, a worker in fine silver, though one would imagine the thing was crafted to be sold, probably commissioned as a special design. If you happen to run into a silversmith on your way to Darkwater, a member of your team might chat to him about such special designs, not mentioning the dobhar-chú, of course, unless the craftsman brings up the subject. Think of some other strange creature, the aonbharr, perhaps, or the ollphéist. One a great horse, the other something like a serpent. The sort of thing a man might want on a buckle or brooch."

I try and fail to imagine myself wearing such an item. "Mistress Blackthorn, neither the king nor Archu seems inclined to have us spend much time investigating the possibility that the prince has crossed a border between worlds. Under the circumstances, shouldn't we be doing that as well as putting the other plans into place?"

If Mistress Blackthorn is surprised, she shows no sign of it. "I understand this argument, Dau. But I think they're right. The most urgent thing is to look at the simpler answer, abduction by human hands. The ferocity of that man's execution troubles me. I hope you will be careful. I know your work is dangerous in its nature; we worry about Liobhan every day, even though we know she's doing what she always dreamed of, and most likely excels at it. We worry about Brocc, so far away and living such a different life. Even though that was his choice." She hesitates, turning her cup in her hands. "Dau, even as you pursue this in the human world, you should keep your eyes and ears open for anything that might suggest the involvement of uncanny forces, and I don't only mean the Crow Folk. I wish Brother Oisín had not chosen to stay away this spring. That man is wise, and he's tolerant in his thinking. Should you encounter him on the road, you should take time to tell him the story and ask him for an opinion. He's entirely trustworthy. I cannot think who else might be consulted on that possibility. Except . . ."

I clear my throat, feeling awkward. "Liobhan did mention that you had an old friend in the Otherworld. Someone you helped as a child."

"Conmael." There's a new warmth in Mistress Blackthorn's voice. "My daughter must really trust you to tell you about him."

"We'd trust each other with our lives," I say. "And with our secrets. Though the family secrets on my side are . . . unsavory. That's a tale for another time."

"I would not call on Conmael except in the direst of circumstances. Not unless it were impossible to save the prince with the resources already to hand. And since this is the king's son, those resources will be considerable."

"I understand. That's what Liobhan said, more or less. But . . . if this did prove to be life-or-death, and it turned out to be a matter of—of spells and charms—would you consider that?"

"Ask me when and if that time comes, Dau. I don't like to presume on a friendship. Conmael is a person of great authority in his own world; his time is precious. Any debt he believed he owed me, he has already repaid several times over. But you can ask. That's provided you and I are both in the same place at that moment. If I were younger, if my son did not need me here, I would offer to go with you. I regret that neither Liobhan nor Brocc is free to help you."

"I regret it, too. Each of them would be able to help in ways none of the current team can. We—Liobhan and I— have seen Brocc within the last year. He came to our assistance when we were in difficulty. On a mission. Not officially a mission, but . . . it required the same sort of approach. Brocc showed himself to be brave and unselfish, as he always was. Then left again once the job was done. He seemed well. Liobhan spoke to him at length; she would be able to tell you more."

"It's good to hear anything at all, Dau. I'm relieved to know Brocc is well." There's a brief silence as she turns those questioning eyes on me. "Am I correct in thinking we should consider you as an extra son now?"

Oh, I wish Liobhan were here to witness this moment. "I would be honored, Mistress Blackthorn. Liobhan and I . . . we have become very close. More than comrades. But she's dedicated to her work."

"And you, Dau?" She's doing that wisewoman thing again, stripping back my layers with her gaze. No hiding from Mistress Blackthorn.

"Swan Island is my home. The community there is my family. But . . . Liobhan is my heart." I look at the ground; I can't meet her eyes any longer.

"We're happy for you both," she says quietly. "Don't get

yourself killed, Dau. There's a future to live, and you're needed."

I bid her good night and leave before I lose my composure entirely. I head for the men's quarters, where I must finish packing for tomorrow's departure. I do not enter until my face is completely dry of tears.

9

BROCC

Niamh has learned to crawl on hands and knees. She wobbles, then steadies. The look on her face enchants me, so solemn and purposeful until she spots Dandelion, offspring of Moth-Weed and Gentle-Foot, capering across her path. Niamh reaches out a hand to grab the little one. Dandelion skips out of reach and my daughter, unbalanced, collapses on the forest floor, gurgling with laughter. I would have cautioned her to go gently; beside Dandelion she is a giant. But even though Niamh is so young, her instincts are good. She has never hurt the tiny being, even on the rare occasions when she has managed to catch him. I seem to recall that human babies put everything in their mouths, and Niamh certainly does that with stones and moss and leaves. When she first caught Dandelion she simply examined him closely, dribbling a little. Then she set him down on the ground again and he scampered off.

My daughter is delighted by her new mobility. Never having known danger, she is entirely fearless. It may not be long before she walks, climbs, balances, runs. Every time I leave the gathering place I worry about her. Even with others watching over her. Even when Niamh is sleeping under the careful eye of Nightshade or Moon-Fleet. But I must continue my work with Shadow. Each time we meet, we grow closer in understanding. Soon, surely, I will learn how I can help the Crow Folk. Soon my strange friend will find a way to tell their whole story.

Today, after our midday meal, Eirne withdraws to her retreat accompanied by Nightshade. My wife's cheeks have lost their rosy hue. Her eyes are shadowed and her skin pale. She is not feeding Niamh as often as she was. Moon-Fleet sends some of the smaller folk out to fetch goat's milk. Where they go for it, I do not ask. Perhaps they milk a farmer's animal while his attention is elsewhere. How they keep the creature calm enough I cannot imagine, but I know many old stories about mischievous folk playing tricks of that kind. It feels extremely odd to be in the middle of such a tale. Indeed, it feels wrong that they must steal in order to ensure my child receives sufficient nourishment. It is just as well Niamh's spirit of adventure extends to food as well as exploration. She savors the goat's milk. She is also happy to drink water. Rowan has made a little cup for her. She has sampled not only the root and nut mash, but also various fruits and berries, and sometimes a kind of porridge. I think the grain, too, is stolen. It will be easier when my girl grows some teeth.

While the small ones clear away the platters and cups, I take Niamh to the bard's hut, where I settle her on my pallet. She is quiet, listening as I sing a song about rowing a little boat along a river and hearing frogs calling and crickets chirping and a lark singing high above. Then I play "Flight of the Fair One" on my harp, watching as Niamh's eyelids droop, and her thumb goes into her mouth, and she falls asleep.

I would like to curl up next to her and sleep, too. With her beside me, surely I would dream only good dreams. Dreams in which my daughter can grow up safely, and my wife is happy and well, and the world is as it should be. Dreams of seeing my human family again. But I cannot spare the time for rest. Shadow will be waiting.

I open the door. "Rowan?" I call softly.

He's there in a moment. He understands. I have the best of comrades here. The longing to go back, to see my parents and Liobhan and Galen, is balanced by the need to stand by this clan, my little family in the forest, my Otherworld brothers, Rowan and True. I cannot turn my back on them.

"I shouldn't be long," I tell Rowan in a murmur. "She won't wake for a while."

"I'll stay by her, Brocc. Go, do what you must."

I still haven't told him about Shadow and Watcher. I haven't told anyone. But Rowan and True have shared some of my strangest encounters with the Crow Folk, and neither is stupid. They know what I want to do. I tread on dangerous ground. Eirne does not know. Her fear and loathing of the Crow Folk make it impossible to tell her the truth, though at some point I must. Rowan was her most loyal retainer before I came to this place. True would never have opposed her decisions. If she believes they were complicit in this all three of us may feel her fury. I can't tell her. Not yet. Not until I understand what the Crow Folk need. Not until I have a plan to present. Soon. It should be soon.

In the clearing, Shadow is ready for me, a solitary spot of darkness amid the fresh greens of the forest. The air is clear and sweet. Bluebells grow here, and snowdrops, and other tender flowers. Without the presence of Shadow, the place would be alive with small birds hunting insects. I glance upward and—yes—Watcher, too, is here, perched somewhat lower in the tree than the usual spot. I have assumed that Watcher is female, perhaps Shadow's mate. But they may be comrades bonded by adversity.

I settle, cross-legged on the flat stone. I am tempted to move closer to Shadow, but no—that is not necessary, and I can't risk losing his hard-won trust. I breathe deeply, then sing the formal verses with which this ritual always begins. I imagine my fingers sweeping across the harp strings; I recall the birdsong that punctuated my last greeting to him. As I think of that, Shadow answers me, not with words, but with a soft sound, less of a caw than three deep notes of song. Tears sting my eyes. A wonder. A wonder like the moment when that young creature, an infant of the Crow Folk, sang back to me as I tried to soothe it with a lullaby.

> *I come in peace.*
> *I come in trust.*
> *I come in friendship.*
> *I am here.*

This greeting is perhaps not needed today; Shadow's contribution to the song tells me he knows my purpose and welcomes me. Still, there is a way these things should be done. Am I starting to think like a druid?

Today Shadow is calmer. His thoughts are no longer a maelstrom of churning seas and wild winds, though the sea is there, a constant wash of sound underlying everything. Perhaps that sound is in his blood, a relentless call. The island remains, a stark form against a sky brighter now, first light touching the clouds with gold and silver and turning the water to a glittering carpet. The wind still blows in that place; the sea is restless. Perhaps it is always thus. On Swan Island there's rarely a day without some breeze, and more often than not it's a strong one. The isle of Shadow's thoughts is far more remote. It must be buffeted from every quarter. A wind like a scourge. I see no trees in that place.

The ledges are empty. No sign of the creatures I saw before, perhaps Crow Folk, perhaps something else. Where are they? Out catching fish to feed their young? But I see no nests, no eggs, no fledglings.

In Shadow's thoughts, the sun emerges from the sea, a golden disk, and all is bathed in light. In that moment the great bird comes, winging over the lonely isle, its flight both graceful and strong. And . . . there they are. On the ledges, in twos and threes, black cloaked, or maybe black winged, I cannot tell, only that they do not have beaks like birds, and their eyes, turned up in awe to gaze at the wondrous creature passing over, are not the eyes of birds. These beings are neither bird nor animal nor human.

"They are your tribe," I whisper. I don't need to make it a question. Deep down, I know it's true. "Your people, Shadow. And that is your home."

Shadow's call sounds out again: three deep, calm notes. And, as I hold my breath in delight, Watcher flies down to perch beside him on the branch, closer than she has ever come before. Then, sheer magic! Another, then another, then yet another voice joins in. I see them above me, the beings we diminished by dubbing them Crow Folk, perched in the trees here and there, some almost hidden by the foliage, some shrinking into pockets of shadow, a few in full sight as they fill the clearing with their extraordinary call. There is a deep longing in that sound. Is it a cry for help? Is it a response to my greeting: *We, too, are here?* I am so full of feelings that I cannot move. Some greater power holds us in its hand.

Then, sudden as a knife in the dark, a furious shriek jolts me from my trance. Eirne. Eirne on the forest edge, above the clearing, spewing out a tirade of vile, accusatory words. Nightshade behind her, trying to pull her back, pleading with her. Eirne thrusts her sage away with some violence. Shadow lifts his wings, flies up toward safety. Watcher is slower, more damaged by the wounds my brother inflicted on her. Eirne raises her hands. I feel the magic pouring from her, furious, destructive, unstoppable.

"No!" I shout, on my feet and running toward her. "Please!" I stumble, I curse, I fall to my knees.

A blinding white light blasts forth. I curl over, arms shielding my head, eyes squeezed shut. Close by me there's a screech of agony, cut sharply off. Above, a flurry of wings. I cannot look. But I must look. I must bear witness. I straighten, open my eyes, rise to my feet to see a dark form diving down on my wife. And there is Nightshade, moving in front of Eirne, arms stretched wide in protection, owl eyes shining with courage. Eirne cowers behind her.

Shadow strikes. It is so quick, so expert, that Nightshade falls without a sound, leaving Eirne exposed. But Shadow does not touch her. Instead, with a few powerful wingbeats he is up and away, and by the time he disappears from view above the treetops, only one of his kind remains here: Watcher, destroyed on the very day she summoned the courage to acknowledge me. She lies in the center of the clearing, a lifeless thing of feather and bone. Up on the rise, crouched by Nightshade's limp form, my wife is screaming at me in fury and grief and denial.

I go to Watcher. I take off my short cloak and lay it over her sad remains. I kneel, searching for words that will not come. Eirne's smaller folk are up there behind her, wailing. Perhaps they were drawn to this place by that strange sound the Crow Folk made earlier, in the moment of understanding: the moment that will never come again, not after this. Eirne's torrent of abuse continues unabated. Then, at last, comes True's deep voice as he tries to establish calm.

I cannot move. I cannot take the next step, whatever it is. I should sing. I should send this poor creature on her way to the Afterlife with words of kindness. But all that comes from me is a whispered, "I'm sorry. Oh, I'm so sorry."

I will not shout. I will not raise my voice. No wild dispute between husband and wife, queen and bard, will sully this place where two innocents have died today because of her prejudice. She curses and rails and shrieks. Without Nightshade, her steadying companion over all the years since that five-year-old girl, half human, half fey, was thrust into this world and told she was queen, without Rowan, her steadfast protector, who is in the bard's hut watching over our child, Eirne is adrift, rudderless, and utterly possessed by grief and rage.

True speaks. "I will carry her back to the gathering place, my lady." He bends to lift the lifeless thing that was once Nightshade. Holds her with tenderness and respect.

"No—no—no—" protests Eirne, flapping her hands in confusion. I think she has lost sight of where she is or what must be decided.

"Come, my lady." Moon-Fleet steps forward, takes Eirne's arm and guides her away from the scene of death. "Your people need you."

Eirne sobs and babbles and curses, but allows herself to be led away. The small ones follow, weeping. And I am alone.

If I touch Watcher, if I move her, will Shadow and his clan swoop down and make an end of me? I have betrayed his trust. Eirne has done the unthinkable. I cannot begin to consider how she did what she did, and why, if such magic is at her fingertips, she remains so fearful of the Crow Folk. It hardly matters. All is changed.

Whether Shadow and his clan are there, invisible high in the trees, or whether they are gone, I do not know. I know only that this poor creature lying at my feet deserves the same respect in death as all beings do. I lift her gently, with my cloak still wrapped around her, and carry her out of the clearing and away down a forest path dappled with sunlight. Under the beeches wildflowers bloom, a carpet of purple and gold fit for a queen to tread. My throat is tight; I am full of tears. But I am a bard, and I sing.

> *May you find safe haven on your home shore*
> *May the light of morning touch you gently*
> *May your heart know the peace of the ancestors.*
> *Your courage was a light in the darkness*
> *Your trust was balm to the spirit*
> *May your tale live forever.*

I find a resting place partway up a rock wall, where fox and badger will not venture. It is like a smaller, more benign version of those cliffside caverns I saw in Shadow's thoughts. I lay the broken body within, tuck the cloak around it. "Rest well, Watcher," I whisper. "I swear to you, by the earth itself, that I will see your clan delivered to freedom. That is my solemn promise."

This death lies heavily on my spirit. This betrayal is beyond forgiveness. I return to the gathering place almost unseeing. My mind is curiously blank, a clean page awaiting I know not what. One thing remains clear and bright: Niamh, my fair one, my daughter. Thank all the gods she was safe in the hut with Rowan and did not have to see that. Let her have slept through the whole thing, though Eirne's shrieks were surely loud enough to fill the whole forest.

That din has been replaced by an eerie quiet. I almost expect to find the gathering place empty, Eirne perhaps being tended to by Moon-Fleet in her leafy retreat, the small ones gone to their safe places, and True at the hut with Rowan. But no. Eirne, white-faced and stern, sits on her willow throne, her eyes glacial as she watches me approach. And all the rest of them are assembled before their queen, hushed, trembling, terror of the unknown written on their faces. True stands at the back, under the council oak. Rowan is seated on a tree stump with Niamh on his knee. My daughter is holding a ball of woven rushes that Moon-Fleet made for her. She is the only one smiling.

Eirne stands. "I do not know how you dare show your face here," she says, and hers is the ringing voice of a queen, cold with fury. It is at the same time the voice of a child suddenly bereft of a beloved companion. I think of what was lost just now, the hard-won friendship, the understanding reached this very morning, and I feel not one shred of sympathy. "You betrayed me, bard!" She raises an accusing hand to point at me. "Because of you, Nightshade is gone forever! How will I go on without her? Who will give me wise counsel, who will comfort me, who will stand by me in times of trouble? How could you do this, Brocc? How could you?"

I do not point out that True and Rowan and Moon-Fleet and the smaller ones have always supported her and helped her. She is beyond listening to reason. I do not speak of the destructive magic she just unleashed. Perhaps she did not know, until now, that she held such power within her. I do not speak of Shadow and Watcher and the fragile bond she broke today. What would be the point of that?

"We all need some time," I say. "We cannot discuss this now, so soon after these cruel deaths. We must—"

"We? We? There is no we. You have brought nothing but sorrow and loss to our clan! I had such hopes! Such dreams!" She's weeping now, the chill control gone. "I thought—I truly thought—that with you by my side I could find an end to this nightmare. But no. You brought the creatures close. Perhaps you were in league with them all along. You have betrayed me, Brocc! And now you will leave this place. I want you beyond my borders this very day. Take your things and go! Return to your own world, bard, and be glad your punishment is not worse. Never set foot in my realm again."

Nobody says a word. The shock on True's face and on Rowan's is a reflection of what I feel. Even the tiny ones are quiet, though some are weeping. Niamh stares at her mother, the ball forgotten. Rowan lifts a hand to stroke the little one's hair in reassurance.

"You wrong me," I say quietly, knowing this is the hardest test I have ever faced, far harder than the decision to leave the human world, my family and comrades, my life on Swan Island. "I have worked only for peace. But I will not offer explanations; you are hurt, grieving." As am I; but in her book, my sorrow counts for nothing. Shadow's grief would be beyond her comprehension. "Let us at least wait until tomorrow and discuss this more calmly."

"Did you not hear me, bard?" Her voice is once more under control, her manner commanding. True makes a sudden movement, then is still. "You will be beyond my borders by nightfall." It is a royal decree. "You have seen what I can do. Obey my command or it will be the worse for you!" For a moment, just a moment, her glance goes to Niamh, and a chill enters my bones.

"I will not leave my daughter."

For a long, long moment Eirne stares at me. I hold my head high and meet her gaze as a Swan Island man should, though my heart is breaking and I am full of fear. Niamh. My precious child, my little girl . . .

"Then take her," says Eirne, and her voice is iron. "Take her and go. I don't want her here."

Cold fingers close around my heart. True's voice, Rowan's, Moon-Fleet's, the higher protests of the small folk ring out around me in a horrified chorus. Eirne makes an imperious gesture, and all fall silent save for Niamh, who babbles and squirms in Rowan's arms, now eager to be set down.

"Do not think to go with the bard," Eirne warns, looking first at Rowan and then at True. Does she not understand the cost—not only to me, but to herself and to the clan—of breaking the bond between the three of us? We are like brothers. "Do not think to offer him assistance. This is his doing and his only. Moon-Fleet, attend me in my retreat. Rowan, True, you will make the arrangements for Nightshade's burial. At dusk we will meet again to honor her." For the last time she looks me in the eye, and I wonder if I ever truly knew her. "I will retire to rest. Before I rise, you and your child will be gone from this place."

10

LIOBHAN

One of the things we learn on Swan Island is to adapt quickly to change. That's just as well, because not long after Dau and the others go off on their mission things take an unexpected turn for me. Haki purchases a Norse trading vessel called a knarr, towing it in from an anchorage further along the coast. It's extensively damaged, and he asks for help with repairing it in the boatyard at our mainland settlement. The regular boatbuilders, Odar and Cairenn, are happy to provide space and tools for this project, but they have their own work to do maintaining our small fleet of fishing boats and ferries. It's no surprise when Hrothgar volunteers to help, as he comes from a seafaring family. But Haki suggesting Elka come with him, provided I agree? That I don't expect.

I can hardly say no to this request from an elder. But Elka's departure would leave me with no more to occupy my time than maintaining my own fitness, being a companion to Justice, and perhaps doing the odd bit of whistle playing. And brooding over how Dau is getting on. I feel like a failure. If Archu were here I'd talk to him, as he's good at setting me straight. Instead I seek out Brigid, who's in the armory preparing feathers for fletching. Her hair is pulled back from her face with a plain linen band and she's frowning with concentration.

"Sorry to interrupt your work, Brigid. May I talk to you?"

"That sounds serious, Liobhan. What's the trouble?"

She knows all about the ship, and that Hrothgar has already gone over to help.

"You may not have heard that Elka's been asked to go, too. If I say yes to that, I can't keep training her. She seems keen to do it. Maybe it would be just as well."

Brigid pauses in her work, sharp knife in one hand, quill in the other, and turns her shrewd gaze on me. "What do you mean by that, exactly?"

"I think we need a pause, both of us. I want to make a success of this, Brigid. Only . . ." I have to say it. I have to be honest. "I wonder if she might do better working with someone else."

"You doubt Archu's judgment? That's not like you, Liobhan."

Tears sting my eyes. "Archu has faith in me, I know that. I want to do a good job. Elka works hard and she has excellent physical skills. But she can be rather remote. A little hard to talk to sometimes. I don't know how she would go in a team, working under pressure, when trust is so important."

Brigid turns her gaze back on her task. "Give her time. People don't learn the ways of Swan Island so soon after they come here. Elka's story is complicated. I take it she hasn't confided in you."

"I'm the last person she'd confide in. If anything at all sensitive comes up, she goes silent on me."

"Mm." Brigid takes an arrow shaft from a storage basket and lays it on her workbench. "What would Archu say at this moment?"

"He'd say, offer me a solution."

She looks at me, brows raised in query.

"All right. We suspend the training I'm doing, we let Elka go over to the mainland to help Haki. I suppose that will be a test of how well she works in a team. And when the job on the ship is done, she returns and we start again where we left off." I hesitate.

"You think she'll speak freely to you once she gets back? Won't you be faced with the same problem all over again later?"

I have no reply to offer. Most likely she's right.

"You know, Liobhan, if I were asked to list your five strongest qualities, one of them would be confidence. That can't be gone solely because your man's away on a mission. You must have known that time would come."

"It's nothing to do with that!" Curse it, now I've snarled at an elder for no good reason. What she said is at least partly true. Dau's absence is like a physical hurt. It's as if part of me has been taken away. "Sorry."

"Courage, confidence, strength," says Brigid, examining the slots where feathers will be joined to arrow shaft. "Sense of justice."

I realize she's enumerating what she thinks are my five strongest qualities, and am stunned into silence. What's the fifth one? Pigheadedness?

"A good heart," she says. "You couldn't sing as you do without that." There's the slightest trace of a smile on her weather-beaten features. "I have a solution to your problem. You go, too."

I open my mouth to protest, but close it with the words unspoken. "To do what? I know nothing about boats."

"You can work for me at the Barn. That way you can continue Elka's training, perhaps only for an hour a day, but enough for you to keep building trust with her."

I try to get my head around this. Working for Brigid, yes, that would be excellent. Staying in the mainland settlement . . . that would make Justice happy. But the cottage usually shared by Dau and Illann, and sometimes by Dau and me, is not exactly capacious. "I think Hrothgar's planning to stay in the cottage, the one we usually sleep in. With Haki. I'm not sure . . ."

Brigid is openly grinning now. "Offer me a solution."

I think fast. There are sleeping quarters in the Barn, of course, but they're both small and communal—not suited to lengthy stays. Nor is it ideal for Elka to stay with the two men.

"I think Deirdre would have room for Elka." Deirdre, the herbalist, shares her cottage with three cats. "And I could sleep at the Barn."

"Good," says Brigid. "Or you might be a little more selfish and make it the other way around, provided those cats will tolerate Justice. You're an established member of the community and Elka is a new trainee. She's already being offered a special job, something she wants to do. She'd be fine sleeping at the Barn. Or the boatbuilders might be able to fit her in. Besides, Deirdre might welcome some help with her work, and you have the required skills."

I realize I would like to stay with the undemanding Deirdre and brush up my techniques in preparing salves, drafts, and the like. I could go out gathering for her in the nearby woodland. Take Justice walking there. Suddenly this rather mad idea is starting to have some appeal.

"I'll speak to Cionnaola for you, Liobhan." Brigid gives me a good long look. "There's something you should know. Every trainer on this island has doubted their own ability at some point along the way. Every one of us has had trainees who challenged us, who didn't want to cooperate, who took a long time to settle into the island way. What about Dau?

He was difficult from the first. Just as well we could see the brilliance behind his unfortunate manner."

"Mm," I say, blinking away a stray tear. "So, if Cionnaola agrees I'll start making the arrangements. I suppose we'll go over tomorrow."

"I suppose we will. You'll be busy, Liobhan. Don't think the stillroom work and keeping Elka up to the mark will fill in most of your day. With Dau gone, I need a reliable assistant."

"I look forward to it. And thank you."

"A smile. That's good. Off you go now, I have work to do." I'm almost out the door when she says, "Bring your bow. I'll teach you a couple of tricks your friends don't know yet."

Folk go out of their way to accommodate my needs, as if the fact that Galen is hurt, or maybe the fact that Dau went on the mission and I didn't, means they should treat me kindly. Working with Brigid is an opportunity I didn't expect to come my way until much later. She's training some of the newer island warriors in spy-craft, which tends to mean uncomfortable exercises—uncomfortable for them, that is—involving being woken up at odd times or interrogated in unpleasant ways or asked to endure periods in complete darkness and so on. It feels weird to be helping put these tests and trials into practice. Even more so when I myself was so recently subject to torture at the hands of Dau's wretched brother. Before we started this work I gave Brigid the full story of that; it seemed the right thing to do. She listened in silence, then asked if that experience would affect my ability to help with this kind of training. I said I'd make sure it didn't. When I'm her age, which I'd guess to be near forty, I aim to be as strong and self-sufficient as she is. I didn't tell her that bit.

I'm staying with Deirdre in her cottage. Elka's staying

with Odar and Cairenn, right next to where she's working. Justice is happily settled with Hrothgar and Haki in what I think of as our cottage. Sensible arrangement. Means the only people sleeping at the Barn, apart from Brigid, who has private quarters there, are the folk we're training.

My days have fallen into a good routine. First thing in the morning it's the usual exercises, done in the outdoor training area at the Barn. Sometimes on my own. But usually with a group, Brigid included—she lets me lead it. It feels odd calling out instructions to one of the elders. Elka attends this every day, often with Hrothgar and Haki. The men who are at the Barn for Brigid's special training are required to join us whether or not they've just had a night without sleep. Of course, that usually means Brigid and I haven't slept much either, since we've been overseeing whatever they've been through. That training can seem cruel, but they're learning to be resourceful; tough; resilient. Sometimes the main point of the tests and trials is to get through them without breaking down. Sometimes it's to work out how to escape or to rescue a comrade. When they succeed we're as delighted as they are.

That work takes up a good deal of my time, and can happen at odd hours. But Brigid allows me to do other things. So, I make sure Elka comes over to the Barn most days to spend an hour or so on combat moves, and sometimes she brings Hrothgar with her so he can keep up his skills. I spend time with Deirdre at the cottage. Helping her teaches me a lot, though I still wish I'd spent more time on my mother's craft when I was younger. When we were at Oakhill I took some risks both in the stillroom and out of it. I suspect I came close to poisoning a whole group of men, Dau's brother among them. I want to be sure I'll never kill someone out of sheer incompetence.

Some days I visit the boatyard to watch them working on the knarr. She looks beyond repair to me, or did when they first brought her in. Still, if Haki is confident they can bring her back to her full glory, then they probably can. He knows his ships, that man. One thing I notice: a striking change in Elka when she's working there. Even the most menial task, the most tedious, repetitive job such as cleaning up old planks or holding tools for Haki, brings a brightness to her eyes and a warmth to her expression that I seldom saw on the island. She and Haki and Hrothgar make an efficient team. The give-and-take is like a dance; it's something I could make a song about. Maybe I will, one day.

My days may be full, but Dau is never far from my thoughts. I never got to hear the details of that mission: who would go where and what they'd be doing, apart from trying to find the prince. I've heard nothing more about Galen. If my brother died, I suppose they would send a message. If Aolu was found, we'd hear news of that. If he was found, Dau would already be on his way home.

The group at the Barn completes its training and returns to the island. Until the next group comes over—experienced warriors who will face harder tests, be set more challenging problems to solve—Brigid gives me time off. I work with Deirdre, making decoctions and infusions, producing salves and drafts, washing dishes and sweeping floors. With three cats in the cottage, keeping things clean is no simple matter. I offer to help at the boatyard, but Odar waves me away with a smile. The knarr is a big project on top of the usual work of the yard, but I suppose that with my lack of skills I'd only be in the way.

I can't settle to anything. Maybe it's the weather; it feels as if a storm's coming, but so far there's not a drop of rain and the wind is only a breath. Everything waiting. Everything as tightly wound up as I seem to be, time off or no time off. So I go back to the cottage, grab a basket and ask Deirdre if she needs any wild-picked herbs. She tells me what to harvest and where I might find it. I stride out into the woods near the settlement, after first advising the guard on duty—there's always someone on patrol to keep out unwanted visitors— where I'm going and why. He reminds me to report in when I get back. This place is an outpost of Swan Island, and while outwardly it looks like any other small coastal settlement, there's nothing ordinary about it.

Gods, it's good to be out under the trees, and even better to be walking fast, moving my body so hard I don't have room for troublesome thoughts. By the time I reach the spot where cresses and other water-loving plants grow by a meandering stream, I'm breathing hard. I pause, stretch, and gather a small harvest for Deirdre. Funny how the moment I stop moving my mind fills up with all those thoughts, foremost among them Dau far away on his mission. A pox on it! Didn't we always say we'd cope? Didn't we say we wouldn't let our feelings for each other get in the way of the work we do? Then why is it so hard?

Right. Had my walk, got my herbs, time to go back. Something makes me uneasy as I pick up the basket. But nothing prepares me for a herd of cattle stampeding through the woods toward me, ducking and weaving, too many for the narrow forest pathways to hold. I dart behind an oak, crouch down, and press myself hard against the trunk, hands over my head. Everything, is thundering hooves, scything horns, snorts and bellowing, and general mayhem. All around me branches snap and twigs splinter. The earth is churned up and flung about and the animals' steaming breath clouds the air. It feels as if the ground beneath me is actually shaking. My heart thuds in time with the hoofbeats. When they've passed me I open my eyes and stand up. There's neither farmer nor herdsman in sight. And the cattle are heading straight toward the settlement. Nowhere to go then except into the sea. Whether they do that or try to turn, it's going to be a disaster. There might be children out on the path, folk in their gardens, the team working on the knarr in that open boatyard, right in the way . . .

A few stragglers pass me, hurling themselves with reckless speed after the others as the herd rampages on through the woodland. The animals crowd one another, risking damage as they force a way between the trees. I run behind, shouting a warning, but my voice is swallowed up by the sound of the herd. I haven't a hope of catching up. The guards at the settlement will hear them coming, but what can they do? Anyone in their path will be reduced to a smear of blood and a heap of shattered bone. Where in the name of the gods is the herdsman?

Ah! A shortcut. I sprint up the side path, hoping I can attract someone's attention before disaster strikes. When I get to the high spot I'm so dizzy I think I might pass out. I bend over, hands on knees, to catch my breath. When I stand straight again, the cattle are passing below me. They fill the road from one side to the other. I can see ahead as far as the settlement. Thank the gods, there's nobody in the way—people must have got into their houses or behind their walls in time. But no. I'm wrong. Where the track ends, alongside the jetty, three children are playing on the pebbly shore, so intent on building a tower of stones that they haven't heard danger approaching. The cattle have slowed a bit, but they're panicky now they're out of the woodland and confined between the low walls of gardens and cottages to either side of the track. They rear up and jostle and let out squealing sounds of distress.

I shout a fresh warning, but nobody hears me. The children don't move. My heart turns cold. There's nothing I can do, nothing.

And then three figures appear. One is tall, dark-bearded Hrothgar, who strides out of the boatyard and down to the shore, where he scoops up the smallest child, takes another's hand, and heads toward the shallows under the jetty with the third child following. The second figure is Haki with a long stick in hand and a grim set to his features, moving to stand protectively between this retreating group and the maelstrom of animals. And the third is a shorter person with fair hair pulled back in a long thick plait. Elka. What in the name of the gods is she doing? My mouth opens in horror as she sprints right across the track, in the path of the unruly cattle, to swing open a gate I'd forgotten. There's a path behind the Barn that leads to the open training area. But how can Elka possibly get them in there? It's barely wide enough to admit one cow at a time. She'll be crushed.

But no. As Haki blocks the way to the shore with his long stick, Elka stands tall, draws breath, and opens her mouth. The sound that comes out makes the hairs on my neck stand on end. It's a high, piercing chant, weaving around just a few notes, so powerful that you might think it would travel all the way to the Hill of Tara. She holds the gate open, the sound pouring from her as if she's a vessel for some unknown force, and the cattle pass through one by one. They grow calm. Even those at the back of the herd stop jostling and snorting and wait their turn to move forward. She sings, they advance. Chaos becomes tranquil order. When it becomes clear the animals are not going to stampede down to the water, Haki lays aside his stick and moves to stand next to Elka, still watchful. Eventually an exhausted farm horse appears at the rear of the herd, bearing a distraught-looking man, who draws his animal to a halt and stares in disbelief. Elka's chant, strong yet ethereal, rings out over anchorage and boatyard and shore, and the cattle move at measured pace through the gate and along the narrow path as if heading to a familiar barn for milking. The last cow goes through. Haki closes the gate. Elka falls silent. I hope Brigid or whoever else is around the back of the Barn doesn't get too much of a shock.

By the time I scramble down the rise and jog along the track to the gate, the farmer has dismounted. I realize I've met him before. He's not a Swan Island man, but he's a trusted friend of our community.

"How did they get out?" I ask.

"Spooked by those wretched birds. Broke through the gate. Dagda's bollocks, someone could have been trampled to death . . ." He falls silent as Hrothgar and the three children emerge from under the jetty, none the worse for wear. The biggest child—it's the son of Odar and Cairenn—is explaining something busily to Hrothgar, who bends over to listen. My friend still has the smallest child balanced on his hip and the middle-sized one by the hand. Those two are the daughters of Deirdre's neighbor, whose house cow can now be heard mooing at the rear of her cottage, perhaps wishing she could have a wild adventure, too. I can hear Justice barking.

Brigid appears with a mildly perplexed look on her face. Haki speaks to her, then they lead the farmer and his horse around to the back of the Barn, a place not generally open to folk from the wider community. Under the current circumstances there's not much choice. I imagine our training area is milling with cattle.

I walk over to the boatyard, suddenly feeling quite shaky. Elka is now sitting on an upturned rowboat, looking a little pale but otherwise perfectly calm. Deirdre and her neighbor come running down the track; the small girls are reclaimed by their mother with hugs and kisses. The children are full of excitement.

"We went right under the jetty! Look, my shoes are all wet!"

"We saw a hundred cows! Two hundred! This many!" The child stretches her arms out so wide she's in danger of toppling over.

"Sorry," I say to Deirdre, and my voice comes out sounding the way I feel, weak and wobbly. "I dropped your basket somewhere in the woods. I'll go back for it later."

"Sit down, Liobhan. That's an order."

So I find myself sitting next to Elka on the boat, with Justice lying on my feet as if to keep me out of trouble, while Deirdre and Cairenn go into the boatbuilders' house to make a brew, and Hrothgar eases his long form down onto the ground beside us. He grins at Elka.

"Haven't heard that in a good long while," he remarks. "Family got cattle, back home?"

Elka bobs her head in a *yes*. Gives him a trace of a smile. What she just did was astonishing. I can't think what question to ask first.

"If this were part of your training," I say, "I'd give you top marks for quick thinking. What is that—that chant?" It wasn't unlike what Brocc sometimes does with his voice. It was deeply uncanny. But if I mention magic Elka will shut the conversation down.

"Special call," she says. "To bring herd in for milking. Or from grazing. Hear from far off. Other call, different, to send them out."

"But these cows would never have heard that." Morrigan's

britches, that was some song. I still can't work out how she makes that sound. It would carry from one valley to the next. From one end of a forest to the other.

"Risky, yes," Elka says, looking down at her boots. "At home, cows know song. They know singer's voice. I try anyway. Nothing else to do. Lucky, cows understand."

"Lucky, yes," I say, because if it hadn't worked, not only her own life but those of several others would almost certainly have been lost. "But also very brave. And resourceful."

"I do not know this word, resorf . . . What is that?"

"It means quickly working out what to do and then doing it," says Hrothgar. "That was remarkable, Elka. Almost like magic."

Elka flinches. "No magic." She makes a small, quick gesture. "Just a call. Like whistle to a dog, or call to hens, *puk-puk-puk*, you know."

That makes me smile. "If you can produce that sound, you can sing," I say. "I hope someday you'll sing with me. A woman who can calm a herd of rampaging cattle with her voice can do almost anything."

Elka looks at me sideways. "I teach you cow call, Liobhan," she says, "you teach me song. Yes?"

"It's a deal." When I smile, she smiles back, with a spark of mischief in her eyes. But she's also got her arms wrapped around herself, and she's shivering. If that gave me a shock, how much more so for her, standing there on her own, not sure if the cattle would obey the call or charge forward and crush her?

"Up to the house, Elka." Hrothgar offers her his arm. "You need a hot drink and some breathing time. You're looking rather pale yourself, Liobhan. All right?"

"I'm fine." I deserve no fuss at all. Unlike the others, I did nothing heroic. Saved my own life in the forest by ducking out of the way in time. Lost Deirdre's basket. Ran hard but got back too late to rescue anyone. Yelled a warning that was drowned in the uproar. *Not your best day, Liobhan.*

Crow Folk. That must be what the farmer meant by *those wretched birds.* Crow Folk here, so close to the island. Elka said the walking shadow wasn't one of them. But Crow Folk spooking a herd, that's all too plausible. It horrifies me that they're here. And it reminds me of their part in the attack on Galen. Something's changing. Something's afoot. I just hope we can find answers.

11

DAU

We arrive at a wayside inn to hear music drifting forth: small-pipes and bodhrán in a lively version of a tune I've heard before on the island. After another long day of riding I'm too tired to recall its name, but it makes me think of Liobhan playing the whistle. She'd know what it is, she knows all of them.

Garbh leads our horses around to the stable area at the back. I remind myself once again that for purposes of this journey I am a chieftain's son, not a Swan Island warrior. Though, of course, I have to be both. Garbh and I must keep ears and eyes open. I enter the establishment and find the host, who takes one look at me then offers a meal of roast beef and a private chamber that will accommodate me and "my man." Seems I still look like a nobleman even when I'm sweaty, saddle-sore, and bone weary.

I demand to see the chamber. When he leads me there, I look the place over with an expression borrowed from my brother Seanan, before agreeing, grudgingly, that since we'll only be here for one night, this will do. I haggle the price down—he is in fact asking too much. When Garbh reappears, carrying our bags, I send him back out to demand private use of the bathhouse, with hot water.

The bath is more than welcome. We've kept up a good pace and it's taking a toll not only on ourselves but also on the horses. Our overnight stops have revealed no hints about Aolu and nothing much about the household we're headed toward. Maybe this place will be different. The closer we get, the more useful the gossip's likely to be.

Clean and tidy in our good clothes, Garbh and I enter the main room of the establishment, where the promised roast beef awaits, along with ale and a company of merry travelers and musicians, one of whom is familiar. It's the piper who performed in my father's hall at Oakhill. As we spoke briefly back then, he may well remember me. What was his name—Rian? Cian? I try to avoid his eye.

I can't get too friendly with any of the folk here. But there's only the one long table, so the son of a chieftain has no choice but to sit down to the meal with everyone else. I find a seat at the end of the table, away from the musicians, and motion to Garbh to sit between me and the next man.

The food is good and we're hungry, so I don't pretend to find it unsatisfactory. No need to behave like Seanan all the time, only give the general impression that I consider myself a cut above the rest. I keep myself to myself, but Garbh talks to the men opposite him.

"Where are you heading?"

"Northern Argialla. You?"

"Passing through, delivering some horses. Gone that way before?"

"Why do you ask?" Garbh is being careful. As it is, not many folk will hear the conversation, because after a short break the band has launched into wild dance music. Feet are tapping under the table, and there's a bit of fist thumping, too. Platters and cups add a rattling accompaniment.

"Some big trees across the road through Hunter's Glen,"

says the man across the table. "Not likely to be moved in a hurry. Came down in a storm. We had to backtrack, go around the longer way, over Blackstone Pass. It's not a bad ride." The man's eyes dart to me, then away. Perhaps he's making assumptions about my riding skills or lack thereof. I gaze into the distance, chewing my food.

"Can you draw me a map?" asks Garbh.

"Here, I'll show you." The man starts rearranging cups, platters, knives, and various other objects on the table. "This is Hunter's Glen and the main road through into Argialla, and here's the higher track you need to use. You'll come out at this point, through a beech forest. It joins the main road again, but further east."

Garbh looks at me.

"And where is Lady Almha's residence on this admirable map?" I ask, clasping my hands before me on the table.

"Darkwater? About here, my lord." The fellow sounds nervous now. I'm making him uncomfortable, and I'm sorry for that. But not entirely, as it means I'm creating the correct impression. The man places a salt container on his makeshift map to represent Lady Almha's place, then traces the way from where we are now—the hostelry is an inverted cup, thankfully empty. It seems unlikely the thing is to scale.

I need to know more, but I'd best not sound too interested. Garbh asks the question for me, without prompting. "How long is the ride, if we take this Blackstone Pass?"

"With good horses, you'd get from here to Darkwater settlement in three or four days. A day's ride to Hunter's Glen—there's an inn, not as comfortable as this one, but clean enough—then half a day's ride to this point." He points to a gap between two greasy platters.

"You wouldn't want to be going straight up to the pass," puts in the man next to the mapmaker. "Get caught up there at night, weather closing in, and you're in trouble. Odd sort of place. My best advice is, camp by the track for a night, rest your horses, head on next morning. Up, over, down again, that's one day's work for your mounts. There's a settlement of sorts on the other side, where you can stay a night. Then two days' easy ride to your destination."

"You know the area well, it seems," I comment, thinking how unlikely it is that anyone could have brought a captive on such a journey without being seen. It doesn't sound like the sort of road you'd travel by cart, with someone bound, gagged, and hidden under a load of market goods.

"Yes, my lord," says the second fellow. It seems he's more confident around nobility than the other man. "My work takes me that way often."

"And what work is that?" Gods, I hate how easily that condescending tone comes to me.

"Messenger, my lord. For Lady Almha's household."

"I see." Could be a useful source of information, though he's probably been trained to keep his mouth shut. It wouldn't hurt for Garbh to befriend the man, if there's time. "Thank you both for your clear instructions. Garbh, commit this to memory."

"Yes, my lord." He speaks with a straight face and an obsequious manner. In fact, *my lord* is incorrect for a chieftain's son. It should be *Master Dau*. But I'm glad he didn't call me that.

We sit drinking and listening to the music a while longer. Then I rise, shielding a yawn, and tell Garbh I'm retiring for the night but he can stay here awhile longer. He takes the hint and calls for another jug of ale. He's been drinking very little himself. But the men will talk more freely without the constraint of my presence.

I'm lying awake, wondering if the prince is dead or alive

and where on earth he might be, when Garbh returns to our shared quarters. We speak in murmurs as he takes off his outer garments and settles on his pallet.

"I didn't get much more. The man did mention strange tales about Blackstone Pass. Odd sounds, like howling or screaming. Things scuttling about. No wonder folk mostly take the other way."

"Aren't the dobhar-chú supposed to howl only at full moon?" I'm not quite sure if I'm joking.

"The general wisdom is that the pass is safe only by day." Garbh stretches out, trying to get comfortable on the too-short pallet. "Sounds crazy, doesn't it? But folk take it seriously. I asked him what people thought it was, ghosts maybe, or tricks of the wind and moonlight. He said all they know is that there's something up there that doesn't like to be disturbed. Couple of disappearances in the past, apparently." After a bit, he adds, "That man, the messenger. He said he thought he'd seen you before."

A pox on it. "Did he say where or when?"

"I asked him, trying to be offhand about it. He said he couldn't recall, but maybe in Darkwater settlement, which is next to Lady Almha's residence."

That had better not mean Seanan's in these parts. Whoever the man saw, I know it wasn't me. "Which way's the messenger headed now, to or from Darkwater?"

"North, he said. So we won't see him on the road."

"I've met that piper before. At Oakhill. With luck, he didn't spot me. At least I'm still Master Dau, if he does have a word."

"If I can, I'll find out where the band's going next," says Garbh. "With the main road blocked, they may be headed the same way we are."

"Could be they'll end up at Lady Almha's place while

we're there, who knows? Morrigan's curse, I hope we're not wasting our time here, Garbh. This whole thing might be a fool's errand. The Crow Folk, the dobhar-chú, and . . ." *And the possibility my wretched brother may somehow be involved*. I can't say that. Am I going to think of Seanan every time I hear of an act of unusual cruelty?

"Sleep well, Dau," mumbles Garbh, pulling the blanket over his head as if to shut out unwelcome thoughts.

"You, too, Garbh." I wonder what demons walk through *his* mind, refusing to be banished.

12

LIOBHAN

E lka's "cow call" requires me to use my voice in a way I didn't know was possible. But I like a challenge.

We find a place to practice, along the coast from the settlement and far enough from any farms to avoid the sudden arrival of herds of cattle—if Elka could summon that farmer's livestock even when they'd never heard the call before, who is to say the same thing may not happen again?

We're on a ledge, just down from a cliff path looking out to sea. It's breezy. Remembering our last experience in this kind of terrain, I'm struck by how quickly things have changed. Trust has begun to grow between us, a tender plant rooted in unlikely soil. We are becoming friends. Perhaps we've each seen qualities in the other that we admire. I've learned that Elka can work hard in a team, and I'm starting to believe they can turn the knarr from a beaten-up apology for a ship to a handsome, practical vessel that could be sailed between Swan Island and the court of Dalriada, for instance, or maybe further. Haki and Hrothgar value Elka's assistance, that's obvious. And I've seen something more surprising: how good she is with children. Who'd have thought it? There are always a few young ones running about in the settlement, and Deirdre tells me they all love Elka. Between work on the boat and training with me, she's as busy as any of us. But during her time off, she can often be found down on the shore with the young ones, looking for special stones or helping to make a little boat from driftwood or teaching them how to stand on their hands. Or she'll be sitting on the upturned rowboat listening as a small boy or girl tells her something of great import, such as the discovery of a shell that looks like the full moon, or the fact that the tall chestnut tree at the back of Deirdre's cottage now houses a nest with baby birds, and that the cats are to be shut indoors until those babies have learned to fly.

"Best if you stand up, Liobhan," Elka says now. "Better for breathing. But be careful."

I grimace, thinking of how often I've warned her about high ledges and how one should always face inward. This one is broad enough for us to sit cross-legged, side by side, looking out to sea. For a person with good balance, it is safe to stand up. But it's a long way down to the water. I make sure my back is against solid rock, and place my feet carefully.

"Now we breathe."

We work through the exercises she's taught me, a routine that helps me to draw in the very deep breath that's needed to produce the high, penetrating tone of the call. There's no way I can produce the sound Elka does. Her voice is naturally higher than mine anyway, but it's not only that. It's the power she puts behind every note, an intensity that sends the chant or song over a great distance.

"At home," she says when the breathing work is done and we're ready to sing, "land is all up, down." She illustrates with a hand. "High mountains. Deep valleys. A long way from farm to farm, village to village. Cows go up hill, find good grass. Far up. They need a loud call, bring them home."

She makes me run through the words softly, for there are words in this chant, in her own tongue, and they translate to the sort of verse Brocc might make up, coaxing the cattle home as if they were beloved children, with visions of the warm barn, the feed of fine oats, the gentle hands of the milkmaid. "Good," she says when I'm done. "Now we call. Breathe slow and deep: one, two, three, four."

I draw in air as she's shown me, starting deep down—more air than I would need to play a whole verse of "Artagan's Leap" in a single breath. Beside me Elka does the same. I keep my chest open, braced. On the slow outward breath, we call together. First the long wordless notes, strong and compelling as the summons of a great trumpet. Another deep breath in, and we sing the verse together. Here on the ledge, our voices must soon be lost in the crashing music of wind and waves. But in a quiet valley, all green grass and sheltering trees, peaceful lakes and isolated farmsteads, the call would ring out far and wide.

Elka falls suddenly silent. I falter for a moment, glancing across to check that all's well, meet her half smile and the challenge in her eyes, and continue on my own. The long, steady trumpet-tones; then another verse, speaking of comfort, shelter, home. And I'm done.

"Very good," Elka says as I lean back against the rock wall and recover myself. "Words not perfect, but almost."

"Thanks," I gasp. "I can't believe you do that twice a day back at home."

Elka doesn't reply, and when I straighten and look at her, I see the reserve creeping into her eyes again.

"Let's go back up," I say. "Unless you want me to do it again."

Elka heads up the narrow path from the ledge, saying nothing. When we're safely at the top and well away from danger, I sit on the ground and drink from the waterskin I left up here. Seems to me that to win her confidence, I have to let down my own guard a little. "I still find the breathing difficult," I say. "My brother would do it better. I wish he could hear you, he would be fascinated."

"Your brother who is hurt, wounded? Guard to this missing prince?"

"No, Galen's not a musician. I mean my other brother, the one who used to be a Swan Island warrior. His voice is . . . remarkable. Almost like magic."

Elka doesn't ask any questions, but her silence is eloquent.

"Brocc is an adopted son. We don't know who his parents were." I'm not quite ready to tell her the whole story. In time, I will. "Now it's my turn to put you through your paces. Let's practice 'High Days of Summer.' First verse on your own, then I'll join in. We should stand up. Remember how it begins?"

"Of course, Liobhan."

I turn a severe eye on her and catch a mischievous grin on her face. She's as changeable as an autumn day. I can't help smiling back, even though my thoughts are on Brocc far off in his strange world, and his child growing up among uncanny beings, under the eyes of the Crow Folk. "Off you go, then," I say, and as Elka's voice rings out in the sweeping, heart-stirring melody of the song, I don't allow myself to cry for my first brother or my second, or for Dau in danger, or for anything at all. I simply lose myself in the music. "Well done," I say when we reach the end. "I enjoyed that." And if one or two details were not quite perfect, I decide not to mention them right now.

We're halfway back to the settlement when Elka says out of the blue, "This brother, he is . . . witch? Maker of spells?"

How do I answer that? "A witch, no. But there is a power in his voice that sometimes seems uncanny."

"Your father not angry with this? Your mother? Not cast him from home?"

I stop walking and stare at her, shocked. "Why would they do that?"

Elka seems surprised by my response. "Because . . . magic, spells, evil . . . they are not afraid?"

I'm tempted to tell her briskly not to be so silly. But I see something in her eyes, and I answer her question with a question of my own. "Is that what happened to you?" Surely not; her cow call must have been invaluable to a farming community. When she looks at the ground, saying nothing, I add, "My parents would never send any of us away, for that or any other reason."

"Your family not scared of magic? Spells to call up demons, charms to poison? Curses on enemies?"

"That sort of magic, my parents certainly would be uncomfortable with. But natural magic, the kind my mother calls hearth magic, is something we know quite well." I'll have to tell her. "My mother is what we call a wisewoman. Not a witch in the sense you mean. A healer, a herbalist, and a storyteller. She tends to the sick. Helps women deliver their babies. Keeps watch over the dying and lays out corpses. That's why she's with my brother Galen now. To tend to his injuries."

For a moment she is speechless. "Truly? Folk do not fear her? Shout foul names, throw things?"

I wonder if it was ever like that for Mother when she was younger. She doesn't talk much about those days. I know some truly terrible things happened to her. "She's greatly respected. She's looked after the people of the district for years, while my father thatched their roofs and listened to their troubles."

There's quite a silence then, but we don't walk on. I wait,

watching the gulls wheel over the sea and thinking of that day on Swan Island when Elka saw the walking shadow.

"My mormor—my grandmother—she is völva," she says eventually, her voice low, almost apologetic. "Wisewoman, magic worker. From her, I learn the cattle call. I learn many things. From when I am small." She indicates with her hand the height of a child perhaps five years old. "My mother takes me up the mountain. Mormor heals the sick; she do the telling—what may come, what should not come—and she finds things hidden. I learn much. But my father is angry. When he find out he beats me. He beats my mother. But I still go up the mountain. Keep the secret."

She pauses to drink from her waterskin. The look on her face tells me she's right there in the past, seeing it, feeling it. I wait, knowing whatever is to come can't be good.

"Father wants cattle call. That much he lets me do. He wants good daughter: spin, sew, bake bread, marry man with big farm. Still I go to Mormor, bring food for her, shawl I spin and weave, beer I brew. One day I go up the mountain and Mormor house is gone. Gone to bones and ashes." Elka falters, pressing her knuckles against her mouth. Draws a deep breath. "I run away. Go to big brother Sigurd. Fisherman, live by the sea. I help with little ones. Work on the boat. Sigurd teach me to fight. Father is angry. Wants me home. Sigurd sends message to Haki, his old friend. I come here."

This is the longest speech I've ever heard her make in Irish. I hardly know what to say.

"I'm glad you got through it and came here. Nobody will judge you on Swan Island, Elka. If you have . . . special abilities, skills that owe something to training as a wisewoman, a—what was the name in your language?"

"Völva. Hrothgar says, seer. Wisewoman and seer."

"Does that mean you can foretell the future?" She looks a

little blank. "You can go into a trance? See what is yet to come?"

"Mormor not teach me this. She walks between worlds. Chant and go away. Still here, but . . . gone other place."

I think of the fey queen, Eirne, who can conjure powerful visions in her scrying bowl. She showed Brocc and me two different futures. Either might have proven true, depending on our choices. For a short while we had the fate of a kingdom in our hands.

"We should head back," I say. Cloud is building above us; rain is coming. And Brigid is expecting our next group for training sometime today, if the weather doesn't stop the boat from getting across. We need to prepare for them. "I'll teach you another song on the way. You know how dogs sometimes go in circles, trying to catch their tails? That's how this song works. We chase each other with the tune and never catch up. The words are easy to learn. Here's how it goes . . ."

13

BROCC

Dusk is falling. My back aches. I must stop, make fire, feed Niamh. How can I keep her warm enough tonight? I should have gone to Mistress Juniper, or walked to the court of Breifne and thrown myself on King Faelan's mercy. But the one was too close to Eirne's realm, and the other fraught with complications. Instead I came north, and now my daughter is crying, and her wrappings are soiled again—the smell lingers, and the warmth against my back, where she wriggles in her sling, tells me the linen bindings are leaking. Why did I head this way? Like a pigeon trained to return to the known loft, the familiar shelter, my steps take me toward home.

I stop walking. Niamh is screaming now, red-faced, protesting the sudden disappearance of all that is familiar, the abrupt cessation of all her comforts. What to do first, clean her up and change her clothes, try to feed her, or make fire? Where can I safely lay her down? Gods, I'm weary. Too tired to think. Too sad, too shocked. Disbelieving still. Bereft.

I maneuver Niamh off my back, juggle her on a hip as I throw my cloak onto the earth. I lay my daughter down in the shelter of an oak, placing the bundle I've carried in my hand to one side of her. A tangle of roots blocks the other side. If I don't get a fire going soon it will be dark; will she stay where she is long enough? Thank the gods she can't walk yet. At least her progress will be slow. I cannot bear her cries. They strike at me, driving home the guilt, the anguish, the helplessness.

I gather firewood, never going far enough to lose sight of Niamh. My hands are shaking; her distress sets every part of me on edge. As I place the sticks, tuck dry tinder under them, find my flint and knife, I sing the songs she loves most. The one about the folk of the forest meeting for revels on Midsummer Day. The counting rhyme with croaking frogs and leaping fish and soaring swallows. A silly one about a buzzing bee. Never has a bard done worse service to a piece. My voice is a ragged croak, my breath inadequate for the simplest ditty. I'm weary to the bone. I could drop in my tracks right here and sleep until morning. But I cannot.

I manage to get the fire going. I place large stones all around it. Niamh is not screaming now, but weeping softly. Danu save me, how am I going to get all the way to Winterfalls? If the clan had obeyed Eirne's orders and refused me help, I'd not have lasted a day. But as I stood in the bard's hut staring at my possessions, scarcely able to think, Rowan came with Niamh in his arms. Helped me pack a bag. As we were doing that, True came to the door with food wrapped in leaves, a jar of the mashed root mixture that Niamh likes, and a roll of linen. That won't last long, but at least she can be clean and dry tonight, before she sleeps. What was Eirne thinking? What did she imagine I would do?

"I can't take my harp," I said to my comrades. As if that mattered anymore. "I can't carry Niamh and the supplies and the harp all at once."

"I'm sorry," True said. "Where will you go?" For all of us knew there would be no reasoning with Eirne; if Nightshade were still alive, that might have been possible, but Nightshade was gone, and Eirne would forever blame me for her killing.

"North to Dalriada. To my family."

Rowan said nothing. He sat there on my pallet holding Niamh. True stood at the doorway; he is too tall to be comfortable in the bard's hut. After a while, as I tried and failed to make choices about the rest of my belongings, Rowan said, "We are your family, too, Brocc. We are Niamh's family." His hand, neither that of a man nor of a creature but a curious blend of the two, came up to stroke Niamh's dark curls, and she made a small sound of appreciation. The look in Rowan's eyes jolted me. I'd thought I knew how loved my daughter was; I'd thought I understood how deep the bond was between me and my Otherworld brothers. But I was wrong. Mine was not the only heart shattered by this severing.

If, later, Eirne in her retreat heard Thistle-Coat and Gentle-Foot and the other small ones weeping as they bade me farewell, if she caught the deep sound of True's voice and the high echo of the tiny passengers who live on his body as they told me they would never forget me, she did not show her face, nor speak one more word to me before I walked away from there forever.

I change Niamh's clothes. All of them, for every item is either soiled or soaked in urine. I cannot wash her, not here in the cold, but I wipe her little body with a handful of moss. There is water a distance away in a stream. Perhaps I can fetch some once she sleeps. Rowan has packed smocks, leggings, little coats in the bag, and there is the linen True brought. Another challenge to face: how to wash and dry these things while we are on the road. That is for later. She must have supper and then settle to sleep.

Niamh will not eat. The mashed root mixture smells as it should, and I have a familiar bone spoon to feed her with.

Lacking a cook pot I cannot warm the food, but I coax her as well as I can. She turns her head away, to the left, to the right, and when I keep trying she bellows outrage, then sobs as if the end of the world is come. Perhaps that is what this feels like for her. Rowan packed her special cup; we have used it already today. I set aside the food, offer water. I make myself breathe slowly, though panic is close. Out here, we are so alone. When she drinks, I feel relief soften my whole body. But the food, she will not touch. Tomorrow I must step out of this world and into the other. I must find a habitation of men, a farm, an inn, a settlement, and ask for help. I have no means to pay save song, being without my harp. But sing before an audience, in my current state of distress? They'd laugh me out the door if they didn't throw me. And what about Niamh? I will not trust her to anyone else. Not even for the length of a performance. I dare not.

I build up the fire as far as I safely can. It will not last the night. It is almost dark, and the forest feels strange to me, almost hostile. I have a strong sensation of being watched, but I will not leave my daughter while I perform a patrol.

I wrap Niamh in a shawl I find at the bottom of the bag, and rock her in my arms. I sing as best I can. Out here, no harsh criticism is likely to come my way. I try to plan, to think ahead. But my mind is full of Watcher, her hesitant steps as she edged closer to me, and in her eyes the long-awaited dawning of trust. Watcher, at last moving toward me in hope. Watcher in a moment destroyed. And Shadow swooping down in terrible vengeance, all hope of under-standing lost. I see it over and over, and know I will not sleep. When Niamh lies warm and relaxed in my arms, having fi-nally given way to slumber, I know I should fetch water, pre-pare for morning, check the fire one more time. Instead I lay her on the cloak, curl myself around her, and pull the blanket over the two of us. "Home," I murmur to her sleeping form. "We're going home." On a high branch of the oak, something moves, then settles.

We sleep two more nights in the forest, though more often I lie wakeful in the dark. I believe we are being followed, tracked. Perhaps by Crow Folk, perhaps by some other kind of spy. I've spotted a dark form among the trees, keeping pace in silence. What it means, I do not dare to guess.

Niamh has eaten almost nothing. A few mouthfuls from the jar, a little hard bread from my own supply, which I soften with water and feed to her in tiny morsels. Water from her cup. I have washed her clothing in a stream but had neither the sunshine nor the time to get it dry. My daughter is miserable. I would rather she bellowed in annoyance than hung passive in her sling as she does now, as if she no longer trusts me to provide for her. We must throw ourselves on the mercy of strangers. We walk out of the forest and into the world of humankind.

When I traveled to Breifne on that fateful mission, in company with Liobhan and Archu, we came on horseback, taking roads used by folk transporting goods in carts and by parties riding from one settlement to another. We passed herders with sheep or cattle, boys moving geese between fields, men-at-arms escorting some lordling about his business. There were wayside inns, places offering a night's shelter, a good meal, a warm hearth fire. I should remember the way. But although less than two years have passed, it is hazy in my mind. Perhaps I am simply too tired to think.

This road is deserted. There are no farms, only fallow fields, forested hills, and, beyond them to the northeast, higher peaks, shadowy purple and gray, stony, forbidding. Goats might inhabit those parts. Birds of prey might hunt there. Are we still in the kingdom of Breifne, or have we crossed the border? I must not go near Oakhill, where I will be remembered by some folk—notably the chieftain and his senior advisers—for giving crucial testimony in a hearing that considered the crimes of Dau's eldest brother, a vile specimen of humankind if ever there was one. And yet, the quickest way home would take us close to that place, then northeast to Dalriada. My heart sinks still lower, imagining the long, weary miles ahead. A thready whimpering comes from my daughter. I must find help.

"Hush, sweetheart," I murmur, walking forward over the uneven ground. "We'll be there soon." Even my daughter, who cannot understand the words, must know this is a lie.

Another day, another night. We take refuge in the meager shelter of a broken-down hut, not far from the road. My belly aches with hunger. Niamh is sleepy, quiet. No longer plaguing me with her cries, no longer making the sounds that tell me she's hungry.

There was a moment of hope, earlier. We stopped to rest at the edge of a grassy field, after my legs refused to carry me a step further. And a bird no bigger than Niamh's hand flew down to perch close by. That brought a shadowy smile to my daughter's face. She made a little sound as the creature moved to perch on her head, then fluttered up to mine. For a moment I thought it might be one of Eirne's messengers, drab though its coloring was, all dun and ochre. My heart was filled with confusion. What message would Eirne send? That she forgave me, that she wanted me to bring Niamh home? That she was sorry for the terrible things she'd said, that she hadn't meant any of it? I watched the bird and waited, even as I knew I lacked Eirne's ability to read its thoughts. After a time, it flew away. Just an ordinary creature, out looking for tasty morsels. But I know what my answer would have been. I miss the clan, my comrades, the circle that kept my girl safe and healthy. I miss the beauty of the forest. But . . . I saw Eirne at her most fey in that moment when she unleashed the fell magic that killed Watcher. I heard her at her least human when she spoke those fateful words: *Take her and go. I don't want her here.* I will not go back. I will never go back. How could I trust her? "It's too late, Eirne," I whisper.

We passed a stream earlier, and a pond. My waterskin is full. In our makeshift shelter I hold Niamh upright on my knee and she drinks, but only a sip or two. I remind myself that I am a Swan Island man, and that a Swan Island man knows how to cross country, how to find the way, how to cope in the midst of disaster. It doesn't seem to help. I'm cold, I'm tired, I'm hungry. Those things will pass. But Niamh . . . what if she dies, right here in my arms? Such a tiny child cannot go long without food.

In the dark, in the cold—I cannot make a fire, it has been raining and there is no dry wood to be found—I hold Niamh close and sing to her. I sing of the first flowers of the spring, and butterflies, and sunshine, and all things good. And when I run out of words, when the night fills with shadows and fears, I offer up a silent prayer. *Keep her safe. Oh, please, keep my daughter safe.*

I am close to sleep, with Niamh against my chest, and so I nearly miss it. The sound of wings is so quiet it seems part of the song I was singing. The disturbance of the air is only another night breeze. But I smell something. Fish? Abruptly, I'm awake. Crow Folk, oh, gods, where is my weapon? I set Niamh down, fumble around me, fail to lay hands on my knife. Faint moonlight shows me a dark form moving among our belongings. Something in its beak. A familiar look in its eye. "Shadow?" I whisper, disbelieving.

In one strong wingbeat he is gone. The moon is rising. And there, placed neatly atop my bag, are a sizable slab of bread and a thick wedge of cheese—an easy cargo for so large a bird. For one day more, we will survive.

It is hard to sing when your head is full of tears. But he may still be close, and this gift is more than supper for a pair of heartsick travelers. It is trust. It is faith in a better future. It is hope reborn. I draw a shuddering breath and sing my thanks.

> *From the bottom of my heart, I thank you.*
> *From the depths of my spirit, I honor you.*
> *May we share the path of peace.*

Later, while Niamh sleeps rolled in the blanket after a meal of crumbled bread soaked in water, I watch veils of cloud as they pass across the moon's perfect face. I eat sparingly of the cheese and the remaining bread. I must set aside enough for tomorrow—who knows how far it may be to the next place of shelter?

Out of the night a sound comes to me, distant but unmistakable: the three solemn notes that are Shadow's call of recognition.

14

DAU

G reetings to you, my lady!" I bend in a graceful bow, every inch the chieftain's son. Garbh stands a respectable three paces behind me—far enough to be appropriate to his station, near enough to make it clear that if anyone so much as glances at me the wrong way, he's ready to deal with it.

Lady Almha's response is not the polite greeting I'm anticipating. Perhaps she hasn't taken much of a look at me until now, when I straighten and meet her gaze. She starts, stands, and says in an accusatory tone, "You!"

Inwardly, I give voice to a foul curse. "I do not believe we have met before, my lady," I say in courteous tones, lifting my brows just a touch. "I have not lived in these parts for many years. Not since I was a child."

Her eyes narrow. They are lovely eyes, dark blue, set in an oval face of some beauty. Her hair is demurely covered by a veil. I judge her age to be little more than my own. Young to be chieftain. She scrutinizes me.

"I do have two brothers"—I have no choice, now, but to tell her this—"and we are somewhat alike. Perhaps it was one of them you were thinking of." Chances are she mistook me for Seanan. Ruarc is a monk, and his hair is not only tonsured, but red. I'm starting to wish we had been less successful in gaining admission to the lady's household and to her hall. "I live far from Oakhill now; I do not see my family."

Lady Almha beckons me closer. Examines me. I half expect her to step forward and feel me over as a farmer might a promising stud bull. "You are a son of Lord Scannal?"

"His youngest son. We had a falling-out years ago. I tread my own path. Which, on this occasion, has brought me to Darkwater. It seemed appropriate to greet you and congratulate you on your chieftaincy."

Her brows rise. "Since my chieftaincy was gained on the death of my husband," she says coolly, "it is hardly cause for congratulation. And I have been chieftain for some while now. You are tardy in your visit, Master Dau."

She remembers my name, which was announced by her steward when we entered her hall. I'll take that as a good sign. "Any offense was unintentional, my lady. I and my man here"—I indicate the silent Garbh—"plan to stay in these parts for some days, perhaps longer. I appreciate the opportunity to pay my respects."

"Come, be seated." The lady indicates a bench close to her own chair. It seems supper is over in this grand house. The seating is placed near a broad hearth on which burns an excellent fire, and various men and women are gathered close by. Judging by their apparel, they are highborn visitors or senior members of the household. Servants come from time to time to refill cups or offer platters of sweetmeats, then retreat. I see no guards. Garbh is not invited to seat himself; he stands at a short distance as before, an imposing, silent presence. "Will you take some mead, Master Dau?" Lady Almha asks. "It's a particularly fine brew, made here last season."

I accept a cup. The lady introduces the other folk by

name—as I guessed, a mixture of guests and retainers. Didn't Garbh mention back at Winterfalls that Lady Almha's senior adviser was a woman? The only other women here are the lady's personal attendant and the wives of her lawman and councilor.

The inevitable question comes soon enough. "What brings you to these parts, Master Dau?"

I attempt an expression of self-deprecating good humor. "An odd errand. There's a young lady whom I wish to impress. She is oblivious to the gifts a man might more usually offer, such as flowers, a fine brooch or necklace, a tame bird for her pleasure. The lady—forgive me if I do not divulge her name—is something of a scholar, and has a particular love for old tales, the more gruesome and terrifying the better. I thought to seek out stories that were new to her, and to write them down and make a little book of them, bound in fine leather with her name embossed upon the cover. This quest has led me far from home, with my loyal man in attendance." I spare Garbh a glance. He's staring into the middle distance, his expression impassive. I drop my voice to a confidential tone, leaning slightly toward the lady. "Lady Almha, you will no doubt think me foolish, but I have come to Darkwater in pursuit of the dobhar-chú."

Someone lets out a yelp of laughter, quickly stifled. I see amusement on various faces. But Lady Almha's eyes are suddenly bright with interest, and when she says, "Indeed," it is with an odd emphasis that I cannot quite interpret.

"How thoughtful!" exclaims one of the women. "It may seem a strange gift to some, but I admire a man who takes the time to discover what his beloved truly appreciates. And to make this little book yourself! Are you something of a scribe, Master Dau?"

"Hardly that. But I can write passably clear script, and I

don't believe the lady will mind if the illustrations are somewhat lacking. I will do my best. The binding, I will leave to
a craftsman." When nobody says anything, I add, "I am
right, am I not, in seeking this strange creature here in Darkwater? Somewhere in the hills, perhaps?"

Now they're all staring, wondering, perhaps, if I am quite
in my right mind.

"Oh, not the monster itself." I allow myself a chuckle.
Gods, I hate this character I'm creating. In a different world,
this could so easily be the real Master Dau of Oakhill. "I seek
only the tales, from any individual willing to tell. I thought
my man and I might venture to those areas where the creature is reputed to lurk. That way my versions of the stories
would have more character. Dare I say . . . authenticity?"

"As to that," says the man Lady Almha introduced as her
steward, Fursa, "we don't encourage folk to wander up in
those hills. Not because we expect the dobhar-chú to make
an appearance, but because the area is dangerous for walking. Much of it is shifting ground, slippery slopes, and sudden
drops. By night the weather often closes in. Folk get lost and
come to grief. It's not the place for a pleasant stroll."

Is he mocking me? Garbh and I don't look like men who'd
have difficulty crossing such terrain successfully; we may be
wearing the best clothing the prince's residence could provide, but we're both long legged, broad shouldered, well
muscled. "We would take the appropriate caution, naturally.
There was a lake up there—we spotted it from the track as
we rode over Blackstone Pass, the other road still being
closed to us. I'd thought I might use that as the setting for
my tale of the dobhar-chú." The lake, we observed in passing, had some of the characteristics of the place where a traveler was eaten by the creature in the tale Master Saran read
to us. The stony surrounds, the lichen, the remote mountain

setting. Though there may be many such spots in those hills. Our own ride over Blackstone Pass was entirely uneventful, with never a howl to be heard.

Lady Almha smiles. I must not be deceived by her friendly look. We're here on a mission. What counts is the fate of Prince Aolu.

"The lakes are many in those hills," the lady says. "But only a few are visible from that track." The smile turns to a frown. "Did you say the main road is not yet passable? How long does it take the local folk to clear a few trees away? Fursa, speak to Gorman straightaway, will you? We'd best send a party of men over there in the morning to make sure it's done." Fursa departs the hall on silent feet. It's clear the lady commands instant obedience. "I'm sorry you were inconvenienced on your travels," she says more warmly, her eyes on me again. "When you have gathered what you need for this book of tales, will you be heading south to visit Lord Scannal? Or back home?"

It's not quite a question about where I live these days, but it is an invitation to share that information. "Home, most likely," I say. I have no intention of visiting my father ever again. Even though, when I left Oakhill last time, there was a fragile civility between us. "I have the facility there to complete my little book and have it bound to my specifications."

"And, of course, the lady is close by. The lucky recipient of your gift."

A smile seems the correct response. I imagine Liobhan listening to this conversation and trying not to laugh. When I get home I'll tell her about it.

I'm about to ask the gathered folk about the local hostelry and whether it's adequate for accommodation but Lady Almha forestalls my question. "You'll stay here with us, of course, Master Dau. We can provide you and your man with private quarters. You'll find this house quite comfortable. You will be welcome for however long you need to be in these parts. That way, we can make sure you don't fall foul of the dobhar-chú. Or any other strange beasts that may be lurking close by."

"Crow Folk, for instance," says one of the men in dour tones. "Sadly, they are not the stuff of curious old tales, but entirely real, curse them for the murderous creatures they are."

"You have many of them in these parts?"

"More than before," the fellow says, "and coming in closer to the settlements. Hard to drive them off; they've no fear of dogs. With a good bow, a person with the right skill can account for one or two. But that's just as likely to bring more to the attack, and it'll be the archer and other human folk they'll come after then, not so much the cattle or sheep."

"You've had people killed in this region?"

"A few. There are tales about Blackstone Pass. You may have heard them, if you had cause to spend a night at any of the inns along the way."

"We heard some tales, yes. But the warning was not about Crow Folk; it was advice not to go that way by night because of howling and disappearances. I took that to mean the dobhar-chú, since those creatures are reputed to raise their voices on the night of full moon."

"A foolish story," Lady Almha says in suppressive tones. "Not to travel over a high pass in the dark, that is common sense, and a warning is perfectly appropriate. Any rider in his right mind would choose to wait until light. The howling folk speak of is born of superstition and fear, no more. For a wise traveler our roads are perfectly safe."

Everyone is quiet after this; perhaps they are accustomed to giving their chieftain the last word. I wait a little, then I say, "But if the Crow Folk are here and folk have been killed, surely no road can be considered safe. Perhaps I am misunderstanding. I had no wish to offend."

"It's nothing," the lady says, her sharp tone suggesting she is indeed offended. Yet not long ago the mood was mellow, almost genial. "Where is Fursa?" She looks one way, then the other, as if she has forgotten she dispatched him on an errand. Have I touched on something sensitive, to provoke such a change in her? "We'll have a chamber prepared for you and your servant. You must be weary after the ride from . . . where did you shelter last night?"

"We stayed one night in the settlement on this side of the pass, after we came down," I tell the lady. "The inn there has good stabling. The next day we found ourselves still on the road at dusk with no dwellings in sight, so we camped in a sheltered spot. Then we came on here. I welcome the offer of accommodation, my lady. It's most generous of you and your household." A nobleman doesn't offer to pay a chieftain for a few nights' lodgings. I'm probably meant to offer a gift of some kind.

"Say nothing of it, Master Dau. Perhaps you can tell us a tale or two after supper, in recompense."

Dagda save me! "I will do my best, my lady, though I am more fluent with the pen than with my tongue, sadly." I regret this remark as soon as it's left my lips; it sounds just a little suggestive, and brings a dimpled smile to the classically lovely face of my hostess. Someone chuckles softly. A shame Liobhan isn't here to tell stories in my place—she has the gift; I most certainly lack it. Still, I have a little time to prepare something and, I hope, not appear too much a fool or braggart.

"It is a shame Mistress Sciath is not here at present," comments the councilor. "She has a great interest in old tales, especially those from our region. I think you would enjoy meeting her, Master Dau."

"Indeed." Should I know who this person is?

"As my senior adviser, she is often called away. At present Sciath is dealing with a matter of some importance, far beyond our border. Perhaps you will meet her when she returns."

Ah. This person matches Garbh's recollections of the household, from his visit here some time ago as Rodan's bodyguard. "I look forward to that opportunity, if I am still here. A female councilor is quite unusual, as doubtless you already know, Lady Almha. And it seems Mistress Sciath is something of a scholar as well."

"There is no reason why a woman should not be perfectly capable at both, Master Dau. Capable, competent, and well-informed. Don't you think?"

It's a challenge. Fortunately I am able to answer honestly, with Liobhan in my mind. "I agree entirely, Lady Almha. The women who lead Christian religious foundations, for instance, generally display all those qualities and more. I was merely observing that opportunities for women to shine as secular leaders offer themselves more rarely than they might."

The lady smiles. "Mistress Sciath would enjoy discussing this subject further, I am certain," she says. "She is as fond of a good debate on a contentious topic as she is of strange tales."

"I will look forward to that." I cannot imagine my father putting one of his councilors forward in this way. In his household, even the loyal Naithí was treated more as servant than friend. But that was an odd household indeed, one in which nobody could let down their guard. I trust the wounds are healing now Seanan has left Oakhill, and all the good folk there are treading a better course. I stifle a yawn, then murmur an apology.

"But what am I thinking? You must go and rest, Master Dau. Avail yourself of our bathing facilities, have a bite to eat—I imagine you and your man have not had supper—and relax awhile. Here is Fursa at last. We need a chamber prepared for our guest, Fursa. Without delay."

"It's being done as we speak, my lady. Master Dau's bags have been brought up from the stables. With your leave, I will escort him and his man to the bathhouse now. I've arranged for them to take supper in their quarters. This way, Master Dau."

I bid the company a courteous good night and follow him out, with Garbh behind me. I sense curious eyes on me as I leave the hall. Being here as myself-but-not-myself is likely to prove tricky. I didn't have the chance to ask the lady whom it was she mistook me for when she first saw me. That's a question best asked away from the circle of listening ears. If Seanan is here, or close, or might arrive without warning at any time, I'll need to be ready for it. I can't let my untidy private business get in the way of the mission. The lady's reaction suggested she knew him well. As if his unannounced appearance would be an unwelcome surprise. All she said was that one word, *You!* But her tone told me a great deal, and none of it was good.

"I'm having doubts about the plan," I say to Garbh later, when the two of us are bathed and changed and sitting over a good supper in our quarters. The chamber is spacious and comfortable and I'm glad of the privacy, which allows us to close our door and discuss confidential matters provided we keep our voices down. "We could waste a lot of time making pleasant conversation, eating good food and living in comfort, and learning absolutely nothing."

"We only just got here, Dau." Garbh picks up a linen napkin and wipes the grease from his lips. He regards his empty platter with some regret. The dish of roast lamb was particularly fine. "If it will ease your mind, we might set ourselves three days, four days to uncover something. I'll go out and talk to folk in the settlement on some pretext. This place is not as well fortified as some I've seen. The gate's guarded, but it looks easy enough to talk your way through."

"Mm." My mind's been running down a different path. "This Mistress Sciath. See if you can find out where she went and when she's expected back. But casually. Don't sound too interested."

Garbh's giving me a quizzical look. "I know how to do the job, Dau," he says with the hint of a smile.

"Sorry. I know that. Garbh, you mentioned a female councilor when you were talking about your earlier visit here. Was that Mistress Sciath? If Lady Almha's husband was still alive then, why did she have her own councilor? Isn't that unusual?"

"The lady may have been called an adviser rather than a councilor. But it was her, yes. She was very close to Lady Almha. Always by her side, and plainly as something more than a personal attendant. It was Rodan who said she acted like a councilor. Being the man he was, he thought it ridiculous that a woman would take that role. And he couldn't understand why the wife of a chieftain would have need of such an adviser. Rodan never held women in high esteem. Perhaps Lord Cernach thought it good for his young wife to have a well-informed, confident companion, rather than be surrounded by a crowd of silly young things."

I raise my brows at him. "Weren't you ever a silly young thing, Garbh?"

"You and me and all of us, comrade. Listen, Dau." He's all

of a sudden serious. "What you told me about your brother. And what she said, when she first took a proper look at you. Could he be mixed up in something here? Even in the kidnapping, if it turns out these people are behind that?"

"I don't know and I can't ask outright why she said that. But if we're here long enough for you to get friendly with a few folk, and if he's been here, chances are someone will say something to you. They'll mention how I look uncannily like Seanan, though he's most likely calling himself by some other name now. I doubt he's been here as an honored guest. My father banished him from Oakhill. But it did look as if he was familiar to Lady Almha. Curse it. We should have a woman on our team. Someone the maidservants and kitchen helpers and laundresses will chat to." If only they'd been prepared to bend the rules and let Liobhan come with us.

"They might chat to me," says Garbh. "You should ask Lady Almha if they have music and dancing here after supper. Seems like the sort of place where they might. I don't mind a dance, myself."

We fall quiet. I'm remembering a certain night of dancing at the royal court of Breifne, and Garbh standing up to partner Liobhan after she had fallen foul of Prince Rodan. Garbh lost his position there for that offense. It was a courageous act, a public recognition that she had been treated unjustly.

"You're right about the evening entertainment," I say, coming back to the here and now. "With luck this is the kind of household where everyone gets up to dance, from chieftains and visiting noblemen to kitchen maids and grooms. Naturally I would allow you to join in. Could be an opportunity."

"For you as well," Garbh says. "How's your dancing?"

"Better than it was before I met Liobhan. I can put in a reasonable performance as a chieftain's son. A ride would be another opportunity to speak with Lady Almha alone."

"Mm. Could be the one you need to dance with and ride with is Mistress Sciath, who likes tales of the dobhar-chú. And the Crow Folk. I wonder where she went."

Something's teasing my mind, something I can't quite grasp hold of.

"Garbh?"

"Mm?" My companion sounds half-asleep. It's been a long day.

"One way or another, it looks as if the attackers made a shambles of their job. Not only did several of them get killed, but one of them earned a gruesome public execution. I'm still failing to understand why. The Crow Folk attack must have been coincidental, based on what we know of the creatures. It could hardly be considered anyone's fault if the prince used that opportunity to escape. And if Aolu was still in their custody, wouldn't they have got out of there as fast as they could once the Crow Folk backed off? Why take the time to kill that man and put him on display?"

"There could have been an argument within the group about how things were to be done. Everyone on edge, trying to make a decision . . . Someone strikes out with a weapon . . ." Garbh is overtaken by a huge yawn.

"And severs another man's head by mistake? Hardly. And another thing. We ruled out a locally based attack. But these men must have known Prince Aolu by sight, and that suggests they had inside help, or someone had been spying out the territory in advance. Watching for an opportunity. If not, how could they spot their target?"

"If either the prince or Galen usually wore something marked with the Dalriadan royal emblem," Garbh says, "that would have been enough, to a man who knew about such things. Signs and symbols."

A flash of memory comes to me, making my belly churn:

the symbol of my own family, branded onto Liobhan's arm by my brother, during the night he held her captive. "The kind of man who would wear a belt buckle decorated with a dobhar-chú," I say.

"Oh, this does me good!" Lady Almha exclaims as we reach a wide, level expanse of greensward and urge our mounts to a canter. It is a day of benign sunshine, of fresh, sweet air and birds caroling in the trees, the sort of day on which one should put aside dark thoughts of conspiracy and killings and lost princes and simply enjoy the fine spring weather. I cannot do so. If I speak with this woman it must be to the purpose. If I spend time with her I must not waste a moment of it. The longer Garbh and I stay at Darkwater, the more doubtful I grow about the theory that brought us here. Why would Lady Almha, fairly new to her chieftaincy and still finding her way as a leader, be involved in the abduction of Prince Aolu? There would be no sense to that, no advantage she could gain. Such an act, if discovered, would blacken her name among the leaders not only of Argialla but of all the neighboring territories.

I want to tell her. I want to ask if she's heard the news about the prince, ask who she thinks might be responsible and assess her response. But I can't. My orders are to look and listen but not to reveal my purpose. So, this morning we ride for recreation. I will talk about other matters and hope to glean something useful.

There was no need to ask the lady about that odd moment when she first saw me and thought I was another man. Garbh overheard a couple of grooms talking in the stables. One observed how closely I resembled someone named Sealbhach—not a name I have heard mentioned in the household. And another man commented that one of Sealbhach was bad enough, who'd want two of the bastard? They agreed, in undertones, that they were glad Mistress Sciath and her men were away from Darkwater, and expressed a wish that the absence would be a lengthy one. So there it is; my brother has become a hired guard, or something of the sort. If this is indeed Seanan. I cannot imagine him earning a living in such a way. He is much too fond of giving other folk orders.

We've come out without our guards. Rain has prevented such an outing until today, the fifth morning after our arrival in this house. I have spent the time as fruitfully as I can, giving Lady Almha my full attention whenever the opportunity arose, dancing with her after supper when some musicians played—Liobhan would not have been impressed by them—and making myself as amiable as possible. Today, while we're out riding, Garbh intends to visit the settlement.

Near the spot where grassy sward gives way to low wooded hills, we slow our horses to a walk. "Might we go that way?" I suggest, pointing to a track that winds uphill between the trees. It looks broad enough to take two riders abreast and the gentle slope should not unduly tax the horses.

Lady Almha hesitates, drawing her mare to a halt. "If you wish. A certain distance. But not to the higher reaches; there are Crow Folk, and we are hardly prepared for that." She has a small but useful-looking knife at her belt; I, a larger one. And other weapons hidden on my person. I'm surprised she was prepared to come out with me and leave the guards behind. But then, this is her land and I suppose she knows the risks. "There's a spot where one can halt, rest the horses and admire the view." A pause. "And speak in private."

"We might ride to that point and take our refreshments there."

In response the lady smiles and urges her mount on, a little more briskly than she might. I wonder if this is some game I do not understand. Her moods are volatile. She can be warm and charming, but it takes very little to upset her, and I have not yet worked out how to avoid that, though I think the touchiness may relate to the presence of the Crow Folk in Darkwater. She is sensitive on the subject of Mistress Sciath, too. On edge, almost. Is her admiration for her adviser touched with fear? If that is so, why keep the woman in her household?

It's quite a long ride to the vantage point. At one point a stream makes its way through the woods not far from the path, and we pause so the horses can drink. Then it's uphill once more until we finally come to a halt, dismount, and tether the animals to a sturdy post set there for the purpose. In this spot the hillside is open and the path has broadened to a wide level area holding a sturdy bench long enough to accommodate three. From my saddlebag I take the provisions supplied by Lady Almha's cook and place them between us on the seat. Ale in a tightly stoppered jug, bread, fine cheese, slices of roasted chicken—it is quite a feast. A pair of platters, a pair of cups, a pair of small knives. A napkin to place underneath. Set out, it looks like a treat for lovers. For a moment I let myself imagine that Liobhan is sitting at the other end of the bench, and that we can eat together, then slip away to the shelter of the trees and lie down on a blanket and . . . I busy myself sharing things out in order to avoid the questioning look that has suddenly appeared on my companion's face.

"A fine view," I remark. "Is that the Blackstone Pass I see over there?"

"Mm," murmurs Lady Almha, shading her eyes as she gazes northeastward. "They've finally cleared the other road, through Hunter's Glen. Folk should not be obliged to use Blackstone Pass. It simply isn't safe. And if they come to grief, the blame falls on me. Then the foolish tales come out again, the howling, the half-glimpsed shapes, the strange lights. And the Crow Folk, of course. But they are almost everywhere."

I turn my head to look up into the nearby trees, as if expecting to see a small army of the creatures waiting to swoop down and seize the food from my hand.

"Not here," she says quickly, "or I would not have risked this path without guards. Higher up, yes. But they are mostly found in the hills above Elderbrook, close to the near end of Hunter's Glen. Indeed, it might almost be said they gather there. More of the creatures flock in season by season."

I pour ale for her, making no comment.

"The Crow Folk give Darkwater a bad reputation. Travelers will not come here if they might at any moment be attacked, or harried until their horses throw them and they break all their bones. Until the recent developments, I wanted to see the wretched things exterminated. If not that, then driven from these parts forever. Mistress Sciath has persuaded me otherwise." She looks at me as if expecting a well-informed response.

A nod, trying for a thoughtful look. How much does she think I know? "Perhaps there is more to the creatures than meets the eye," I say, doing my best to sound wise. "We are, in general, at somewhat of a loss to understand their behavior."

Lady Almha stares out over the broad acres of her territory, toward the far hills. She glances around as if to ascertain that we are truly alone. "We can talk freely here," she says eventually. Her voice is just above a murmur. "Your reference to the dobhar-chú, when you first arrived here . . . Have you spoken to Mistress Sciath? I assume you have heard something of her plans, or you would not have made your way here."

Think quickly, Dau. "I have yet to meet the lady in person. I'm here on the strength of some information of which I became aware through a source best not named. I imagine you want to keep this quiet." I look one way, then the other, as she did earlier. "A chance meeting with a man I will likely never see again. My interest was piqued. I had sworn never to visit Argialla again. But here I am." A rueful smile, a shrug.

"Sciath takes great personal risks in her pursuit of answers. She has been following this path since we witnessed a certain occurrence in Breifne. From that time on, she has been firm in her belief that destroying the Crow Folk would be wasteful. Hence her quest to harness their power, rather than exterminate them."

What in the name of the gods . . . ? I gather myself to respond. "It is indeed a bold idea, my lady. Both bold and fascinating. I have wondered how Mistress Sciath might put this into place. What the steps might be. One would need a means of control . . ." A wild theory starts to form in my mind. Breifne. Where Brocc sang and won a true king his rightful crown. Where he kept the Crow Folk at bay by . . . "You refer to the use of song, yes?" I must go with great care here.

She smiles. "It was a song that gave her the first clue, long ago. Not that she explained this fully to me at the time. Sciath is clever, Dau. Sometimes her mind darts ahead so swiftly I cannot follow." Lady Almha glances over her shoulder again, though in this secluded spot only birds and insects can hear us. "She has pursued this since a time before I was chieftain. Even now she searches for the agent she requires to set the plan in place."

"Remarkable!" I am walking on shaky ground indeed. A plan to control the Crow Folk? Can this be related to the attack on Galen and the prince? One wrong question, one wrong move may expose me as a spy.

"We should eat," I say, playing for time. "This food looks delicious. And then perhaps you will tell me more—I'm all ears."

I eat and drink, I watch birds circling in the sky, I breathe slowly and practice patience. I consider how long Mistress Sciath has harbored this wild ambition, and wonder why she decided to propose her unlikely plan to Almha rather than to her husband, then chieftain of Darkwater. More malleable? Easier to convince? I don't ask questions, though I have plenty. It's not until we've both eaten our fill, and I'm starting to pack things back into the saddlebag, that Lady Almha speaks again.

"Sciath has traveled far away, Dau. She was drawn by a rumor. She hopes to find the source of it. A story about a minstrel with unusual powers . . ." Lady Almha breaks off, looking away from me. "You may find this hard to believe."

"Why not try me?" I will my heart to slow. This may not be what I suspect it is.

"Perhaps you attended the coronation of King Faelan in Breifne. I imagine Lord Scannal would have been invited, as my late husband was."

"Sadly, I was not there," I lie. This fine lady would hardly have noticed me undercover as a lowly stable hand. "At that time I was estranged from my family and living far away."

"There was a musician at the court of Breifne. At the ritual he played the harp and sang. The performance was . . . it was remarkable beyond anything you might hear from the most celebrated of bards, Dau. Everyone present felt the power of it. The magic of it. Folk talked about it long afterward, though the minstrel himself disappeared shortly after the ritual and was not seen again. Some people said he must have been part fey, to coax such sounds from his instrument."

"Indeed." Oh, gods. Seems my suspicion was right. Just as well Brocc is safe in his Otherworld refuge.

"A tale began to spread. That the same man, the singer, had used his voice to ward off a flock of Crow Folk. Someone thought they heard strange chanting. And some horses were returned to the stable in a terrified state, not long after."

I remember that part all too well, since I was the one who led the horses in. Fortunately, almost the entire household was in the ritual area at the time. I slipped in and out of the stables without alerting anyone. Who spread this rumor? Who heard us shouting and the Crow Folk screaming, up on the edge of the forest? It's easy enough to imagine the occupants of an outlying farm being woken before dawn, wondering what was going on but too terrified to rush to our aid. We were luckier than we thought, getting away from Breifne with our cover intact.

"I attended that coronation ritual with my late husband, Lord Cernach. Mistress Sciath was with us. We heard the power in that man's voice. Sciath says that if the rumor is true, about the Crow Folk, perhaps the same man—they told us his name was Donal—could teach her how to control the creatures. How to use them to our benefit. A person with that ability could surely wield great power."

I stare at her, struggling to mask my shock. "Indeed. And the purpose would be . . . ?"

"To create a fighting force, of course. That would be a greater army than Erin has ever seen in all its long history."

I can see she's surprised that she needs to explain this. She expects me to consider it an excellent idea. Has Mistress Sciath put these notions in her chieftain's head? Are they both so insanely ambitious that they really believe others would fall in with such a plan? But then, Sciath has had a long time to work on her mistress; she's been in the household since before Almha's husband died. I can imagine how it might have been: a lonely young wife wed to a husband whose days were perhaps taken up with long councils, meetings with advisers, and the like. She might well have been bored, disaffected, in need of a friend and confidant. Along comes a clever woman who soothes and flatters and listens at first, then gradually persuades her mistress to her own extreme plan. Lord Cernach would have been harder to convince, I suspect. I can't imagine my father ever considering such a possibility. But Lord Cernach died. And now . . . Yes, I can see it. But why would Almha confide in me?

Oh, gods. I am the son of the neighboring chieftain. Estranged from my father, yes, but as far as Lady Almha knows, I might still become his heir. I am of around her own age and as yet unwed. I remember the sparkle in her eyes as we danced, her sideways glances. The place of honor allocated to me at table. Right now, I wish I were anywhere but here.

"Dau?" She turns a quizzical look on me.

"A bold plan indeed," I say lightly, moving to untether the horses. "Is there an enemy threatening the borders of Darkwater, that such a force would be required?"

"At present, no. But as your father's son, you must know how quickly these things can change. Mistress Sciath's plan stretches far into the future. Her journey is a search for the truth; an attempt to discover where this man with the so-powerful voice went when he disappeared from Breifne on the very day the new king was crowned. She would find him and bring him here." A pause, as if she's choosing her words carefully. "So we may learn from him."

"Perhaps we should head back." I've packed the saddlebag, and now I help the lady mount. "I look forward to meeting Mistress Sciath. She sounds like a person of strong will and great independence." I clear my throat.

Lady Almha glances at me sideways as we begin our descent of the path. "I am pleased that you do not add *for a woman*, Dau." Again she leaves out *Master*. Is there a purpose in that?

"Experience has taught me that it does not pay to underestimate a woman, my lady."

"Oh, please call me Almha, at least while we are on our own. *My lady* is for the house, when others are nearby."

"I'm honored, my—Almha. May I ask a question?"

"Of course."

"Does Mistress Sciath travel alone?"

"She generally takes two guards for protection. This time she has a larger escort. Five or six men." Her tone is awkward again. There's something she doesn't want to say. I don't ask; I wait.

"Not our own men-at-arms; she would not take so many from my household guard for a mission of this kind. Hired men from elsewhere."

I don't ask whether Mistress Sciath's hired men wear the dobhar-chú on their belts. I don't mention my brother. I must not leap to conclusions, tempting though it is to put the pieces of this together and end up with that unsavory scene in the woods at Winterfalls. I must play along with this, do what she perhaps wants me to do, even as I struggle to accept the horror of it. Does this woman riding at my side not understand what power a leader might wield with an obedient army of Crow Folk at her bidding? If that is what Mistress Sciath intends for the chieftain of Darkwater, she must be out of her mind. Perhaps they're both crazy.

But it won't happen. It can't. What Brocc did that day when the Crow Folk attacked us was to raise his voice in a powerful chant that made them back off. It was astounding, yes. Magical, probably. Cooperative, absolutely not. That morning Brocc's song was a weapon. And a little later, he used his voice and his harp as remarkable instruments of celebration, of recognition. Brocc is a Swan Island man, a warrior. But he would never use music to command an army, whether of men-at-arms or hired fighters or Crow Folk. He's an entertainer, a storyteller, a true bard. To use his gift in self-defense or to save a comrade is one thing. To use it as Lady Almha suggests is quite another. The very thought would sicken him. Just as well he is in the Otherworld, where Sciath cannot reach him.

I remember that other scene, on my father's land at Oak-hill, at the time when an injury had rendered me blind. Brocc insisted on releasing some captive Crow Folk my brother had hurt. It was an exercise fraught with peril, for the birds were distressed, confused, and strong enough to damage us. I heard him speak gently to them, almost tenderly; he prom-ised them freedom and safety. He could not sing that day, so Liobhan sang for him, while he gave the Crow Folk a healing draft. The cage was opened and they flew out into the day. I felt the wind of their passing as I crouched in the doorway with my arms over my head, fearful of beak and claw. They did not touch me.

We halt, the lady and I together, at the foot of the hill. "A minstrel is not generally the kind of man who makes a good war leader," I observe quietly.

"A war leader?" She sounds shocked. But she cannot be so innocent. The woman is a chieftain. "I do not believe that is what Sciath seeks, Dau. She travels only to find this man, Donal, so she can speak to him about his ability. So he can show her how he does what he does. No more than that." When I make no comment, she adds, "Dau. I have told you this in confidence, since you hinted that you already knew something of the plan. There have been times when I had doubts, I confess. But Sciath is sure of its importance and confident of its success, and I am convinced she should at least attempt it. You realize this must be kept secret. Not a whisper, either in my household or beyond it."

"You have my word, Almha. I'm honored that you would trust me with this, and I understand the importance of keeping it private. I will hope to hear more at some future time." Swan Island training, along with my brother's example, has taught me to tell smooth lies and be believed. "We should ride on," I say with a smile. "And I should start calling you *my lady* once more."

She laughs, tossing her dark hair, which has escaped its confinement during the ride and is falling in curls around her face. "I suppose you should, Master Dau. I've enjoyed the ride. We must do it again."

"That would give me great pleasure, my lady."

Oh, this world of pretty manners and pretense. Lady Almha has a secret so shocking I am still struggling to believe it. I suspect Mistress Sciath has her own secrets, not to be shared even with the chieftain over whom she has such influence. Lady Almha is right to have misgivings about the quest her councilor pursues with such diligence. I can hardly comprehend a plan of such grandeur and ill intent. Were it possible to assemble and train such an army, this minor chieftain newly come to her position might become the scourge of all Erin. She might unseat the lawful High King and usurp his place. She might be responsible for the deaths of hundreds. Thousands. A person would have to be mad to want that kind of power. I see little in Lady Almha to suggest she would wish to pursue such a course, nor indeed that she would have any aptitude for it. Sciath is either ruthless, devious, and intent on evil, or out of her mind.

The Swan Island elders need to know about this. But there's no safe house near here; the one we were told about is in the smaller settlement of Elderbrook, a day's ride away at the near end of Hunter's Glen. That leaves me with no way to get a message out quickly. We should have brought a backup team. Maybe Garbh can find a pretext to ride to Elderbrook without me.

Can this be linked with the missing prince? There's no reason he would be caught up in it, apart from that wretched belt buckle. It must have been my mention of the dobharchú, perhaps along with the Crow Folk, that made Almha think I knew more than I do. So there is a link. I pace our chamber, to and fro, struggling to set my thoughts in order. We have to get a message out. There are pigeons here, as at most great households, but I cannot request the use of them. I'm the estranged son of a noble family, wandering on my own with no grander purpose than preparing a special gift for my sweetheart. To make such a request would be to arouse suspicion, especially when Almha has asked me to keep things secret. Curse it!

At last Garbh returns. I've been at the stables on the pretext of checking our horses' welfare, but my real purpose was to keep an eye on the gate, watching for him. I motion to him and we go to walk around the field where the animals are let out for exercise. There's nobody in earshot. It's not a problem if someone sees us together, since he's my personal guard. I'm about to tell him what Lady Almha told me, but Garbh speaks first.

"No useful gossip, sadly. I asked about fishing, and a couple of fellows took me out across the fields to show me a good spot. Then back to the inn for another jug of ale. The host thought at first I wanted a bed for the night, was very keen to offer his best. Disappointed when I told him I was in your employ and staying in the chieftain's household. He said there were far fewer travelers these days, because of the Crow Folk. His accommodation's been empty for the last five nights."

"I have news," I say. "Something troubling, and from the lady herself." I tell him the story, not advancing any theories, just repeating what she said.

When I'm done Garbh curses under his breath. "We've stumbled into a real nest of snakes, Dau. A nasty, tangled one. I hope you were careful in what you said to that woman."

I grimace. "I did my best. There's no way to get a message back to Winterfalls, unless we can find a plausible reason to go over to Elderbrook and send it from the safe house there. If we can, we should send to the island for reinforcements. A backup team if they can manage it. At the very least we should get some kind of warning out. Maybe Liobhan can work out a way to send word to Brocc."

We're at the far end of the field, by a stile. We stop in the sunshine, leaning on the drystone wall. "We need to give it a bit longer," Garbh says. "Another day, two days. After what the lady's told you, she'll be suspicious if we head off tomorrow. Even if I go on my own. She's likely to think I'm off to pass the secret information straight on to someone else. Which, of course, would be quite true. We can afford to wait for a better opportunity. Mistress Sciath's not going to find Brocc, and without him, nothing can happen in a rush." He falls silent, looking over toward the stable block. He's not seeing it, though; he's thinking hard. "I did overhear a mention of Mistress Sciath's men, while I was using the privy at the Darkwater inn. Not much. Just that they're not exactly popular in these parts, and nobody's in a rush to welcome them back."

"Mm. If she's hiring men from outside the area and paying

them well enough, the locals might have cause to feel some resentment." I think of Seanan again. My brother as part of a venture to tame the Crow Folk? That's the least likely thing I can imagine. He fears and loathes the creatures. He subjected them to his foul experiments. "The prospect of more time in the lady's company is not appealing. It's a thin line to tread, pretending I'm here because I knew something about the plan. I'm amazed she leaped to that conclusion simply because I mentioned the dobhar-chú." Something's nagging at me. This feels like a puzzle I could solve, if only I could fit the pieces together the right way.

"Speaking of the dobhar-chú," says Garbh with a grin, "I know a perfect way for you to fill in those two days. Aren't you meant to be making a little book for your sweetheart? What better time to make a start?"

15

SCIATH

Extraordinary. After all the slow and careful work, the delving, the subtle questioning, the knitting together of the disparate and fraying threads of rumor and custom and daily observance, after the endless, meticulous search across forest and farmland, inn and great house and anywhere a bard of fey ancestry might possibly have sought a bolt-hole, at last she had him. If this was indeed the right man. He hardly matched the image in her memory. This person was no merry, smiling minstrel, but looked worn to shreds, his face ghost-white, his hands shaking with exhaustion, his eyes desperate. And this man carried not a harp, but a child.

She watched as he settled the two of them into a make-shift camp. He changed the infant's clothes, he washed it, he fed it some sort of pap. The child cried, and he soothed it. Sciath's heart sank. Surely this could not be the man she sought. This was a pathetic specimen of humankind, a wan-derer, a wretched vagrant. The minstrel had been a hand-some fellow, a person of power, with magic at his fingertips. Such a one would never be reduced to this. Her informant had lied.

It was getting cold. There had been rain, and a chill damp hung over the fields. The man she was watching had made camp not far from the road, in the meager shelter of a crumbling drystone wall. A lone elm grew there, and its branches formed a roof of sorts over the man, the child, and their pitiful belongings. Sciath shivered, cold despite her woolen cloak. Time to retreat. Bitter disappointment lay like a stone in her heart. To be robbed of success now, when she had believed herself so close . . . It was intolerable.

The child had fallen silent. Perhaps it was asleep. The man wrapped it in a garment of some sort and cradled it in his arms as he sat with his back against the wall. Sciath did not move. To step away was to accept defeat; she could not bring herself to do it. And as she watched, still and silent under the trees, the man looked up, not toward her, but into the elm, where a dark form perched. One of *them*.

The man showed no sign of fear. He took no action to shield his child from attack. He did not move at all. But he opened his mouth and sang, and it was no gentle lullaby but a resonant call that made the hairs on Sciath's neck stand up.

> *I come in peace.*
> *I come in trust.*
> *I come in friendship.*
> *I am here.*

And in the silence that followed, there came a reply from the bird: three low, deep notes that made their own grave tune of recognition. *I, too, am here.* Oh, gods, that she was hearing this, watching it, capturing the moment of proof! It *could* be done, it *had* been done! The creatures could be tamed, they could be made to listen and to obey! Sciath's heart beat like a marching drum. She held herself stone-still, hardly daring to draw breath.

The musician sang on; the child in his arms did not wake.

> *Three gifts in parting:*
> *The gift of friendship*
> *The gift of understanding*
> *The gift of trust.*

Simple words, a simple tune, hardly a song. But full of power and longing. She must learn to channel that power. To transform that longing into what she needed—an unquenchable determination. A ruthless drive to win.

There were no answering notes from the bird this time. The three stayed unmoving, in silence: crow on branch, minstrel in his wretched wayside camp, child in his arms. She wondered if they were speaking to each other, man and bird, in some way she could not understand. The fellow did not lie down or close his eyes in sleep. Moonlight painted the three of them silver and black, and Sciath was aware again of the creeping cold, the dark of the forest, the predators that might strike without warning. Should she approach the bard now? Call in her men? Not with that creature perched overhead; if the thing was his friend, who was to say it might not swoop down to attack her the moment she came close? The child was another complication. What to do with it, how to deal with it . . . But then, it was a very small child. Portable. And too young to form words of accusation or blame. The child might prove extremely useful.

She thanked the gods that she had dispatched Sealbhach back to Elderbrook and kept only the other two with her. How fortunate that Ruairi and Scoithín were waiting at a distance, as she'd commanded. Now was not the time to take this prize. She would wait until tomorrow, and choose her moment. Ruairi could stay with her; the bard might think it odd if she appeared to be traveling entirely alone. Scoithín could go ahead and get everything set up. The two of them were, on the whole, reliable. Not that any of the wretched crew she'd hired had proven entirely trustworthy. They'd made a complete mess of things in Winterfalls, thanks to one fool's choice to act without waiting to consult her. Because of that they'd wasted precious time. And taken an unnecessary risk. There had been two men missing when they'd come back to the meeting place where she was waiting with Ruairi. And while they were still stumbling through an account of the disaster, the Crow Folk had struck again, leaving two more men dead and the rest reduced to mindless terror. Fools. Useless apologies for fighters.

When that attack was over, Sealbhach, a man not without intelligence, had told her the unvarnished truth about which of the group had led them forward without her authority, and she'd made an example of the offender. Then she'd dismissed most of them, warning them to get out of the area quickly and to keep their mouths shut if they knew what was good for them. Not one of them had dared ask for his pay. Even the most woodenheaded must have realized the only reward a failure like this deserved was contempt.

Sciath had kept but three with her: Sealbhach, Ruairi, and Scoithín. They'd performed a search of the area where their quarry had escaped capture. The other man, perhaps a guard, lay motionless where he had fallen. Dead, Sciath assumed. There had been no sign of their target. Perhaps, while they were deeper in the woods, he had circled around and made his way out to the nearby settlement at Winterfalls. Then, in the distance, they had heard men's voices and the excited barking of a dog. A search party. Sciath had snapped out the order to retreat. As they'd fled through the forest to the spot where their horses waited, she'd heard the searchers shouting, and the name they were calling was not Donal. It was Aolu. The name of the king's son, the crown prince, whose home was only a stone's throw away. It could not be coincidence. Her men had not only disobeyed orders then let their target escape, they had wasted their time and effort on the wrong person. A person whose disappearance was likely to bring out a whole army of searchers.

She'd slipped out of the forest and moved on southward with her three remaining men. A few days later, when Sealbhach's helpful suggestions were starting to get on her nerves, she'd sent him back to Elderbrook to await further orders. The other two she'd retained. Scoithín combined the useful qualities of silence and brute strength. Ruairi was not an imaginative man. He would follow orders, whatever they were.

Tomorrow, then. She'd have to hope the fellow could keep his infant alive that long. She'd make sure she was in the right place at the right time. Not here, and not too early. On the road, later in the day when he was footsore and weary.

A cloud covered the moon, and shadow fell on the little camp. Sciath slipped away from her hiding place and headed for shelter. For all the chill wind, her body was warm with anticipation. Tomorrow. Oh, tomorrow!

16

BROCC

Anortherly gale drives the rain sideways as if it would turn us to icicles. I was a fool not to go to Mistress Juniper. I was a fool not to challenge Eirne. I was a fool not to run to the court of Breifne and throw myself on King Faelan's mercy. I must have been out of my mind to take my child on this wretched, plodding, miserable walk, for it has turned her from merry, rosy-cheeked infant to pale and shivering ghost of a child. Danu help me, what if I lose her?

Shadow trails us, sometimes seen, sometimes unseen. Often he stays in the cover of trees until dusk, then comes swift-winged to roost beside us. Today he is nowhere in sight. I tried to convey to him, as I held Niamh close in hope that she might gain some warmth from my trembling body, that he should not follow me near any habitation of man. My plight is of my own doing, and I would not have my friend endanger himself in his efforts to help me. It is wonderful, miraculous that we have this means of speaking to each other now, first the formal greetings, then the silent exchange of images, the wordless storytelling that opens to each of us the other's world. If the circumstances were different I would be full of joy. But if he stays with us Shadow puts himself in peril. Each time he seeks out food for us, he risks attack by pitchfork-wielding farmers or villagers with burning torches. And he must live. He must survive. I believe, I truly believe that in Shadow lies the hope of his tribe.

I am no longer a Swan Island warrior. My journey has become one failure after another, a chain of wrong decisions. I plod along, every part of me aching, my clothing soaked through, my feet blistered, my heart leaden. Niamh had the last of our food this morning. I must reach help today or I will lose her. Why is there nobody on this road, no cart, no flocks or herds, no riders passing from settlement to settlement? Why are there no farmsteads, no wayside inns, not even a barn under whose roof we could shelter? This is the loneliest of paths. If I stop, I may not be able to walk on. But I must stop, if only for long enough to check that Niamh still breathes. By the side of the road, in the persistent rain, I halt, set down my sodden bag, and untie the sling that holds my daughter. My fingers are numb with cold; I struggle with this simplest of tasks. When I maneuver Niamh around to the front I nearly drop her, but manage to scoop her back into my arms. This slight effort makes me dizzy. My knees are like soft wool; my legs will not hold me any longer.

Niamh breathes still. Each time she draws in air there's a little sound, a tiny rasping cry of woe. I sink to the ground, wrapping my arms around her. The rain falls; the wind blows. My throat is tight with grief. But I am a bard, and I will not let my daughter go without music. With tears spilling down my cheeks, I hum my shaky way through the tune I made for her: "Flight of the Fair One." I did not think, when I penned this joyous piece, that the flight might be her last.

And then . . . oh, gods, hoofbeats along the road, the jingle of harness, and voices. I struggle to my feet. I tuck Niamh into one arm and hold the other hand high. *Let them not ride straight past, let them see us, let them stop . . .* "Help!" I call, and my voice is harsh as a crow's. "Stop! Please!"

The riders halt by us. There's a woman clad in a plain gray cloak, her hair covered with a hood. A well-armed man of burly build rides behind her. She dismounts; he follows. I don't need to say a word. The fellow takes off his fur-lined cloak and drapes it around both me and my daughter. The woman says something to him and he responds. I am beyond understanding anything but the blessed warmth of this garment, and the unexpected, wondrous return of hope. I stand there wordless, on uncertain legs, until the woman says, "There's a place where we can take you, not far from here. Our friend is already there. A roof over your head, food for you and the child, a comfortable bed for the night. And if we can help you on your journey afterward, we will. Come, now. Pass me the baby, there. It's all right, I will keep her safe. Ruairi?"

The big man leads me to his horse. I know I can't mount by myself. I can barely support my own weight, standing. I lean against the warmth of the animal. "Wait there," the fellow says.

The woman passes Niamh to her husband, or bodyguard, or whatever he is. She removes her cloak, for all the chill. "Tie her to my back, put the cloak around us both, then help me mount," she says crisply, and he obeys, using the sad, damp sling in which I have carried Niamh.

"But . . ." I protest. They choose not to hear me. Somewhere deep down, I know the arrangement makes sense. I am too weak to carry Niamh and sit on a horse. And the woman did say it wasn't far. But I don't want anyone taking my daughter, not even if I can watch them every step of the way. "But I . . ."

When woman and child are settled in the saddle, Ruairi boosts me bodily onto his own horse and mounts behind me. The animal is strong and sturdy; it makes nothing of the added burden.

"Ready?" the woman calls.

"Ready, Mistress Sciath."

"Move on, then. The sooner we're out of this weather the better."

I am so tired I almost miss it; I am slumped against Ruairi's chest like some fainting damsel. But through the pounding drumbeat of the rain, the eldritch whistling of the wind, I sense it: high overhead, a steady beating of wings.

I wake with a start. Daylight shows between the shutters. Where am I? My head is fuzzy, my limbs are leaden. How long did I sleep?

It comes back slowly. We're at a house, not a wayside inn but a farmstead. A woman and a man brought us here . . . oh, gods, the warmth, it was so wonderful. They fed Niamh goat's milk sweetened with honey . . . I was so tired, too tired to explain myself . . . *Niamh.* I'm suddenly awake, throwing off the blankets, struggling out of the bed, groping for the shutters . . . Light floods in, illuminating the modest chamber, some garments draped over a bench—not my clothes, I've never seen them before—and showing me the cradle in the corner, the little bed into which I tucked my daughter last night. Niamh has slept late. But that is no surprise. She will be hungry when she wakes.

I approach softly, not wanting to startle her. I look down. The cradle is empty. My daughter is gone.

I blunder out of the room. The crash of door against wall brings several people into the hallway, including the woman who provided our food last night and helped me bathe

Niamh. This house is her home. I can't remember her name. Mistress Sciath is here, too, and a man who is not Ruairi, but who looks equally formidable.

"Where is my daughter?" The voice of common sense says Niamh woke before me, they took her out so I could sleep on undisturbed, they have her safe in the warm kitchen. A darker instinct is not to be denied. Dread rises in me.

The kindly woman starts to speak, but Sciath silences her with an imperious gesture, then motions to her to depart. The woman obeys, not before turning a look on me that combines helplessness with pity.

"Where is Niamh? What have you done with her?" A wave of dizziness comes over me; I put a hand against the wall for balance. Morrigan's curse, what is wrong with me? I need to be strong, strong as iron; I need to be a warrior. I need all my wits about me.

"She's safe, my friend." Sciath's tone is calm, level, de-signed to reassure me. As if anything could, until I hold Niamh in my arms and know for myself that all's well with her. "The child is with another family. All comforts will be provided for her. The woman has a babe of her own and is happy to act as wet nurse, having sufficient milk for two. Little Niamh will be well looked after." When I say nothing but simply stare at her in disbelief, she adds, "They will keep your child until such time as she can be returned to you. Don't concern yourself, Master Donal. I paid them well."

I struggle to make any sense of this. Perhaps, to an out-sider, what she says might sound reasonable. But . . . "Why didn't you wake me? How could you make such a decision without consulting me? Niamh is my daughter!" Did she just call me Master Donal? How can she know that name, my mission name from our time in Breifne?

The large man clears his throat. Sciath regards me with

her brows raised. Without words, both convey their opinion that I was not doing a very good job of looking after my child. I try to rein in my feelings; to act as a rational man should. "Thank you for your kindness in rescuing us yesterday. For bringing us to shelter. My apologies for what may seem ingratitude. But as her father, it is for me to decide where Niamh goes and with whom. You did not have the right to take her away without my approval. She and I will be moving on as soon as I can make the arrangements." I draw a deep breath; I am failing to keep my voice steady. "I need her back here, Mistress Sciath. Where I can watch over her myself."

"Come," she says, nodding to her man, who opens the door to the kitchen with its fire and its savory smells of cooking. The other woman, the kind one, is nowhere to be seen. "We have matters to discuss, Master Donal. Serious matters. I have a proposition for you." She looks me up and down. "Perhaps you should dress first. Scoithín left clothing in your chamber. Scoithín, you might show Master Donal where the privy is, and wait until he is ready."

My belly is churning with a queasy mixture of fury and anxiety. A proposition? What proposition? But I am barefoot, wearing a nightshirt I don't remember putting on. Did someone have to undress me last night? Morrigan's curse! I allow the hulking, silent Scoithín to escort me to the privy and back. He waits while I dress in borrowed clothing that is warm, if ill-fitting. I tell him I want to see Niamh this morning, and to leave with her as soon as possible. In response he offers a grunt.

Back in the kitchen, breakfast is waiting for me. The others must have eaten earlier. I cannot eat, hungry as I am. I sit with the platter in front of me and Mistress Sciath at the other end of the table, regarding me with a carefully schooled expression that tells me nothing at all. Did I meet her in Breifne? Did she perhaps hear me playing music with Liobhan and Archu, when we were employed as musicians? I was gone from the court for some time before the coronation, returning only to play the harp and sing on the fateful day itself. After that we went to ground, and the next morning we left that place. The only time I used the name of Donal was on that mission. I must tread carefully. I must not dive in with a thousand angry questions. "Mistress Sciath. Thank you again for taking pity on us yesterday, when we found ourselves in difficulty. I'm sorry if I addressed you less than courteously before. My daughter is my whole world. It distressed me to find her gone when I woke. I do not understand why you took this decision without first consulting me."

"The offer of a wet nurse was too good to turn down, Master Donal, and it required swift action. Folk stopped here for a bite to eat, on their way to deliver some goats to that holding. They offered comfortable transport for Niamh. A farm cart, a girl to sit in the back and hold the child. You were sleeping heavily. We hadn't the heart to wake you." Her tone suggests this argument is quite reasonable.

"I am Niamh's only family, Mistress Sciath." My mind fills with images of True cradling my daughter in his stony arms, his gaze tender. Of Rowan bouncing her on his knee. Of the little ones leaping and twirling to "Flight of the Fair One." Of Moon-Fleet playing a game with her poppet of twigs and vines, and Niamh laughing in delight. Of Eirne. My heart twists. "It is for me to decide where she will be safe. We found ourselves in dire circumstances, for reasons that are irrelevant now. I would ask of you a little more help, which I believe you promised when you brought us here. Assistance with the rest of our journey. The means to hire a horse, for which I can repay you later. Some provisions. Perhaps . . ." I hesitate. After what has just occurred, I'm not sure I want to stay with these folk any longer. But I must, for a little. "Perhaps one of your men to escort us to the next hostelry. Once there, I can earn our keep by singing."

A strange look crosses Mistress Sciath's features. She has a striking face, the cheekbones prominent, the nose long and straight, the dark eyebrows arched. Her hair is dark, too, plaited up so severely that not a wisp dares break free. In her eyes I see something I do not like at all, and I wait for her to present her proposition. But she does not speak of that, not yet. "Where were you taking the child, Master Donal?"

She doesn't know who I really am. I'd like it to stay that way. But with Niamh to think of, I am obliged to give her a truthful answer. Or at least partly truthful. "Northeast. To a place near the Dalriadan court."

"You surprise me. So far from home, on your own with such a tiny child?"

I say nothing. My guilt is burden enough; it provides me with more than sufficient punishment. I do not need the chastisement of this stranger.

"You have family in those parts, Master Donal?"

This time I'm the one who offers a grunt in reply. I will not name Winterfalls. I will not name my parents or any of their friends.

"As it happens," says Mistress Sciath, "we may be heading that way ourselves. Master Donal, eat your breakfast, please. Whatever happens, it is likely you will have another long ride ahead of you. You need your strength." It's plain from her tone that alongside her two brawny companions, I cut an unimpressive figure. Given the circumstances, that is hardly surprising. "Eat," she repeats.

"I'd like to see Niamh this morning, straight after breakfast. I want to be on my way again later today."

There's a pause. Sciath sits straight-backed, watching me as an owl might watch a mouse far below on the forest floor. Scoithín has not moved from his position by the door. It's becoming obvious he's here as a guard, to stop me from going anywhere that doesn't suit them.

"As to that," Sciath says in crystal-clear tones, "where you go from here, and who accompanies you, will depend very much on your response to my proposition. Eat your breakfast while I lay it out for you."

She proceeds to do so, step by chilling step. I soon stop eating. I am frozen in place, disbelieving. She heard me sing and play at Faelan's coronation; she deduced there was some magic in what I do, some power beyond the strictly human. She heard rumors about me. It seems someone overheard me early that morning when I chanted to stop the Crow Folk from killing the three of us: Liobhan, Dau, and myself. And . . . oh, gods . . . she saw me in the woods not long ago. With Shadow. She heard me singing to him. Heard his response. She can't know what passes between my friend and me in silence, Danu be thanked. But she knows enough. She knows that despite our vast differences, he and I can talk together. I pray that Shadow did not follow me here; that he heeded my warning and kept to the relative safety of the woods.

"And so, my proposition," Sciath says. "You have something I want, Master Donal. And now, I have something you want. We might reach an agreement. I so much prefer these matters to be settled amicably."

I use a trick Liobhan taught me for such moments: counting up to five before I speak. "I hope you are not intending to involve my daughter in this, Mistress Sciath. I do not bargain with human lives."

"Your daughter is already involved, Master Donal. A click of my fingers could end her life."

I'm on my feet, barging toward the door, my heart racing. Scoithín blocks me with his forearms. I know I'll never get past him, not with all the tricks I learned during that rigorous training on the island. The journey has taxed me badly; the deep sorrow of what happened, along with lack of sleep and inadequate food, has robbed me of more strength than I can afford to lose. Ride on today? I'd be a fool to try.

I turn back to face Sciath. "You would threaten the life of a child not two seasons old? What is it you want from me so badly that you would sink so low?" I'm shivering. I straighten my back, relax my shoulders, lift my chin. I am no Swan Island warrior now. But I can play the part.

"Come back with me to Darkwater. Show me how you talk to the creatures, how you reach them. Work for me and for my great purpose, Donal. Teach me to do as you do, or if that is not possible, stand by my side and use your gift to help me."

I think I want to be sick. What is she suggesting? "Your great purpose—what purpose? The Crow Folk cannot be bidden, Mistress Sciath. It is not for humankind to tell them what to do."

"But you are not of humankind," she says quietly. "Not entirely. Or so I surmise."

I wait, my heart thudding.

"I want an army the likes of which no leader in Erin has ever imagined. An army of Crow Folk, fearsome and strong, unstoppable. It can be done. You have shown me the way. Your voice could command such a force. They would do your will. Or mine, if you can teach me the trick of it."

"Impossible." Shock renders the word hoarse and strange.

I clear my throat. "It couldn't be done. Nobody could sustain that kind of control for long enough, or widely enough, to induce a large body of Crow Folk to act together. And . . . why? Why would you want to do such a thing?"

"Not I; I am a mere adviser. I speak on behalf of my mistress, Lady Almha, chieftain of Darkwater."

A long silence, during which the woman I saw earlier puts her head in the door, perhaps thinking to clear away the breakfast things, and at a gruff word from Scoithín retreats.

"It can't be done," I tell Sciath bluntly. "It isn't possible. And . . . it would be deeply wrong. If your mistress has asked this of you, I'm afraid she is deluded as to how much influence I have over the Crow Folk."

"Are you telling me you can't?" There is a delicate threat in her tone. "Or won't?"

I sit in silence, counting. She meant what she said about Niamh. Why else rush my daughter away while I still slept? I don't doubt that she can do it, and would. The look in her eyes is chilling. I must shut down the shout for help, the urge to attack, the surge of feelings that stops me from thinking clearly. I may be worn down in body, but Swan Island taught me there are other ways of fighting. And my time in the Otherworld was not wasted. There, folk don't stick to yes or no, black or white. They make bargains.

"What benefit might I expect to gain from this arrangement, other than a promise that my daughter will be safe?" *You're playing a game, lady. I, too, can play games.*

A tiny smile curves Sciath's lips, then disappears. "Ah. You are prepared to listen, then. A good first step. Scoithín, explain to Master Donal how I reward loyalty."

"We're well compensated for our services, Master Donal."

I realize this is the first time I've heard Scoithín speak. His voice is very deep and surprisingly soft, with some sort of accent, perhaps a southern one. It unsettles me to realize it reminds me of True's. "Compensated in what way?"

"The sort of payment you'd expect as a trusted man-at-arms in a chieftain's employ, though we work directly for Mistress Sciath. And additional benefits for exemplary service."

I nod thanks, then turn back to the lady. "But you are not offering me the same kind of employment as that of Scoithín or"—What was the other fellow's name?—"or Ruairi."

"Indeed not, as you are no warrior. The recompense would be appropriate to the special duties you undertook. Closer to the sum a royal adviser might expect." She names a figure; it sounds ridiculous, the sort of trove a questing hero might find in the keeping of some fearsome dragon. Ridiculous because it is too much. Ridiculous because the whole idea is corrupt, vile, just plain wrong. First a threat to my daughter's life; then a task that, even if I could achieve it, would sever entirely my hard-won bond with the Crow Folk, itself the fragile beginning of a true mission. To do as she wishes would be an utter betrayal of trust. To refuse would be to sacrifice Niamh.

"Let us assume I will consider this plan." I sit straight, head high, eyes calm. I breathe slowly. I keep my voice level, even as my heart screams in pain. "My cooperation would be under certain conditions. Were those conditions not met, I would be unable to attempt what you require of me."

Sciath opens her mouth to protest, and I hold up an imperious hand.

"Wait! This is not *won't*, but *can't*, Mistress Sciath. To work with the Crow Folk, to communicate with them, I need to be at peace, calm, relaxed. I must be able to open my mind to them. If I am constantly worried about something, such as the welfare of my child, I cannot hear them and they cannot hear me. For such a grand exercise as you have outlined, one that would inevitably take up a great deal of time—months, perhaps years—I would need that peace of mind maintained throughout. Where were you thinking I would carry out the work? And what were your plans for my daughter?"

"Has not the child a mother to care for her?"

I do not reply. I keep my back straight; I keep my eyes steady.

"Years," she says. "Truly? As long as that?"

"You propose an exercise on a grand scale. I assume much of the work would be done covertly; it is not the sort of plan a leader would want broadcast to influential neighbors."

"We would go to my mistress's territory. Crow Folk live there, in the forest. There is a place where we could work. I have already considered the issue you raise. I would take appropriate measures to prevent the knowledge of this from reaching unfriendly ears."

I wait. She knows she hasn't answered the most important question.

"Your daughter would stay where she is. Among kindly folk who can provide for her."

I can't help tightening my mouth, clenching my fists. "That is unsatisfactory, Mistress Sciath. Niamh is little more than a baby. If this task took a year, two years, three, she would have forgotten me entirely by the end. She would have become some stranger's child. Unless your mistress's territory is only a stone's throw from here, so I can see my daughter every day, what you suggest is unacceptable."

Her eyes narrow. "Have you forgotten what I said?" The iron is back in her voice. "I can dispose of the child as easily as *this*." She clicks her fingers.

I will not shout. I will not attack her. I will not attempt to escape. *Haggle. Make terms. That's the way these things are done.* "Act thus and all you have lost is a child you care nothing about," I make myself say. "If she dies, it will be both *can't* and *won't.* I love my daughter above the moon and stars, Mistress Sciath. Harm her, and you lay on me a guilt and grief that would render me incapable of doing any work of this kind for the rest of my life. Harm her, and nothing in the world could persuade me to assist your efforts. Harm me, by torture or other means, and the result would be the same. To succeed in this work I must be sound in body and mind. I hope I make myself clear."

A long silence. I've surprised her. I've surprised myself.

"You seem to believe that I am offering a choice, Master Donal." Sciath's tone is icy. "Your pathway is quite clear to me. Entrust your daughter to those who can provide her with the comforts a small child needs: nourishing food, a good roof over her head, safety and companionship. Take up this challenge, the mission of a lifetime. And if you fear achieving the goal will take too long, work harder. Do better. Who knows, what could have been a task of years may be achieved far more quickly. Then you can take your daughter and set this behind you." A pause; her gaze is ironhard, implacable. "Do as I wish, and she will be safe. I give you my word. Refuse, and you lose her this very day."

Horror holds me silent. There seems no way out. Can I play along with this, wait for an opportunity to escape, rush back to Niamh . . . No. If Sciath can do what she threatens, if there is the least chance of that, I am bound to her will. I am bound to a mission of unspeakable evil; I am bound to betray those I have worked so hard and carefully to understand. What will my life be worth, if I obey? Act thus and I will be unfit to be Niamh's father. *Gather your wits, Brocc. You are not some helpless wayfarer. You are still a Swan Island man.*

"Master Donal?"

There is a way out. A long and difficult way, a perilous way. All hangs on the fragile bond I share with Shadow. "You give me no choice," I say, forcing myself to look her in the eye. "I will come with you."

17

LIOBHAN

Just as I'm starting to feel settled on the mainland, things change again. Cionnaola comes over on the ferry. Soon after, Brigid calls me and Haki to a private meeting at the Barn.

"We've had news from Illann," Cionnaola says when we're all seated. "Archu has been injured and is out of action. He's at a safe house in Ulaid and won't be able to travel for some time, but he's in good hands. Illann believes there's no point in continuing to investigate the situation in Lakelands. He didn't give reasons, such messages needing to be brief. But he's coming back to a central point, and he wants one or two folk sent out to meet him there. The plan would be to provide backup for Dau and Garbh, and perhaps also look into something we haven't yet followed up."

I wait, making myself breathe slowly. A little self-restraint may be my best friend right now. I don't fully understand this, having not been briefed on the mission, though Dau did tell me quite a bit in the privacy of the bedchamber, the night before he left. But I can guess what's coming.

"I refer to portals to another world," Cionnaola says. "The possibility that the prince has gone beyond our reach. With no ransom demand so far and nothing of significance coming in from the various parties sent out by the king, I believe it's time to act on that possibility. Illann's message was sent first to court, so King Oran and Master Donagan know about this and they've agreed to my suggestion, with some reluctance. To them, I suppose it feels like giving up."

I nod. Breathe. Keep my mouth shut.

"We're short of people at present, as you know. There are five teams out in the field on various missions, and I've just had a request I can't refuse, for an old friend in the south, which will require at least eight men. Besides, this is a specialized job." Another weighty silence.

"Just tell her, Cionnaola, for the love of the gods," says Brigid. She may be the only person on Swan Island who can speak to our chief in such a manner.

"Both Illann and Archu believe we should bring you in at this point, Liobhan, despite our reservations. Indeed, we haven't much choice, since there's nobody else here with your understanding of the uncanny. I'd need to be satisfied that you could adhere to the Swan Island code and keep your mind on the job, despite the fact that Galen is involved."

I hold back the *yes* that's bursting to get out. "I'm confident I can do that, Cionnaola. Would I go on my own?" Oh, to have Brocc by my side on such a mission. But he is far beyond reach.

"Am I right in thinking I'm present not as an elder who can provide wise advice, but as the man who took two capable fighters off the island to work on a nonessential task?" Haki has a rueful smile on his face.

"You're here for both reasons, my friend—your ideas are always welcome. But yes, Hrothgar would be well suited to this. I won't send Liobhan alone. She'll go undercover, and that means she'll need a companion who can plausibly carry a good amount of weaponry, that is, hers as well as his own if required. A traveling musician and her protective husband. A fine lady and her trusted bodyguard. Either would work well."

My heart's beating like a galloping horse. "How soon would we go?"

"As soon as you can be ready. Tomorrow, if that's possible. An overnight stop at Winterfalls, so you can talk to your mother and work on your story. I have a map; I'll show you where to find Illann. Mistress Blackthorn can advise you on your task. I know these portals are not easily found. If you go southward beyond the previous search area and over toward the Argiallan border, you'll reach the meeting place, and from that point you and Illann can work out what comes next."

"It's not a simple matter of going out and searching," I say, remembering the exhausting, remarkable day when I sang and played outside such a doorway deep in the forest near the court of Breifne. It was hours before Eirne finally decided to let me in. "We'd need to use songs, tales, games . . . If only we had Brocc."

"Indeed. When this is over, we'll give some thought to adding more expertise of this kind to our community. It's a weakness we must address. We're glad you are willing to help, Liobhan. You and Hrothgar have a strong bond already. You'll work well together."

"I know. Thank you, Cionnaola. We'll do our very best."

"Good," says Cionnaola. "We'll send word to Winterfalls to expect you. Go over to the island today and collect any items you need. Appropriate dress for both noblewoman and traveling minstrel, as well as clothing suitable for tracking in forested areas. The necessary weapons, but don't overload yourself. You may as well sleep over there and come back on a morning ferry. Take time at Winterfalls to prepare your cover story and make sure it's well rehearsed before you head on."

As I walk back to Deirdre's cottage I'm still taking in the enormity of what's just happened. I never thought for a moment that they'd change their minds on this. Not once. Can I actually achieve something? Hunting for portals in an unknown forest would be like looking for grains in a haystack. It's all very well when you know something's there. But this is all supposition, and unless someone's leaving helpful clues—the Fair Folk do that if they actually *want* someone to come in—you could end up wandering about for a very long time and finding absolutely nothing. Let's hope my mother has some useful ideas.

When I've gathered the few possessions I have in Deirdre's cottage I head down to the boatyard, where Brigid has already broken the news to Hrothgar. Justice greets me by jumping up and licking my face with enthusiasm. Poor Justice; he'll be adrift with both me and Hrothgar gone as well as Dau.

"Don't fret, Liobhan." Brigid's there, turning a shrewd gaze in my direction. "That animal will be just fine. He has work here guarding the boatyard, and if Haki doesn't want him in the cottage, he can sleep at the Barn."

The ferry isn't due for a while, so I sit and watch Haki and Elka doing something complicated with ropes. Justice lies heavily across my feet, enjoying the sun. Hrothgar goes off to pack up his belongings. Out to sea, birds fly over the steep cliffs of Swan Island, calling as they go. At least there are still birds there; not all have been scared off by the walking shadow or whatever it is. Ah. There's something I need to do over on the island before we leave, and I want Elka to do it with me.

I wake before dawn. Elka is already up and dressed, her hair in a neat plait. I'm not sure what Haki thought of my sudden request that he release her for the day to help me with an unspecified task on the island—entirely true—but he said yes, and so did she when I asked her. I wash and dress, and as soon as it's light enough we slip out of the women's quarters and head for the cliff path. The sky brightens as we go. Birds wake and fly out from their roosts; down below, the sea is restless, pounding in on the rocks, and the breeze is sharp. I set a good pace and Elka keeps up without difficulty. She didn't ask questions about this expedition, and I'm glad of that. I want to do this, I need to do it before I go. Just why, I can't quite put into words.

We pass the druid's house, where there's no sign of life. Brother Criodan and Guss must still be abed. It's not until we reach the Dragon's Egg that we pause to catch our breath. I lay a hand on the stone in respect and recognition, and Elka does the same. I'm glad she's overcome her reservations about the cavern. I hope I'm not getting her into trouble. I might be stripped of the opportunity to lead a team before I've even started.

We look down over the pebbly stretch of shore to the sea. The tide is high; the water churns up over the rocks, carrying swaths of seaweed and assorted debris. We must tread carefully or risk an uncomfortable demise from cold, drowning, being pounded to death, or all three. Or, at the very least, an embarrassing return to the settlement soaked to the skin.

"Sure you're happy to go right in with me?" I ask. It's only fair to give her the chance to back out. My voice is almost drowned by the wild music of sea, sand, and stones. "You can wait here if you want."

"I come with you."

We're not exactly breaking a rule, but we all know Brother Criodan prefers us to go no further than the cave entry. If there's something in there, whether it's one of the Crow Folk or a walking shadow or a desperate fugitive, going in holds additional risk. We've left our weapons behind. Carrying iron in the presence of uncanny folk is not advisable. It can harm them. It can frighten them away. It's pretty sure to rule out gaining their trust. Yes, this is risky. Some would call it foolish. But I'm heading off later to look for portals to the Otherworld. It would indeed be foolish not to check this first.

We pick our way across the rocks to the cave entrance, which is quite well concealed from curious eyes. I don't want to creep in and perhaps terrify anyone who might be there. Nor will I call out, announcing our presence.

"We'll sing our way in," I murmur in Elka's ear, and take a few deep breaths, relaxing my shoulders. If there's nobody here, not even a sad ghost from times past, we'll have done no harm. If there is an uncanny presence in the cave, music may help smooth the way. Elka makes a gesture, not the one she made when she saw the walking shadow, but another, perhaps a sign of protection.

The first song that comes to mind is "The Farewell," not at all appropriate to the occasion. But it feels right, so I sing it—not the words, just the tune to "la-la." It's a wistful melody, reflecting the theme of love and loss. Elka hums along behind me. As we walk into the cavern, I'm mindful that the being Brother Criodan saw here was something like the Crow Folk. In my thoughts I make an image of Brocc releasing captive creatures from a cage: wild beings that my brother treated with respect and compassion.

In its stark way, this place is beautiful. The roof arches high; an opening far above us lets in pale morning light. The rocks on which we stand side by side are as smooth as if they'd been polished by some giant hand, and in the center of the cave a pool catches the light in its clear depths. I can still hear the wash of the waves, the movement of the stones as they are turned and turned again in the sea, but that sound seems distant now. Within these walls I don't feel uneasy. I feel protected, as if a guardian spirit from long ago still lingers here, its work not yet complete. Perhaps generations of quiet folk, druids and the like, have spent time here praying or meditating or thinking their way through problems. Perhaps it has provided a haven for folk in trouble. A refuge. A hiding place.

No sign of life now. No scuttling crabs between the stones, no tiny fish in the pool. No movement save faint ripples on the water. But . . . there is something after all, a small winged creature fluttering far above us. A bat? A moth? No, it's a tiny bird, perhaps flown in through that high opening and now unable to find its way out. As it descends I lift my hands, thinking to usher it toward the cave mouth. It circles my head, then comes down to perch on my right forefinger. It is so delicate. Its little claws are gentle against my skin. Something in its beak. Danu save me. This has happened before, when a bird stole some of my hair and carried it to Brocc in the Otherworld as a cry for help. And now this little thing, not bright of plumage like Eirne's messengers but clad in earthen colors, drops hair onto my palm, along with a leaf. Its duty done, it spreads its wings and flies straight out through the cave opening. Not trapped, then. On a mission.

Beside me, Elka is staring round-eyed. "What is that?" She breathes the words.

The wavy dark hair is Brocc's, I'm sure of it. But there is a second curl, the same color but much finer and softer. Baby hair. The leaf is long and pointed. It's from an elder tree. "A message," I murmur. "My brother's in trouble."

"Oh!" Elka makes a soft sound of wonder. She slips past me to the water's edge and seats herself on the rocks, cross-legged and straight-backed. Beckons me to sit beside her. "We wait," she whispers.

I settle beside her, not sure what is coming. Elka's hands are in her lap, palms up, relaxed. I try to match her calm pose, though my heart is thudding with the shock of what just happened. I hold the bird's gift in my cupped palm and struggle to rein in my racing thoughts.

Elka's breathing slows. She reaches out and takes my right hand, making a link between us. She closes her eyes. She told me she lacked her grandmother's gift as a seer. But maybe she was wrong. With my own eyes shut, I count silently to a hundred.

When I open my eyes, someone is watching us from the far side of the pool. Someone clad in dark feathers, someone who is most certainly not human. But not one of *them* either. This is no bird—the feathers are a garment. The being has hands with long, sharp-nailed fingers, and features that are a curious blend of bird and rodent and human. What I can see of its skin is hairless and matches the rocks it stands on. The robe or cloak conceals the shape of its body. Its luminous pale eyes gaze across the water. I cannot read their expression.

My mind is teeming with questions, but I hold myself still. If there are visions to be seen, it's Elka who will make it happen, not me. But I incline my head in recognition. That feather robe . . . the face . . . This may not be one of the Crow Folk, but it surely has something to do with them.

The being seems to be waiting. It gestures toward the pool, almost as if suggesting we step in.

What is it I want to see? What is it I most need to know? I try to picture it. *A missing man . . . the Crow Folk . . . a plot . . . a portal to the Otherworld . . .* But my mind cannot set aside the small bird's gift: the delicate items in my hand. My brother. His child. Can Brocc be somehow connected with our mission?

Elka's hold tightens. Something new is visible in the water. Not my reflection. Not hers. Not that of the creature now seated opposite, still fixing us with its strange, bright eyes. I see a traveler on a lonely road by twilight, with a pack on his back and a small child in his arms. As he adjusts the load he looks up. A gasp of horror escapes me. It's Brocc, but so terribly changed I would hardly know him. He's gaunt and drained, the merest shadow of his old self. I can't hold back a sound of distress. Elka's firm grip steadies me. The image in the water shifts to show a forest clearing by daylight. Tall dark pines encircle it, and on their branches perch Crow Folk, a host of them crowded close. A woman stands below. Youngish. Black haired. She wears a long cloak. A man beside her. Brocc again, without the child.

The woman speaks to him, and Brocc looks up toward the Crow Folk. I think he's singing. After a while he lifts his hands and the Crow Folk move as a great army might move to its leader's command, up and away. Is this the flight to freedom my brother once spoke of? The homing song? Why, then, does Brocc look so wretched, as if he would die rather than do this?

The image changes again. A troop of men-at-arms rides along a well-made road. Ahead lies a settlement, and beyond it on a rise is a grand fortified house surrounded by a stone wall. It's familiar. So familiar. The riders are wearing blue tunics, and one carries a banner well known to me: a blue field on which is the household emblem of a sword and dagger crossed. The sun shines; the men are talking and laughing as they ride. Then the Crow Folk are on them, a dark, fell tide. Elka makes a little sound of horror. I sink my teeth into my lip, not wanting to see this, unable to look away. Crow Folk attacks are usually untidy, with no obvious pattern to them. This is quite different. It's a ruthless, planned assault that leaves every man dead, every horse dead or dying, their straight road home turned to a blood-drenched charnel house. When it's over, the birds wheel in unison and fly away. And just for a moment we're back in the forest, where the woman in the long cloak, with a triumphant smile, claps Brocc on the shoulder in congratulation. The image fades and is gone.

I want to be sick. But I can't. "Tell me this isn't happening now, as we speak," I whisper, staring across at the uncanny being. "Tell me there's time to stop it." But the creature is silent. Perhaps it cannot understand human speech. Perhaps it believes, quite reasonably, that such visions are best inter-preted by those who ask for them. Not that I did so in words, but there's no doubt this was meant for me. Gods, I'm cold to the bone. I can hardly breathe. How could Brocc allow himself to be used like that? He's the last person to be cor-rupted, the last to be bribed into turning his gifts to such an ill purpose. "He wouldn't," I say. "Brocc would never do that, never. He wants the Crow Folk to fly free. To fly home." But even as I speak, doubt creeps into my thoughts. That was Brocc's child, surely; an infant two seasons old at most. What if someone threatened her? To keep his daughter safe, per-haps there is nothing my brother would not do.

The being raises its clawed hands. Its bright eyes are fixed on me and the suddenness of its movements shows it's angry. It points to the pool, as if to remind me of what I saw, then makes a swift, strong gesture of negation, arms crossed, then hands sweeping down and out. It points to me. *Stop him. You stop him.*

"What can I do?" I ask. "I don't even know where he is. Is this now? Or is it yet to happen? Is there time to stop it?"

The being repeats the sequence of movements. This time they are still sharper, more furious. *This cannot be allowed to happen. You must act.*

"You're angry," I say. "I understand. But . . ." Even as I speak, the creature fades back into the depths of the cavern and is gone from sight. "Oh, gods," I murmur, as Elka re-leases my hand and bows her head, putting her own hands over her face. For a little, I cannot move a muscle. *Brocc. Oh, Brocc. Oh, Dau. This on top of everything.* For those were Dau's father's men. That was his father's house. What am I to do? Then Elka straightens, drawing a deep breath. Together we rise to our feet and make our way out into the morning. The wash of the waves feels too loud; the sunlight is too bright.

"Come," says Elka, holding out a hand. "We go back, yes?"

She's recovered far more quickly than me. I'm dazed by that vision, confused and horrified and unsure what to say. When I decided to come here, I was hoping for something to explain Aolu's disappearance; some wisdom that would help our search for portals or other clues. Not this. If that was a true vision, Brocc is in dire trouble. He needs me. And Dau's kinsfolk are under threat, perhaps imminent threat. But I have a mission, an important one, and for the first time ever I am leader. Do I tell Cionnaola what I saw? Do I tell anyone?

At the Dragon's Egg, Elka stops. "You all right, Liobhan?"

"Not really. Did you see what I saw?"

"Man with a baby, in trouble. He sings to make Crow Folk attack." A pause. "This is your brother? The bard?"

I nod, miserable. "Brocc, yes. And I don't know what to do. He could be anywhere. If it's true, if someone's trying to make him do that with the Crow Folk, then . . . Elka, the only time I've seen that kind of vision before, it showed the future. It showed not what was happening, but what might happen. Two futures, one good, one bad."

"I never do this before. I cannot say if picture is now or other time." She sways as if dizzy, and I remember that she was the one who called up the vision. Without her, I would not have been given this knowledge.

"Are you all right, Elka?"

"All right, yes. Tired. Surprised. I not know I can do this."

"The child," I say, thinking aloud. "Brocc's child. I guessed they were expecting one and it seems I was right. It would be about the age of the one we saw. So this is either happening now or will happen soon. I have to do something. If he's really training the Crow Folk to attack, it must be breaking him, heart and mind."

"It is bad," says Elka. "Crow Folk army, terrible. You tell Cionnaola? Tell Brigid? What about your mission?"

Without thinking, I've clenched my fists, and the precious items given me by the little bird are scrunched up together. The leaf is crushed. The leaf. Elder trees. Why would the bird bring me a leaf, unless it was a clue?

"We don't tell them yet. We tell Hrothgar on the way to Winterfalls. And then I talk to my mother."

"We?" echoes Elka, eyes wide.

"I want you to come with us. If you're willing." She's a seer and a warrior, not to speak of her other talents. We need her. Just how I'm going to convince Cionnaola without telling him the full truth I have yet to work out. I set aside the very real possibility that this breach of trust will lose me my place on Swan Island. I have to save my brother. It's urgent. That creature in the cave made it pretty clear that this was for me to deal with, not a task for the team. I can't tell Cionnaola or Brigid or any of the elders. But Elka saw the vision, too, and she saw the little bird's message. She understands how important this is. If she comes on the mission I'll have two capable comrades, and Illann would make the team up to four. It must be possible to ride to Oakhill from Darkwater, where Dau and Garbh have been sent. The two territories share a border. Maybe we can split up, maybe we can . . . Oh, gods, there's too much whirling around in my head.

"Breakfast," Elka says. "Then we talk, yes? Make a plan." She puts an arm around me, awkwardly, and I'm so glad of the gesture that tears come to my eyes. "Now come, we walk back."

We head along the cliff path in silence as the birds rise and fall in the air, and the sea washes in far below us, and the northerly wind stirs the grasses. What is to come seems immense, impossible, ridiculous. I may be sacrificing my whole future for something that will never happen. But the bird . . . that part was real enough, and I know such messengers can be trusted. Brocc . . . I can't leave him at the mercy of that woman, I can't. I have to save him. But what about the prince? Isn't he, too, in jeopardy? What about getting a warning to Dau's father? I'm supposed to be team leader.

What would Archu say? For once in my life, I have absolutely no idea.

18

DAU

We're stuck. Can't leave in a hurry, not now Lady Almha has shared such sensitive information on the mistaken assumption that I knew something about the plot already. Can't split up unless things get really difficult; only a fool reduces his team to one. But we must get a message to Winterfalls. For that, we need an excuse to ride to Elderbrook and the safe house.

Garbh does his best to gather information by chatting with serving maids and grooms as well as the folk he meets over a jug of ale at the local inn. He listens out for talk of Sciath's men and why their presence in the area seems generally unwelcome. If he can find out where those men and their mistress may currently be, and how soon they're expected back, so much the better. I'm not going to ask Almha directly for that information.

I occupy myself with reinforcing my cover. I talk with various members of the household about the dobhar-chú, the Crow Folk, and any other strange creatures they might happen to know of. I talk about my sweetheart without telling them anything at all, apart from the fact that she loves old tales and unusual gifts. Much of this is ridiculous, and it's hard for me to remember why it's important when my mind is on Mistress Sciath's monstrous mission with the Crow Folk. I spend time in the chamber used by Lady Almha's scribe, who's happy to lend me a corner of his worktable, some sheets of parchment, and the use of his pens and inks. He's a short man with a long nose, his name is Suibne, and he's not talkative, which pleases me. He does tell me a tale of Suibne Gelt, who was cursed into the form of a bird-man and spent the rest of his life running wild in the woods. Suibne's a good storyteller—far better than I prove to be when I start to work on the little book I'm supposed to be writing—and his quiet company provides a blessed respite from that of Lady Almha, with whom I have to watch every word, every look, every gesture.

I cannot escape the lady's company entirely. To achieve that would be to arouse her suspicions. They seat me at her right hand for every meal; clearly, she has given instructions that I should be treated as a particularly honored guest. When there's music and dancing in the evenings I find myself partnering her more often than not. I cannot ignore the looks she gives me under her lashes, or the way she holds my hand just a little longer than necessary at the end of a dance. I try to avoid being alone with her, but I can hardly refuse when she asks me to accompany her on a walk or a ride. She asks me about the progress of my little book; she probes for further details of my sweetheart, to whom I give an appearance and character as unlike Liobhan's as possible. It is becoming difficult to hold back information about whose daughter she is and where she—and I—live. The lady also asks about Oakhill and my father. It's becoming clear that her intention is somewhat more serious than amusing herself with playful flirtation. The scribe's workroom is a welcome refuge.

Four more days pass, five, six. I've written a tale of the

dobhar-chú—how Liobhan would laugh at my efforts—and one about the Crow Folk, taking care not to include anything about how music may or may not affect them. I've set down the tale of Suibne Gelt, which might provide Liobhan with material for a song or a whistle tune, and I've written a story about a fisherman being turned into a frog, based on something one of the locals told Garbh. If Suibne glances across the worktable sometimes with a slight smile, he makes no judgments. He has not asked to read my work.

Garbh and I talk in our chamber, in lowered voices.

"Is there an alternative to the safe house? Somewhere else we could get a message out?" he asks me.

"The monastic foundations use pigeons, but I've no idea if there's such a place nearby. And you know why I can't request the use of Lady Almha's pigeons, even if they have birds trained to fly to the court of Dalriada."

"Would it need her approval? Couldn't you speak to the pigeon-keeper in person? Send a love letter to your imaginary sweetheart?"

"At a royal court?"

"Why not? She might be one of Queen Flidais's personal attendants."

I grimace. "Risky. Could be everything goes back to Lady Almha. If it did, she'd learn that we had a connection with that area. It's a small step from there to Prince Aolu."

Garbh is silent for a while. Then, "Dau," he says, "maybe we should go back to Winterfalls. What you found out, about Mistress Sciath—if what the lady told you is true, it's big. We need to take it to the elders. It's not something we can deal with ourselves, just the two of us. And we're getting precisely nowhere with the mission. Not a hint of a captive prince anywhere."

"A pox on this!" I slam my fist into a small table, hurting

myself. "Mistress Sciath's scheme is horrifying, but it's a wild fantasy, like those tales of the dobhar-chú. Something that couldn't happen. If it's Brocc she's searching for, she's not going to find him. How could she, unless he happens to step out into the human world while she's passing by? And how likely is that?"

"We do this step by step." Garbh sounds much calmer than I feel. "We ride over to Elderbrook tomorrow or the next day. Find a pretext that will convince the lady. We send a coded message to the elders about Mistress Sciath and let them decide what to do about her scheme. That was never our job. As for the prince, there could be messages for us at the safe house. Who knows, he may have been found by now."

There's music after supper again, and dancing. I partner various ladies of the household, doing my best to steer clear of Lady Almha. But I can't keep avoiding her all evening, so eventually I step out with her. She's wearing forest green, with her hair caught up in ribbons as if she were a girl of fourteen looking to charm a suitor. Gods help any man snared in that web. With Mistress Sciath probably watching every move, his life wouldn't be worth living. But a man less wary than I might be dazzled by the lovely face, the bright eyes, the elegant figure. She is a graceful dancer, deserving of a more skillful partner.

"How is the little book progressing, Master Dau? I hope Suibne is providing you with all you need. He can be somewhat dour at times, but he's an excellent scribe."

I don't find Suibne dour in the least. He's tactful, down-to-earth, and blessedly quiet. "Master Suibne has been most helpful, thank you. Would that I had his skills. My book is progressing at a steady pace. Two more tales and it will be ready for binding."

"Exciting!" she exclaims. I turn her under my arm—a maneuver that is much easier with Almha than it is with Liobhan, who is of similar height to myself—and wonder at this response, until she adds, "There is a saddler in Elderbrook, a fellow who does excellent leatherwork. He and his assistant make all manner of goods: bags, gauntlets, belts. I imagine he could supply a very nice piece of tanned hide for this cover, and you could bring it back to Suibne to do the binding."

I stumble, swallow a curse, apologize nicely. Elderbrook. A man who makes belts. She's provided me with exactly what I need. And also an ominous clue.

I wait until the dance is over before pursuing the subject. Garbh has been dancing, too; his partner, a rosy-cheeked servingwoman, stands on tiptoes to whisper something in his ear, and he laughs merrily. I think he may be better at this game than I.

Almha and I seat ourselves; someone brings mead.

"I could do with a new belt myself," I say, looking down at the perfectly serviceable one I'm wearing. "Something better suited to special occasions. My young lady does complain, sometimes, that I dress too plainly when we are out in the public eye. She takes great pride in her appearance."

"Ask Ferchar for one of his special buckles," says Almha, and I feel a trickle of ice down my spine. "He doesn't make those himself, there's a silversmith fashions them. If your sweetheart likes strange old tales, she'd love the designs. They're all creatures, curled-up dragons, selkies, merrows, and so on. You might purchase one for her as well."

I make myself breathe slowly. I count to five. "An excellent idea," I tell her, and force a smile, while my mind examines the link between this style of buckle and a certain brutal execution and finds it compelling. If not Mistress Sciath in person, then surely her hired men were behind that bungled abduction. Could it be they chose the wrong target? "If the weather is good, I might ride over there tomorrow and have a look. I imagine it takes Master Ferchar a while to make items to order. The book cover and two belts—that might be some days, or even longer if he has other work on hand." I won't think of Seanan. I'm on a mission, and I won't let the past get in my way.

"Tomorrow? Oh." The lady sounds crestfallen. "I would have enjoyed that ride; I had thought I might come with you. But I cannot go tomorrow, I have a council with some of the local landholders. Could you wait a few days more?"

"I'd best go soon," I say, "to allow this craftsman time to do a proper job. Perhaps you could accompany me when I go back to collect the items; I would enjoy your company, Lady Almha." I hope I strike the right note, warm, courteous, but sufficiently formal to set a distance between us.

"Of course. And the weather should be set fair for a while now. You'll need to stay at Elderbrook for a night, maybe two—you won't get there and back in a single day. I'll give you a small package to take to Master Ferchar. It will ensure you receive prompt service. Who knows, he may even complete the work before you need to return here. He does keep a stock of buckles on hand, including the fine silver ones."

I don't ask how she knows all this. I don't ask if she's seen a buckle shaped like a dobhar-chú. "They're warming up for a jig," I say, smiling. "Shall we attempt it?"

Next morning Garbh and I ride out toward Elderbrook. I've been mulling over my ideas about the abduction, and once we're well clear of Darkwater I share my thoughts with my companion. "Maybe they targeted the wrong man. I only met Prince Aolu once, but superficially he does look like

Brocc—dark curly hair, pale skin, an intensity about him. Brocc is taller and broader in the shoulders, but a person who hadn't met either face-to-face might make the error. And it would explain the aftermath. The . . . punishment."

"Weren't the prince and Galen singing just before they were attacked?"

"Morrigan's curse, so they were. Laughing and singing. You're more than just a pretty face, my friend."

"Dagda's britches," murmurs Garbh. "If your theory's right, it's all tangled up together: the abduction of Prince Aolu and the Crow Folk scheme. But we're still left with a missing prince. Where in the name of the gods did he go? Have they got him locked up somewhere so he can't take the tale back home? Or worse?"

Remembering that sickening scene in the woods above Winterfalls, I wonder if Mistress Sciath would think nothing of dispatching a king's son simply for being in the wrong place at the wrong time.

"Dau. What if we're still in these parts when Mistress Sciath gets back? If she's as sharp as she sounds, it might be better if we're gone. Especially without a backup team. Lady Almha's sure to tell her friend about your interest in the dobhar-chú, the Crow Folk, and all other things strange and magical. And from the sound of her, Mistress Sciath's going to be a lot more suspicious of your motives than the lady is."

"Let's get today out of the way first."

Garbh refrains from comment. I sounded sharp. I know I'm getting edgy. I need to stay calm and focus on the task. Go to Elderbrook, purchase a belt, chat to the saddler. And possibly to the silversmith, if he's somewhere nearby. I'd thought we might stay long enough in the area for the craftsman to complete the work, despite what I said to Lady Almha. That way, we need not make a return trip to collect the items. It would provide the opportunity to take a better look around. But Garbh's got a good point. We don't want to meet Mistress Sciath face-to-face. Better to gather whatever clues we can in Elderbrook, then head straight back to Winterfalls. Wherever Prince Aolu is, I'm pretty sure he's not here.

The settlement of Elderbrook lies at the Argiallan end of Hunter's Glen, a forested river valley whose road is the main route through to Ulaid. By the time we're getting close, light rain has started to fall and everything is bathed in a fine, misty damp. So much for the lady's prediction of fair weather. The hills behind Elderbrook are not as high as those of Blackstone Pass, but they're high enough. Heavily treed on the lower slopes, rocky above, from what I can see. Streams splash down the hillside to join the river Elder; I expect this area has its own mountain lakes, its own possible haunts for strange creatures. Its own portals, who knows? There's a feeling about the place, something I can't put my finger on, but it reminds me of the woods near the court of Breifne. That place is full of magic.

The main thing right now is getting our horses to shelter so we can give them a good rubdown and a feed. I wouldn't mind some dry clothes and a warm fire myself. It's late in the afternoon; we won't be visiting any craftsmen today.

We find the local inn and a host who is more than happy to provide us with lodging for a night or two, though he looks at me a little strangely when I give my name. We're in luck; there's only one private room, the other accommodation being communal quarters, but there's talk of Crow Folk gathering and people are staying off the roads when they can, so the room is available. Now doesn't seem the time to pester our host with questions; instead Garbh takes our horses around to the stables, and I allow the man to show me the chamber in question.

"You've a look of someone else, Master Dau," he says. "A fellow that comes by here sometimes. Don't know his name, but he's as like you as a brother. Got any kinsmen in these parts?"

Oh, gods. "Not in Darkwater, that I know of. What company does this man keep?"

His expression darkens. "A crew of . . . I don't like to use the word *disreputable*, Master Dau, in case the fellow turns out to be a long-distant cousin of yours. Fighting men, you might call them. Not the sort a body would want to meet on a dark night. You'd be safe enough, I expect, given the size of that man of yours."

With an effort I find something to say, though I feel as if I've been punched in the gut. "Yes, Garbh would soon see away any miscreants. Thank you, this chamber will suit us well. When the horses are settled we'll be wanting some supper. No need to wait on us; Garbh will come and fetch it."

"Thank you, Master Dau. I hope you'll get a good night's sleep."

Not likely. As soon as I drop off I'll be dreaming of my wretched brother. What am I going to do if he walks into the place while I'm here? I can't know for sure that he's off traveling with Mistress Sciath. I still can't imagine him as one of her hired men. He's no fighter. He's more the kind who stands back and watches while someone else does his dirty work for him. If he's in these parts, if he really is involved, I'll have to step right out of this. Garbh's suggestion that we go straight back to Winterfalls from here is starting to look good. I've played a part passably well with Lady Almha. I may be able to deal with the more challenging Mistress Sciath. But put Seanan on the scene and everything changes.

Garbh returns with our bags and I tell him what happened. He listens in attentive silence.

"I'm not sure I can do it if my brother turns up," I say at the end. "Maintain a pretense of civility, explain calmly that I'm in these parts simply to pay a call on Lady Almha. It'll be far, far better if he and I don't meet."

Garbh starts methodically unpacking the bags. "No choice but to stay here tonight," he says with reassuring calm. "The horses need a rest and so do we. But it may be best not to hang around in Elderbrook for too long. How about this: you go and see this saddler in the morning and talk to him about belt buckles. I stay close in case of trouble. You order your goods, and you tell the saddler you'll come back and collect your belt when it's ready. At some point we make a covert visit to the safe house, which I hope we can find, and send a message to Winterfalls. Then we go back to Lady Almha's and wait a while longer. If there's a reply to our message, the folk at the safe house should have a way to get it to us."

A shiver runs through me. I imagine a dozen, two dozen ways Seanan might suddenly step out and confront me. I imagine as many ways I might react, and none of them are good. "If I come face-to-face with Seanan, I won't be able to play a part," I tell Garbh. "I don't have it in me."

Garbh shakes out a crumpled shirt, lays it flat on a storage chest. "You're a Swan Island man," he says. "One of the best. Don't doubt yourself, Dau." Glancing over at me, he adds, "Look at it this way. There's a lot of bad blood in the past between you two. But if you let that hang over you and stop you from taking action, then even if he lost, you're letting him win."

I want to throw something at him. But I don't. Because, uncomfortable as it is to hear, he's talking sense.

* * *

Morning sees us on the doorstep of Master Ferchar's workshop. It's at the back of his cottage, opening off a small courtyard. We're on foot, since this establishment is within walking distance of the settlement. No rain this morning, though a damp mist shrouds Elderbrook. Before we go in, Garbh gives me a direct sort of look, the kind that says, *You can do this, brother.* I nod in response.

The workshop has a half door and we can see two men already busy inside. There's a sturdily built, middle-aged person with a measuring stick in hand, doing something at a workbench, and a younger man putting some finishing touches on a beautifully crafted saddle. As we approach, the older of the two workers looks up and sets down his tools. Behind him I see tanned hides hanging from tall frames, an array of implements whose uses I can only guess at, and shelves on which lie samples of Master Ferchar's secondary work: the bags, gauntlets, and belts Lady Almha spoke of. There's a hearth here with a small fire burning, to keep these craftsmen's fingers from going numb on cold mornings like this. On the top shelf, something gleams in the light of the flames: set upright against a length of wood stands a neat row of silver buckles. I imagine he locks them away at night.

"Good morning to you," I say. "Master Ferchar? I trust this is not too early to call on you."

As the saddler comes to open the half door, I see a variety of expressions cross his face. First welcome; then recognition, shadowed by doubt; then a curious blend of dislike and courtesy. All this in a matter of moments. "Master Sealbhach! I did not expect to see you so soon. Another commission for me? Please, come in." As we enter, and as I'm still trying to work out what to say, Master Ferchar glances at Garbh with a half smile. "Perhaps congratulations are in order? The Brotherhood of the Dobhar-chú has a new member?"

"Hush," I say quickly. "We don't speak of such things." And thus I am committed, for a day or two at least, to becoming the man I loathe with all my heart and soul. For what better way to find out what Seanan is up to than to step into his wretched shoes? I think quickly. A new commission. Some sort of brotherhood. Not hard to put those things together, though if I'm wrong this will quickly grow awkward. "Oh, and I have a package for you. We are hoping you may be able to make what we need quickly. This is from the chieftain herself." We opened the package last night, at the inn, and checked its contents before sealing it up again. Why Lady Almha would want to send the saddler a goodly number of silver pieces, I have no idea. I found no note or other clue with the funds. The trust she places in me is alarming; might Garbh and I not have simply pocketed this windfall and left Darkwater forever?

Master Ferchar takes the package without a word, weighs it in his hand for a moment, then sets it on a shelf. "I could have a belt finished for tomorrow," he says, eyeing Garbh's impressive form. "There's a buckle ready. We can take the measurement now, if that suits you."

In response, Garbh removes his short cloak and unfastens his own belt. He stands still as Master Ferchar puts a band of linen around his waist and marks on it not only the finished length, but also the points at which one might want to attach various items. Distracted as I am by the need to play the part of my brother, I can't help admiring the orderliness of the workshop and the efficiency of the craftsman.

"Very good," he says now. "One of the longest I've made; though Mistress Sciath's men are all on the big side. If not broad, then tall like you, Master Sealbhach. I've a couple of fine cowhides ready; either would be suitable. If you weren't in a rush, I could make you a new pouch to match." Garbh's existing belt currently holds his pouch and his dagger, but it also has room for another weapon and a waterskin.

"We won't have time for that," Garbh says. "A pity. You do fine work."

It occurs to me that if we're going back to Lady Almha's I must at least ask about the other item. "I'm also seeking a piece of good leather suitable for covering a small book, Master Ferchar. That may seem a strange request, but it's for a special gift. I know a scribe who can do the binding; and I can give you the dimensions required. I don't expect that in a hurry. We might return to collect it some other time. I would pay in advance." I realize the saddler is looking at me a little oddly; I spoke in a manner far more my own than Seanan's.

"I could do it, yes. When you say small, how small exactly?"

I show the size with my hands, knowing how unlikely is that this project will ever reach fruition. "Only twenty pages. A gift for a lady. Tales of strange creatures."

Master Ferchar smiles. "Then I can guess what you might be wanting on the cover, and if it's Master Suibne doing the binding for you, I'm sure he has the skill to execute it. Best if I give you a bigger piece of leather and let the expert cut it to the size you need. That will save you the trouble of a possible return trip. At least, until such time as the brotherhood has cause to expand its numbers again."

It seems prudent to make no comment. Instead I interest myself in the items on display, and glance casually at the range of silver buckles, hoping Lady Almha won't think it odd if I do not purchase a belt for myself. There's a buckle shaped like a toothsome sea creature, and one fashioned as a dragon breathing out flames, and another that's a horse with too many legs. But no dobhar-chú that I can see. I don't ask; chances are Seanan already knows where the saddler keeps his special items. Brotherhood of the Dobhar-chú! Morrigan's britches, do grown men really play such games?

Master Ferchar is showing Garbh various hides, offering him a choice. Garbh asks which will be the hardest-wearing, and selects that. "Might I see the buckle before we go?" he asks with just the right combination of eagerness and restraint.

A box comes out and is opened with some ceremony. I note the sturdy lock, in which the key turns without a sound. The saddler lifts the lid; Garbh approaches and looks in.

"May I touch it?"

"Of course, lad. It won't bite." Master Ferchar grins as Garbh reaches in to take the silver buckle in hands so careful you'd think he was handling priceless gems. The expression on his face suggests he is awed, honored, thrilled. He is indeed good at this.

"Thank you," he says after a little, and sets the gleaming buckle gently back in its place. There are three of them in the box, which is lined with silken cloth. I wonder how often this brotherhood acquires a new member. If my theory is correct, and I'm becoming surer by the moment that it is, they'll be needing to bolster their numbers after that catastrophe at Winterfalls.

"Do you require payment in advance, Master Ferchar?" I ask. "Full or partial?"

For the first time, the saddler looks taken aback. Awkward. "No, no, it will be the usual arrangement for the belt. And Lady Almha has been generous enough to add a small consideration for your piece of hide, Master Sealbhach, so no further payment is required. She must approve of your lady friend."

"The two have not yet met, Master Ferchar. But perhaps my description was sufficient. Thank you for your time. Should we return late tomorrow? The next morning? I know you must be busy."

"You're at the inn?" When we nod, he says, "I should be done by late tomorrow, but you won't be wanting to ride back at night. If we make it the next day, you'll have plenty of time to show your comrade around the area. Perhaps a stroll up the hill? Or a ride?"

I won't ask any questions about paths or places to visit or where anything is. Master Sealbhach may be entirely familiar with Elderbrook and all points around it. I have to hope the saddler and his helper don't chat much with the folk from the inn, where I've given my real name. A tangled web. Garbh and I had best spend the rest of the day out of doors, on our own. "That sounds a good plan. Thank you once again. You'll see us the day after tomorrow. It might be quite early; we'll have a fair ride ahead of us."

Garbh murmurs his own thanks and we make our departure. Once we're well clear of Master Ferchar's premises and away from curious eyes and ears, I say, "Brotherhood of the Dobhar-chú, hm? Otherwise known as Mistress Sciath's band of disreputable henchmen. You know what this means."

"I hope you're not expecting me to wear the thing and pretend to join this brotherhood. If they make a habit of hacking off each other's heads, I might not last long."

When I don't respond to this, he says, "Might not have been the best idea, letting the fellow think you were Master Sealbhach. If he's one of *them*, I mean."

"It looks that way, Garbh. A risky move, certainly. But it gained us vital information. We should return to the inn for some supplies and then make ourselves scarce. A walk up into the hills. A good look around."

"For the dobhar-chú?"

"That's our excuse, if anyone asks what we're doing. Material for the book of tales. But since we're stuck here for another day, we should find the safe house. And investigate this brotherhood. They must meet somewhere; they surely don't have their base at Lady Almha's establishment. She made it quite clear what she thinks about her friend's rough company."

I have a supply of small coin. At the inn I pay for a portion of bread and meat wrapped in a cloth. We refill our waterskins and head out again, talking loudly about a walk along the river to check likely fishing spots for the future. Once we're out of Elderbrook settlement, we take a side path that goes between fields, then up the hill through a forest of old oaks. In the village the mist was starting to lift, but under the trees pale shrouds hang and waver, and the eerie half-light makes the place less than welcoming.

"Path's well-trodden," observes Garbh. "Seems not everyone's afraid of these hills."

"It's Blackstone Pass that's supposed to have the dobhar-chú."

"Blackstone Pass has the screaming at full moon and the ghostly presences. But this place matches that tale Master Saran read. I bet there's a lake further up."

We pause to exchange a glance. The light is too poor for me to read Garbh's expression, but a sound comes as we stand there: no bestial howl, but something suspiciously like the cawing of a crow. "How's your singing voice this morning?" I ask Garbh.

"You're joking." A silence. "You're not joking. It's about as good as yours, based on past performances. I can't sing like Brocc. You know that."

"You may not need to sing at all. But be ready, just in case. And keep your weapon to hand."

"We're going on up, then?"

"That's what we're here for."

We don't go straight up, because there's a point where this path splits three ways. One ascends steeply; it seems the most direct route to the top of the hill. One meanders off to the right, losing itself under the trees. The third, to the left, is blocked by a heap of debris: fallen branches, dead leaves, heaped soil and stones.

"Wait a bit." I pick a way around this unlikely pile and go on a short distance to find, not entirely to my surprise, that the track beyond is well-trodden and clear of any rubbish. "Garbh," I call, keeping my voice down. "This way."

We go on. The path rises gradually, taking us around the hill in a roughly westward direction then curving back toward the northeast. Oak gives way to mixed forest as we climb, and then to more open ground, though low bushes and rock formations provide cover. Where the track crosses a stream, there's a small but sturdy plank bridge in place. It would be possible to ride this far, though you'd need a steady horse to do it, and getting around that blockage at the start would require some care. Higher up, the terrain looks too steep. I'm glad we came on foot.

"How long do we go on?" asks Garbh as we pause to catch our breath. "What are you expecting to find?"

"Any sign of activity. I may be quite wrong about this."

"Someone blocked the path. Not wanting visitors."

"Exactly. Meaning that up here somewhere there's something they want to keep secret."

"What happens if we meet the brotherhood face-to-face, Dau?"

"We ask them where the best fishing spots are, I suppose."

Garbh refrains from pointing out that if I look so like Master Sealbhach, no member of this brotherhood is going to believe that excuse. We walk on. The path branches again, one track going downward into the forest, the other straight ahead. The trees grow more sparsely here; there's open, rocky ground not far ahead. No sign of that early mist now. The sun has emerged and a deceptive peace lies over the land. We walk on, and a vista opens up: across many miles of farmland I can see Blackstone Pass and the mountains where things howl in the night. We're looking right across the territory of Darkwater.

"Would they come all the way up here to do whatever they do?" asks Garbh.

"If Mistress Sciath wants to control the Crow Folk, then she's got to work somewhere there are Crow Folk nearby. And it can't be close to Lady Almha's establishment because the work needs to be secret. Maybe she's bribed every single soul in Elderbrook to turn a blind eye. Sounds as if her fellows are well known here."

"Can't be too well known, since the saddler thought you were your brother. You can't be identical."

"We're not. But we're alike enough so a person who didn't know us well and didn't see us often might get us confused. See ahead, there? There's a spot where the path leads under trees, and I think there's a waterfall." I point, and we listen. Sure enough, there's a faint rustling, splashing sound. "We'll go that far at least. If there's nothing to be found bar a good fishing spot, we can eat this food and take a rest before heading back."

But there is something to be found. Not only the water-fall, which dances down the mountain in a slender thread of silver, but level ground at the foot of it, and a lake into which it spills. A lake small enough to be well concealed by its shield of elder trees, but large enough to cause any passerby to halt and rethink his route. We do exactly that.

"The track continues on the other side," Garbh says, pointing, but we don't move forward.

"Mm. As if a person's being invited to wade straight across. Or swim, perhaps."

"Maybe there was once a bridge. Or stepping-stones. But more likely it's a strategy for keeping folk away. An effective one. If they aren't convinced by the heap of rubbish back at the start, they will be by this. That's if they've heard of the dobhar-chú."

"I won't suggest we sit down for a bite to eat, then. But I do want to see what's on the other side. Let's make our way around." I don't believe in the dobhar-chú, I never have. But there are plenty of indications that someone doesn't want uninvited guests, and that has me on edge. The whole place feels odd. Even the graceful elder trees seem to rustle a warning. And surely the sound from that waterfall is louder than it should be.

"At least there are no Crow Folk," murmurs Garbh, fol-lowing me as I walk cautiously around the strip of open ground at the lake's edge.

"Don't speak too soon." True, there's been nothing from them since that call we heard earlier, but if the locals say they're up here, they probably are. And we're a fair distance from any help. "Stay on your guard."

On the far side of the lake we pick up the track again. It soon curves back along the tree line. I can't help looking over my shoulder a couple of times, imagining some dripping monster following us. If we don't find something soon, we should consider a retreat.

"Dau," says Garbh suddenly. "What's that?"

There's a rock wall up ahead, where the hillside becomes suddenly steeper. Against it there's a man-made structure. We approach with caution. I may have joked about it, but meeting the so-called brotherhood face-to-face would be almost as bad as encountering the lake monster. All remains quiet, save for the voice of the falling water. The structure is long and low, a hut of mud and wattle roofed with deteriorating thatch. There's a wooden door and a single shuttered window. A short way into the forest I glimpse a cleared area surfaced with hard-packed earth.

"Training ground?" suggests Garbh.

"Looks like it. I wonder what they keep in here?" I'm tempted to break in the door of the building, but this might be nothing more than a storage area for local fishermen, and it could be hard to explain our way out of such an act of wanton destruction.

"That roof's not going to last long," Garbh observes, stepping back to take a good look at it. "Going to holes here and there. I bet you could see right in if you wanted to. I'll give you a boost up if you're game."

Since the alternative would be me boosting my somewhat larger comrade, I agree. He heaves me up—we've practiced this kind of thing before—and I fumble around until I find a crosspiece in the timber frame of the roof. I haul myself up to crouch precariously on the roof's edge, making sure my feet are on solid wood. Falling inside the place and being trapped is certainly not the plan. I feel less like a Swan Island man on a mission and more like a small boy out on an ill-considered adventure.

Garbh was right about the thatch; it's moldering away and

full of gaps. I widen one, sneezing as I do so, and peer down into the dim interior of the hut. Straw pallets piled up—they'll be damp—cook pots, platters, cups. Blankets. There's no hearth, and it's just as well, since a stray spark would see the whole lot go up; the place is full of stuff. There are two big storage chests, but there's no telling what's in those. I see what look like targets for archery. There are coiled ropes, and poles that might be driven into the ground and used as some kind of markers. I hadn't expected weapons—they wouldn't leave anything of value here if they had any sense—but now I spot some staves propped up in a corner, and racks where, while men were in residence, swords, bows, or other weaponry might be stored. The Brotherhood of the Dobhar-chú may well use this extremely modest structure as its headquarters.

I signal to Garbh that I'm coming down; he stands in position to ensure I don't break an ankle in doing so, and I'm glad of it. The time when I fell off a ladder is still strong in my memory, though Liobhan only reminds me of it when she thinks I'm being pigheaded. I tell Garbh what I've observed. "We'd best be off," I add. "Find somewhere to eat the provisions, well away from here."

"Dau?" Garbh is sounding worried.

"Mm?"

"You know that tale about the dobhar-chú, the one Master Saran read to us? Remember how the woman left an offering by the lake and the creature didn't attack her?"

"Are you suggesting we give up our midday meal? I was getting hungry."

"Not all of it, just a share. It may sound stupid, but there's a right way to do things. We do have to walk past the lake again on our way back."

I manage not to sigh as I undo the cloth around our food supply and divide what was meant for two men into three parts. I pass one of these parts to Garbh. This was his idea so he can be the one to place the food at the water's edge. In fact, I think his instincts are sound. We retrace our steps to the lake. The day has warmed up. Sunlight turns the unsettling spot into a benign place of fresh green leaves, clear water, shining pale stones. Shining pale stones in small, orderly piles. They're closer to the trees than to the water, and they weren't here when we passed by on our way in.

"Garbh." I point; we both halt.

"Danu save us," Garbh whispers.

Isn't there a song about piled-up stones being used by uncanny folk as a marker or message? A warning? Or maybe a pathfinder, because I think I can see, over there in the shadow, another way leading straight into the forest. A shortcut to Elderbrook? Or something entirely different? My skin prickles. I sense unseen eyes watching us.

"We should still make the offering," Garbh says.

He walks slowly toward the water with the food held before him on both palms, as if he's enacting a ritual. Though every instinct shrinks from it, I go with him. If Liobhan were here she wouldn't hesitate. We halt an arm's length from the lake's edge. Garbh crouches to lay down the offering, using a hand to indicate the crusty bread, the strips of meat, the berries glistening in the light. As he speaks I bow my head, though I feel somewhat foolish. I imagine the dobhar-chú deciding we're the tastiest part of the surprise meal.

"We come in peace," Garbh says. "We mean no harm to those who dwell in this place. Please accept our humble offering."

On the water's surface, not a ripple. In the forest, not a leaf stirring. Garbh rises to his feet, then stands in silence while I fight the desire to turn and bolt. At last Garbh nods to me and we walk away.

"You're a braver man than I am," I murmur, glancing back over my shoulder.

"Just seemed the right thing to do. Now what? Back the way we came, or take a look down there? What do you think those stones are for?"

"I'd guess they're track markers, and I'd guess further that whoever set them there meant us to see them. Are they the sort of sign the brotherhood might use? I doubt it. I'd like to investigate, but we'd want to be very careful. And it's not an ambush I'm thinking of."

"Mm. It's the sort of place where you might take one wrong step and end up . . . somewhere else."

"Exactly."

"What would Liobhan do?" asks Garbh, putting my own thoughts into words.

"She'd take a look, at least. With caution. We should stay together and watch out for other signs, too. Things like knotted grass or markings on bark."

"Should we sing?"

"My past experience, limited as it is, suggests that would not be a good idea." A song might be appropriate if we did want to walk into the Otherworld; that's how Liobhan got in eventually. Right now, the mission needs us in our own world. "It might draw the brotherhood straight to us. We may be two foolish friends out for a stroll in an unlikely spot, but someone might notice the damage to their roof and get suspicious. We go slowly, hoping this path will eventually take us back down to Elderbrook."

"And hoping it reveals more clues," says Garbh. "As well as a safe place to sit down and eat. I don't know about you, but I'm starving."

This pathway is narrow and winding, as if designed to confuse. Here and there the oak forest opens up to stands of whitebeam or rowan. When we reach a point we judge to be far enough away from the lake, we sit beside a stream—not too close—and eat the remaining food. We've seen more of the pale stones as we passed, sometimes neatly piled, sometimes scattered. Following the stream and keeping to a downhill course should lead us back to the open fields around the settlement. While the stones are troubling in their implications, we haven't spotted anything that resembles a portal. Liobhan got into Eirne's world through a wall that seemed impenetrable. After she'd sung and played for hours, it eventually opened for her. But the tales tell of mushroom circles, of hollow hills, of folk simply falling asleep in the wrong spot. If there's such an entrance to the Otherworld here, will we know it when we see it? Might we already have passed through?

"Best be moving on," I'm saying when Garbh suddenly freezes, finger to his lips. Someone's coming, or something. No time to get away; the sound is just down the hill. We dive for the nearest cover, Garbh behind some rocks and me flat on my belly in a shallow depression between the trees. I hardly dare breathe. Anyone with the slightest skill at tracking can't miss us. Silently, I maneuver my knife from its sheath.

Footsteps. A faint jingling sound, perhaps from clips attached to a person's belt, or from a weapon striking some other metal object. Can't be a horse, not on this narrow track. The steps come close then move away. I lift my head with caution, look down the hill, and glimpse a man moving onto a side path, heading away from us. A man of around my own height, clad in colors that provide good concealment in this woodland. He's wearing a hooded tunic. As I watch, he pushes his hood back. His golden hair is a bright flag in the darkness of the forest.

I flatten myself again and count to fifty. When I rise, he's gone. No sign of anyone else. "Garbh," I call softly as I rise to my feet. "Did you see him?"

"Was that him? Your brother?"

I think I may be sick. I bend over, hands on knees, until the feeling passes. "Master Sealbhach in person. And alone, from the looks of it. But the others may not be far behind. Maybe he's been sent to open the place up. That's if the path he took leads to the hut. We'd best get out of here." Which way? Return past the lake and risk walking into Seanan, if that is indeed where he's headed? Or continue downhill and perhaps meet the rest of the brotherhood on the way up?

"Maybe the stones mark the safe path," Garbh says. "Safe for us, I mean."

"Why would the Fair Folk be doing you and me any favors? Maybe they lead to a place there's no getting out of." Liobhan suspected Otherworld beings might be involved in Aolu's disappearance. But he vanished from the forest near Winterfalls. Is there a possibility they might have brought him here? Why would they do so? I can't believe the Fair Folk would play a role in Mistress Sciath's plans. At least Prince Aolu wasn't in that hut. Still, I wish I'd climbed through the hole in the roof and done a proper search. Thinking of those storage chests, I shiver. You could hide a body in there, if you cut it up first. Could Seanan have planted these stones, leading us into a trap? "We'll have to chance it," I say. "Don't step in any mushroom circles, Garbh. You might end up dancing with the clurichauns for a year and a day."

There are no mushroom circles, but there are plenty of side paths, and in places the trees grow so closely that it's hard to guess which is the true way down. There are streams to cross, stony outcrops to negotiate, and steep slopes that slow us. At each meeting of pathways, one track is marked

with a single white stone. We follow these markers, trusting
that whoever set them there is kindly disposed toward us.
This method takes us downhill in what I calculate to be the
general direction of Elderbrook settlement.

"Dau?" Garbh pauses, looking up into the trees. We're
back in the lower reaches of the forest, under oaks, and as I
follow his gaze, I see them up there on the branches: Crow
Folk, too many of them to count, perched in groups and
looking down at us. I bite back the foul oath that springs to
my lips. We may be armed, we may be Swan Island men, but
if this mob decided to attack we wouldn't stand a chance. I've
never seen so many of the creatures gathered together before. I motion to Garbh to keep on walking. I wonder if being
a Swan Island man at this moment might mean using my
wits, not my sword arm.

Down the hill. Between the trees. Over a narrow bridge
across a meandering stream. I try not to glance upward too
often, but I can't help checking. More of them, more and
more. On every tree. On almost every branch. My heart
sounds a fast drumbeat. Cold sweat breaks out on my skin.
Surely one wrong move on our part will see them dive on us
with beaks and claws ready for slaughter. Rough terrain or
not, the instinct to run is hard to ignore.

The path forks again, one branch straight ahead—is that
open ground I can see between the trees, perhaps the fields
around the settlement?—the other off to the right, toward a
rock formation that somewhat resembles a bent old woman.
It wears a green cloak of mosses and creepers, and there's
even a long root or vine at one side that looks like a staff. The
oaks grow close, but not close enough to conceal the crone.
The white stone at my feet does not indicate the obvious
pathway back to Elderbrook. It's set squarely on the track
toward her.

"Morrigan's curse," I murmur. "If ever there was a spot for one of those portals, that's it." Despite myself, I'm torn. So far, the stones have led us on a safe path. No further sign of Seanan, no sightings of the brotherhood, and the Crow Folk are doing no more than watch us. I don't need to ask myself what Liobhan would do. She has a habit of marching forward heedless of personal risk. I want to go and look. I want to know why these woods are full of Crow Folk and what has brought them here. If they knew what Mistress Sciath planned for them, surely they'd be heading away from the area as fast as they could. But with Seanan close by, we need to get out of here. It would be foolish to linger.

"Down this way," I say. But before I walk on, I pick up the white stone and place it on my palm, in awkward imitation of Garbh's ritual at the lake. I look at the rock woman and bow. "Thank you," I whisper. I turn and look up toward the dark throng perched in the trees. "Thank you." *For not killing us. For letting us pass.* I lay the stone back where it was, and the two of us make our way down the hill, out of the forest and back toward the settlement.

19

LIOBHAN

The moment my mother sees me she knows something's wrong. There's no hiding secrets from her. Master Donagan greets us on arrival and offers the amenities of the household. Our horses are led off to the stables. And right after that, Mother appears in the courtyard with Galen beside her—Galen upright, walking, his head bandaged and his expression a little wild. I embrace each in turn. Tears are shed. I introduce Hrothgar and Elka to my family. But we can't talk openly with so many folk close by, even if they are trusted members of Prince Aolu's household. That will have to wait.

There's no official meeting planned, I guess because this mission is of a kind that kings and councilors aren't well equipped to advise on. Donagan says he'll speak to us later, just to check we have everything we need. Hrothgar and Elka go off to stretch their legs after the ride and work on the cover story. And I follow my mother and brother into the little walled garden that's one of our favorite spots at the prince's house. Galen's acting strangely. He's up, he's moving, I should be delighted. I am delighted. But he has a trapped look, and he's strangely quiet. He settles himself on a low wall near us, saying not a word.

I hardly know where to start. I hate giving them more bad news. Though it's not news exactly. A vision is not the same as fact. "Might we be overheard here?" I ask in a voice just over a whisper.

Mother lifts her brows. "We're among friends in this household," she says.

"Even so. This can't be shared with anyone else. Not anyone. Elka and Hrothgar know. Nobody else." I draw a steadying breath. "It's not about the search for Aolu. It's about Brocc."

I tell them about the cavern and Elka and the winged messenger. I tell them about the vision and see on my mother's face an expression I wish I could take away. But if I trust anyone I trust her, and she needs to know. I dip into my pouch and bring out the little silk bag in which I'm keeping the two curls of hair and the broken leaf. I tell them the story.

"Brocc would never use his gift as a weapon," Mother says when I reach the end. "Never. If what you saw is happening now or about to happen—if he's been taken away so he can turn the Crow Folk into a fighting force—he must be acting under coercion."

"When we saw Brocc working with the Crow Folk, there was no sign of the child." Saying this aloud fills me with horror all over again. "This woman must have threatened to harm the infant unless he does what she wants."

"Would he give in to such a threat?"

I hesitate.

"Tell me the truth, Liobhan. I haven't seen Brocc since the two of you went off to Swan Island, bright-eyed and full of hope. Has he changed so much that he would perform a monstrous act in order to keep his child safe?"

Curse it, the tears are flowing again. "I don't know. I don't know what to think. Brocc is full of love and warmth and joy.

When Dau and I saw him at Oakhill—a whole other story, it can wait—he told the truth and acted with honor. He was committed to helping the Crow Folk. He believed them misunderstood; frightened rather than malign. To use them as a fighting force . . . It's hard to believe he would do that. But he loves his child, that was plain. An impossible choice."

"Mm." Mother's thinking hard; I know that look. "Brocc has been living in the Otherworld. Choices there aren't a simple yes or no. You make bargains. You set terms. And if that doesn't get you out of trouble, you resort to trickery. Brocc may be playing a game of his own." She falls abruptly silent. I have my sleeves rolled up a little, and she's staring at my right arm. "What is that?" she asks, her tone shocked.

"A scar. From a burn." Oh, gods, I didn't want to tell this story. What happened is over, it's done with. "It's healed. It's fine."

"Show me." There's no denying her. I hold out my arm; she peels the sleeve back further and turns her expert eye on the long, raised scar with its angled branch. "Deliberate," she says flatly. "A symbol of some kind. Who did this to you?"

"It happened when we were at Oakhill. It's a long story. The man who did it was torturing Crow Folk, marking them in much the same way. Dau proved his guilt, with our help, and the man was banished. Disinherited. Sometime I'll tell you and Father the whole tale, but now is not the time. You have more than enough to worry about; no need to add me. I can look after myself."

"Hmm." She narrows her eyes at me. "Why would Brocc be out in the human world with a baby? Why take it away from its mother and the rest of her clan?"

"I have no idea. When I saw Brocc at Oakhill, before he even knew there was a child on the way, things were already strained between him and Eirne. She was terrified of the

Crow Folk, he said; fearful for her people. That makes it all the more odd that Brocc would leave."

"Liobhan." For the first time, Galen speaks. "You said nobody knows about this, about Brocc, except you and your two comrades. So . . . did you lie to your superiors? Are you telling us you're giving up the search for Aolu?"

I make myself meet his gaze. He has something of the look I saw on Brocc's face in the vision. He looks haunted by demons. I wish I didn't have to answer. But I must. "If it's possible, we'll do both. But there are many people out looking for Aolu, and Brocc's situation is dire." I touch the damaged leaf with a gentle finger. Mother has taken the two curls of hair—I've fastened each with a knotted thread—and laid them on her palm. She's never seen that baby. Not even in a vision. Her first grandchild. "The vision in the cavern . . . it did contain clues to where that Crow Folk attack might happen. It's not far from the area we've been told to head for, to meet up with a comrade." After my mother's reaction to the burn, I'm not going to tell her the attack the vision showed was at Oakhill. "Brocc may be in a place with elder trees. Or named for them."

"There's the river Elder," says Galen. "It flows through Argialla and Ulaid. Starts up in the hills above Hunter's Glen. I think there's a settlement called Elderbrook."

"Illady Falls," Mother says. "That's one of the spots where the dobhar-chú is supposed to lurk, according to a tale Master Saran found for us. Could that be an old name for Elderbrook?"

"Could be," I say as my heart beats faster. "Where is Elderbrook, Galen?"

"Close to the river, at the Argiallan end of Hunter's Glen. It's all forest around there, except in the higher reaches. Liobhan, this talk of portals . . . You mean the king has finally seen sense?"

I hesitate. The change of plan has come about, I'm pretty sure, not because the king or Donagan or Cionnaola realized the portal theory really was the best fit for such a sudden and complete disappearance, but because they were running out of leads in the human world. I see the desperation in Galen's eyes. I hear it in his voice, and I know I can't tell him that. I don't want to lie to him. He's my brother, too, and perhaps his love for the prince is as strong as Brocc's for his child. But there's more than a personal loss hanging on Brocc's situation. Whole kingdoms might be at risk. "That's why we've been called in. To look for signs suggesting the prince has gone to the Otherworld. I'm hoping you can set us on the right path, Mother, since you know more about these things than anyone."

She looks at me; I look at her. She doesn't need to tell me it's an impossible request. She, too, doesn't want to say certain things in Galen's hearing. "Dau asked me about this before they left," she says. "At that point I was in agreement with the king. I believed the more obvious possibilities should be investigated first. I did tell Dau such doorways only open up when someone on the other side wants to let a person in. I can't point things out to you on a map. All I can do is suggest the kind of places a portal might be found. But you know that already. A person can't learn as many songs as you have without picking up a great deal of wisdom on such matters." A pause. "Weren't you ruled out of that mission because of Galen? Or because of Dau?"

"What did Dau tell you about that?"

She smiles. "Let's just say I gather you two are very close now, and that means you don't get sent out together. I believe your man was of the opinion that you would be an asset to this particular job because of your knowledge of the Other-world and your musical ability, and he was sorry you weren't with him. But also relieved. And if that burn is anything to go by, I understand his attitude very well."

"Mm. Yes, I was ruled out. Then they changed their minds."

"You changed their minds for them," puts in Galen, with a small spark of his former self.

"Something like that, yes."

"I know of a portal at Wolf Glen," Mother says. "But that's in the other direction, and it's not a doorway you'd want to be messing about with. Whatever lives on the far side is in no way sweet and cooperative. It's possible that entering any other portal on or near Winterfalls land might take you to that same unfortunate place. That might even happen be-yond the border. There's no knowing. Folk do say both time and space are different in the Otherworld. Changeable not only between worlds, but within the uncanny realm itself. So you must exercise extreme caution. Don't even think of crossing over unless you have a very strong indication that you'll find Aolu in that realm. Otherwise you might find yourself among the not-quite-so-fair folk, with no way back."

"I understand that." I glance Galen's way. His jaw is tight; his hands are clenched into fists. "I am concerned about Elka," I say. "I was the one who suggested she come with me, once I saw what she and I could do together. But she's new and I shouldn't lead her into trouble."

Mother manages a smile. "That from a woman who's bro-ken rules quite fearlessly all her life? I shouldn't joke about it, I know. Liobhan, if I were in your shoes I'd go after Brocc as soon as I could and save him from whatever foul enterprise he's got himself mixed up in. That child needs its father back

safe and well. Brocc's a good boy. He doesn't deserve all this."
For the first time, there's an uneven note in her voice. "And
as you say, there are many folk out looking for the prince
already."

"I'll probably lose my place on the island. That'll happen even if I don't succeed in rescuing Brocc. I held back information from the elders, I got myself and my friends sent
on a mission, and we're going to do something entirely different."

She looks me straight in the eye. "Sometimes you have to
make a hard choice. Follow the rules, play safe, and perhaps
lose something irreplaceable. Or break the rules, do what
you know is right, and risk a calamitous fall. I know what I
would choose. Have done, often, and sometimes paid dearly
for it. But it's not my choice. Not this time."

Abruptly Galen stands. He turns and walks out of the garden without a word. The set of his shoulders speaks for him.

A shiver runs through me. "If only I could be in two places
at once. He'll never forgive me for this. For abandoning
Aolu. That's the way he'll see it, even though we'll look for
portals on the way. But I have to find Brocc. I have to."
There's something further I want to ask my mother. Need to
ask. I'm not sure I should.

"I could ask Conmael for help," she says, speaking the
name I've been reluctant to mention. I know she hates to
impose on her old friend. "With Brocc at such risk and the
child in danger, too, I think it's time to try. Not here. We'll
go over to Dreamer's Wood. He may not come. He may not
have answers. But the situation is dire, so we'll attempt it, if
you agree."

We're both standing now. I give her a hug, which requires
me to bend a long way—can my mother be getting smaller?
"Thank you," I say. "For everything."

★ ★ ★

Dreamer's Wood is an easy walk across the fields from the prince's residence, and on the edge of the wood is our old house, where my parents still live, though they're staying at the prince's house until Galen's fully recovered. Nobody questions us, since it's perfectly natural for me to want to visit home before I head off on the mission. As luck would have it, my father is there with our old dog, Trusty. Father throws his arms around me. Trusty is warier, having not seen me for a long while, but eventually lets me rub the special spot behind his ears. It's so good to see Father. I wish we had time to sit before the fire for a while and share a brew along with several years of news. But it's not to be.

"Brocc's in trouble," Mother tells him. "I'll explain later, before we walk back over. It's confidential. Liobhan is heading out on a mission tomorrow. I need to talk to Conmael. Liobhan, we'll do it now. Come with me." She gives Father a smile I know well, one that is just for him. It's like a warm light in a dark place. "We'll be ready for a brew a bit later, if you have the time."

"Always," says Father, his blunt, plain features reflecting that glow.

Mother leads me into the wood, under the pale-barked birches and down to the narrow strip of shore beside Dreamer's Pool. The place is quiet; birds seldom sing here, such is the powerful magic of this body of water. She bids me wait at a distance, then closes her eyes and stands very still. I make myself unclench my teeth, relax my balled-up fists, slow my breathing as I know she must be doing so she can send her silent call to Conmael. She wouldn't try this if things weren't so desperate. She's always tried not to lean on their friendship, which started with a long-ago favor she did him as a child. I wait. I think of Brocc as he was in the vision, and I think of us when we were young: a brother and sister only a couple of moons apart in age. There's no blood bond between Brocc and me, but we are as close as any siblings can be. We grew up together, we sang and played together, we were sparring partners as we learned to fight. Together we shared a childhood in this place, safe and happy in the care of the best parents any child could possibly hope for. Galen, too. He was big brother and protector to the two of us.

"Blackthorn."

The voice is not my mother's. I open my eyes. There he is, standing beside her on the shore, a tall, pale figure in a swirling dark cloak that moves of itself, strangely. I have seen Conmael once or twice at a distance, when he came to speak with Mother of his own accord. But never so close. He is indeed imposing. And quite obviously not of this world.

"Conmael, greetings." Mother addresses him not as the proud Otherworld lord he is, but the friend she has known since they were children living in an ordinary village in the south. "We need your help. We believe Brocc is in serious trouble. His child, too. Liobhan will tell you what she knows."

Time to step up. I mustn't be overwhelmed by the grand look of the man; I've dealt with my brother's wife, Eirne, who is an Otherworld queen. I move closer and set out what I know: the vision, the clue brought by the bird. Oakhill. Galen's mention of the river Elder. I can't assume he knows about Aolu, so I tell him that story, too. "My comrades and I have been sent to look for places where the prince might have traveled beyond the human world. Portals. But the search area is huge and it could take a very long time. Brocc's need is more urgent. I must stop that woman from using him in such a vile way. Think what might happen if the Crow Folk were trained to be an army, a strike force. Years of unrest. War and terror. Doing this goes against everything

Brocc believes in, Lord Conmael. He wants to understand the Crow Folk and help them, not exploit them. It would break him to act in this way. And yet, in the vision, he was doing it. Probably under a particularly evil kind of coercion."

Conmael nods gravely. "I would help you if I could, please believe me. But this lies outside my influence. I know of Brocc's interest in the Crow Folk; we have spoken together since he crossed into the Otherworld, and he told me of his belief that the creatures are not evil, only lost and misunderstood. I told him then that I sensed the riddle of the Crow Folk might be his to solve; that it might be his mission to save them. They live under a curse, or so I believe. Learn how to break that curse and you learn how to set them free. I believe the task is his and his alone."

I can't hold back the words. "But—but what about that woman, the one who's making him control the Crow Folk? There isn't time for Brocc to work out his own solution. He's in deadly danger right now, and so is the child!"

There's compassion in Conmael's eyes, which are of darkest blue and most definitely fey in appearance. Compassion and regret. He's going to say no again, I can see it on his face.

"I do not intervene in the matters of the human world," he says. "It is against an ancient rule. This woman is of humankind. She seeks power, I imagine, for some reason of her own. Though such power, as you point out, would ultimately be to nobody's advantage. I do not play a part in the rise and fall of kings and queens, chieftains and druids and priests, in this world. In my own world it is a different matter. One thing I will do, and that is inform myself of what may have occurred in Eirne's realm. I wonder greatly what caused Brocc to leave that place and take his child with him. A messenger, you said. From his wife? Would she send such a creature to you?"

"I doubt it. Eirne didn't exactly warm to me when we met. There was a time when a bird stole some of my hair and took it to Brocc. A time when I was in bad trouble." Poisoned, beaten, tied up with maddened Crow Folk not far off. I won't mention those details with my mother listening. "I've wondered who sent that bird. It couldn't have been Eirne. It may have acted of its own accord. That was at Oakhill. Brocc and his friend True came to save us."

"Ah, True," says Conmael. "A good soul. Might not he or another of that clan have dispatched this messenger? Brocc has comrades there, loyal ones."

"Does this matter right now?" There's an edge in Mother's voice. "This woman, whoever she is, wants to turn my son into a monster. Can you at least give us some advice, Conmael?"

"If you did find Brocc, what would you do?" Conmael sounds as calm as the still water at his feet. Though both may be deceptive. "It seems this woman has a powerful hold over him."

With difficulty, I match his tone. "I'd use every weapon I had to stop her. I'd get my brother out of trouble, whatever it took." I am a warrior trained. I am strong. I am a musician, and while I may not have Brocc's skill, I have used my voice and my whistle to deal with the uncanny before. I have good comrades; three of them, if Illann joins us. But . . . this is not their mission. I blink back sudden tears, hating my weakness. "I know not to barge in without a plan. I'm trained in strategy. I just need to find him, then I'll work out how to do it."

Conmael turns to Mother. "You've raised strong children, you and Grim. Trust them with this. All three of them will play a part in setting things right. Liobhan, make use of the clues you have been given, and of the help you have at hand. Follow your instincts. I believe you are already on the right path. And remember, visions can be deceptive. They generally owe something to the one who conjures them, and in this case that is complex. What you saw was based on three elements: the questions to which you sought answers; the mind and heart of your companion, the seer; and the being who watched, the creature connected in some way with the Crow Folk. Of the three, you are the only one who knows Brocc. Only you know the exceptional strength that lies deep inside our boy. Go and find him. But tread carefully. This may not be what it seems. Brocc may be playing a long and perilous game. To step in at the wrong time may put his plan in jeopardy. Have courage, my friends. I must bid you farewell now."

"Farewell, Conmael." Mother gives him a little bow; he returns the courtesy.

"Farewell," I say. "And thank you." As I watch him walk away under the trees, I realize that even though he said he couldn't help, he's done just that. His words have given me confidence in my risky choice.

Back at the cottage, I sit in the warmth and drink the brew Father has ready, aware of how little time we have to spend together. Mother outlines the complicated story for him. Confidential this may be, but the two of them have no secrets from each other. Besides, with all three of his children involved, he needs to know. He's a quiet person, but we know that when there's a decision to be made or a challenge to face he may well come out with some piece of wisdom that nobody else has thought of.

"Were those Conmael's words?" he asks now. *"All three of them will play a part?"*

"That's what he said." Mother tucks her graying hair back behind one ear. "Brocc's in the middle of it. Liobhan's about to rush to the rescue, or rather, tread carefully to the rescue. But Galen? Not long out of bed, still needing his wounds tended to, and swinging between moody silence and outbursts of wild anger? He's not dealing with anything right now. He's convinced Aolu has been taken to the Otherworld and furious that nobody's followed up that possibility. When you were speaking earlier, Liobhan, he must have thought: *At last, at last someone's looking for him where they should look.* And then you made it clear you were going to find Brocc. I don't know what Conmael meant about all three of you playing a part. Galen must be torn; he's desperate to find Aolu, but Brocc is his brother, too. I only know I don't want him going off on his own. He's threatened to do that often enough since he was injured."

"That's Galen's mission," Father says quietly, looking at me. "To keep Aolu safe at any cost. Not as grand as Brocc's hopes for the Crow Folk, but worthy all the same. Aolu's the future king of Dalriada, and a good king he'll be if he gets the opportunity. You might weigh that up, Liobhan, as leader. Maybe there's a way the two missions become one." He always was wise.

All too soon we have to say good-bye. Father envelops me in a big hug as if I were still the small daughter whom he taught to plant a garden and thatch a roof and dig a drain, as well as how to defend herself. Although I am a very tall woman and quite strongly built, he dwarfs me. With his arms around me, I lay my head against his chest and listen to his heartbeat, strong and steady.

"You can do it, Liobhan," he says. "Trust yourself and trust your brothers. And come home safe, will you?"

"I'll do my best. Better go now." I turn away, fighting tears. Falling apart will be no help at all. I am indeed mission leader. I'd better go and talk to my team.

* * *

The day is passing quickly. I go looking for Elka and Hroth-gar and find them outside, in a secluded, sunny area up near the prince's grazing fields. Nobody around. It's safe to talk. We've told Hrothgar about the vision, of course, and why it's so important to reach Brocc quickly. At the time, he made no comment on the fact that my plan did not match the mission we've been given. Now I pass on my mother's warnings. "Finding Brocc feels urgent to me. But we should be cautious. Mother thinks he may be carrying out a plan of his own. Though if the attack we saw was real, the cost of that plan would surely soon be more than he could bear." It was a sight fit to break your heart, all those fine men scattered like discarded dolls, the road awash with blood and strewn with body parts, and the Crow Folk flying away, their work complete.

"While we were waiting, Elka told me a story," Hrothgar says. "Tell Liobhan, Elka. She needs to hear it."

"It is a story Mormor tells me long ago. An island, far out in ocean, small folk live there. Not birds. Not human. Different. They live on cliffs, in little caves. Eat fish, look after babies. Make fire by night, sit in a circle, old ones tell stories, sing songs. Hard life but happy, you know? Watching over them is a great bird, is . . . ?" She turns to Hrothgar.

"Sea eagle," he says.

"Sea eagle, yes. Aake. Spirit, guardian. Aake tells them, live in peace, respect others, take only what you need, be kind. Long years they do this, never break the law. But one time, a man is washed up on shore, human, from wrecked ship. Still alive. One of the island folk finds him. Should call for help, save man. But no. Man has strange patterns on his face. Small one is afraid, thinks he is monster. So small one picks up a rock and kills man, like *this*." Elka mimes the act, all too convincingly. "Ancient vow of peace is broken. There is unrest. Fighting. More die, more hurt, all get angry. Aake pays the price for this. She is torn in three parts, cast to earth, sky, ocean. As she goes, Aake curses small folk, turns them into birds. She curses them to fly on, one place, another place, never can stay long. No new home, always restless."

I'm holding my breath. Isn't this almost exactly what Brocc believes about the Crow Folk?

"Small folk fly long, long time. Old ones, young ones tired, drop in sea and drown. Others fly on. Nobody knows where they go, Mormor say. Only away, far away."

"Banished forever? Or did this guardian spirit give them a way to break the curse?"

"Island folk must learn to honor vow of peace once more. No hurting, no killing, no angry. Then Aake will be made whole again, and come for them, and they fly home. When Mormor tells me story, she say they are still lost, still flying. You think this is Crow Folk, Liobhan? How long are they here? Mormor tells me this when I am small girl." With her hand she indicates a child maybe seven or eight years old.

I consider an awful possibility: after such a grueling ordeal the Crow Folk—if indeed this is their story—may have been driven so far out of their wits that they are no longer capable of flying home. Maybe they can't mend their violent ways even though they want to. "They've been in these parts a few years," I say. "Not very many. But the story says they were condemned to fly from one place to another, never settling for long. Who knows where they were before they came here?" Danu save us, if the Crow Folk are the tribe from this story and someone really does intend to turn them into an instrument of destruction, this would become a tale without redemption or hope. The guardian spirit could never be made whole again. The tribe could never fly home.

For a moment I feel drained, helpless, unable to take in the monstrosity of it. Then I consider the walking shadow, the being in the cavern. I mustn't forget the vision. "That's one future," I murmur, more to myself than to the others. "But there's more than one possible future. A story can be told a hundred ways. There can be all sorts of endings, depending on whether people are brave, or take risks, or let themselves be paralyzed by fear. Depending on how hard people try, and how good they are at solving puzzles. How clever they are at playing tricks. The Crow Folk may seem a lost cause, savage and unbiddable. But they're not all like that. It's possible for them to feel hope." I think of the wounded birds we helped to release. We were careful, fearing that the moment the cage door was opened they would attack us. But they flew straight out to freedom, leaving us silent with wonder. Oh, gods. I see it, though I know it's all but impossible. A great flight homeward. If only . . .

"The being in the cavern," Hrothgar says with some hesitation. "The walking shadow. That may once have been one of them, perhaps an elder, a druid or something similar. A walking shadow is between worlds. Anchored to this life because there is work to complete before they can rest."

"Waiting," says Elka. "Waiting for tribe to turn to peace. Waiting for others to come, to be ready. An elder, a druid, yes . . . or a spirit. A shadow of Aake. You think?"

A shadow of their goddess . . . it's an astonishing thought. I want to believe it, but I'm not sure I can. "Why weren't we shown the good ending as well as the bad, the way Dau and I were in Breifne? That offers a choice. It gives a person time to act, for good or evil. Aren't visions provided to help people make wise decisions?"

"What you saw might be taken as a warning. *Act now, or this is what will happen.*" Hrothgar's deep voice is thoughtful.

"The being in the cave could see a possible future, yes. But perhaps not all possible futures. That being, too, may be worn down by the long wait. That being does not know Brocc. It doesn't know what kind of man he is. It doesn't know what he would do."

I can't stop my tears from flowing. "Sorry," I mumble, feeling stupid, but so profoundly grateful for his words that I don't mind making a fool of myself. "Seems to be my day for crying." I wipe my face with my sleeve. "Of course, the Crow Folk may not be the tribe of Elka's story, though they do match it well. That being had a look of them, even though it wasn't a bird. Even if they're not the same, something similar may have happened to them. It's close to Brocc's idea, and his Otherworld heritage gives him a better insight than we might have." Danu be thanked, these wretched tears are finally drying up. "Maybe we can actually do this."

"You, daughter of wisewoman." Elka turns a very direct look on me; today, her eyes are like still water, calm and deep. "I, granddaughter of seer. Hrothgar, son of storyteller. Warriors, all three!"

"A stirring call to action!" says Hrothgar, smiling. "Now we'd better go back in. I think I see Master Donagan down there, and he's waving a hand in our direction."

Donagan clarifies Illann's request: we're to ride as far as an inn called The Three Pipers and wait there for our comrade. It's a travelers' hostelry in Ulaid, near the border with Argialla, and only a few days' ride from the place where Dau and Garbh went. It's also well situated for a ride further south to Oakhill, should it come to that, which I very much hope it won't. If that vision comes true, Dau's father's men mowed down by the Crow Folk, this will become too big for us to deal with and I will have made a monumental error.

We're to take forest tracks as far as we can, staying off the main ways. And we're to look out for any sign of uncanny folk, including possible doorways to the Otherworld. Should we find anything, we're to act only if there's cause to believe Aolu might have gone that way. Otherwise we make a note of the place and move on. After we meet up with Illann we regroup, providing backup for Dau and Garbh as well as following any leads we may have discovered.

If we obey these instructions to the letter it will be a slow journey indeed. If we can't visit settlements we'll need to carry food for the horses as well as all our gear. And we can't ride all day every day; our animals have their limits. Hrothgar says he'll go and talk to the stable master about a packhorse, and Donagan agrees that would be wise. In Donagan's hearing I say nothing about the need for speed, or how helpful it might be if we could change horses on the way. I don't say our search of the forest will be a lot sketchier than it should be. My stomach churns with the need to keep holding back the news about Brocc. If it leads to disaster I'll never forgive myself. I did wonder earlier whether Galen, who was clearly furious with me, might rush off and blurt out the whole sad story to anyone who might be prepared to listen. So far it seems he hasn't done that. I haven't seen him at all. He's gone to ground somewhere, like a creature licking its wounds.

Later we check our belongings and rehearse the cover story. I'm to be Lady Oonagh of Willowvale, somewhere in the south, and I'm traveling with my personal maid and my bodyguard, who are a married couple. Should we be seen and questioned about why we're wandering around in the forest, I'll admit to a fascination with local plants, especially curative ones, and go into an elaborate explanation of what we're looking for—as my mother's daughter I'm well equipped to do that convincingly. As for where we're headed and why, we're all trained in staying polite while not answering questions, and vague mentions of heading back south should be enough.

I have one good gown with me; it's the one I wear to sing and play. It's hardly the garment of a fine lady, but at a pinch it's good enough for Lady Oonagh. We decide the lady is somewhat eccentric, and given to expeditions on horseback in search of rare specimens of plant life. That means I can wear my riding outfit with trousers under a divided skirt. The same for Elka. Hrothgar may be carrying most of the weaponry, but we all need to be ready for action. I borrow a second overdress from one of the bigger women of Prince Aolu's household. It fits, just. I take my whistle with me, in the small pack I'll carry on my back. We may not be intending to spend much time in the forest seeking out portals, but I'd never forgive myself if we did find one and I wasn't ready for it.

The three of us take turns firing questions at each other, trying to trip each other up. Elka's hesitant Irish proves an advantage to her. When she's stuck, she can convincingly hide behind confusion about the meaning of a word, or seem to be hunting for the correct way to put something. In fact her Irish is getting better by the day. I've noticed she and Hrothgar don't always revert to Norse now when talking together.

Galen is not at supper. Mother says he's sleeping in his own quarters, since he no longer needs her to watch over him during the night. It looks as if he's decided not to speak to me again before I leave. I understand his fury. I've made a hard choice. A risky choice. It must seem to Galen that I don't care about the prince. I wish I could say to him, *Just wait. Let me do this, let me save Brocc, and then we'll go searching for Aolu,*

I promise. But I can't promise. I don't know how this will work out. I only know what I have to do.

He's not there in the morning when I bid farewell to Mother and Father. He's not there when our horses are brought around from the stables and we get ready to ride off, or when we thank Master Donagan and Finnian and various other members of the prince's household. And he's nowhere to be seen as we ride out, heading south on a forest track with the harsh cries of Crow Folk ringing in our ears, a stark warning of what may lie ahead.

I go first. Elka follows, leading the packhorse. Hrothgar is the rear guard. We've planned out a route of sorts. We've agreed to change the plan if it's too slow. The more I think about this, the less I want to spend time looking for portals. The chances of success seem slim and we need to move fast. I have a couple of ideas of my own, not ready to share with the others yet. I'm keen to reach The Three Pipers before Illann does. That way I can try a few things out before he gets the opportunity to say no.

We've been riding for half the morning when we hear hoofbeats coming up behind us. I rein in my horse and turn, my hand going to my weapon; Elka and Hrothgar do the same. A lone horseman is approaching, a tall, red-bearded man with a shaven head, astride a long-legged chestnut mare.

He rides up and halts his mount beside Hrothgar's. "I'm coming with you," says Galen.

20

AOLU

I have been here many days, many restless nights. Wherever *here* is. At the end of that long uncomfortable journey, my bearers brought me to a clearing surrounded by tall pines. There's a shelter, a low hut built from all manner of materials: fallen timber, cunningly woven withies, mud and grasses and leaves. It is small but remarkably weatherproof. They have given me a straw-packed mattress, a blanket, a strange little jug for water, and a cup fashioned from bone. They bring meals twice daily—such are my circumstances that I have set aside my doubts about eating Otherworld food. On balance, I would rather be stuck in this realm forever than die of starvation. And stuck I am, for now at least. My ankle is damaged. I can barely walk.

The small folk are of many shapes and forms. The one called Robin seems to be their leader. He talks to me kindly, but like the others he cannot, or will not, answer certain questions. So, while I recognize that I am in the Otherworld, I do not know how far they carried me—this question seems to baffle him. For much of that journey I was falling in and out of consciousness, shocked and confused. I do not know how any of this matches the times and places of my own world. Was Galen killed that day, the day I fell into this place?

He was badly hurt, he must have been, but did he survive it? Who were those men who attacked us? To these questions, Robin answers, "I do not know." What were the creatures I first encountered in that dark place, after my fall? To this he responds, "Bad things. We saved you, Prince."

As soon as we reached this place, the small folk called for their healer. Her name is Mother Ash. She is bigger than the others, as tall as a child of eight or so, but in form an old woman, wrapped in shawls and scarves and aprons, with a necklace of tiny skulls interspersed with feathers, acorn cups, and other talismans. I was hot then, rambling, flinging myself about in a most unhelpful manner. Feverish, Mother Ash told me later, after I came back to myself. She dosed me with a draft, and then she strapped up my ankle—drugged though I was, it took several of the small ones to hold me still, for the pain was fierce. I slept. Mother Ash set rules and made sure I followed them as the days passed. No arguing, no trying to get up, eat the food provided, drink water, use the bucket to relieve myself. Swallow the drafts that dulled the ache and brought merciful sleep.

Gradually the pain receded. She made me wriggle my toes, flex my foot. Gave me more exercises to do and set two of the small ones, Hazel and Thorny, the duty of watching to be sure I went through the sequence at least three times a day. Hazel has a long nose and lovely limpid eyes. Thorny has hair that stands up in spikes and a tail with bristles at the end. Each time, one of them would perform the exercises alongside me, matching move for move, while the other stood observing and making ridiculous comments. Though still in some discomfort, I could not keep from laughing, and that set my companions off, too. By that stage I was succumbing to the belief that going mad would not be such a bad thing. Eventually, when the ankle was growing stronger and the exercises becoming less painful, they brought me a walking stick beautifully crafted from walnut. Carved up its length is a tall tower of creatures, with a stag at the bottom, and a badger balanced on its back, and a terrier standing precariously on the badger, and so on. At the very top is a tiny bird with its wings spread, ready for flight. This, they made for me together. It is the most magical gift I have ever received, save for Galen's love.

I will not be flying anywhere, but I can get about with the aid of this fine thing. A few steps one day, a few more the next, and so on until the day when I limped to the edge of the clearing and discovered I could go no further. Not because I was too exhausted or sore to walk on, or because the terrain was too steep or the way too full of growing things, but because I walked into a wall. An invisible wall. I could see the forest in front of me, I could see leaves stirring in the breeze, I could hear birds chirping up above and smell the bracing scent of pines. I even heard, from a distance, a harsh cry that sounded like one of the Crow Folk. But the wall was there, as solid as if it had been made of stone, and I could not get so much as my little finger past it.

The small folk do not live in the clearing. Nor does Mother Ash. They come in and out to tend to me, using forest pathways. But at no spot can I pass the wall; I am a prisoner among those who have helped me. I ask why, and they have no answers. But it seems they were only waiting for me to be back on my feet and clear of mind, because Mother Ash comes to see me one day, and when she has checked my ankle and professed herself satisfied with my progress, she sits down beside me on a fallen tree and fixes me with her bright eyes, solemn as an owl. "Prince of Dalriada, will you help us?" she asks.

It comes back to me then, something I had all but forgot-

ten: the words Robin spoke when he and his companions
rescued me that day above Winterfalls. At the time I was in
a haze of misery and I hardly understood. Help them? I cannot refuse. I owe these strange little folk my life. But . . . this
is the Otherworld. What impossible task might this be? Perhaps I should bargain. *I will help you if you promise to set me free.*
But that would be churlish. It would be unworthy of the
prince I am. "What can I do?" I ask.

"There is a creature here. She has come among us and
will not leave. A dark thing full of sorrow. She has led Crow
Folk onto our territory. They make the small ones restless
and frighten away the creatures of the woodland. They are
on every tree, on every branch, watching us with their evil
eyes. We want them gone. We want the creature gone from
this place." Her hand comes up to touch one of the little
skulls on her necklace; I think of my own talisman, lost on
that terrible day.

"Why would you ask me? You are a . . . a wisewoman, a
healer. Can't you talk to this creature?"

"I do not know if the being can speak as we do. She is not
like any creature known to me, nor anything in our tales.
Not of our kind. Not of humankind. Neither fish nor fowl nor
earth-dwelling animal. She has a look of the Crow Folk. But
she is not one of them. They roost close to her dwelling. All
day, all night they stay there. We are afraid."

I give this some thought before I answer. "Did Robin's folk
rescue me in the belief that I could help with this, Mother
Ash?"

Her mouth twists into a rueful smile. "Not so. You came
to grief in your own world, it seems; you fell into a dark
place. Robin's work is to keep the troublesome folk of that
place away from our borders. If sometimes he and his assis-
tants come upon a wayfarer in strife, why would they not try

to help? So it was with you. Robin and his helpers found you hurt, lost, and being harried by hostile beings. They brought you to safety and passed you over to me for healing. And now you are almost mended again."

"And I am deeply grateful, both for the rescue and for the good care. I am very much in your debt, Mother Ash, and Robin's. I want to help. Tell me, if he and his team can keep these dark creatures at bay, why cannot they help with this other difficulty?"

Mother Ash's face tells me she believes this a foolish question. "Do you not know the power of the Crow Folk? How easily they kill, and with what little reason? Our folk would be destroyed. And the creature who has come among us will not talk to us. She will not listen. I have tried."

"Then why would I do any better?"

"You are a prince," she says simply. The trust in her voice is terrifying.

I cannot imagine I look at all princely right now, though at least I have my clothes back—for quite some time in the early days I lay naked under a blanket, until the small ones brought me my shirt, trousers, and tunic, washed, dried, and neatly folded. Did I tell the small ones who I was, on that day of flight and pain? I must have done. And now, gods help me, I must act like the prince I am. A creature akin to the Crow Folk! I might step up to address the thing only to have my head bitten off.

"I will try," I say. "Where is this being?"

"I will take you. It is outside the wall."

"In the human world? Then why—"

"No, no. The wall is for your own protection. Our world stretches beyond that barrier, Prince. You could wander and wander and never find your way home. To cross over is not a simple matter of walking on."

Ah. Now is the time to ask whether, if I persuade this creature to leave the area, I might be given instructions as to how the way home might be found. But I cannot ask. She needs help. I am a prince. I must not put a price on this. "Lead on, then," I say. "I'll do my best."

The wall can be opened at a touch. Her touch, that is, not mine. Mother Ash leads the way toward the forest; I walk behind, using my stick for support. Above us, Crow Folk line the limbs of the pines, perched close together in a way I have never seen in my world. Immobile. Not the blink of an eye; not the twitch of a claw. This is curious indeed. It disturbs me.

At the base of a rock formation there is a small cave, and Mother Ash halts a few paces from this simple shelter. "The creature is in there," she says quietly. "Be wary. She has long claws and sharp teeth. She has committed no acts of violence here. But she seems full of sorrow. When she came to this place, she brought a shadow that has lain over all of us. There is something amiss about this being, something lost. Speak to her, Prince. Tell her to go away and take her Crow Folk with her. They disturb us. They perch there, staring. They do not fly. It is as if they are waiting."

I can't see the being; if she's in this modest shelter she must be right at the back, in the darkness. I take a few steps closer and squat down, peering in. "Will you stay with me, Mother Ash?"

"The being does not trust me. Better if I go."

Is this a trick? "I hope you will let me back through the wall, then," I say. But she is already gone.

Within the cave, something moves. A rustling, a scratching. The old tales are full of scenes where men and women encounter fey folk and speak with them. Sometimes it's easy, as to some degree it has been with Robin and Hazel and the rest. Sometimes it's hard, and the humans need to use tricks or make bargains. Sometimes they sing. I doubt my voice is up to that at present. The being may not speak our language. She may not be able to speak at all. She may not be able to hear. I could draw with a stick in the soil, but how could I convey anything beyond the most basic message? *Think, Aolu.*

I try words first, hoping to coax the creature out. Trusting that the sharp teeth and long claws will not be deployed against me. "Good day to you. My name is Aolu, and I am the prince of this land." I speak more in hope than in certainty. I may be far beyond the borders of Dalriada. "I want to help you. Will you come out and talk?"

A sigh, more rustling, a muted clicking. I can see the being now, or at least, I can see a clawed hand and a swath of dark feathers. Is this in fact one of the Crow Folk? Clicking again. Five and three and five. Three and one and three. And the same again. A pattern.

I cast around for something I can use. A stone, another stone, both of them coated with dried mud. I tap them together, but the sound is no more than a dull thud. I set them down and clap softly instead. Five and three and five. Three and one and three. Then, taking a guess, seven and five and seven. I wait.

The being emerges to squat in the entry to her cave, looking not at me but down at the two white stones she holds—those hands show plainly that this is no bird. And the feather plumage is not part of her body, but a robe that spreads out on the earth around her like a pool of shadow. Her eyes are bright; her ears are prominent; her skin is grayish in hue and hairless. I do not know why Mother Ash seemed so sure this was a female; was it perhaps a necklace that somewhat resembles her own? In place of the threaded skulls and acorns and other forest items the healer wears, this being has tiny shells and fronds of dried seaweed and water-smoothed pebbles strung around her neck.

She taps again with her white stones. Seven and five and seven. I nod, smile, wonder if this is a standard greeting or a coded message. I make a guess and clap five and three and five. The being bares a set of dazzling white teeth. They look sharp as blades. She taps three and one and three. I seat myself cross-legged, not too close, and relax my hands in my lap. Slowly the being sets her stones down.

"Greetings," I say quietly.

She makes no reply. The smile, if smile it was, is gone now. She sits and waits. Oh, for Galen to be here. The stones are the key. It would take him only a moment to work out what to do. Lacking his strong presence by my side, along with his flair for games, I must do my best. Galen would have his own stones with him; I have none. I point to the two on the ground, raise my brows in question. I try to show a message in signs: *I want to talk to you. Those—may I use? More stones?* I glance around as if seeking a supply in this unlikely part of the woods.

She covers her two stones with protective hands.

"I would not steal them. Only borrow."

No response; she guards her treasure and is silent. Perhaps I can find some pebbles nearby. Maybe there's a stream. I think I can hear running water; that may be where the small ones refill my jug. I gesture, *Wait*, and rise to my feet, wondering how far I might go before I hit another invisible wall.

Something's holding me back; is my tunic snagged on a thorn? No. The being has come forward from her cave and has hooked a claw into my clothing. The message is clear.

You wait. She reaches into the dark recess of her shelter, bringing out a handful of stones, then another. They lie in a pile between us, neither as clean nor as varied as those Galen keeps safe and polishes and handles every day, but still, I think, with sufficient variety to be used in . . . what is it I need to do? Make a picture? Tell a story? Perform some feat of magic? Surely Mother Ash would be better for that.

But maybe I need only watch and listen. This being may be a maker of magic. She may be the one with a story to tell. *Show me,* I gesture. I lower myself to the ground again. My ankle protests the movement but I set the pain aside. I settle to watch.

She moves a larger rock into the space between us. On this she sets many small stones, placing each with care. All of these are dark in color, black or charcoal gray. The being uses her long-fingered hands to make graceful motions around the rock. I copy her, making a gentle sound as I do so: *shh, shh.* She nods. I've got it right: the sea.

She moves the dark stones about on their rock or island, placing them sometimes in groups, sometimes apart. I see them going about their daily business, perhaps fishing, if this is a remote spot, perhaps tending to children—the smallest stones—perhaps cooking. Sometimes they lie down at the very edge of the rock, which seems an odd place to sleep. I see a daily routine. Before sleep, they gather all in one place, forming a great circle, and one of them—the being points to this brown stone, then to herself—walks about, perhaps telling a story.

I do not know how to mime *wisewoman*, but that is what I am starting to think. If I'm right, why is it that this being can't talk with Mother Ash the way she's doing with me?

Something's happening in the world of these island people, these tiny things in their precarious home. The being places a stone—it stands out from the others, being close to purple in hue—on the ground at the foot of the island-rock. She makes the wave movement again, but this time it's harder, faster, a violent storm. The purple stone, the stranger, is buffeted against the rock, then lies still.

I mime *dead*, my eyes closed, my arms hanging limp and my hands loose on the ground. She shakes her head. Makes the purple stone move weakly. I change my position to show *hurt*. She nods; gives another smile, full of teeth. I'm starting to understand. Her recognition of that awakens a strange mixture of emotions. I feel humble, honored, hopeful. Awed at the revelation of a mystery she has not disclosed to Mother Ash and Robin and the others. Why me? *You are a prince.* The truth seems weightier than it ever was before. I gesture again, inviting her to go on.

One of the small dark stones, the island people, comes down to the shore. Finds the stranger. Is confused, frightened. The creature—I think of her as the Storyteller—reflects this on her face as she makes the small one move around the fallen one, occasionally touching, perhaps kicking or prodding. Then she looks across at me and mimes something she cannot show with the stones, using her hands instead: she points to the small one and the stranger, then makes a hard fist with one hand and brings it down with some violence on the other, stopping just before she does herself an injury. She makes the stranger float out to sea, carried by the waves. Away, away. *Dead.*

What comes next is a catastrophe. The Storyteller's hands are deft, moving here and there. She shows a terrible punishment falling on the island people for the killing of this stranger washed up helpless on their shore. First, she uses both hands to mimic a great bird flying over the island, a creature that dwarfs the small folk below. The Storyteller's face, which itself has something of a bird about it, and something of an earth-dwelling creature such as a mole or rat, and something of a human woman, conveys anger and grief and loss. The passage of the great bird leaves the island folk in chaos, the stones lying everywhere in a jumble. The Storyteller indicates them, then shows with her hands that they rise and fly off all together. Away, away. No cause for joy; her face shows this is a great sorrow, a loss, a waste. She tips the scattered stones off the rock and sets them aside in a heap. *Gone.*

Gone where? I spread my hands, shrug my shoulders, raise my brows in question. I want to ask if she is one of those folk, but I cannot think how to show it.

The Storyteller rises to her feet. She is taller than I thought, but under the enveloping feather garment her form seems thin, delicate. Bird-like. But not a bird. Oh, gods. Is she telling me . . . ?

The Storyteller lifts a hand, indicating the tall pines of the forest around us. I look up. Every branch is crowded with Crow Folk. They perch close to one another as if seeking comfort. They watch us, silent.

It's easy enough, then, to ask a question. I motion to her heap of dark stones. I motion up toward the Crow Folk. I point to her.

She bows her head in acknowledgment. Lays a clawed hand over her heart, then gestures toward her little cave, her safe place among strangers. She lifts both hands up toward the dark trees and their silent inhabitants, almost as if to embrace them. *Mine. My people.* Then points with startling ferocity toward the clearing. She crosses her arms, palms outward. *No. They must keep away. They must leave us alone.*

So much for helping Mother Ash. She wants me to rid her clan of the creature. The creature wants to stay. She has some kind of duty toward the Crow Folk. Exactly what that might be, I have no idea. Is her presence somehow keeping those wild beings safe? Mother Ash said, *She watches them, like a guard.* To me, the Storyteller seems powerful but benign. Fixed on her own purpose, whatever that may be. Is it her presence that attracts so many Crow Folk here? That would be fair grounds for Robin's clan to want her gone, and the birds with her.

I must consider this. I must try to work it out. Sometime, if—*when*—I return to my own world, there will be quite a story to tell. Often, I have wondered if the whole thing is a mad dream: the attack in the forest, a fall to some evil underground place, Robin's folk rescuing me and bringing me here, Mother Ash, the Storyteller, the Crow Folk . . . But what about Galen? I heard him shout. I saw him fighting for his life. That part was real. And I still don't know if he's alive or dead.

I rise to my feet, wobbling as pain lances through my ankle. I'm not as well recovered as I thought. I stand on one foot and bend to pick up my stick; the Storyteller is quicker than I, and puts it in my hand.

"Thank you," I say aloud, then incline my head in respect. "I will speak to Mother Ash." *If she lets me back in.* I cannot use both hands to gesture; if I let go of the stick I will fall. Mother Ash will not be pleased with me, after her hard work.

The Storyteller returns the courtesy, dipping her head in turn.

"Farewell now." I look up toward the trees. I offer the Crow Folk the same little bow of recognition. Maybe I'm mad. With Crow Folk, you can never be sure if they'll ignore you or swoop down and slash your eyes out. But . . . the Storyteller is here, and they are calm. Calm, attentive, somber. Waiting. But for what? I turn and make my way back toward the clearing. At the point where I judge the wall to be, I put a hand out in front of me and slow my pace. But this time it's different. This time I walk straight through.

21
DAU

I've made a strategic error, and it may come back to bite me. With Seanan in Elderbrook and involved in this brotherhood, I can't risk staying around long enough to collect my goods from the saddler's workshop. I should have told the man straightaway that I wasn't Master Sealbhach, only a lookalike kinsman. But then we wouldn't have gleaned the valuable information about Mistress Sciath's men. So what now? I must at least obtain the material for the book cover, and Master Ferchar will think it odd if Garbh doesn't collect his belt. A pox on this. I want to stay another day in Elderbrook. I want to find out what Seanan's up to. But I can't risk meeting him face-to-face. Mistress Sciath's plot looms large in my mind. Though I hate to say it, Prince Aolu's strange disappearance seems less important. I'm tempted to break the rules and mention him to Lady Almha when I get back, quite casually. *Have you heard the rumors that the prince of Dalriada has vanished, perhaps been taken for ransom? Who would do such a thing?* As the son of a chieftain, I might well know of this. But undercover is undercover, even when a man's acting as himself. It's fine for the lady to know I'm Lord Scannal's son. She mustn't know I'm a Swan Island man.

"I could stay one more day," Garbh suggests as we sit in our chamber at the Elderbrook inn, talking in lowered voices. "Long enough to pick up the things from the saddler's and find the safe house, since we didn't manage to do that today. Then back the next morning. And you head off first thing tomorrow. Easy enough to make up an excuse."

"What if Seanan's been at the saddler's? What if he's heard how someone came in impersonating him, and someone who isn't part of the brotherhood purchased one of the special belts? You'd be a target, too."

"You said before that your brother wasn't much of a fighter."

"He's not. But he's cunning. And he hates losing. If the rest of them turn up you might be one against twenty."

"What's the alternative? If I don't stay to collect the goods we have to make a return trip. And didn't you say the lady would want to come with us then? That's something to be avoided. Unless you're tempted by her little smiles and sideways looks."

"All this must have addled your brain, friend." He has a point, sadly.

"You must have seen it. She fancies you, Dau. And I bet it's for more than a quick roll in the hay. Lady Almha's young. She could marry again. You're eligible; she doesn't know you'll never be chieftain of Oakhill, unless you told her you'd refused your father's offer."

"I said my father and I were estranged and that I no longer lived there." He must be wrong. Lady Almha viewing me as a prospective husband? Surely not. But . . . she's certainly shared a lot of confidences with me. She's put a remarkable degree of trust in me. If our positions were reversed, I'd be far more cautious.

"Probably thinks she could talk you back into it," Garbh

says. "Or that your father could. There'd be enormous strategic advantage to both chieftains in such a pairing. Especially if Mistress Sciath's grand plan succeeds."

"You're crazy," I say, but his theory is uncomfortably convincing. And deeply unsettling. If Garbh is right, I could make use of the situation. Coax even greater confidences from the lady. Would I lie with a woman if it was key to achieving my mission? The idea appalls me. "Morrigan's curse, Garbh," I murmur. "I may not have a high opinion of my father, but I know he'd never agree to be tied to such a mad venture. If Mistress Sciath managed to make it work, and if Father refused to be part of it, Oakhill could well be the first target of Lady Almha's Crow Folk army. That makes strategic sense, if the word *sense* could be applied to such a plan." Dagda's bollocks! I can even see where Seanan fits into the scheme. He's one of Mistress Sciath's men. Most likely a leader among the brotherhood, by virtue of his noble birth. He'd love the plan. He delights in playing cruel games, in manipulating folk, in using fear to exert control, whether it's over Crow Folk or men and women. For Seanan, this endeavor could provide a path back to power and status. I know him well. I know exactly why he's here.

"All right, we'll go with your idea, Garbh. I leave in the morning, you collect the goods from Master Ferchar tomorrow afternoon, stay one more night, then follow me back. Keep your head down as much as you can. Don't spend too long looking for the safe house or you might draw the wrong sort of attention to the folk there as well as to yourself. At least Seanan doesn't know you by sight. And how likely is it that you and he will both visit the saddler's workshop at the same time? Still, have a story ready just in case."

"You were embarrassed when he thought you were Master Sealbhach, and it felt too awkward to put him right? And if Seanan challenges me, I tell him I met Mistress Sciath on her travels, I did her a favor, and she offered me a place in the team. And I hope he doesn't ask me a lot of questions or decide to ride back to Darkwater with me." When I make no comment, he adds with a smile, "I'll try my best not to walk into the man, Dau. Trust me, will you?"

"I do. But you don't know my brother. He's a vile apology for a human being, Garbh, and he'll stop at nothing to torment me and mine."

"This may not be as bad as you think. If Mistress Sciath can't find Brocc—and if he's in the Otherworld, how could she?—she's got no way of controlling the Crow Folk, unless she can find some other bard out there with the same sort of gift. So this remains what it is, a scheme, a plan, highly unlikely ever to come to fruition. We'll report it to the elders, of course. King Oran and the leaders in Tirconnell and Ulaid would need to be informed. Your father, too. But unless we find some sign that Aolu has been brought to Darkwater, we're surely best to get out of here promptly and with as little fuss as possible. If there's no message for us at the safe house, we should ride back to Winterfalls and report in."

His suggestion is entirely sensible. Why, then, do I have the skin-prickling sensation of something not right? Why do I want to go back up into that forest and take a better look around? With Seanan in the area, that would be like sticking my head in a noose.

I arrive back at Lady Almha's residence at dusk next day, tired and travel-stained, but with certain awkward topics of conversation to raise. I take supper with the household, avoiding the clear though unspoken invitation to sit at the lady's right hand and instead seating myself between Master Suibne and one of Lady Almha's attendants. I chat to Suibne about the little book, letting him know the leather will be coming in a day or so, and asking questions about the method of binding and how long it will take—oddly, I find I would like the book to be finished so I can take it home as a gift for Liobhan, even if all it does is make her laugh. I do not want to waste this kind person's time and skill on a project that was never genuine. Suibne says the binding takes some while because of the need for glue to dry fully, not to speak of the rather painstaking work of tooling the cover. But there's preliminary work that can be done with the pages and the boards before we have the leather; he can start on that tomorrow.

Almha's attendant knows I'm just back from Elderbrook and asks me, joking, whether I spotted the dobhar-chú. I turn the conversation to possible illustrations for my little book, and whether she thinks otter-dog or serpent-dog would look better. Suibne is drawn into this discussion and offers to ornament my work with one or two small pictures. For a little while the situation feels almost normal, though I wish Garbh were here. He's big and capable, he can look after himself, I know it. But he's too close to that forest and that hideout. He's too close to Seanan, and it sets unease in my bones.

There's no music or dancing tonight. When supper is over, Lady Almha invites me to sit by the fire awhile and take a cup of spiced mead. Others who have lingered soon disperse, leaving only the two of us and her most senior attendant, who seats herself at a distance—out of earshot, I judge—and works on some embroidery. I wait for Almha to start the conversation.

"You returned without your man," she says, surprising me.

"Garbh has remained behind to collect the completed work from Master Ferchar and bring it here. It didn't suit me to stay a second night at Elderbrook. The inn is . . . satisfactory. But I found myself longing for my comfortable bed here, Lady Almha."

"Almha, please." She glances at her attendant, whose gaze does not rise from her work. "Let us not be formal, Dau. Were you impressed by Master Ferchar's work?"

"Oh, very much so. A fine tradesman. But . . . there was a little awkwardness, largely of my own doing. I have a question to ask you. I hope you won't be offended."

She waits, brows raised, not quite smiling.

"When we first arrived here, when you first saw me, Almha, I think you mistook me for another man, one you were far from delighted to see in your hall. At the time I mentioned my brothers, but we dismissed the possibility that you might have met either. Will you tell me whom it was you mistook me for?"

She looks surprised, but not unduly disturbed. "In appearance, you are very like a certain man of my acquaintance. But now, I am astonished that I made such an error. Your manner is quite different from his."

"Might that man's name be Master Sealbhach?"

Now her lip curls. "I would not address him as Master. But yes, that is his name. One of Sciath's band of . . . helpers. Why do you ask?"

"When I met Master Ferchar, he, too, assumed I was that man. Almha, I believe this Sealbhach must be my eldest brother, Seanan. I will be honest with you. One of the reasons I returned a day early was my very strong wish not to encounter Seanan face-to-face. Our father disinherited him. He was banished from Oakhill. I'm astonished to find him living so close to the family holding. There's very bad blood between us. I never want to see my brother again."

She takes her time to absorb this, regarding me with what looks like genuine concern. "Sciath's men do not enter this house as guests," she says. "Occasionally they provide an escort for her or make arrangements for her longer journeys, so they may enter the grounds, visit the stables, and so on. When it is necessary for them to stay here, they are accommodated in an outbuilding. I should not be surprised that Sealbhach is your brother, since you are so alike. But I am surprised, Dau. I have met him more than once, and have wondered why Sciath retains his services—he seems more quick-witted than some of the others, but his manner sets my teeth on edge. He has altogether too much to say for himself. Disinherited, you say? And now he is working as a . . . a hired man. You would not wish to better his situation? To offer him opportunities?"

"Anything I might have to offer, Seanan would not want. He goes his own way and I go mine."

We sit in silence for a while, drinking our mead, which is more than welcome after my day's ride, and watching the bright play of flames on the hearth. The hall is dimmer now; candles burn here and there, but the corners are shadowy. I wonder how much the lady really knows; how far her understanding stretches. I wish I could give her my honest opinion about Mistress Sciath's plans and the dark prospects they might mean for her own chieftaincy and the territory of Darkwater. But Almha and her adviser are friends. She praised Sciath's wisdom. So I do not take that risk; instead I take another.

"Almha, I heard an odd rumor at the Elderbrook inn. It concerned Aolu, the prince of Dalriada. Have you heard mention of him recently?"

The lady does not appear surprised or concerned. "I know of Prince Aolu, of course. Heir to the Dalriadan throne, only son of King Oran. Why do you ask?"

"I don't know how reliable this is; it was a chance remark by a man at that hostelry, and I did not engage him in conversation. He said something about the prince going missing. There was even a whisper that there might have been foul play."

Her brows go up. "There have been some rumors in the district, yes. How credible they are I don't know. Very worrying for Prince Aolu's family, if this is true. When Sciath returns I will ask if she knows of this. I believe she has been traveling in that general area."

"You're expecting her home soon, then?"

"Quite soon, I hope. I look forward to introducing the two of you."

"I will be most interested to meet her. From what you've told me of Mistress Sciath, I take her to be a person of strong opinions and considerable depth. Note, I do not add *for a woman*."

Almha bursts out laughing, startling her attendant, who was perhaps drowsing over her handiwork. "Well said, my friend! And that, I think, is an excellent note on which to say good night and sweet dreams. I am glad you came back early. I missed you."

"And I you," I lie, taking her hand and lifting it briefly to my lips. Gods, I hate this! As I make my way to my chamber, I wipe my mouth on my sleeve. We'll leave as soon as Garbh gets back. I saw nothing amiss in Almha's response to my mention of Aolu. We're not going to find the prince in Darkwater. We need to take ourselves out of here and back to Winterfalls, so we can tell the elders, and through them King Oran, what Mistress Sciath is up to. And while Lady Almha clearly views me, at the very least, as a trusted friend, her councilor will be quite a different matter. We'll go. Not tomorrow, because Garbh won't be back here until evening. But the next morning, without fail. We won't ride through Elderbrook; that's riskier with every day that goes by. We'll take the track over Blackstone Pass.

22

BROCC

I can't let down my guard for a single moment. I can't think of Niamh, alone among strangers. I can't think of the little clan back in Eirne's realm, shattered by the terrible thing that happened. There's no point in wishing Liobhan or Dau or any of the Swan Island team could come and rescue me. I won't ask for Conmael's help as I did once before, when True was at death's door. When we spoke together, he told me the puzzle of the Crow Folk might be mine to solve. Now is the time to prove that. I will do it on my own, even with Niamh's life in jeopardy and the urge to rush to her rescue strong in me. I must pray with all my strength that the folk who have her will keep her safe. The path I'm walking is perilous. A single misstep will be disaster.

The ride was long; I lost count of the days. We went by narrow paths through forests, by farm tracks, our route clearly chosen to keep us away from folk's eyes. Our overnight stops were with householders who knew Ruairi or Scoithín, and who provided food and a roof over our heads without asking any questions and, indeed, without saying much at all. I assume payment changed hands.

I expected eventually to reach the home of Lady Almha of Darkwater, the chieftain on whose behalf Mistress Sciath hopes to enact her monstrous plan. Instead Sciath and her two men have brought me through deep forest to a deserted camp. The last part of the journey was on foot. Our horses were left at an isolated dwelling on the edge of this forest. A silent man opened a gate for them, nodded at Ruairi, accepted a bag of coin.

The woods in these parts are full of Crow Folk. It's plain Sciath expects me to start working on her grand endeavor straightaway. Does she know Shadow has been following us? I was torn when I saw him. I thought he had left me. I wanted him to go, to fly away from danger. But I need him. He is my link to the others. My only link, now Watcher is gone. My voice might calm the rest of them, up to a point. I might persuade them to wait. But I cannot communicate with them as I do with Shadow. It is only through him that my true intention can be realized, the fulfillment of a plan that twists Sciath's scheme into something quite different. I doubt my ability to convey the complexity of what we must do, even to Shadow.

Sciath saw me with him in the woods, of course, before she brought me and Niamh to shelter. She knows we have a bond. But the light was not good, and perhaps she did not notice his scars. I doubt she could distinguish him from any other of the Crow Folk. Safer for him if she has no idea of his importance. On the long ride here she peppered me with questions. I gave bland answers, revealing as little as I could. Her presence exhausts me. It leaves me with nothing to give. And to achieve the task, I must give all I have in me.

Now she sees us settled in the somewhat basic quarters of the camp, where a lanky, silent man named Muna is waiting to let us in. The place has been recently stocked with food and fuel, enough to last us a good while. Sciath tells us she will return to Lady Almha's residence to report to her chieftain. She warns Ruairi and Scoithín, not for the first time, that if I escape their custody there will be dire punishment. Then she leaves, taking Muna with her.

As we unpack what little we brought with us, Scoithín explains that it's a full day's ride to the chieftain's establishment; Mistress Sciath will need to stop somewhere overnight and head on tomorrow. I ask about the horses. It's a fair walk back to the place where we left them. But it seems Mistress Sciath will obtain a fresh horse for the ride and have the others brought back when they're needed.

Of the two guards Scoithín is the more approachable. But I trust neither man. They are armed; I am not. Both are considerably bigger than I. I may be Swan Island trained, but my combat skills are rusty. I might prevail against one of them. But the two together? Hardly. On the other hand, I'm pretty sure I could outrun them. And once in the forest I could quickly lose them.

In the course of general conversation I learn that there's a settlement not far off, but that the folk from Elderbrook don't often venture up this far. Grazing fields extend from the foot of these wooded hills to the settlement. We're in the north of Argialla. Dau's father's territory of Oakhill must lie to the south of this chieftain's holding. There are some curious references to the dobhar-chú, with which I'm familiar from old tales. Scoithín shows me, with some pride, the image burned into the wood above the door to this humble dwelling. It's a creature with a dog's head and the tail of a fish, though Scoithín says the dobhar-chú can also be a blend of dog and otter. Either way, he tells me it was seen in these parts in olden times, and warns me to be careful around streams and lakes, of which there are quite a few in the area. Ruairi expects me to greet this with scornful laughter. I can see it in his expression and his folded arms. Instead I congratulate Scoithín on the image, which I am guessing is his work, and tell him I know a song about the dobhar-chú if he'd like to hear it after supper.

"No time for that nonsense," Ruairi grumbles. "You're not here for fun and games."

"Indeed," I say, forcing a smile. "But I can't work with the Crow Folk after dark. I certainly can't do it when I'm tired, and that was a long day in the saddle." Not to speak of the fact that it's getting cold and there's no hearth in this place. There are holes in the thatch; my father would be appalled. I dare not ask about hot water and the means to have a wash. I've already been told that if we want to relieve ourselves we go out under the trees to do it. Which, in my case, means taking one of the guards with me every single time.

They draw lots to decide who's preparing supper, and Scoithín gets the short straw. He builds a fire within a ring of stones, and soon has a pot hanging over it with an unidentifiable mixture bubbling away inside. It smells surprisingly good. The flames' heat gives comfort to my cold, tired body, and the flickering light brings a welcome memory of better times. I imagine myself standing by a fire on Swan Island among my comrades, listening to Archu drumming and Liobhan playing her whistle, a high, pure echo of home. Or I might be basking in the warmth of a fire from long ago, on the modest hearth of my parents at Dreamer's Wood. We'd all be there: Mother telling a story, Father working on one of the tiny creatures he carves, Galen seated beside him watching and learning. Liobhan and I would be waiting for the pauses in the story, so we could sing and play to illustrate. I miss my harp. My fingers ache for the strings. Will I ever play again?

"You look as if you need sleep more than food, Donal," comments Scoithín.

"Food will be welcome. It smells good. You must let me take a turn cooking sometime, Scoithín. It's not one of my special talents, but I can do passably well."

"Mistress Sciath's got other things in mind for you. She wouldn't want you wasting your time cutting up onions and the like." A pause. "Do you really know a song about the dobhar-chú? Did you know they can swallow a man whole?"

"I did not. Remarkable. And people believe they still live around here?"

"I couldn't say."

"Plenty of Crow Folk in these parts, though. That must trouble the local farmers. You're isolated up here. In danger of attack, surely." I'm not sure how far I can push this. Any moment Scoithín will say, *Too many questions*, and shut the whole conversation down.

"They stay clear of us, mostly. This keeps us safe." He indicates his belt buckle, an ornate thing that looks to be made from real silver. I've noticed it before, without looking too closely at the design. Ruairi wears a similar belt.

"May I see?"

Scoithín sets aside his ladle and comes over to show me. His pride in the thing is obvious. "Sign of the brotherhood." He's speaking in a lowered voice now, perhaps afraid of Ruairi's scorn. "Mistress Sciath gives them for outstanding service."

The buckle is beautifully made. I can see it's a dobhar-chú, though this one is a dog and otter combination rather than the fish and dog creature depicted over the door. "That's very fine," I tell him. "Who made it for you, Scoithín?"

"Fellow in Elderbrook made the belt. He gets the buckles from a silversmith in another settlement. Makes them up specially for Mistress Sciath."

And so she wins their loyalty. With fine gifts and a sense

of belonging. The brotherhood. Who knows where these men were before they caught her eye? Who knows what lay behind them when they signed up for this misguided adventure?

"Scoithín." Ruairi's in the doorway of the hut. "You're not here to make friends."

I want to challenge him but I can't. In effect I am a prisoner, even if I did agree to come with Mistress Sciath. Niamh's life depends on my compliance. I make no response to the remark. But after we've eaten our meal and had a basic wash in some water warmed over the fire, I ask Scoithín if he'd like to hear the song about the dobhar-chú, and he nods *yes* before Ruairi can get a word in. Music builds bridges. Some of them stone-strong, some as delicate as a single note from a harp.

We sit by the embers of our cooking fire, with the forest dark and quiet around us save for the faint rush of water from some nearby stream, and I sing the song. In truth, I don't remember it very well, but a bard is always ready for such times. Where there are gaps I improvise. The song tells the tale of a dobhar-chú who grew lonely in his isolated home on the shores of a mountain lake, and crept off in search of company. Most of those he encountered, he ended up eating. Some tasted better than others; the hedgehog hurt his mouth, the eel was tough and chewy, and the snake left him with a sore belly. As he crossed the hills he became more and more aware of his loneliness, and more and more illtempered. At full moon he spent half the night by a stream, howling, only to realize, during a pause to draw breath, that someone else was howling along with him. There on the opposite bank stood another dobhar-chú, a female, her pelt gleaming in the moonlight, her eyes bright as stars.

I give the song a happy ending. He did not eat her; she did

not eat him. It was love at first sight, and they settled down and raised a brood of tiny otter-dogs. The long, lonely time was over.

I've added a catchy refrain of the kind audiences can't help joining in with. *The chú, the chú, the dobhar-chú,* and then some melodic howling accompanied by foot stamping. By the end even Ruairi is singing. It's not the ideal activity for a secret headquarters, if that's what this place is supposed to be, but I'm glad it has left us all in a better mood.

We cover the embers with earth and go inside to sleep. I dream of my daughter lying awake in the unfamiliar house, her wide eyes searching the darkness for signs of home. Where is the mother who was once tender toward her and then turned cold? Where is the father who played his harp to her and sang her to sleep and carried her on his back? Where is Moon-Fleet with her intricate games, and True who cradled her so gently in his great arms, and Rowan who loved her as if she were his own? Where are the dancing small ones who delighted in her presence? *Be strong, Niamh. When all is done, I will come and fetch you home.*

Morning. After breakfast and a cursory wash in cold water, I explain to my guards that I cannot work close to the hut, and I cannot work in the broad cleared patch nearby, a spot used by the brotherhood for combat training when they're here in numbers. When I ask how many make up their group, neither man gives me a real answer.

"Enough," growls Ruairi, who seems averse to any kind of conversation with me.

"Mistress Sciath will be needing a few more," says Scoithín. "She doesn't take just anyone."

"You lost some men?"

"Too many questions!" Ruairi snarls.

"Only two," I point out, "and I asked only out of concern for the welfare of your brotherhood. It seems to me that between the Crow Folk and the dobhar-chú, your training ground is more than a little vulnerable."

"That's why you're here, isn't it? Get the wretched creatures in order, teach them to obey, make good use of them instead of leaving them to rampage everywhere and upset ordinary folk going about their business. So stop poking your nose into what doesn't concern you, and get on with the job she's hired you for." Ruairi stands with hands on hips and legs apart, staring at me in a manner designed to put the fear of many gods into me. Odd how my fear for my daughter has reduced other threats to nothing. These men do not scare me. I have their measure.

"Very well. The job Mistress Sciath has hired me to do requires a natural clearing within the forest. It should be a spot with tall trees close by where Crow Folk can perch high enough to feel safe. Somewhere for me to sit—a fallen tree, some flat stones. It must be a place where I can work uninterrupted for long periods. You need not keep constant guard. I will not attempt to escape. You must know that if I do that, Mistress Sciath has said my daughter will pay the price. I am not so heartless as to put my own welfare above that of my child."

"She's with kindly people," says Scoithín, frowning. "They'll keep her safe."

"Niamh won't be safe until this whole thing is over. Now, will you find me such a place to work in, or shall I seek it out?"

We find it not so very far from the hut. I can hear a waterfall somewhere nearby, and there's a stream running across the clearing, with a small pool among stones. I judge this body of water inadequate for any but a miniature dobhar-chú that might perhaps nibble on a man's toes, should he decide to dip his bare feet in the water. If I get through this, if I survive with my wits intact, I will make a song about that, a silly one for Niamh. I imagine the little ones of the clan jumping about and squealing at this, and I wonder if I will ever see them again.

A brief debate ensues as to how much space I need around me and why the men must stay quiet while I am working. I cannot explain to them. If I attempted an accurate description, the whole thing would sound ridiculous, fanciful, the stuff of dreams. The two men know I will be communicating with the Crow Folk. They know the Crow Folk are to become an army. I hope they understand that such a process must be extremely gradual.

"It may look as if I'm sitting there doing nothing most of the time," I tell them. "But you mustn't interrupt me unless there's real danger. Sometimes I will sing. Crow Folk may fly down close to me. They are not our enemy. So, no setting arrow to bowstring, no throwing of knives, no rushing forward. Do that and you will almost certainly provoke an attack, and you know what damage these creatures can do. You must leave this to me."

Neither looks convinced. I hope Mistress Sciath doesn't bring a lot more men. Not only is there limited space in the hut, but the more of them there are, the less likely I am to have all of them respect my rules. It will be hard enough to do this with Niamh weighing on my mind. It will be harder still with the brotherhood constantly on the edges of my vision, distracting me from the work during the day and asking unwelcome questions by night.

"Go, then," I tell the two of them. "I won't bolt, I promise. If you must, keep watch from a distance, ideally somewhere I can't see you."

"Don't tell us how to do our job," says Ruairi. The two of them go off all the same. I can't see them in their hiding place, but I know they haven't gone far. What I fear most is that they won't be able to distinguish between Crow Folk attacking and Crow Folk flying in to talk to me. The creatures are arriving in numbers now, settling a little awkwardly on the upper branches of the pines, which clearly provide less comfortable perches than oaks do. Is Shadow here?

I seat myself on the stones near the pool. I breathe slowly. It is hard to summon the necessary calm. It is hard to slow my pounding heart, to still my rushing thoughts. So much hangs on this. Almost too much to bear. But I must do it. I close my eyes, and when the time is right, I sing. Three blessings. Three hopes. And the invitation:

> I come in peace
> I come in friendship
> I come in purpose.
> I am here.

I sit in silence, waiting, hoping. My thoughts are on Shadow, his loss, his courage, his unwavering trust in me. What I need to tell him cannot be spoken aloud. From this moment, if he agrees, he will join me on this perilous pathway, and unless we understand each other perfectly we are doomed.

I feel the change; I open my eyes and there he is, perched on a fallen branch some distance away. He is cautious. Aware of my minders' presence, I think. "I am here," I whisper. I clench my fist against my heart, bowing my head. Then I look straight at Shadow. *This is the future I wish for.* In my mind, I show myself singing, and Shadow flying above me, and the rest of the Crow Folk rising from the trees to follow him. They fly a long distance, all the way to the sea and out across the water. I show the sun rising and setting; I show the remote island with its rock shelves and the great bird in the sky above. I show the Crow Folk going home.

I wait, then. Shadow lifts his wings and moves his feet, and I think perhaps he did not see any of that, I think he's about to fly off, but no: he hops down from his perch and comes a little closer, then dips his head briefly in acknowledgment.

I make a new image. Mistress Sciath in her hooded cloak, her face pale and solemn, her eyes full of blazing ambition. *And this is the future she would have me make.* This part is the hardest to convey. I show Mistress Sciath giving me orders; I show the two guards watching. And then . . . oh, this hurts. I show myself surrounded by Crow Folk, gesturing, instructing them. I show Shadow helping me. And then I show a party of riders on a road, a troop of men-at-arms with their leader bearing a flag. Their heads are high, their faces bright with resolve. I show the Crow Folk swooping down, not in a straggling group of three or four, but in serried ranks, fifty, a hundred, more. The men have no time to mount a defense. The thing is over in a flash. The road is dyed scarlet. Corpses of men and horses lie scattered like so many discarded playthings. The attackers fly away, their formation tight and orderly. My last image shows Mistress Sciath beaming with delight as she puts a bag of silver pieces in my hand. I let that picture fade away. My eyes are full of tears. How can I explain about Niamh? But perhaps I need not explain. Shadow saw us at our lowest. When I was in despair, he brought sustenance and hope. In time of greatest need, he was my friend. I think he can guess what Sciath held over me to ensure my compliance.

For some time the two of us are still and silent. I can't be sure he has understood. This could mean freedom for his people. It could spell disaster if anything goes wrong. But I see no other choice. We must do what is right, whatever the risk.

Shadow moves again, one step closer. In my mind, I see a white-faced man with a small child in his arms. Dusk is close; rain is falling. I gaze into my own despairing eyes. The vision slips away and is replaced by another: that same man carrying a tiny, cloth-wrapped body through the forest. I know it for the sad corpse of the young bird I tried to save; the little one cruelly killed on Eirne's orders. I see myself lay my pitiful burden down in a safe place and sing farewell, sweet dreams, swift flight to the Afterlife. As the image fades, I feel tears running down my cheeks. Shadow looks at me as if in query.

I must make another picture. I show him myself in my parents' cottage, with a warm fire on the hearth, a lamp burning, everything bathed in mellow light. Niamh is on my father's knee, held safe by his big hands, her own hands waving in delight as the old dog, Trusty, comes over to lick her foot. My mother is there, stirring porridge on the fire. I am singing a song of love and freedom, my hands nimble on the harp strings as my daughter listens, bright-eyed.

Now a new image: the small, broken creature becomes a bright spirit bird, whole and perfect, flying free in open sky. Below it the ocean sparkles under summer sun; high above it flies the great guardian, watching over the young one. *We are brothers. Brothers in sorrow. Brothers in hope. Let us do this together.*

Shadow gives his special call: the three solemn notes. He

flies up to the pines, where he finds a perch amid his fellows. I wait. I pray. I will Ruairi and Scoithín to stay out of sight. And after some time, Shadow returns. After him—oh, wonder!—come seven others to settle on the ground close to me.

It has begun.

23

LIOBHAN

We reach The Three Pipers just in time to get the horses into shelter before heavy rain blankets the area. Our animals have worked hard today and are overdue for a rest. The facilities are good here; we can be sure they'll be well tended to.

Galen is still with us. He's surprised me. When he first appeared we argued, of course. About his state of health, about the fact that he's dispensed with the bandage even though his wounds aren't fully healed, about the fact that he's not a Swan Island man, so can't simply attach himself to our team without any knowledge of how we work or what rules we follow. Galen disposed of that argument quickly by inquiring whether I'm following those rules right now. I could have refused to let him ride on with us. But I didn't. I did make it clear that our first concern, for now, was Brocc's safety, not Aolu's. I hated saying that. Galen didn't comment. He just shrugged his shoulders and set his jaw, and we all rode on.

We looked out for portals or signs of them. We took forest tracks, mostly. But when those were too slow we took the main road with everybody else, keeping to our cover story. Since there's no disguising the fact that Galen and I are close kin—we look like the brother and sister we are, and we do stand out in a crowd—he's traveling as my kinsman, Ban. Hrothgar and Elka are Torvald and Helga.

Our cover has not been truly tested along the way, but now it must be. I'm the one who steps up to address the host, while Elka stands beside me carrying her bag and mine, and the two men provide a formidable presence behind us.

"Lady Oonagh of Willowvale," I announce. "With my kinsman and our attendants. We require accommodation for a night or two, if you please, and stabling for five horses. Two private chambers adjoining would suit us well." And as the man gawps at me without a word, I add, "I will pay handsomely, provided you can meet our requirements."

"Well now, my lady, I'm sure we can come to an arrangement to suit you." The innkeeper glances at my companions, then clears his throat. "We have a private chamber, just the one. Apart from that it's shared quarters, men in one area, women and children in another. Very clean. Warm bedding. No fleas."

"Only one private chamber in an establishment this size?" I cast a haughty look around the entrance hall, which, by standards of wayside inns, is solid and well-kept.

"There are two, but the other's occupied, my lady. That party will be moving on tomorrow, so it's yours from then, if you can manage with the one room tonight."

That's inconvenient, but at least Elka and I can sleep behind a closed door. And if Illann's here, the men may find it easier to talk to him if they're all in the same quarters, provided they can get away from listening ears.

"Very well, I suppose that will have to do. I'll want hot water for bathing, and a good supper. And I'm cold. I hope the sleeping quarters are not drafty."

The innkeeper has recovered himself a little, though the

intimidating presence of Hrothgar and Galen is plainly making him uneasy. "I trust you'll find it warm and comfortable, my lady. A good bed for you, a pallet for your maid here." He glances at Elka with cautious admiration. Even after a long, uncomfortable ride, she manages to look quite fetching with her golden hair braided up and her cheeks pink from the cold.

Some while later, after a welcome wash and change of clothing, Elka and I go to the communal area where folk take food and drink and catch up with the news of the road. This inn serves travelers heading through Hunter's Glen into northern Argialla. Galen and Hrothgar are seated among others at a long table. We spot Illann near the hearth fire drinking ale and giving the occasional nod as some fellow tells a tale. He spares us a brief glance, then turns back to his companions. I realize there's one thing I haven't thought out properly. I'll have to tell Illann everything. He'll take the news about Brocc seriously, I'm sure. But this will mean I have to confess that I deliberately withheld information from the elders. To make matters worse, I drew two of my comrades into a mission of my own making. I feel queasy at the prospect.

Elka and I attract more attention than I'm quite happy with. We've changed into our spare gowns and tidied ourselves up, and what with my height and red hair and her undeniable charms, it's perhaps not surprising quite a few of the men try to engage us in conversation. The evening then becomes a balancing act; the need to play a part is at war with the natural instinct to retaliate when they overstep the mark. Elka's the victim of this more often than I am, since she's here as a maidservant, while as Lady Oonagh I can make use of a quelling gaze and the occasional sharp comment. To tell the truth, I'd rather be up on that little platform with my whistle, playing tunes and singing songs. If I have to go undercover, I'd far rather do it as a bard.

Galen looks remarkably relaxed, conversing with the men sitting near him, and later proposing a game to be played on the tabletop with the colored stones he happens to have in his pouch. It's no surprise to me that he would bring them on a venture like this. Those playing pieces have long been a prized possession. At home he spends hours inventing games. I sit quietly beside Elka, hoping this activity does not provoke any disputes. Galen tells the other men there won't be any wagers—wise of him—since some of them will be learning the rules as they play. It's no game I've ever heard of. There's an intriguing mix of moves based on a strategic conflict, with attack and defense, small teams held in reserve to be deployed as required, and a treasure to be guarded by one team while the other attempts to seize it. Playing in teams rather than as individuals means everyone at the table can be part of it if they wish. I restrain myself from joining in. Sometime, if things go back to anything resembling the way they were, I'll ask Galen to teach me. If they throw me out of the Swan Island team I'll have time for that kind of thing. Considering his distress over Aolu, my brother's doing a remarkable job of joking and laughing and being kind to those who are struggling with the game's complexity. He'd make a good spy. The scars on his brow and ear attracted a few comments earlier. He explained that he'd had an argument with a stable door.

Later, after Elka and I have retired to our chamber, leaving Galen and his new friends still arguing amicably over their moves, Hrothgar taps quietly on our door. I let him in and close the door behind him. Nobody in the hallway.

"Illann will talk to us all in the morning," he says in a murmur. "He's been here since yesterday, had a good look around and listened out for anything useful. No word of Dau and Garbh. They must be still in Darkwater, at the chieftain's house. Possibly can't get messages out. We'll need to make contact somehow."

"Did you tell Illann about Brocc? About what we're doing?"

Hrothgar's mouth twists. "I'm leaving that to you. Just told him we've come as the backup team. He didn't ask about Galen."

"He doesn't know Galen. As far as Illann's concerned, that's just some local man who likes games."

"He says we'll make plans tomorrow. We'll meet out near the stables before breakfast." He lowers his voice still further. "About Elderbrook. There's some talk, apparently."

"What sort of talk?"

"Something going on in the forest nearby. Nobody's quite sure what, or they're not prepared to say. Word's got about that someone powerful doesn't want ordinary folk going up there. Certain men come in and out of the settlement for supplies, but they don't mingle much. Also, there are Crow Folk in that forest. More of them all the time. Which means people are happy to keep away."

I swear under my breath.

"So, we go there?" Elka has been listening intently, making sure she follows every word.

"Tomorrow, I hope. Hrothgar? Make sure Galen doesn't rush off on his own, will you? No solo quests. Tell him to wait for this meeting."

"Yes, my lady." Hrothgar gives me a wicked grin, wishes us sweet dreams, and goes quietly out.

I don't sleep well. When I do drift off, my dreams are a splintered mixture of Crow Folk and dobhar-chú and screaming victims, along with images of myself getting things terribly wrong. A lake with surging water, a glimpse of many teeth, claws slashing as Brocc yells, *Attack!* A tree that looks like an old woman, or an old woman who looks uncannily like a tree. She's beckoning. I see Galen running. I shout, *Stop!* But he doesn't hear me, and in an instant he's gone.

"Bad dream, Liobhan?" That's a real voice, Elka's, and I sit up, shivering, to see her crouched beside my bed, her face illuminated only by a narrow strip of moonlight between the shutters. In this light her hair is silver-bright. She looks like something from an ancient tale.

"Mm." I reach for my shawl and sling it around my shoulders. "Too much to think about. Sorry if I woke you."

"No matter, I am awake, too. Think of tomorrow, what to do."

"Some of us need to meet up with Dau and Garbh. And we should investigate those woods near Elderbrook. The ones that are full of Crow Folk. Galen will want to keep looking for Aolu, though I can't think why he'd be in these parts. And Illann may want the same, since that's the mission we've all been sent out for. This is messy, Elka."

"Messy?"

"Untidy. Disorganized. Not well planned."

"Don't they say, a Swan Island warrior can make impossible happen? Five of us here. Then Dau and Garbh, is seven. Can go . . ." She makes a gesture, hands flat, fingers stretched apart, moving forward.

"Can go several ways at once. Maybe even attempt two missions at the same time. True. And we'll need to. I think the chieftain's house, where Dau and Garbh are, is quite a distance from Elderbrook. Besides, the more we all stay together, the likelier we are to attract attention." It's hard to think ahead when so much is uncertain. Illann may well expect us to comply with whatever plan he comes up with, and that might include dispatching me straight home as soon as I tell him what I've done. But he didn't see that vision of Brocc. He didn't see the haunted look on my brother's face, the look that visits me over and over in my dreams. "Did you pack something you can wear if we need to be invisible in this forest?" I ask, trying to banish that image from my mind. "Something you can move freely about in?"

"Same trousers as for riding. Tunic, green like leaves. You?"

"I have clothes that will do. But we can't track in our cloaks. So, no hoods." Elka's hair is the most visible thing in this dimly lit room; it seems to gather the moonlight. In the forest it will stand out, and so will my bright red-gold locks, even tightly plaited. "I should have dyed my hair."

"Scarf for hair," Elka says. "Brown, green. I bring two." She fingers the bedcover, whose color is indeterminate in the dim light. "You?"

"I have a felt hat, close-fitting. Hope it stays on." I wonder what Dau would think if he saw me with dark brown hair, or maybe a short crop. Gods, there really will be seven of us. Together, we would certainly draw the eye. Most of us are unusually tall, strong-looking individuals. Elka is striking in her own way. The only one who blends easily is Illann. "Now we'd better try to get back to sleep. We should sing a lullaby. But on second thought, no. That might wake all the other guests in this place, even from behind a closed door. I wish I could play my whistle. I did bring it."

"I tell a story, if you like to hear."

"Could you tell that one about the eagle spirit again?"

So she does, in a voice just over a whisper, and quite eerie it sounds in the quiet room, with only that sliver of cool light in the darkness. Toward the end I can tell Elka is falling asleep, as the pauses grow longer and longer. As soon as she's told the part about the Crow Folk flying from place to place and never finding rest—I'm convinced now that this is their story—she falls silent. I think of the cavern on Swan Island, and the awful prediction of that vision in the water.

I dream, not of my brother commanding the Crow Folk to ruthless, bloody violence, but of a different end to the story: a high, clear call, and the dark birds rising from the clifftops to fly away northward over the ocean, winging a pathway home.

24
DAU

Master Suibne expresses delight that the leather will be here later today, and says he will start work tomorrow on the cover for my little book. I feel both sad and somewhat guilty; Garbh and I will be gone before the thing can be finished, and the scribe has already trimmed and stitched the pages and prepared the supporting boards. Partly in order to stay out of Lady Almha's way, I spend much of the morning watching him work and chatting about one thing or another. I ask for his opinion on the Crow Folk—what are they, where do they come from, why are they here?—and he gives the considered responses one might expect from a man who loves to read. Are the creatures uncanny? Perhaps. Are they violent in their very nature? In their deeds, certainly. But there can be many reasons for a person, or a creature, to strike out at others. Fear. Confusion. The demons of the past. It's all too easy to apply that theory to me and Seanan.

At a certain point I leave Suibne to work undisturbed and head for the stables to check on my horse—unnecessary, really, as I know she is being well looked after, but I'm restless, and I want nothing to impede a prompt departure tomorrow. The last thing I want is to be here when Mistress Sciath arrives, perhaps accompanied by my brother. I know Garbh can't be back before this evening, but the wait feels endless. I go for a walk around the grazing fields in hopes of calming myself. I make up possible excuses for our sudden decision to leave. It will have to be some news brought by Garbh that makes it imperative for me to go home immediately. But the more I think, the more I realize that I'll be asking too much of my comrade. After a full day's ride today, neither he nor his horse will be ready to head off again in the morning. And if we're not planning to come back, he can't leave his horse here and take one of Almha's in its place. One more day, then. And pray to those gods I don't believe in that if Mistress Sciath returns before then, she doesn't bring Seanan with her.

The foolish part of me, the part that thinks of Liobhan all too often, wishes one more day were long enough for Master Suibne to finish binding my book of tales.

Dusk is falling when Garbh rides in. I've been watching out for him, and after he's taken his weary horse to the stables we go to the bathhouse together and are lucky enough to be the only occupants. As we wash, we talk in lowered voices, alert to the possibility someone may walk in.

"Bad news, Dau. I didn't get to the safe house. I've collected the goods from Master Ferchar, but I spotted your brother out and about with some other men, so I stayed out of sight for the rest of the day. Couldn't pass on a message, couldn't get one in return."

A pox on Seanan. "Any sign of Mistress Sciath? The lady's expecting her back here soon. I imagine they may come through Elderbrook."

"I didn't spot such a party in the area. But when I collected the goods Master Ferchar said he supposed you and I would be pretty busy soon, what with all that was going on. I said *yes, maybe*, or some such. Admired the belt, thanked him on

my behalf and yours, and got out of there as quick as I could."
He steps out of the shallow tub and wraps the drying cloth
around his body. "Gods, that's better. Got aches and pains all
over. Long ride."

"Rest day tomorrow. We'll head off the next morning toward Blackstone Pass. King Oran needs to know what Mistress Sciath's up to."

There's silence for a little. I dry myself while Garbh tips
the bathwater out into the drain. As I'm getting back into my
clothes he says, "Sciath and her fellows went off searching
for Brocc, didn't they? They might be coming back because
they've found him."

"Shit, Garbh. You'd better be wrong. It's hardly likely,
considering where he is."

"I hope I am wrong, since that man's Liobhan's brother
and a friend to Swan Island."

"Sciath can't ride around endlessly. She's answerable to
the lady here; she'd need to report back." A councilor is answerable to her chieftain, yes. But what happens when the
councilor has grown so high in the chieftain's trust, and has
influenced her so greatly over the years, that she who was a
servant is now in effect the master? I ponder this as we return
to our quarters. If it came to a disagreement over the plan,
would Almha stand up to Mistress Sciath? Forbid her to go
on with it? Somehow I doubt that. And I wonder what Mistress Sciath will have to say if and when she learns how much
her mistress has revealed to me.

"We pack up quietly tomorrow night and leave as early as
we reasonably can next morning," I tell Garbh. "I'll find an
excuse. But no word of it until then. Act as if we're staying
on awhile longer."

"I hope there's no dancing tonight. I'd fall asleep on my
feet."

I deliver the leather for the book cover to Master Suibne, who exclaims over the quality and says he may make a start on the work tonight. I'm impressed by his enthusiasm.

Garbh nods through supper, too tired to eat much although he must be hungry. I excuse him from duty and send him off to his bed. And when Lady Almha suggests she and I might sit and chat over some mead again, I apologize politely and tell her I am too tired to be a good companion. She suggests a ride tomorrow; I feel obliged to say yes, since no excuse comes readily to me. I can hardly tell her I would rather sit in Master Suibne's workroom and watch him at his mysterious and exacting craft. The look in her eyes makes me glad I am not staying longer. If she seriously views me as a potential lover or, gods forbid, a prospective husband, it would be a most unwelcome complication. One I'm relieved I need not prepare for. I retire to my quarters, where Garbh is sunk so deep in sleep he doesn't so much as twitch when I come in. I doubt I will sleep so well.

25

AOLU

When I am finally released from this place—a benign sort of prison, but a prison nonetheless—what will I have learned? To be more patient, certainly. And I have a new insight into what it means to be a prince. I have not charged to the rescue like some hero of old. I do not blame my injury for that; even at my best, I am no fighter. I've made no rousing speeches, nor have I gathered these small folk together to drive out the threat. But I have done what I see my father doing when, as king, he presides over councils and resolves disputes. He is calm and wise. When folk talk, he listens. When the situation requires it, he exerts his authority. He keeps a balance. He keeps the peace. That does not mean laying down the law, though reminding folk of the law may, at times, be useful. My father helps his people find a path through disagreements and challenges. So, in my lesser way, do I, when I hold my councils for the landholders and other folk in the Winterfalls community.

Maybe Robin and Thorny and the others believed I would be a hero of that other kind, a man of swift action. Maybe Mother Ash expected me to wield a sword, or use magic, or believed my very presence would send their unwelcome guests cowering away. Instead, I called a different sort of council, asking Robin to bring the small ones, along with Mother Ash, to meet me outside my little hut in the clearing.

"You should let this being stay," I told them. "She's waiting for something. She needs a safe place. I do not believe she means you harm."

"Waiting," says Robin. "For what, Prince?"

"That, I can't tell you. I hope to speak to her further—I can do so only in signs, and it is slow. But I don't think you need fear her. She is a wisewoman, like Mother Ash. Concerned only for the welfare of her people."

There's a weighty silence. Then Thorny pipes up with the inevitable, "What people?"

Before I can find the right way to break it to them, Hazel points to the pines with their rows of silent Crow Folk, and there's a babble of protest from many voices.

"Hush," says Mother Ash. "This is not the prince's fault."

"But he was meant to—"

"But he should have—"

"Crow Folk killed Buttercup! They killed Catkin! They tore Conker limb from limb!" This from Robin. "*She* may mean us no harm, Prince, but what about *them?*"

Draw a deep breath, Aolu. Straighten your shoulders. Be like your father. "I know the Crow Folk can be cruel. But . . . how long is it since these deaths occurred?"

"None in these parts since autumn," says Mother Ash. "But the creatures are not to be trusted. They strike without warning and without cause."

I think of the tale the Storyteller told me with her stones and wonder if my interpretation was correct. That story had no *what next*. The island folk flew away, that was all. Where did they go? Did they find a home? Did they find forgiveness for that act of violence? And should I tell the tale now? Perhaps it is not mine to tell.

"When folk act wildly," I say, "there is always a reason for it. Yes, even with the Crow Folk. This being, the Storyteller"— I make it a title, a name, for surely she deserves that—"is waiting, and the Crow Folk are waiting, and we must wait, too. Sing your little ones to sleep with sweet songs; lie beside them if you will, be there to frighten off bad dreams. Be kind to one another; help one another every day. Remember the times of joy. This will pass. I believe it." I'm suddenly, inexplicably choked by tears. So much for the calm, wise prince. "I—" I put my hands over my face.

There's a sudden hush. Then someone is hugging my leg, and someone else is weeping, and I take away my hands to see Mother Ash proffering a handkerchief. "Sit down, Prince. Rest that ankle, wipe your eyes, and tell us your own story, if you will. What brings these tears?"

So I tell them. "A long while ago, when I was younger, a boy called Galen came to live in my house . . . He had the reddest hair and the cheekiest grin you ever saw . . ."

26

BROCC

Brothers in hope. I must remember that message, even when despair comes close to drowning me in its shadowy waters. Even when my mind fills with images of all I have left behind: Niamh, so small, so perfect, with her trusting gaze and her delight at the marvel of a speckled leaf, a scurrying beetle, a dew-brightened spiderweb; my brothers back in Breifne, sturdy, kindly True and quick-witted, faithful Rowan; my family at Winterfalls; my warrior sister on Swan Island; my harp, my music, my soul . . . I cannot say that. A bard's soul is in everything he sees and hears. It is in the spreading oaks and the darting insects, the gleaming surface of the pond by moonlight, the deep darkness of the cave, the great arch of the sky. It is in the high, clear song of the lark, the drumroll of thunder, the crash of ocean waves. It is in our bonds with those we love, and it is also in our fear and disquiet and anguish, for music does not tell only of sunny days and laughter, of joy and contentment. The beat of the drum can be a call to battle, the pipes a stirring reminder of loyalty to king or clan. The whistle may keen of sorrow one day, and the next day set feet tapping in a jig. Brothers in hope. Hope of a brighter future. Hope of liberation, hope of freedom. We can do this, if only she gives me time.

So far, only the two familiar guards have remained. Once a man came in with supplies, but after a word or two with Ruairi he left, looking keen to get out of the place. There are many of Shadow's folk here now. With each day more of them join us in the meeting place, down on the rocks or perched on the limbs of the surrounding trees. I cannot communicate directly with any but Shadow, but it does seem he can pass on my thoughts to many of them, and theirs to me. I have learned a bitter story of error and loss. I have learned how one wrongful death led Shadow's clan onto a track of terror and violence, and how their guardian spirit, in banishing them from their island, herself entered a form of exile, for if I understood correctly, she broke in pieces and was swallowed up by earth, sea, and sky.

That story is lodged in the heart of every one of them. To win back her protection, to open the pathway home, they must prove themselves worthy. They must show they are ready to return. Yet what Mistress Sciath wants me to do, what she believes I am doing right now, would not prepare them for that. It would do quite the opposite.

Today I have called Shadow with the customary greetings, and he is here, close by me. His scars show less starkly now; feathers will not grow back over the places where Seanan burned him, but his plumage is glossy in the morning sun and his eyes are bright. Around us the clearing is full of Crow Folk, silent, watching.

She will come back. I show Shadow an image of Mistress Sciath standing beside me, hands on hips, gaze sweeping around the clearing. *She will want me to show what you have learned. A demonstration.* This is hard to illustrate. I do my best, showing myself standing alone in the middle of the clearing, eyes closed, arms outstretched with palms up—the position I usually take when I call Shadow. Then I show, sudden as lightning, seven or eight Crow Folk swooping down on me, flying in tight formation, so low their talons must surely take out my eyes or rip the flesh from my face. In the image, I do not move. I do not cover my head or throw myself flat or take any evasive action. I wait and they pass, rising to perch in the pines on the far side of the clearing. *Like that,* I tell Shadow. *To show her you can attack. But not a real attack. Because, to go home again, you must show that you can live in peace.*

I wait. Shadow remains still and silent; I know, now, that he is passing on my message to the others, perhaps in some form that is easier for them to understand. Then he gives me a new image: the same attack, only this time one of them flies too low, and I am wounded and fall to the ground with blood streaming from my head. Then men run into the clearing with bows, and arrows fly, and Crow Folk fall from the trees like so many overripe fruit. The image fades.

We will practice. At first with the center empty. Then with a branch. Then with me standing there. I show him the pictures. I don't allow myself to be afraid. *We can do it.*

We work on it. Exactly what Shadow passes on to the others I can't be sure, but most of them retreat, either to the trees or to the undergrowth at the clearing's edges. Seven remain, along with Shadow himself. "Your Swan Island team," I murmur, and I make the warrior's gesture of greeting, fist clenched against my heart, head bowed. When I see them dip their heads in response, tears spring to my eyes.

I convey to Shadow by thought and gesture that we'll start now, with the area empty. As I retreat to the edge I spot Scoithín further back under the trees, watching wide-eyed, and frown at him, a finger to my lips. *Silence.*

The eight rise to perch high in a giant pine on the far side of the clearing. Four on one branch, four on another. They are as disciplined as any team of warriors preparing to charge. I draw a deep breath, waiting, then at some unspoken signal they move, swooping down and over the stones where I was standing not long ago, then up to land above me on this side. Quick as a breath. Silent, save for the whisper of their beating wings.

Shadow makes them do it again, this time a little higher over the stones, and then a third time. After that, he flies down alone and waits in the center. I drag a fallen branch across and jam the limb between the rocks so its needled foliage sticks up to roughly the height of a man standing. Shadow helps me, using his beak to maneuver the thing into place and to make some small adjustments which, when I step back, do cause the branch to assume a vaguely human-like appearance. Once more I retreat to the edge.

They dive again, skimming the standing branch, which shivers at their passing. I do not see a single twig, a single needle drop.

Shadow returns to my side. No choice now; trust earns trust. I walk to the center, extract the branch and lay it flat. I stand in its place and lift my hands as before. I close my eyes. I remind myself to breathe. In my mind, I play the tune I wrote for my daughter: "Flight of the Fair One." I'm on a high note when they pass over me. The hair on my head stirs as if in a strange wind, and between one heartbeat and the next they are away. When I open my eyes, Shadow is still beside me, though the others are settling once more on their high perch. This time they have done it without him.

With song and gestures I thank my friend, and I thank the seven, and I stretch my arms to indicate the whole host of them, watching from the branches above. I bow my head in recognition. This is a great step forward. It is far more than I expected so soon. And it frightens me more than I can put into words. Sciath would be impressed, I am sure of that. And she would realize that achieving her goal might not in fact take the seasons or years I spoke of, but a far shorter time. Shadow's people are new to this way of working. After their long ordeal, their sorrow and loss, and then the years of blood and wildness, they will not so easily fall into a peaceful way of being. Here in the sanctuary of the forest, maybe. But out there in the realm of mankind, where sheep and cattle graze and folk travel the roads, folk who fear and loathe their kind and who may be well armed? Crossing that ground will be quite a test. If it comes too soon, I cannot be sure we will pass it.

I'm tired. I've barely moved, but body and mind feel worn out. I bid Shadow farewell, bowing again and placing a hand over my heart in a gesture of peace. He dips his head, then flies up to join his clan. And I walk back toward the camp, knowing I must sit down or I will fall down. Scoithín steps out from his ineffective hiding place, takes one look at me and puts out a hand in support.

"All right, Donal? Looking a bit pale. Came close, didn't they?"

"Close but not too close. They did as they were asked to. I'm tired, yes. Need to sit down and have something to eat and drink."

"Doesn't look like much. What you do, I mean. But it is, isn't it? Wears you out."

"Mm." I appreciate his concern. But he's one of *her* men, and that means I can't tell him anything. "It tires me. Scoithín, when do you expect Mistress Sciath back?"

"Can't say. Careful, don't trip on those roots. She might be away a while. Has to report to Lady Almha. And it's almost a day's ride each way. But now that you're here, she'll be eager to get back and watch what you're doing."

"She knows it will take a long time. I told her that. She won't be wanting to stay up here at the camp, surely."

Scoithín grins, and for a moment I glimpse a brother, a father, a son. "She doesn't stay up here and she doesn't stay at the inn. Got friends in the neighborhood. Takes a man with her for protection."

"Won't that leave you a bit short here?" It would be an ideal time to quit Elderbrook, if Shadow's people can be ready.

"She'll bring more fellows with her. When she sees what you're doing with the creatures, she'll want a stronger guard set on the place. Five or six at least, maybe more."

That's not good news. The more folk linger around the camp, the edgier the Crow Folk are likely to become and the slower my progress will be. But that's not a matter for Scoithín to deal with. I suspect he's told me more than he was meant to. If necessary I'll have it out with Mistress Sciath. She needs me. Without me, she can't get what she wants. If I say fewer guards, then there will be fewer guards. If I say give me more space, I get more space. Just as long as I don't push things too far.

27

LIOBHAN

We meet in the stable yard behind The Three Pipers, a good excuse having offered itself—Illann, who was a farrier before he joined the Swan Island team, is checking my horse for a possible sore foot and taking his time over it. It's plausible that all of us might be here together, preparing for the next part of the journey. It's early. There's no sign of the grooms employed at the inn, and no travelers coming in or out as yet.

"Four of you," Illann says, keeping his voice down. "I was expecting two."

"About that . . ." I'd better tell him straight out, get it over with. "Brocc's in really bad trouble. At least, I think so. And there's a plot underway, something the king needs to know about. It's like this." I set out the story as concisely as I can, wondering if Illann will order me to go straight back to Swan Island and confess all.

When I'm done, he looks up at me for a while, then murmurs, "Morrigan's curse, Liobhan. You all knew about this? Hrothgar? Elka?"

"Important." Elka speaks up. "I see this vision with Liobhan. It is dark, terrible. We must go."

"And you?" Illann looks at Galen. "What are you doing here?"

"In the absence of anyone else," my brother says, "I'm searching for Aolu. I'm convinced he's been taken beyond the human world. I don't have much to go on but my own instincts, but right now they're pushing me toward Elderbrook. If necessary I'll go on my own."

Illann releases the horse's leg and gets to his feet, giving the animal a reassuring stroke on the flank. "We'll all ride through Hunter's Glen to Elderbrook today. The rumors about that place are enough on their own to require investigation, and Liobhan's story only adds to my suspicions. We'll go to the safe house and get the folk there to send a message to Master Donagan. Tomorrow, two will ride to Darkwater and make contact with Dau and Garbh. They haven't sent any messages out, so we don't know what their situation is, and they need to know what we're doing in the area. Two will stay in Elderbrook to make some inquiries and do a search. We won't ride as a group today. We'd be too conspicuous. We'll split up but stay fairly close."

"Who's going to Darkwater tomorrow?" asks Hrothgar.

Illann looks across the courtyard. Someone's opening doors, coming out with a broom. We must get moving. "We'll make that decision when we reach Elderbrook. It seems we now have two missions, and if I rule out anyone who's personally connected to either, the team will be too small to split up. There are some hard choices ahead. As for you, Galen, you choose your own path. If you stay with us, you play by our rules. And if you get in trouble you're on your own."

"That's harsh," I can't help saying.

"It has to be or he puts us all in danger. Any questions? Keep it brief, folk are moving about the place."

"Who leaves first?" This is from Hrothgar, and it's a good question. Illann's talking sense about splitting up, but we came in as a party of four. If anything's going to be conspicuous, it's Lady Oonagh, her kinsman, and their attendants heading off separately.

"The rest of you ride out of here as a group and I'll follow a distance behind," Illann says, straightening up. "At some point between here and Elderbrook, you split into two pairs. I'll stay in the rear. Once we reach Elderbrook, you might pause at the local inn. Galen, probably best for you to lodge there. I'll give the rest of you directions to the safe house."

I see the wisdom in that, though I know we need to be careful in our use of such friendly households. It's all too easy to bring down trouble for them if we rely too heavily on their support. "Galen needs to be able to contact us, Illann. We're all on the same side."

Illann's mouth twists. "How much training did you go through to join the Swan Island community, Liobhan? Hrothgar?"

"If you want me to leave you now and go my own way, I will," Galen says. "I've no wish to endanger you. But I believe we can help each other."

"Perhaps. Your sister has a reputation for impulsive actions. Thus far they've always turned out to be well judged. One of you in a team might be an asset. Two, I'm not so sure about. Ride out with us if you wish and I suppose we'll find out."

The ride through Hunter's Glen goes smoothly. The place has a deep serenity about it. The river is a ribbon of silver on the valley floor. The forested hills to either side rise to bare rocky tops, where the sun strikes gold and purple from carpets of lichen. I have too much on my mind to give the beauty of it the attention it merits. We ride into the settlement of Elderbrook and draw our mounts to a halt outside the inn. Galen dismounts and leads his horse around the back, looking for the stables.

We've planned this with some care, since we can't all go to the safe house at the same time. Illann's given us all directions. Now he and Elka ride off, leading the packhorse. Hrothgar and I take our horses to the water trough set there for the purpose, wait while they drink, then tie them up in the shade. We head inside for some refreshments; we'll follow the others later.

We're taking our time over a jug of ale in the near-empty dining area when we hear the host welcoming someone at the door. There are several voices and one of them sounds vaguely familiar, though I can't place it. I can hear baggage being brought in, and a discussion about what time they should play tonight, and I remember who that voice belongs to. Someone who'll know me as a lowly bond servant from Dau's family home at Oakhill. A woman who can sing, and who made the error of doing so in full voice when a crowd was singing along with a band.

"What?" asks Hrothgar, seeing something on my face.

"If a man comes to talk to me, I'm not a fine lady." They're heading this way. I speak in a rapid undertone. "I'm a singer. And you're my friend."

"Always," says Hrothgar with a quick smile, and returns his attention to his ale.

They enter the room, three of them, led by a curly-haired man of slender build, whose bright blue eyes and dimpled smile reveal him to be just the person I expected. "Ah!" he exclaims, looking straight in my direction. "I remember you! The girl with the lovely voice, who wouldn't sing with me even when I begged. I trust that's changed. We'll be playing here tonight and tomorrow night, and we'd be most glad if you'd join us." He pauses, perhaps trying to remember my name. I get ready to say no. I can't sing in public in a place where Seanan might turn up. "I'm Cian," says the minstrel. "Not that you'd remember, I suppose. It was some while ago." He seats himself beside me. I tell him I'm Oonagh, and introduce my friend Torvald. The other musicians settle at the far end of the table.

"I don't think I can join you tonight or tomorrow. I'm so sorry." *Think, Liobhan. There's an opportunity in this somewhere.* "I'm rather out of practice, but I'd love an opportunity to sing. Where will you be after Elderbrook?"

"We're sure of a few nights' work further south, either in Darkwater settlement or at the fine house nearby, the chieftain's residence. We're regular visitors there. If you don't mind the ride, why not come with us and stay as long as it suits you? Do I recall correctly that you play the whistle as well?"

"I do, yes." My heart's racing now. Let Illann not say no to this. Let me not have to break the rules again. And let Galen not walk in and ruin everything. "What do you think, Torvald?"

Bless Hrothgar, he doesn't so much as twitch an eyebrow. "Fine with me, if you want to go. I had hoped to stay here a bit longer than that, get some fishing in . . ."

"Oonagh can ride with us," Cian says, exercising his charming smile. If he's recalled that I had a different name at Oakhill, he's keeping it to himself. "Stay on and catch all the fish you want, Torvald, and come to Darkwater in your own time."

"Wonderful," I say, and know I'm beaming. Ridiculous,

under the circumstances. "We're staying elsewhere, but I'll meet you here the day after tomorrow at breakfast time. Tell me what you'll be playing, so I can get some practice in."

It's quite a while before Hrothgar and I go on to the safe house, following the directions Illann gave us. The road to Darkwater settlement branches off to the southeast; we head south through Elderbrook village, which is small. We turn onto a farm track bordered by well-maintained drystone walls. Our pace is easy.

The weather is fair; at last there's a hint of summer in the air. To either side of the track spread grazing fields tenanted by well-fed sheep, many with frisking lambs close by. Copses of elder and willow break up the open ground. Beyond the fields rise forested hills in imposing array, mostly clothed in oaks, with more of a mix higher up. Higher still there's open ground, as in the glen. It's easy enough to see that as a haunt of the dobhar-chú. If I have cause to explore that place, I'll make sure I take something to offer as a gift, even if it's only the last bite of my bread, presented with respect.

The safe house is so well hidden it would be easy to ride right past it. Trees shelter and conceal both dwelling house and outbuildings, and it's not until we're almost there that we see a stable block at the back, a secluded kitchen garden, and a chicken coop in which healthy-looking birds are having a good scratch about. And there's a pigeon loft.

A sturdily built, strong-jawed man comes out to meet us. If he's armed, he has his weapon concealed. But this is no ordinary farmer; I see that in his stance and in his wary eyes. "Ah," he says. "Good day to you. Come in, we were expecting you."

A little later, we're sitting over a hearty meal in the farmhouse with Master Colm and his wife, Morna, a lean, sharp-eyed woman who puts me in mind of a younger Brigid. Illann and Elka are also at the table. Seems they all waited for us before eating. I should apologize for spending so much time talking about which songs might work best with me added to Cian's band, and who should play or sing what. But I'll save that for when I have to tell Illann I'm going to Dark-water.

"Our son and daughter are out working on the farm," Colm says. "You'll see them from time to time. They're part of what we do here, and they won't ask questions. You mentioned rumors, Illann. I should tell you that there's been some odd activity up in the forest, other side of the settlement. It's been going on awhile. If that's your area of investigation you'd be wanting to tread carefully. The spot in question is defended by a group of armed men who haven't made themselves popular in these parts. The locals give it a wide berth, and no wonder."

I know the folk who run our safe houses are trustworthy. But Illann may not want to tell them everything.

"We have a double mission on hand," Illann says, keeping his voice down even in this safest of places. "There's a man missing, a man of high status; he's being sought widely. He may have been abducted. He may have fled and come to grief. Our attention's been drawn to that forested area you mentioned, not only in our search for this man, but for other reasons. We know there's been unusual activity, and not just by Crow Folk. We'll be wanting to take a good look around." He glances at Colm and Morna in turn. "You can trust us to exercise all caution. Covert observation is the extent of it for now, unless our missing man turns up. What we need from you, apart from a safe place to stay, is a rough guide to the terrain in that part of the forest: the paths, the waterways, the clearings, the obstacles. If these people have a base, we need to know all the possible ways in and out of that spot, and which they most commonly use."

"Mm-hm," says Colm. "We can give you most of that information. Big area to cover."

"And full of Crow Folk," I say. "Are they hostile in these parts? Likely to attack us?"

The farmer grimaces. "If you'd asked me that question before autumn turned to winter, I'd have said yes. But the creatures have grown quieter of recent times, even though there are more of them; more every day, it seems. No attacks on travelers. No attacks on stock either. Makes you wonder what the things feed on."

Remembering Elka's tale of the islanders cursed for acts of violence, I feel a chill run through me. Are the Crow Folk holding back, waiting? Trying to prove that they will no longer follow that path? The fate of an entire clan might rest on Brocc's shoulders.

"I have a question," I say. "We know there are tales in the region about strange creatures, not only the Crow Folk, but things like the dobhar-chú. Do you know if those local tales touch on doorways to another world?"

There's silence for a bit, then Morna says, "Folk don't take that sort of talk seriously."

"But there is talk?"

"When the fellows in the settlement have taken too much ale, you do hear about some fisherman spotting the dobhar-chú and being scared out of his wits. Or a woman gathering mushrooms, by mistake setting one foot into a neat little circle of them and feeling a hand fasten around her ankle, though there's no one to be seen. Folk find piles of white stones. Or so they say."

If Galen could hear this he'd be off into the forest like an arrow from the hunter's bow, alight with hope.

"Since we're going to be looking right through the area," Hrothgar says, "it would help to know if there are any particular places to keep an eye out for. I mean, spots where these mysterious occurrences are supposed to have happened."

Our hosts seem unsurprised by this line of discussion. "When I was a lad, growing up in these parts," Colm says, "every second lake was thought to have its dobhar-chú. They're supposed to howl all together, first full moon in springtime. Never heard it, myself. But there were those who swore they did. A sound fit to set a chill in your bones, or so they said."

"But no Crow Folk, back in those days," says Morna. "They came later." She looks down at her hands as if wondering whether to go on. "As for crossing over, my grandmother always said there was a place. But she'd never tell us where it was. I think she was scared we'd go through and never come back out. She used to say that if we went in, the little folk would get us."

I consider this. "When you were a child, Morna, did you and your friends play in the forest? Climb trees, collect acorns, catch tadpoles?"

She grins. "And look for places we'd been told not to seek out? Yes, we did. We thought we'd found it, once. A portal of the kind you mention. Local folk sometimes call that place the Hag of the Hill. It's a rock all overgrown with creeping things, and a tree up above sending bare roots down over it. If you look from a certain direction it does seem like an old woman, and if you look from another you can almost see a crack that a person could slip through. We told one another stories about the terrible things that would happen if we went too close. Frightened ourselves so much we never did try. The Hag's no more real than the dobhar-chú."

Morrigan's britches! Morna may have dismissed it as a portal, but I dreamed of this very place. Galen needs to know about this.

"I suppose you have writing materials here," says Illann. I'm surprised for a moment, until I remember the pigeon loft and the transfer of messages.

"Thinking of a map?" asks Colm. "You wouldn't want to be carrying that with you when you went up there."

"I'm thinking of a rough sketch that we can commit to memory before we go out. If you have the time."

"Surely. Morna and I will do it together. You might sit by us, Illann, and tell us the sort of detail you want."

I help Morna clear the table. Colm fetches a sheet of parchment that looks as if it's been scraped down and reused almost to the point of no return, and spreads it out. They're just getting started on drawing the map when we hear voices from outside, and one of them is Galen's.

"He's with us," Illann says as Colm jumps up and heads for the door. "Not part of the team, but a friend. I'll have a word with him."

"I will." Not that it's entirely my fault that my brother is here, but I feel responsible. And of course, he would have heard the instructions for getting to this out-of-the-way house.

He's been talking to a young man who has a look of Colm and is most likely the son he mentioned. Colm comes to the door behind me and gives the lad a nod, and he goes away across the yard.

"I'll talk to Ban out here, Master Colm. You'll be wanting to get on with what you're doing." It's plain that Galen, who was so calm back at the inn, is now on edge again. He's shifting his weight from one foot to the other, twisting his fingers together, rolling his shoulders, glancing around for invisible enemies. His horse is nowhere to be seen. If he came from the inn on foot he must have kept up a fine pace.

"Take a few deep breaths, Galen. You won't be good for much if you can't keep still to a count of two. Especially up in the forest where we need to make sure we're not seen or heard."

"And you won't be good for much if you forget your comrade's mission name so quickly, Oonagh. Aren't we meant to use only those from now on? Though I notice Illann doesn't have one."

"That's his business. Listen. It's up to Illann whether you hear everything we get told. And he won't say yes to that unless you keep a good control of yourself. Yes, the forest's just up there." I motion to the hills that rise behind this farm's grazing fields. It's not much more than a stroll to the tree cover. "Tempting, I know. But you don't go off on your own, and you certainly don't go before morning. Getting caught in that area when the light starts to fade would be plain stupid. It wouldn't help you find him. It would more likely end up with us having to search for you." Galen looks down at his hands. I can't tell if he's listening. But I know what he's thinking. His face gives it away. "Why have you decided Aolu's up there somewhere, Ban?"

"Just a feeling. Based on your theory about portals. To vanish so completely, he has to have gone somewhere nobody could find him. At least, not with the usual kind of search."

"Did Mother tell you what she told me, that the only such place she knows about near home leads somewhere bad?"

Galen's lips tighten. "At Wolf Glen. I talked to Brígh from Longwater about it once. But it's too far from Winterfalls. The signs suggest Aolu disappeared completely while he was still within our own part of the forest. He went somewhere dogs couldn't track him. On purpose, by accident, who knows? Or maybe someone took him through."

I think about this for a while. Galen's expression tells me he's waiting for me to understand. "Ah. Portals in all sorts of places. You might go in one door and come out a different one. And because of the quirks of time and distance in the Otherworld, a journey that might take days in this world might take far less time in that one. Or the other way around. I understand that. But . . . I hate to say it, but doesn't that mean you could be searching all over Erin for him? How would you know where to start? Why decide this is the place? That's not what you were saying back at Winterfalls."

Galen looks at me quizzically, brows up. "You'll only laugh."

"Try me, *Ban*."

"These," he says, dipping into the pouch at his belt and taking out a familiar drawstring bag. As he opens it and reaches in, there's a clicking, clattering sound. "Not only useful for getting folk to talk in the drinking hall, but for other purposes, too. Or so it seems."

"What . . . are you using them to perform auguries now?" I don't tell him he's crazy. After what happened in that cavern on Swan Island, I need to be open to anything.

"I tried casting them, the way a Norseman might do with rune stones or a druid with ogham rods. Fixed my thoughts on Aolu, closed my eyes, threw the stones out on a tabletop. And . . . maybe to you, maybe to anyone else, the result would have looked as you'd expect—entirely random. But it wasn't. It showed Aolu boxed in, a prisoner. It showed Crow Folk nearby, many of them." He glances at me, perhaps expecting scorn or doubt. "And a pathway to reach him," my brother goes on. "You know I have many colors and shapes of stones. I could see it, a dense forest, small lakes here and there, and . . . a gate or doorway. Beyond that an open space, like a clearing. The . . . the enclosure, the prison, was in that clearing. I memorized all that, gathered up the stones and cast them again, this time with a question in my mind: *Where is this place?* And was shown, roughly, a map. This area matches it. The river valley, Elderbrook settlement, the wooded hills beyond. He's here. Somewhere close." He gazes out toward the forest. His face is full of shining hope. Sudden tears sting my eyes. Perhaps he's choosing to see only what he wants to see in that jumble of stones. But logic and common sense haven't won us much ground in the search for the missing prince. Perhaps it's time to put some faith in the uncanny. "I've tried it three times," he says. "It came out the same, more or less, each time. It's at least worth the attempt."

"Why didn't you say earlier?"

His mouth twists. "Thought I'd be doing it on my own. You're on a different mission, and so are your friends."

"You'd better come inside, Galen. The woman here, Morna, was talking about portals. A place called the Hag of the Hill. That might not be the only one of its kind in this forest." I won't mention the dream. Not yet. Tell him about that and there'll be no holding him back.

"Thank you," Galen says. "Thank you for believing in me."

"I always did, silly. But I'd like a promise, before we go in. Don't head out on your own, don't go before morning, and follow the rules. If you want me to help you, then be part of the team. Please."

"Didn't you hear Illann? I never was part of the team, and I never will be."

"You rode here with us, you're at our safe house, we relied on you not to do anything stupid when we stopped at that inn. We trusted you with our plans. I expect you to reciprocate by doing what you can to keep the team safe. Have you forgotten that Brocc is your brother? His daughter's in danger. You're that child's uncle, her close kinsman. If you act on your own and ignore the way we do things, you could not only be endangering us, but them, too. What I'm asking is entirely reasonable." And when he simply looks at me, his expression unreadable now, I add, "On a personal level, I would rather you didn't get yourself in any more trouble than necessary."

At last Galen smiles, though it's a wan sort of thing. "That's good, coming from you," he says. "Over the years I've extricated you from too many sticky situations to count."

"Yes, well, I'm not a small child any longer, in case you haven't noticed. When I bend the rules, it's well calculated. Carefully thought out."

"Mm-hm."

"Promise. Please." I don't like using such tactics, but I roll up my right sleeve and show him the mark Seanan set on me, that terrible night when he held me captive. "I never showed you this, but it was done by Dau's brother. A long story that need not be told again. A brand of ownership; he did the same to various creatures, including Crow Folk. I don't know if Dau was right when he said he recognized Seanan's particular kind of cruelty in that man's beheading, back at Winterfalls. But if he was, his brother may be wandering around in those woods as we speak. If he got the chance to hurt me again he'd do worse than this."

Galen's jaw tightens as he looks at the scar, which is an unsightly thing. Hurt like hell at the time, even though I was drugged. "If that man might be here, then you shouldn't be on the mission," he says.

"But I am on the mission. So don't do anything that will draw their attention to us before we're ready. Agreed?"

Another silence. Then he says, "You always were bossy,

even when you were this high." He puts a hand down to knee level. "I'll do my best. Tonight, at least. You really think Brocc might be here?"

I roll my sleeve back down. "Maybe tomorrow we'll find out."

28

DAU

H old this for me, will you, Master Dau? That's it—keep it firm—good, good." Master Suibne's smile lights up his face as he lays tooled leather over glued board and eases the two into perfect alignment. "Ah, yes. A second pair of hands does help at such times. I'm pleased with that result. I hope your young lady will be of the same opinion."

"She'll be delighted. And surprised." Not that I'll ever be in a position to give Liobhan the book. Various steps in the binding process still lie ahead, including punching holes in both boards and pages, then fastening all together with a complex arrangement of cords. Suibne, meticulous craftsman that he is, plans to glue narrow strips of linen, dyed to match the leather, around those holes in the cover before he inserts and knots the cords. A much neater look, he's assured me.

"You look a little downcast, Dau. Take heart; the process is gradual, I know, but the result will be pleasing. And since this is such a small book, it can be ready far sooner than, for example, a scholarly treatise with many pages. We do have some time to wait now while the glue dries. And while we wait perhaps I might add those illustrations we spoke of. You have spaces between the tales that seem ideal for that purpose. I'm thinking of black ink with a touch of red. And perhaps an ornamented title? Ideally that would have been done earlier, but if I work carefully I can still achieve a good result."

I want to tell him he's wasting his time. I want to say I won't be here to see this. But he likes the project, that's plain, and he's been kind to me. Provided a welcome refuge. "That would be wonderful, Suibne. Just one or two would do very well. A title page . . . I had not really thought about a title."

"A Book of Strange Tales? Beasts Weird and Wondrous? A Collection of Curious Creatures?"

"I cannot better those, my friend. A Book of Strange Tales might be the lady's preferred choice. But I will leave it up to you. Please don't take too much trouble. I know you have your own work to do."

"It's a pleasure, Dau. My own work can be somewhat dull at times, though I recognize the necessity of it. A project such as this allows a man to stretch his imagination a little. To have, dare I say it, a bit of fun."

It's at that moment, when the two of us are laughing together like old friends, that Lady Almha's steward, Fursa, taps on the door.

"Master Dau? Lady Almha asks you to come and speak with her. She's in the small council chamber; I'll show you the way." A pause. "Mistress Sciath has returned."

Oh, gods. I school my expression. Let neither man see my dismay at this news. Let neither see me scrambling for what I will say to this woman. Let neither see my bitter disappointment that Garbh and I have missed the chance to extricate ourselves from Darkwater before she came here. And let her not have Seanan with her. As I follow Fursa out and along the hallway, I tell myself that one good thing may come from a delay: Suibne may complete his work on the little book, and I may yet take it home.

I wish the walk were longer. I consider how to present myself; I think of what I need to know and what I must not say. I think of everything Brigid taught me about playing a part. I slow my breathing and make my body calm.

Fursa announces me and departs. Almha calls, "Enter!" I walk into the chamber, where the two women are seated together, Almha at the head of a long table, Sciath on her right. Both rise as I approach. Mistress Sciath is a striking-looking woman, high-boned, dark of hair and eye, taller than Almha. Her scrutiny is intense enough to be uncomfortable. I smile and give a little bow. "Greetings, my lady. Mistress Sciath."

"He is indeed unsettlingly like his brother," Sciath says to Almha. "But I would never mistake one for the other. Come, be seated, Master Dau. I'm told you and Lady Almha have become quite close friends."

"Lady Almha has been generous with her time." I seat myself on Almha's left, which leaves me looking straight across the table at her adviser. "We've had some interesting discussions."

"So Almha tells me. And I have learned something new. I did not know that one of my hired men was a chieftain's eldest son until I spoke with her just now. Disinherited, yes?"

"If we speak of the man who is now calling himself Seal-bhach, it does seem he is my brother Seanan, whom my father not only disinherited but banished from Oakhill some while ago. I was surprised to learn that he had not traveled further away, Mistress Sciath. Did Sealbhach come with you on the ride to Darkwater?" I do my best to sound casual.

"You were hoping to see him?"

"Indeed not; we are on very poor terms, and have been for a long time."

"Then you'll be glad to learn that Sealbhach is not with

me at present, though he is still in my employ. But let us not speak of him. Tell me of your circumstances, Master Dau. Almha tells me you do not live at Oakhill. Were you, too, disinherited?"

This question makes me deeply uneasy. "I was not. But I have made it known to my father that I have no desire to become chieftain after him. That life is not for me; I go my own way."

"And the third brother is in a religious order, I gather?"

Gods, while I was passing time with Suibne these two have been discussing everything I told Almha. "He is the second brother; I, the third. Yes, he became a monk. Meaning my father has no heir. Forgive me, ladies, but I do not see how this can be of any interest to you."

"No?" Sciath fixes her somewhat alarming gaze on me. "I judge you to be as quick-witted as your eldest brother, Master Dau, or possibly more so. Can you really not see it? Let me ask you a question. Before I do so, please understand that I know Lady Almha has shared the details of my current project with you. We have no secrets from each other."

Dagda's bollocks! This is like crossing a raging river on a bridge no wider than a handspan. From the look on Almha's face, she's not enjoying it either. Has she been crying? "Ask, then," I say.

"To the best of your knowledge, what would Lord Scannal's opinion of my venture be, assuming he had the same information as you have?"

I count silently to five before answering. "I have not spoken to my father for over a year, Mistress Sciath. But I believe he would consider your venture to be a threat, as would any of the local chieftains. Every chieftain maintains a force of men-at-arms appropriate to the nature of his holding; that is expected. But for a leader to build a great private army, whether of men-at-arms or uncanny beings—that would be seen as a hostile act. Unless, of course, there were a threat from outside, to which all leaders might wish to respond in concert. A powerful invader from across the sea, for instance. I am not aware of any such threat at the present time."

There's a silence. Almha turns an empty cup in her hands, around and around. Sciath keeps her gaze on me, as if expecting more. "Lord Scannal would not see this venture as, perhaps, an opportunity?" she asks delicately.

Great gods! *Stay calm, Dau.* "You refer to a possible alliance? He supports your venture, perhaps with funds, perhaps with other resources, and you share in the benefits, whatever they may be? Territory seized, enemies annihilated?"

"Do you judge me, Master Dau?" Sciath remains perfectly composed, but she cannot keep the wintry note from her voice.

"No judgment, Mistress Sciath. I simply sought clarification of your meaning."

"Your interpretation is correct. Your father holds the neighboring chieftaincy. I imagine he might be inclined to work in cooperation rather than face the alternative."

"Ah, so it's a threat now?" I keep my tone light.

"Of course not!" Almha speaks for the first time, and the distress in her voice is plain. "You are a friend, Dau. Sciath simply wishes to learn whether your father might consider working with us. The venture is truly remarkable. Lord Scannal may be getting on in years, but if he is anything like you, he will be ready to listen to new ideas and new strategies."

Strategies like using an army of Crow Folk to terrorize your neighbors. Strategies like employing violence in place of wise discussion. "I cannot speak for my father. But I believe he would take quite a cautious approach to the matter.

Have you discussed your project with other leaders in the north, such as those of Ulaid or Dalriada?"

"We have not." Sciath is sharp now. "And you will not, Master Dau, nor will you speak of it with your father unless and until we request it of you. I believe Lady Almha asked you to keep details of this particular topic to yourself."

"When I came to speak with you, I did not expect to be given orders, Mistress Sciath." I use a tone appropriate to the chieftain's son I am.

"Sciath, he's a friend." Almha is clearly disturbed. "A dear friend."

Oh, gods, how I hate this. Mistress Sciath may only be an adviser, but she's in charge here, I see it plainly. "Believe me, I understand the requirement for confidentiality on such matters. What little I know from Lady Almha, I will most certainly keep to myself, both now and after I leave Darkwater. But surely you need not be so concerned about word getting out. It was my understanding that it might be some time before you could begin real work on this project. Are you not lacking a key element at present? The one person with the ability to work with the Crow Folk?"

Both of them smile. Almha's smile is tentative, as if seeking my forgiveness for her friend's manner. Sciath's is a smile of triumph. It turns me cold to the bone.

"The situation has developed," Sciath says. "All is in place, and the work begins even as I speak. I have great hope for this, Master Dau. Boundless hope. Were you to broach the subject with Lord Scannal now, you could make a far stronger case." She gives a little cough, as if what is to come is rather delicate. "If I were you, I would reconsider the situation between yourself and your father. Lord Scannal could only benefit from an alliance with Darkwater. Surely he would be delighted to rebuild his bridges with you. And to see you settled." She glances at Almha, whose cheeks flush rosy pink. "This would ensure you were well able to establish yourself prior to . . . a change of leadership."

Prior to my father dying. "I will give it some thought, Mistress Sciath." I loathe this so much, the careful dancing around a plan so dark and evil and entirely lacking in concern for others that the very thought of it makes my gut churn. But I can't ignore it now. If I leave Darkwater too abruptly, they'll assume I'm off to tell the whole world about this scheme. Does this really mean they've found Brocc and brought him back? He'd never agree to work with them. Never. "You say the work begins now. You realize, I am sure, that it might greatly influence my decision if I could observe that work in progress. I am still somewhat doubtful as to the ability of any man to control the Crow Folk to the extent that would be necessary. To train these wild beings as one might hunting dogs. Might there perhaps be an opportunity for me to watch this person in action?"

The women exchange a look.

"Lady Almha and I will discuss that possibility," Sciath says. "We do not undertake the work here. You'll understand why. Our training establishment is a long day's ride away and well out of public view. I will return there soon. But not immediately, Master Dau. I'm weary from today's ride." When I make no comment, simply wait, she adds, "What you request may be possible. I will let you know." Her manner tells me I am dismissed. I rise.

"I'll bid you ladies farewell for now. I'm happy to have made your acquaintance at last, Mistress Sciath." I bow again, hoping I'm not overdoing it.

"We'll have music and dancing tonight, Dau." Almha smiles at me, but something's gone from her face. She has the look of a person walking on eggshells, fearful of saying a wrong word. I believe her respect and admiration for Sciath to be quite genuine. But in her friend's presence, it seems the chieftain of Darkwater is also afraid.

I give Garbh the news in the privacy of our quarters. We haven't many options. If it's true that Sciath's men already have Brocc in their custody, we can't afford to wait too long. But we must act with great care.

"Seems I have Lady Almha's trust, for now," I tell him. As usual, we keep our voices down, despite the closed door. "But Sciath will be cautious. I don't think she was pleased that I'd been told so much, but the two of them already seem to be planning to include me in the scheme. My father, too. Forget the sweetheart I've mentioned, the one for whom I'm making the little book. They have their eye on a marriage between me and Lady Almha, with my father's holding allied to hers, and the Crow Folk army working for us all. I did tell Almha I have no desire to become chieftain of Oakhill, ever. Mistress Sciath must think me weak enough to be persuaded into anything."

"Dagda's bollocks, Dau. So we pretend nothing's amiss, enjoy the music and dancing and good food, and if Mistress Sciath says yes, we ride to Elderbrook with her for a demonstration of Brocc's work with the Crow Folk. And when he sees us—what? There are only two of us."

"Three. Brocc's a Swan Island man, too."

"And how many fellows is Lady Sciath going to have there, while her prize bard is working his magic on the Crow Folk? A lot more than three, I'll bet. The Brotherhood of the Dobhar-chú will be at record numbers."

"I'd be glad of the backup team right now, I admit. We do what we can. If that means no more than observing what's going on, at least it's a step toward getting Brocc out of very bad trouble. Archu would say, see this not as a problem but as an opportunity."

Garbh grunts in reply.

"And if you notice me acting as interested suitor around Lady Almha, don't despise me for it, Garbh. I'm only playing a part."

He gives me a quizzical look.

"No need to observe every little thing and report back to Liobhan. When we finally get back home, I'll tell her myself."

There is indeed dancing. Garbh looks genuinely cheerful as he partners one woman after another. I find it more difficult. Anytime I glance across at Mistress Sciath, she's watching me, assessing. At least she won't raise difficult topics here, with other folk around. I dance twice with Almha, once early on, and again later when the entertainment is drawing to a close and folk are retiring for the night. I'd have to be blind not to notice the way she looks at me; the way she touches me when we're hand in hand, weaving around other couples in the patterns of the dance. I hate the need to dissemble. But I have a job to do, and that means going along with Mistress Sciath's scheme. She won't want me at Elderbrook watching her work in progress unless I show convincing interest in the alliance with Oakhill. I can't do that unless I'm seen to consider, at least, the idea of a marriage between Almha and me.

As soon as the dancing is finished I make my farewells and head out of the hall. I don't want another private conversation with the two of them, sitting by the fire. But Almha comes out behind me. Briefly there is nobody else in view. She lays a hand on my arm, and I have to stop.

"You won't stay a little longer?" She tilts her head on one side, turning the full force of those charming blue eyes on me.

"I'm weary tonight. Maybe tomorrow. Sweet dreams, Almha." I bend and plant a chaste kiss on her cheek.

"Good night, Dau." There's a sparkle in her eyes now; she gives a dimpled smile. "Dream of good things."

"I surely will." I turn and walk away. I'm getting to be as adept as Seanan at telling lies. An essential skill for a Swan Island man. But at this moment, not something to be proud of. Whichever way this sorry tale turns, Lady Almha of Darkwater is not headed for a happy ending.

29

LIOBHAN

Illann's not happy with me, but he doesn't waste time over it. He's the sort of man who just gets on with things. We've been comrades on a mission before and we respect each other. Besides, now that he knows what drew me here, he's as keen as I am to find out what's going on in Elderbrook. When I explain about Cian and his fellow musicians, he agrees that they'll provide me with excellent cover not only for a trip to Darkwater, but for entry into Lady Almha's house. He does insist that I take Elka with me in case I need my own backup. Once I'm in the house I'll find an opportunity to talk to Dau in private. Depending on what that reveals, perhaps he and Garbh can come back here straightaway. I want to see Dau so badly. I want to know that he's all right. I remind myself that there's no place for personal feelings when I'm on a mission. No place at all.

I've got one full day to work with the team before I go. Elka stays behind at the safe house—I'll explain her to Cian as my friend who sings a little, and who's with me for company on the road. She's going to spend the day working on the songs she does know, so she can join in the choruses with confidence.

With the map memorized, the four of us head into the

woods early, making sure nobody else is within sight. Morna shows us the best path to take from the farm to the forest, with cover provided by copses and drystone walls. Once under the oaks we move more freely, but as the day brightens we exercise caution. It takes only one false step—a boot sole cracking a twig or a foot sliding on uneven ground—to alert a listener. It takes only a careless moment—a quick sprint across open ground without checking all around, or the removal of a head covering when the day gets warm—to draw the eye of a watcher. Thus, gradually, we familiarize ourselves with the tracks, the hiding places, the sudden drops and unexpected bodies of water, the narrow log bridges and the looming rock faces.

Colm was right; it's a huge tract of forest. The fact that it's teeming with Crow Folk doesn't make getting around any quicker, since we need to watch out for them as well as for signs of human activity. Though it seems Colm was right about the Crow Folk, too. They make no attempt to attack us, though whenever I look up into the trees, there they are, watching from their high perches. Only once, later in the morning, does this change. Without warning they all take wing at once, flying off in the same direction. What sparks this I have no idea. After a while they come back to alight in the trees once more. I note how long they're gone, the direction they take, the time of day. This may be part of a practiced routine. Can Brocc already be training them?

Later we see two men moving on an uphill track. Their plain clothing blends with the brown and green of the woodland, except for one thing: they're wearing fancy belt buckles that look to be made of real silver. From time to time the sun finds a pathway between the canopies of the oaks and awakens a glint in those buckles. I bet they're the ones Cionnaola told me about, shaped like a dobhar-chú. The men are armed and they're carrying supplies. Big, solid fellows both. Neither one is Seanan. Seeing that, I breathe again. When they're gone, the four of us move in close and confer in whispers.

"We stay off that path," says Illann. "Might be the quickest route to their base."

"We could take that steeper track, the one we spotted earlier," I suggest. "Go higher, maybe get a look from up above."

"Or split up." Galen's been good about keeping his promise so far, but he's getting restless again. "Go two ways, cover more ground. Isn't the camp our target?"

"Until we know what they're up to, we keep our distance. The place is probably guarded, and we don't know how many men they have. We'll go with Oonagh's idea. Backtrack, then up the hill and find a concealed vantage point. Observe, retreat, plan. Ready? Ban, wait till I'm up above that big rock before you follow. Torvald, same again. Oonagh, you come last."

As we climb higher I see more signs of activity: men moving on the paths below us; men standing under the trees, plainly on watch. Illann's right; moving too close to their camp could be disastrous.

No sign of Brocc. Beyond taking a look at us from time to time, the Crow Folk aren't moving. I set my feet down carefully. It's not possible to be completely silent, but the small sounds of the forest—the wind in the trees, creatures rustling through the undergrowth—provide a shield of sorts. The Crow Folk themselves have nothing to say; not a squawk, not a screech from any of them. The oddity of that sets my teeth on edge.

I move through a stand of pines, with a soft carpet of old needles underfoot. It's darker here. Keeping Hrothgar in sight is a challenge. I catch myself cursing under my breath and clamp my jaws firmly shut. A long, annoying climb later, I find the three of them waiting for me, still in the cover of pines. We've reached the upper edge of the forest; above us the hillside is mostly bare. Lichens of green and pink and purple spread over the rocks. I hear the splash of a waterfall not very far away. Is there a lake at the foot of it?

"Beyond this point we'll be too exposed," Illann whispers.

"Look." Galen points, and after a moment I see what he sees: a crevice or chimney going up toward what looks like a high, level area. There's a thicket of tough-looking trees up there, though all around it is bare rock. "Up there we'd be out of sight. Might get a view down into their camp, if it's where we think it is."

"You're crazy." Even as I say this, I feel the urge to climb.

"Wait." Illann risks a step out from cover, a quick glance in the general direction of the camp. He steps back. "Oonagh, you go up first. Once you're out of the chimney check that we can get to the point we need without leaving cover. If it's a yes, signal and we'll follow you. If not, come straight back down."

I check both ways, then dart across to the chimney's base. I scramble up to the point where the opening narrows. I shift my bag so it hangs on my chest, not my back. With my shoulders against one rock wall and my feet braced against the other, I work my way gradually upward, glad of the fact that I'm in trousers and tunic. This will be easy enough for wiry Illann. It may be harder for Galen and Hrothgar, both bigger men.

I'm at the top. Can't signal a *yes* yet; I need to stick my head out and check the terrain. I do so cautiously, aware of how exposed I may be on this featureless hillside. But . . . it seems Galen's instincts were good. The chimney opens to a level area, still lichen-crusted, and it's not far to that stand of trees, the hardy kind that know how to find soil in the tiniest cracks. The waterfall is louder here, the sound seeming to echo from the stone. I climb out very slowly onto open ground. Crouched here, I can't see the camp or base or whatever it is. But over the splashing of the water I can hear another sound. Singing. My skin tingles; my heart leaps. That voice is Brocc's.

A moment later the Crow Folk fly in. From all over the forest they come, a dark tide rising, flowing over the treetops, gliding down again to settle. For a moment or two I can't move, can't breathe. My training quickly asserts itself: the bare hillside, the scant cover, the need to be quick. I scan the terrain ahead once more. I judge that if we keep down, we'll be able to move forward shielded by a low ridge until we reach the shelter of those trees. With luck, anyone down at the base will be distracted by the Crow Folk. I duck back in, give a thumbs-up signal to Illann, then scramble out again and lie flat on my stomach in the concealment of the ridge.

Down there in the forest, Brocc is still singing, or rather chanting. It sounds like a formal greeting. Is that what brings the Crow Folk in? *I come in peace. I come in friendship. I come in hope.* If I'm hearing correctly over the sound of the waterfall, then those men down there must be hearing it, too. They're hardly going to think that's a message for a strike force in training. I need to see what's happening. If I'm right about what Brocc is up to, it's so risky even I wouldn't be prepared to try it.

Illann's out of the chimney. Hrothgar follows. The singing and the splashing of the waterfall are punctuated by the odd grunt from Galen as he makes his way up. Considering he was attacked by Crow Folk and knocked unconscious not so very long ago, he's doing remarkably well. Illann's expression is something to behold. He looks at me and mouths, "Brocc?" and I nod. That voice could belong to no one else.

Galen squeezes himself out of the shaft and pauses to catch his breath, smiling in wonder as he hears our brother's voice. Then we move, belly-crawling over the rocks in the concealment of the ridge. The chant rises and falls. It stops for a while, and we hear a series of single notes, deep and resonant. Can that be a response from one of *them*? The beauty of it astonishes me. But then, if this really is the lost tribe from Elka's story, they're not crows. They're not even birds. What we see is the result of Aake's curse, a transformation that will last, I assume, until they can return to their remote island to live at peace once more. What we hear now is the voice of a being as wise and calm and thoughtful as Brocc himself. A thinker. A peacemaker. A leader.

We reach the wind-battered trees, which shelter a small pond, probably fed by a mountain spring. Mist from the waterfall hangs in the air. This spot provides a good view of the forest, and a wider one down toward the valley. Elderbrook settlement is not in sight, but I can see a stretch of the road we took through Hunter's Glen. There's movement down there: oxen drawing a cart, a group of riders.

Closer at hand, we can see what must be the camp. Men are moving about, maybe returning from some other part of the forest. Several of them are wearing those belts with the shiny buckles. There may be a building below us from which they're coming in and out, but from our position it's out of view, tucked under the hillside.

Brocc is not singing now. There's neither sight nor sound of Crow Folk, but they can't be far away.

We wait for a while. And it happens again, no less startling for the fact that we've seen it before: the sudden dark-winged rise into the air, the flight in close formation. They make a wide circle over this part of the woodland, then spread out and come down again, vanishing into the trees. Practicing maneuvers, as a body of men-at-arms might do. The vision we saw in the cavern wasn't from long ago. The child's age made that plain. How on earth has Brocc achieved this so quickly?

"Move," murmurs Illann, and we do. More men are coming into the camp, and it's time we were gone. I wish I could see Brocc, if only for a moment, just so I can know he's all right. That can't happen. But I've learned something. I know now where he's working. The Crow Folk rose from a spot right beside a very tall pine, a forest giant of great age and character. It's head and shoulders above the rest of them—my father in the form of a tree—and at its feet there must be a clearing. As I wriggle back toward the chimney and the way down, I wish I could be at that place tomorrow and watch Brocc's work close up. The others will have to do it. I wonder if he's surrounded by guards when he's with the Crow Folk. There was no sign of that woman, the one in the vision. Does she, too, watch and listen?

We retreat. There are too many people around, and now we know Brocc is already here, we should get right out of the area and talk about what comes next. Illann suggests a different route, one that won't take us so close to the track those men used coming up. He tells us to put more distance between us this time. He leads, Hrothgar and Galen follow, and as before I'm the rear guard. As I go I can't stop thinking of Brocc up there on his own among enemies. I wish we could march in and demand that they free him instantly. I wish we could mount an attack and rescue him. I wish . . . But their numbers are far greater, and although our training is almost certainly superior—even Galen's—that spot they're in would be easy to defend. Besides, all they need do to stop us is threaten Brocc. We have to stick to the plan. I could bring Dau and Garbh here in just a few days, and I hope I will. But no surprise attack, even then. That song of Brocc's was not about war and blood. Quite the opposite. Brocc is a bard. His voice, his fingers on the harp strings, those have always been his most powerful weapons. He's probably desperate to escape. Longing to find his daughter. But not yet. I suspect he has a plan of his own to execute, and it involves staying here until that woman arrives, the one in the vision. Intervene too early and we may bring the whole thing falling down around him. We have to wait.

Somehow, on the way back, we get separated. It's not hard to do, since in order to evade possible pursuit Illann has chosen to lead us through a maze of barely visible tracks, some of which require negotiating steep rocky inclines or crossing gushing streamlets. Losing track of him is not a disaster as we can all find our way back to the safe house. I'll spend some time with Elka, working on the songs. I'd better put in some practice on the whistle, too, so I can keep up with Cian and his band. I can just see Galen, a fair distance ahead, but both Illann and Hrothgar have been out of sight a while. I keep on down the hill, hoping I won't fall foul of the Crow Folk that are still up there, watching. Eventually I spot what may possibly be an open field, just visible lower down between the oaks. No sign of Galen now. Maybe he's already reached the safe house.

But no. He's left the track, such as it was, and taken a narrow branching path to the west. He's standing completely still, staring at something ahead of him. As I come closer, he says without turning, "Look."

I follow his pointing hand and suck in a breath. It's the Hag of the Hill, without a doubt. A fine old woman she is, with stone for a body, a tree root for a staff, and a shawl of green growing things to warm her shoulders. She looks as if she's stood guard there for generations—since long before Morna's great-great-grandmother was a little girl exploring forbidden places with her friends. She's eerily close to what I saw in my dream.

We move forward without another word. Galen's tense. All his attention is on the Hag. I go more cautiously, alert to danger. As we come closer to the rock formation we slow our steps. At the foot of the Hag, on the mossy ground before us, lies a single white stone, smooth and perfect as an egg. Without a doubt, it's a sign.

"Respect," I murmur. Galen hasn't had the same experience of the Otherworld as I have. And neither of us has lived there as Brocc has. But our mother is a wisewoman, so we have a better idea than some of how to act.

Galen kneels beside the stone. Reaches to touch it gently. Whispers something with Aolu's name in it. He stands, and together we move toward the rocky crone, looking for chinks and cracks, for possible doorways. If there's any portal to the Otherworld in this forest, then surely it's here. Still, I'm not surprised when we see no such opening. These things are not a simple matter of turning a key or knocking on a door or calling out politely.

"He's here," Galen whispers. "I know it. We have to get in."

"I do have my whistle in my bag. But that will draw every man in this forest; the sound carries."

"You could sing," suggests Galen. His voice is shaking. His hopes are pinned on this. The logic seems fragile. But this may be a situation in which logic does not apply.

"Singing would carry, too, if it was loud enough to be heard on the other side of the portal. If there is a portal.

And . . . if it does open, we can't just walk in. What about the others? What about Brocc?"

Galen says nothing.

"I'm not going to sing. There must be some other way."

"He's there. I know it. You think I'm going to turn my back and leave him?"

"Shh, keep your voice down. We need to think about the old tales. About how people cross that barrier between worlds. How to deal with uncanny folk. We can't charm them with music. Not this time. But that isn't the only way."

Galen can't keep still. He paces to and fro, and as he walks there's a familiar clicking.

"Your stones. Use them. I'm not thinking of an augury or a game. More of a . . . a demonstration of your goodwill. Courteous, but with a very clear meaning."

He halts. Takes his bag off his back, opens it, reaches inside. The stones are in their smaller bag, fastened with a drawstring. He squats down beside the Hag and brushes aside leaves and twigs to clear a patch of earth.

"I'll keep watch," I tell him, though my brother is concentrating so hard I don't think he hears me. Keeping watch is essential. While he performs this task, the two of us will be targets for anyone who should happen to walk up from those open fields. I keep a hand on my knife hilt; I scan all around for signs of movement. But I can't help glancing down from time to time to see what Galen is doing.

He's made a barrier. On one side there are two reddish stones, one smaller than the other. Galen and me, I assume. The barrier is all of pale pebbles, small round ones from light gray to ochre to cream. Beyond it, on the far side, a single pebble sits on a fallen leaf. The pebble is pure white with a particular shine to it, as if it held the sunlight within. Not hard to guess who that is.

"Sure you can't sing?" my brother asks, and his tone twists my heart.

"I could hum a tune, softly. And why don't you say something? They'll hear us." I speak with more confidence than I feel.

"Please."

I hum as quietly as I can—the tune is "The Farewell," a song Brocc wrote about the sorrow of parting and how our loved ones are always with us in spirit. I keep my eyes on the pathways under the trees, the places where someone might hide, ready to leap out with bow drawn. If I were a praying sort of person, I'd offer up a prayer now.

"We come in peace," Galen whispers. "We mean no harm. Lady of the Woods, please open your door to us. I search for the dearest of friends, a kind man, a man of good heart. He is a man open to wonders, to worlds beyond his own. A prince among men, and sorely missed. If I must, I will seek him to the ends of the earth. I will shed my lifeblood for him. If he is here, please let me in. Please let me bring him home."

I keep my tune going for a while longer, then let it fade away. I recall again the endless time of waiting at the border to Eirne's realm. We cannot wait long here; Illann will expect us back. Not to speak of the risk of being spotted.

Galen has his eyes closed, his arms outstretched with palms up. So he doesn't see when the crack appears in the rocks to one side of the Hag, from her shoulder down to her feet. It's just wide enough for a big man like my brother to get through, edging sideways.

"Galen."

He opens his eyes. Steps forward as if he would run straight through to the unknown place beyond. I feel as if I'm being ripped in two. "Galen, wait!"

"I have to go, I have to—"

"Take these, you might need them." I scoop up the stones and return them to their bag. "Here." I put both bags into his hands, the smaller and the larger. I blink back tears. "Go safely. I hope you find him."

Galen nods. Does not speak; perhaps cannot. He turns and walks through the doorway. I want to leap forward, to go with him, to stand by his side. But I hold myself back, and in an eyeblink he is gone. The portal closes. I'm alone with the Hag of the Hill. Finding the prince was my mission, yes. But, like it or not, my true mission lies elsewhere. I won't dwell on the possibility that I've just lost a second brother to the Otherworld. I won't consider that Galen's confidence may be misplaced. He must follow his own path, as both Brocc and I have done. He's big, he's strong, he's grown up. It's not for me to be his guardian.

I bow to the Hag and offer words of thanks. I'm shivering as I walk away. I want to wait for Galen. But that would be foolish. I might wait for a hundred years.

I head off down the hill and back toward the safe house. Tomorrow I ride to Darkwater. Tomorrow I see Dau, and we start to play another game.

30

LIOBHAN

We reach Darkwater settlement after a long day's ride to find that the innkeeper is keen for us to play this very evening, since he has a party of travelers staying overnight. Cian agrees without consulting the rest of us; a full hostelry means more coins tossed our way, in addition to what the host pays for our services. We have time for a quick wash and some food, a change of clothing, and a warm-up out the back, but that's about all. I snatch a moment when Cian's alone to have a private word. It's unlikely we'll see Garbh or Dau tonight, but not impossible, and I need to warn him.

"You remember that day at Oakhill, when you asked me if I'd like to sing? Do you remember the man who was with me?"

Cian runs a hand through his mop of curls, rendering them even more tousled. "Son of the house, wasn't it? Master Dau?"

"I forgot what good memories musicians have. Yes, it was. And I think he may be in these parts now, most likely at Lady Almha's house, but possibly here. This may sound odd, but— it will be much easier if both of us can act as if we've never met him, or at the very most give a polite nod. He's likely to do the same. I can't explain why. Personal reasons."

Cian lifts his brows at me, gives a crooked smile. "Mystery woman, hm? My lips are sealed. You look very fetching in that outfit, may I say?"

We play to an appreciative crowd, and they dig deep to reward us. It seems that even when we're tired and saddle-sore we can do the job well. I remember the times when Brocc and I played and sang for weddings and festivals. That feels so long ago. Before Swan Island. Before I met Dau. Before Brocc left us. A different world. But it's the same world, of course, just as I'm singing some of the same songs. We're the ones who have changed.

I sing love songs and think of Dau. I look for him or Garbh in the packed room while trying not to be obvious about it. Cian and I give a lively rendition of "Artagan's Leap," him on the pipes and me on the whistle, with the other band members on bodhrán, knee harp, and bones. They also have a kind of rattle made from a dried-out gourd. Cian, delighted that Elka is able to help with the choruses of several of the songs, has entrusted this instrument to her, and she wields it with both enthusiasm and perfect timing. I'll be asking her again to join our regular performances on Swan Island; she's good, and I think she might say yes now. That's if we don't both lose our places on the island because I broke the rules.

No sign of Dau or Garbh all evening, but I do notice one thing. Among the crowd of happy drinkers there are two men around whom others leave an empty space, as if nobody wants to get close even in such a crowd. Both of them have silver buckles on their belts.

Cian tells us next morning that we're to play at Lady Alm-ha's house at suppertime. Chances are I'll see Dau at last; probably most of the household will be there for the music. Pretending the man I love is a stranger to me will be quite a test of self-control. Of course, Dau and I are both trained to go undercover. But this feels different. It feels so different that I'm in danger of thinking that unspoken rule about Swan Island relationships is actually a good one. But I dismiss that annoying thought. I always believed we were strong enough, and now we'll prove it.

Cian has said we'll be based at the inn and will move between there and the chieftain's residence as required. I told him Elka and I might not be available in the long term; he replied with perfect courtesy that we'd be an asset for as long as we chose to stay. The first time I met the man I wondered if he had some fey blood, and I haven't changed my mind. There's something about the smile and the dimples and the bright eyes that suggests it, not to speak of his skill on the pipes. Could I go back to being a traveling minstrel if I lost my place on Swan Island? Or would I be too sad, too angry, too furious with myself to do the job well? I hope I never have to find out.

It's evening, and we're at the grand residence of Lady Almha of Darkwater, in an anteroom to the great hall where folk eat and mingle and dance after supper. The place brings up unwelcome memories of Oakhill, home of Dau's unpleasant family. We check our instruments. Elka and I are dressed up for the performance. I'm in my russet gown with its embroidered overdress. I've left my hair loose save for a couple of little plaits from my temples around to the back, where they're held by a clasp. Nimble-fingered Elka did those for me. Her good dress is deep green with bands of dark blue around hem and sleeves, and she's plaited her hair and pinned it up in a sort of crown. The bodhrán player can't take his eyes off her.

We're called into the hall and instantly I see Dau. My heart does a complicated dance in my chest, and I drop my gaze quickly. Shit, this really is going to be hard. We take our places on the musicians' platform, and I feel glad, so glad, that Cian's the one doing the talking, introducing the pieces, making jokes, keeping the crowd happy. Back home, that's my job. I've asked him not to make any special mention of me and Elka even though we're not regular band members, and he complies. Gods, how can I gather myself enough to play properly? I can hardly breathe. *Focus, Liobhan. Remember your training.* Dau's sitting at what must be the high table, with a group of rather grandly dressed people. Illann told me Dau and Garbh were traveling under their own names on this mission. Seems Dau's had no problem settling right into this household. How he must hate playing that role, though he gives every appearance of enjoying it now, smiling back at the sweet-faced woman on his left as she shares some secret. *Concentrate, Liobhan.* I nearly missed an entry then. I force my attention back to the task in hand. I don't want to let Cian down. This feels so different from last night's performance at the inn. My stomach's tight with nerves and my breathing's all over the place. *Get a grip, Liobhan!*

Garbh's standing behind Dau; he's acting as both bodyguard and personal attendant, I think. Maybe I can snatch a word with him later. Pity I won't be able to get up and dance; that can be a good opportunity for a quick exchange of information. Looks like it's nearly time for that now; folk are standing up and moving around. And I see someone I recognize. A dark-haired woman, not the one who's giving Dau all her attention, but another. Just as well we're between pieces, because my blood goes cold and my breath hitches in shock. It's her. The woman we saw in the vision on Swan Island, in the cavern, congratulating Brocc on a job well done. She's there at that table with Dau, seated on the other side of the pretty one. Who is she?

"Time for some dancing?" Cian asks the crowd, giving them his most winning smile. "We might begin with 'Thread the Needle.'" It's an easy circle dance, which most of them will know. Not too fast, and no need to choose partners, though Dau and the pretty woman rise together and head toward the dance area. She's very finely dressed in a cream-colored gown and purple overdress, and is wearing quite a lot of silver jewelry. Matching purple ribbons in her hair. Can that be Lady Almha?

"The lady herself," Cian murmurs as he adjusts the pipes. "And . . ." *And your friend,* is what he means but doesn't say. "Everyone ready?" he asks, then counts us in.

Right. I won't look at Dau and his partner. I'll keep my gaze well away from the expression on her face, which may or may not be genuine. She looks as if she'd eat him up given half a chance. I keep an eye on that other woman, the one from the vision. She's not dancing. She's watching, thinking, making no attempt to talk to a couple of other folk who are choosing to stay at the table. Am I reading too much into this? What on earth is Dau up to?

Next number is a showy jig for pipes and bodhrán. Cian wants me playing whistle in the refrains. Elka's not in this one. She's sitting on the edge of our platform having a break, and that offers an opportunity I hadn't thought of. Garbh strolls over, holds out a hand in invitation. Elka rises, a vision of gold and green, and the two of them step out together. Excellent. I hope they manage to have a word. We need to warn them about that woman. She may be a friend of this household, but the vision showed a person with an evil purpose. They need to know. Maybe we can have an accidental sort of meeting at the inn, or somewhere else in the settlement. Maybe . . .

I play. I don't miss a beat, though my thoughts are whirling with the possibilities, some of them dire. I even add new embellishments to the refrains, different each time. Cian feels obliged to reciprocate, a glint in his eye as his fingers fly on the chanter. If the circumstances were different, I'd be having a lot of fun.

Out there in the crowd of dancers, Elka and Garbh look as if they really are having a good time. They're a striking pair, Garbh tall and broad, a fine figure of a man, and Elka golden haired, rosy cheeked, and as it turns out, rather a good dancer. We gradually speed up the pace of the jig. Our bodhrán player is grinning; Cian and I can't help trying to outplay each other. Some of the dancers give up, laughing helplessly as they feign complete exhaustion. Garbh and Elka make it through to the end and win a round of applause from others on the floor. Dau and the lady did not attempt the jig. They're standing to the side, watching. He meets my eye for one brief moment, then blinks and looks away, bending to hear what the lady is saying. Oh, his face, suddenly ablaze . . . I hope nobody else saw that. But now he's attentive to her. Solicitous. Admiring. I think I want to be sick. *Don't look, Liobhan. He's playing a part, just like you.* I want him out of here. Away from *her*, and away from that other woman. I want him safe. Safe with me, where he belongs.

Three more dances. Dau partners the lady in two of them and stands chatting to her during the third. Elka comes back to join us. Garbh has a different partner for each dance.

We finish with a slower dance, done to the tune "The Lady of Lough Cuan." I play the main melody on the whistle; it's a lovely tune, full of longing, and somehow both sad and hopeful. It's hard to get through it; as the dancers move around I catch glimpses of Dau and his partner holding each other more closely than is strictly necessary. I see the flush on her cheeks as she looks up at him, and the way she sometimes rests her brow against his shoulder as if overcome with emotion or desire or both. I want to give her a smack on the face. But I manage not to let that get in the way of the music. Instead I put my love for Dau into my playing; it floods through me, shaping every note, and when we reach the end I have tears in my eyes. Morrigan's curse, I think I want the old Liobhan back, the one who thought Dau was a stuck-up opinionated pig who didn't know when to keep his big mouth shut. We argued. A lot. But . . . no, I don't want that. Not even when he puts a protective arm around her shoulders as they leave the floor. Not even when she slips her own arm around his waist. That doesn't seem very appropriate behavior in public. Not for a chieftain. Not unless you're married or betrothed, and even then . . .

It's over, thank the gods. I got through it. The household gradually disperses. It looks as if the lady and her inner circle—this includes Dau, it seems—plan to sit by the fire awhile, but everyone else heads off on their own business. Some supper has been provided for us, not in the hall but in the antechamber where we prepared for our performance. Ale, cold meats, a vegetable pie, fruit. Significantly better fare than we'd get at the inn. Cian says to take our time. He's pleased with the performance. If he noticed how distracted I was, he makes no comment on it.

We're still eating when there's a tap on the door and Garbh comes in. "I wanted to pass on congratulations," he says, with a smile that takes in all of us. "My name's Garbh, traveling with Master Dau of Oakhill. He thought the performance was most entertaining. Enjoyed the singing in particular." He turns the smile in Elka's direction. "Me, I love dancing, and you made a fine partner. Will you be playing here again tomorrow evening?"

"If that's what Lady Almha wants," Cian says. "We're staying over at the Darkwater inn for a while. When we're not required here, we'll be entertaining the drinkers."

"Busy life. I don't suppose the young ladies might have time for a walk, perhaps tomorrow morning? Lovely area. The flowers are especially pretty at this time of year." He looks at Cian. "Honorable intentions, my friend—why else would I invite two ladies together? Who knows, it might be inspiration for a song."

"Ask the girls, not me," says Cian. "I don't expect my folk to rehearse all day. What about your Master Dau? Doesn't he require your services?"

"He'll be otherwise occupied. What do you think, ladies?"

I look at Elka; she looks at me. "Fine," I say. "Not too early, though—we've had a long day. Come and look for us an hour or so after breakfast. What was your name again?"

"Garbh. And you are . . . ?"

"Oonagh. I'll look forward to it, Garbh. Some fresh air will do us good."

We're in communal sleeping quarters at the inn, so there's no chance to talk. Elka and I have pallets next to each other, and we're sharing the chamber with four other women, one of whom has a babe at the breast. I settle down to sleep, but although I'm tired my head is full of questions. That woman from the vision, here in Darkwater. Galen gone through a portal. Galen convinced that he'd find his beloved Aolu on the other side. Dau and that woman, the chieftain. What in the name of the gods is he playing at? And Brocc. We need to get back to Elderbrook fast.

The oddest part of this is that it seems the two missions— the hunt for Prince Aolu; Brocc and the Crow Folk—are more closely linked than anybody thought. If Galen's instincts are sound, both tracks lead to Elderbrook.

Elka and I are up early. We're first in the bathing area, where buckets of hot and cold water are provided along with soap, brushes, and drying cloths. When we're clean and dressed in our least obtrusive clothing—plain skirts and tunics—we visit our horses in the stables, where they're enjoying a well-earned rest. Then breakfast. There may be quite a crowd staying here but they're not early risers, it seems. There's a group of three men who look as if they're going back on the road straight after the meal, and a few others scattered around. Elka and I chat in lowered voices, so nobody realizes we're listening to what everyone else is saying. One man comes over and thanks us for the performance on the night we arrived. He asks when we'll be on again and we tell him we hope it will be tonight. I mean that. I don't think I could cope with another evening watching Dau and that woman. Though, of course, if we are required again at the chieftain's house that's exactly what I'll do. And I'll do it well, or I'll end up proving the theory that couples shouldn't work together on a mission. Seems I have a jealous streak, and I don't much care for that. I was jealous of Justice for a while—Dau lavished such attention on him in those first challenging days—but with a bit of help I got over that quickly. This won't be so easy.

Something on Elka's face alerts me. With my gaze firmly on my porridge bowl, I sharpen my ears.

". . . always thought there was something not right about it." The speaker is a gray-haired man whose weathered face suggests an outdoor life. He's talking to a younger man as they share a platter of bread and sliced cold meat. "He wasn't young, Lord Cernach, but he was a fit man, sturdy and strong. To go like that . . . there were rumors about at the time, plenty of them. But they were hushed up."

The younger man makes a crude remark about old men

wed to much younger women, and how such a phenomenon might shorten a man's life.

"Bollocks," says the older man mildly. "If you ask me, someone arranged it. Lord Cernach would have known that flight of steps like his own right hand; been up and down them hundreds of times. Why would he fall?"

"What, you're telling me someone pushed him?"

"Keep your voice down. There's as many versions of the story as there are folk to ask. Nobody admits to seeing or hearing anything, though my lord was in a chamber with his councilors not long before and not far away. Next thing a servingman finds him at the bottom of the steps with his neck broken. Something fishy about it if you ask me."

"And his wife steps into his place. Neat."

They fall silent as a servingman crosses the dining room carrying a stack of platters. I pass Elka some bread; she busies herself spooning honey from a jar.

"Nobody's suggesting it was her. Have you seen the lady? Sweet young thing, wouldn't hurt a fly. If I was pointing a finger it wouldn't be her I'd point it at. Though it wouldn't be so very far away."

The interesting conversation turns to other things. I look at my companion across the table and mouth, "Shit."

"Don't swear, Oonagh," murmurs Elka, making a face. "More honey?"

Garbh appears not long after we finish eating, dressed very plainly and wearing a weapon at his belt. We head out of the settlement and onto a track that runs beside grazing fields toward a patch of woodland. Apart from the sort of remarks commonly exchanged by folk who are virtual strangers, none of us says much until we're in the cover of the wood and have done a check to be sure there's nobody else around.

We exchange information. That woman, the one from the vision, is Mistress Sciath, Lady Almha's adviser and confidant. And the plot is precisely what I feared. Including a suggestion that both Dau and his father might be drawn into the whole thing; seems these women see Dau as the future chieftain of Oakhill, despite his telling them that's never going to happen, and they have their eye on him as a second husband for Lady Almha.

I tell Garbh about the vision that set me on this path. I describe the attack on Lord Scannal's men at Oakhill. "If Dau says no to her—to them—that's how it could be. That's if they manage to persuade Brocc to do as they want. Oakhill would be attacked. If they can't ally themselves by marriage, they'll take what they want by force."

"Crazy," murmurs Garbh. "Why would the lady want such power? That's the part I don't understand. Sometimes it seems like Mistress Sciath is pulling all the strings. If I were the chieftain I'd dismiss the woman."

I glance at Elka. "We heard something at the inn. Men talking. Garbh, if you get the chance to ask questions about the late Lord Cernach and how he died, that would be useful. There's a suggestion it might not have been an accident. That it might have been all too convenient for Lady Almha. I wonder if there are any maidservants who've been here since Lord Cernach's time. I'd like to know when Mistress Sciath joined the household, and how things were before."

"Sciath was at King Faelan's coronation with them," Garbh says. "That's where she heard Brocc singing and playing. She's been in that household since before Lady Almha was widowed."

We all think for a while, to the accompaniment of birdsong and the distant lowing of cattle. "It's easy to make a story out of it," I say, thinking that story feels rather more plausible than the one about taming the Crow Folk. "Almha was young, newly wed, perhaps her husband didn't treat her as an equal, didn't bother consulting her on serious matters. Mistress Sciath is an ambitious woman. She sees an opportunity, works hard to get close to the lady, becomes a trusted friend and confidant. Then gradually persuades Almha that her wild schemes are not only possible, but desirable. There's only one problem: the husband, Lord Cernach."

"They kill him?" Even after hearing what those men said, Elka sounds shocked. "Just like that, they push him down the steps?"

"I've met Mistress Sciath," says Garbh. "I could believe it of her. I think she'd stop at nothing to achieve her goal. But Lady Almha? I'm not so sure about that."

"Any woman do this," Elka says. "Any woman. Warrior, serving maid, washerwoman, mother, any woman. If the husband is cruel, if he does not understand, if he does not listen. If he treats her like a slave. She chooses. Be that slave, die of it. Or stand up, make action. Walk away, leave husband behind. Or . . ."

"Or kill?" I see in Elka's eyes an echo of her own past, though her oppressor was a domineering father, one with no understanding of his daughter's extraordinary talents.

"Or kill. But she would not push him. She is a small woman, not strong."

I can see it. Mistress Sciath offering to make the problem go away. *Leave it to me. I will ensure nobody talks. It will be an accident.* And . . . "Oh, gods," I whisper, with a sudden image of a white-faced Brocc in the rain, clutching his daughter to his chest. "No wonder Lady Almha is supporting the venture with the Crow Folk, mad as it is. If this is true, Sciath could make Almha agree to anything. All she'd need to do was threaten to expose Almha's role in her husband's demise."

We're all silent. This was a snippet of gossip, no more. But it's all too believable.

"You and Dau need to get out of there," I say eventually. "Quickly." Garbh doesn't say anything, just looks as if he's thinking hard, and that troubles me. "That woman's dangerous. Dau's getting himself embroiled. If he doesn't extract himself soon he might find it hard to get away."

"She's taking him to see Brocc at work," Garbh says. "Soon. Sometime in the next few days. Dau's not going to pass that up. We have proof that Sciath's men are tied up with the prince's disappearance. You know about the belt found in the woods near Winterfalls, the one with a silver buckle? Used to display a severed head? Sciath hands out those buckles for loyal service—they're specially made for the purpose. Her fellows call themselves the Brotherhood of the Dobhar-chú. They were there at the scene of the crime, without a doubt. And now they're gathering at Elderbrook. Dau will be wanting to see what they're doing, find out how close Brocc is to a result. Looks like it's all one mission, though how the pieces fit we have yet to work out. I need to talk this through with Dau. But I know he'll want to ride to Elderbrook when Sciath goes."

"So we need to go back."

"Wait another day or maybe two. I'll come and find you at the inn, or we can have a word if you're performing in the hall again. By then I may know when Sciath's leaving, and we can avoid meeting on the road. Dau has the final word, but I see us all heading for Elderbrook. He and I will probably be at the local inn. You two would return to the safe house and make plans with the others. Might be best if I act as messenger; Dau's brother Seanan is in the area, and you'll know what that means."

A pox on it! That's all I need, wretched Seanan thrown

into the mix. Seems Dau's hunch about him being involved was right. Rather than utter the foul words that come to my lips, I say, "If we get to perform at the lady's house again, you can play the part of Elka's new admirer. Dance if the opportunity arises. You made an eye-catching pair."

Garbh glances at Elka. "Easy enough. Playing the part, that is."

Elka cuffs him on the arm, not very hard. She's smiling.

"We'd better move," I say. And I want to add, *Don't fall in love with one of your comrades,* but of course I say nothing of the kind. Didn't Dau and I once say we'd make the impossible happen, in keeping with the philosophy of Swan Island? "Please pass on my regards to Dau."

Garbh grins. "Regards? Is that all?"

"That's from Oonagh, the traveling musician, to Master Dau of Oakhill. I'd say it's more than enough. Shall we go?"

31

DAU

I can't do that again. If Liobhan's here, if she sings, I won't be able to get through the evening without somehow giving myself away. Just as well Garbh took the initiative. Now we know they'll be in Elderbrook when we get there, and how to find them. As for the theory about the old chieftain's death, it seems that may be true. I heard something nobody was meant to hear, and it chilled me.

I was in the workroom with Master Suibne, who was still finishing the delicate illustrations for my little book. In truth, I was hiding from Lady Almha, whose demands on my time are greater by the day. I'd asked the scribe if there was anything I could do for him, and he, unperturbed, had given me some documents to copy.

"You write a fair hand, Master Dau. Tutored by your father's scribe, perhaps?"

"I was. I'm not sure what Master Fiachna would think of my most recent effort."

"Ah, Fiachna. I should have guessed. I knew him well when we were younger. How is he faring?"

I trust Suibne, so telling the truth felt safe. "It's over a year since I last saw him, and he was injured at the time, but recovering. I believe he may now be serving as a lay brother at

St. Padraig's, near my father's house. There have been many changes."

"Mm." Suibne's brush moved with greatest care on the parchment as he put in a tiny detail. He was working on an image of the dobhar-chú, both fearsome and a little comical. "Should you see him again, please give him my regards, and tell him he did a good job with you. Life in the monastery would suit him, I think."

"I hope it does. He was a good friend to me, back in the early days." A trusted friend, at a time when friends were rare. I will always remember his kindness.

We worked on awhile, but it was late, and I wondered if I was keeping my companion from his bed, so I said good night and left the workroom, thinking that with luck, both the lady and her adviser would be abed, and I could creep back to my own room unnoticed.

It was as I passed the door to the council chamber that I heard them. The door was ajar, and the argument within so heated that although both women were trying to keep their voices down, I could hear them clearly. On Swan Island we are trained to listen. I stood in the shadows by the door— there was a lamp on a table further along the hallway, but it did not light this area—and as I listened my heart went cold.

". . . it feels wrong! I like him very much, Sciath. He's a good man, a fine man."

"Indeed. Young. Handsome. Virile, no doubt. A man who could give you sons. Heir to a chieftaincy. Why in the name of the gods start having doubts now?"

"I . . . I am not having doubts about *him*, Sciath. If he asked me to be his wife I would say yes without hesitation. But . . ."

A charged silence. I held my breath.

"But what?" Sciath's voice was heavy with threat.

"To involve him in the plan . . . to draw in his father . . .

Could this not be a simple matter of alliance between two territories? The marriage would increase our influence; give us a stronger voice in disputes with neighbors. Is that not enough? Could we not abandon this plan? I don't want Dau drawn into . . . I see no real reason to . . ."

Silence again. Then Sciath spoke. "Do I understand you correctly? You ask me to give up my great vision, the plan I have worked on and dreamed of almost since the first day I joined your husband's household? The mission we have pursued together, you and I? All because you discover soft feelings for a man? I think you forget something, my lady. I am in possession of certain knowledge I have chosen not to share. Should you break our agreement, I will make that knowledge public, starting with your precious Master Dau. Of course, if you wish to face the consequences of that, go ahead. Act as the chieftain I made you and dismiss me from your service. You have that right."

I heard a crash from within the chamber, perhaps a chair falling over. As I retreated rapidly along the hallway Almha cried out, "No, Sciath! Wait!" I moved as I've been taught, on silent feet, keeping to the shadows, until I was out of sight. Along the maze of passageways, up a short flight of steps, and to the chamber I share with Garbh. Inside. Door closed behind me.

Garbh was still awake, a candle by his bedside. "Morrigan's curse, Dau, what happened to you? You're breathing as if you've run a race."

I collapsed onto my bed. I waited until my breathing slowed and steadied. "Garbh. There's something you should know."

32

GALEN

He's here somewhere. I know it. *Be strong, Galen. Forget the drumming in your head, set aside the weakness in your body, just keep on going. Keep on until you find him. Be like your father. He would never give up.*

Foolish, to think all I needed to do was step through the portal and all would instantly be to rights. But I was confident of just that. I expected Aolu to be there, smiling, saying *well done*, throwing his arms around me and holding me tight. I thought I would bring him back that very day, the spell broken by true love. Hah! Instead, I'm still wandering in this place with no real idea of which path to take or where any of them might lead me. Days of walking. Nights sleeping under the trees. Foraging for what I could find, eating roots that turned my bowels to water, learning the taste of leaves and grasses. I tried to trap a rabbit, catch a fish. I stayed hungry. I can imagine what Liobhan would say.

Maybe I could find my way back. If I got as far as the portal, whoever let me in might push me out again. But my feet keep moving me forward, one, two, and I tell myself it can't be much further. He must be here. I know he's here.

I've come to a place where the trees are full of Crow Folk, perched all along the branches like the ones we saw on the day we found the brotherhood's camp. Since I came through the portal I've seen Crow Folk flying in the distance, all together as they did when Brocc sang. But these ones don't fly off when those others do. They don't move at all. Not a shake of the feathers, not the twitch of a foot or the blink of an eye. They're so still they might be part of the tree itself. I know I'm in the Otherworld. But this is surely the same forest, the one where Brocc's working with the Crow Folk. Right next to Elderbrook settlement, where ordinary folk live ordinary lives. I thought creatures could move freely between worlds if it suited them. What is holding these birds here?

I crouch by a stream to refill my waterskin. Here elders grow, a respite from the dark heaviness of the pines, and filtered sunlight falls on the clear water. The streambed is all pebbles, gray, green, dun, and brown, some with swirling patterns, some marked as if with ogham signs, some perfectly plain. Ah! I got into this place by using my stones. Perhaps they can help me now.

I climb to the top of a nearby rise and scan the territory ahead. I think there's a clearing over there, though the trees obscure the view. I'll go down that way, find a patch of level ground and do what I can. At the very least using the stones may calm me.

As I approach the clearing I can see a sort of dwelling there, a low hut made of all kinds of materials, and I wonder what outlandish being might live in it. Thus far I've seen only the odd elusive squirrel and, one day at dusk, a badger. But now, as I near the open area, a rustling sound in the undergrowth halts me. I glance down, trying to identify the source. I remember, rather too late in the piece, that I'm carrying a weapon. A person doesn't bring iron into the realm of the Fair Folk and expect them to be friendly. *Should have left it behind, Galen. Should have given it to Liobhan.* Now what?

I'm not going to throw away a favorite dagger only to discover that the thing in the bushes is a hedgehog or a rat.

I remove the dagger from my belt, sheath and all, and lay it down beside the track, checking that I'll be able to find it when I want it. There's a pile of white stones on one side of the path and a young elder bush on the other. I take a step forward, then another. More rustling. Maybe someone's trying to tell me something. Maybe this is a doorkeeper or a guardian, and the thing to be guarded is up ahead, in the clearing. So maybe . . .

Ah. At the foot of a rock wall there's a little cave, half-hidden by ferns and creepers. The spot puts me in mind of the Hag of the Hill, though this is much lower and more modest. The faintest sound of movement from within. That's not Aolu in there; he may not be a big man, but he most certainly could not squeeze into that space.

I won't speak. I won't walk past. I set down my bag and lower myself to sit on the ground. I fish out the smaller bag that holds the stones. The weight of them is a comfort; their clicking language reassures me that I'm not powerless, even in this place, even under the baleful eyes of many Crow Folk. I straighten my back, brush some forest litter aside, make a clear patch. I set the stones out much as I did at the portal: the barrier, myself on one side, Aolu on the other. I add a larger stone to represent the Hag of the Hill.

Someone's watching. When I risk a glimpse toward the cave entrance I see a pair of bright eyes in the shadows. What the thing is, I have no idea.

I deploy the stones as they were outside the portal and recommence the story. I move Stone Aolu far out of reach, hidden behind a wall that I make from forest-colored stones: brown, gray, greenish. Stone Galen crosses the first barrier and starts to search. Goes high, goes low. Sleeps in a makeshift shelter—I pluck a few grasses and leaves to suggest this. Stone Galen then searches again, up and down, in and out, and finds nothing. I lay him down. I mime weeping and tearing out my hair.

The creature is at the entrance to its cave. Its eyes are still on my dumb-show; its posture is wary. The being has a strong look of the Crow Folk, though it is no bird. It looks like a small woman, if a woman were made up from parts of several different creatures. I acknowledge her presence with a dip of the head, then go on with the story.

Stone Galen gets over his bout of wretchedness and heads out again. Searches for another day; is weary, thirsty, hungry, and sad. Sleeps another lonely night. Comes down a hill and finds—ah! I place a smaller stone right in front of him, such a dark gray as to be almost black. I look at the being and make a gesture of bafflement. *Where is he?* I point to Stone Aolu, shining white, all alone, and mime a tender hug. *I need him home. Help me, please.*

Her eyes carry out a piercing assessment of me. I can't tell if she understood any of it.

"Please," I say quietly. "Please help if you can. And I will help you, if there's a need."

Quick as a flash, the being scoops stones from her cavern, her own collection, and piles them at the entry. I thought I was good at this game, but beside her I'm a novice. She tells her story, and I see it in my mind every step of the way.

The being leaves my stones in place, save for Stone Aolu, whom she sets aside. She waves her long-fingered hands up toward the trees, then shows with gestures that a broad area of forest surrounds us. With her stones, she shows that within the forest there are two parts or regions, and that in one of them she (the dark stone I chose for her) is a protector or guardian of the Crow Folk. *Safe.* She motions to the trees with their immobile tenants.

Prisoners? I ask by trapping a stone in my hand, making it fight to get out. Pointing up to the trees.

No. Safe. The being's gestures are clear.

Why? I indicate the being, the Crow Folk, the barrier. *Why hold them here?* There's something deeply unsettling about the stillness of these creatures. It's unnatural; how can they not be prisoners? They look drained of life. I can't help feeling sorry for them.

The being's hands move quickly with the stones, showing a sequence of events. Crow Folk gathering, not where we are now, but in the other part of the forest. If I hadn't heard about Brocc and this woman who's using him, and if I hadn't been up in the forest with Liobhan and the others to look, I wouldn't understand. Crow Folk flying in, Brocc singing, the Crow Folk flying off all together on some kind of mission. It's still happening. I've seen them pass over a few times each day.

The being shows me, *Bad.* She shows me, *They must not go,* meaning *her* Crow Folk, the ones who must be under some spell of immobility, if such a thing is possible. Or perhaps she means, *They cannot go.*

I can't keep asking why. It *is* bad. Or will be, if Brocc obeys that woman's will and turns the Crow Folk into an evil army. Brocc. My brother. I'm with Liobhan on this—I can't believe he'd do it. But he wouldn't sacrifice his own child, either. Who could do that? He must have a plan. And if his plan is what Liobhan thinks it is, this being is not protecting her Crow Folk. She's depriving them of their chance at freedom.

I lack the skills to convey this message. And I might be wrong. It all depends on Brocc. On his courage and integrity. On his strength. On his bond with the Crow Folk.

With gestures I request permission to touch her stones, and she nods a yes. I lift Stone Galen and Stone Brocc, and try to convey *brothers*. She may interpret it as friends or comrades. But I think she has some window into my thoughts, and perhaps she understands. Her expression conveys doubt; perhaps horror.

I'll have to show the whole thing and hope I'm right about Brocc. I set his stone back where it was. I make sure the stone army of Crow Folk is gathered around him. I show him singing; I show the Crow Folk rising together, circling the area, then flying right away, as far as my arms can take them. When I set them down, I make wave motions to show the sea. Elka's vision, and her tale, had the Crow Folk exiled from a far island. I pick up a larger stone and place it just within reach. I lift the dark stones, a few at a time, and set them on it.

For a brief moment I see longing in the being's eyes, hope, a dream. But the hope is dashed in an instant with a series of sharp gestures. *No! This cannot be!* She reaches up as if to embrace the silent birds above her. *They cannot go.*

Have I misunderstood something? Have I failed to explain? And how is it that the question I most wanted answered seems to have been forgotten, for there is Stone Aolu, set aside on the earth, all by himself, and I am no closer to finding my dear one.

I reach to retrieve the white stone, to get on with the search, for there's no help to be had here, and I don't know what this being wants from me. Before I can touch Stone Aolu the creature's hand is around my wrist, holding me back. Gods, she's strong!

Wait.

I resist the urge to free myself from her grip. I breathe. I wait.

The being reaches out her other hand toward my face. I try not to flinch; those claws could pierce an eyeball. But she does not attack me; she brushes the place where I bear the scars of that terrible day. Crow Folk wounds. There's a look on her face that says plainly, *I am sorry.*

I mime that I am better, that my injuries don't matter, that all I want to do is find Aolu. But she's not finished. It seems I haven't understood, not fully. She lets me go, and uses my stones to illustrate. Myself and Aolu together. Crow Folk swooping to attack, Stone Galen falling. Then a sweeping gesture toward the silent birds in the trees. *My people did this to you.* And, to make it clearer still, she holds up one finger. *One of them did it.* Her hands imitate flight; then she makes that gesture with hands crossed again. *They cannot go.*

The meaning seems clear, but I don't understand the significance. I've heard the story that may be the Crow Folk's history. Banished because of acts of violence. Not to return until they prove they can be peaceful. But . . . holding them in place with a spell, if that's what she's doing, is hardly a demonstration that they've changed. What does she plan, to keep them frozen in place forever? What they need is to be put to the test. Set free and given the chance to prove themselves. Though I have to admit, that prospect fills me with dismay.

I have too many questions; I have too much to say. The stones are not adequate for this. And while I sit here with this being, I am no closer to finding Aolu. I point to the white stone, raise my brows in question, then wave a hand north, south, east, west. *Where is he? If you know, please tell me.*

In the end, it is simple. She picks up Stone Aolu and places him on our small map, not with Brocc but within the area I judge to be where we are now. She collects a handful of forest debris and tucks it around and over him. She places Stone

Galen and the dark stone I chose to represent her not far away from Aolu. Then she points toward the clearing twenty paces away, with its little shelter made from branches and mud, mosses and leaves.

"He's there? So close?" My heart leaps. I make to rise, but something in her face halts me. I said I'd help. What does she want me to do?

The being uses my stones to answer this unspoken question. She moves Stone Galen to stand beside Stone Aolu, then tells me with gestures and expressions, *Talk. Talk to him. They cannot fly.*

She follows with a gesture I cannot interpret, waving again toward the clearing, then out into the far part of the forest beyond. *Talk! Talk!*

I don't understand, but I nod anyway. At this moment I might promise anything: the moon and stars, a lifetime of obedience, the head of her most fearsome enemy on a platter, if only I get Aolu back.

The being gathers up my stones. I hold the bag open and she tips them in, not dropping a single one. She is deft with those sharp-clawed hands. Not only a player of games, like me, but some sort of magic worker. If she has found Aolu for me, I owe her a great debt. Even if it was one of her folk that attacked me. I place a hand on my heart and give a little bow. *Thank you.*

She nods. Mimes with hands shaped into beaks, *Talk.* Points toward the clearing. *Now go.*

I turn, and he's standing there, at the edge of the clearing. Alive. Oh, gods, alive! He looks so thin and pale, and he's leaning on a stick. He's sprouting a fledgling beard. Staring at me as if I'm a ghost. He has one hand up, oddly, palm toward me.

"Aolu" I whisper, and start to walk. "Aolu!" I shout, and

begin to run, the stones clicking wildly in their bag. Oh, gods, let this not be some ghastly trick. "Aolu, it's really you," I gasp as I close the distance between us. Three more steps, two—

As I reach out toward him, my hand hits a wall that isn't there. A wall keeping me out. I can't believe this, I can't . . . Tears flood my face, but I don't wipe them away because I'm pushing, searching for a gap, groping for anything that might open the wretched barrier, anything, anything—

"Galen." Aolu's crying, too, crying and laughing at the same time. "Put your hand here." With his left hand he indicates his right, which is palm out against the wall. On the other side.

Hardly daring to believe the answer is so simple, I place my palm against his. For a moment I feel a surface hard as glass and cold as ice. Then it softens and warms, and Aolu's hand touches mine. Our fingers lock together. I step forward, weeping unashamedly, and take him in my arms.

33

DAU

At last we ride out toward Elderbrook: Mistress Sciath with five of her men, along with Garbh and me. We will stay in the area for a few days. Sciath explains that if, and only if, she is pleased with what she sees there, she will allow me to watch the bard, Donal, working with the Crow Folk. In my role as Master Dau of Oakhill, I thank her for the opportunity, then do a little negotiation over the terms. I insist that Garbh accompany me, not only on the trip to Elderbrook, but on the excursion to see the bard in action. I point out that Garbh is an experienced bodyguard, bigger and stronger than any of her own men, and can only enhance both my security and hers. I suggest that I might observe the bard on more than one day, provided her assessment at her first visit shows there is indeed progress being made. Sciath greets this remark with raised brows and pursed lips and says she will give it some thought. Later—after she has spoken with Almha, I suspect—she agrees to it.

Ah, Lady Almha. I don't suppose I will ever see her again. More than anything, I feel sorry for the woman. Who knows what drove her to the perilous path she's on? Once that first fatal step was taken, she must have been Sciath's puppet, too terrified to disagree as her adviser's plans became more and more grand and misguided.

I thought she might decide to come with us, to observe in person what Sciath is up to. But I'm glad she stayed at Darkwater. Her absence will make my job easier. I farewelled her with kind words, I kissed her hand, I acted as if I would be back in a few days' time to sit by her side at table and dance with her after supper and become more than a friend. I was careful not to make it obvious that the bags Garbh and I brought with us contained all of our belongings. In my case, that included a certain little book. I was sad and sorry that I had to remove this item from Master Suibne's workroom when he was absent and hide it deep under my folded clothing. When this is all over, if circumstances permit, I will write him a letter of thanks for his craftsmanship and his kindness.

And so we ride. A long day's journey, during which we see many other folk coming and going, on foot, on horseback, driving flocks of geese or herds of cattle, riding in ox-drawn carts. Liobhan and Elka should already be in Elderbrook; Garbh managed to give them advance notice of Sciath's plans. Their arrangement with the band was a casual one, so their rather abrupt departure shouldn't have ruffled any feathers. If matters come to a head in Elderbrook for one reason or another we'll have quite a strong team, with Illann and Hrothgar as well as those two. I've yet to find out how many men Sciath has there.

We ride into the settlement before dusk. Sciath is tired and out of sorts; she has told me she will be staying with friends at their home nearby, but holds back from inviting me to go with her, appropriate as that might be for Master Dau. Garbh and I will stay at the inn, where we know our horses will be well looked after. I tell Sciath we'll wait for further instructions. She bids me farewell with no ceremony at all, and rides away with one of her men in attendance. The rest of them stay with us as we head for the inn. I'd hoped they would go straight up the hill to their secret headquarters, but clearly that's not to be.

The inn is all very well for a meal and a night's shelter. But the longer I stay here the edgier I feel. Every time the door opens I find myself expecting Master Sealbhach to walk in. From the way Sciath spoke of him I gather he's out of favor right now. But the saddler gave the impression that Seanan is usually part of the brotherhood, and possibly high in the pecking order. Maybe he lives close to Elderbrook these days. What in the name of the gods will I do if he does turn up? The truth is, I don't trust myself. For a Swan Island man that doesn't sit well at all. Self-control is part of our code.

We're in luck with one thing—the private chamber is available. We don't stay to converse with our traveling companions or the assorted locals after supper, useful as that might be, though we note that the men who rode with us are known to those locals. I wondered, as they joined us for the journey, how many of them knew Seanan and whether Sciath had told them not to mention the resemblance between him and me. She must have done, surely, or someone would have commented on it by now. As it is, Garbh and I say a general good night and retire early to our sleeping quarters. We're both too tired to watch our words.

Liobhan will be staying at the safe house, along with the rest of the team. She's so close. I could walk there. I could see her now. But of course I can't do that. I may not even see her tomorrow. Garbh and I should stay near the inn in case Sciath appears, demanding to know where I am. I'm in Elderbrook as her guest, even if she doesn't offer me shelter under the same roof. I've gained a position of something close to trust, though I doubt Sciath ever fully trusts anyone. That position, if I can maintain it long enough, may be greatly to our advantage.

We don't hear from Sciath again until the second morning after our arrival. We haven't learned much during that time; it's too risky for either of us to go to the safe house, though at least we know where it is now. On the second evening we stay in the communal area after supper and listen to the talk. Only two members of the escort are there. I assume the other four went up to the camp, since with Sciath in the area and wanting a demonstration, they'll need numbers on hand. No Seanan as yet. I begin to hope, cautiously, that he's no longer in Elderbrook. The locals aren't talking to Sciath's men. They give them a wary glance from time to time and pass the salt on request, but that's about it. They do remember Garbh and me. Garbh chats to one or two of them, but the fact that we came in with Sciath's people this time has changed things; there's a caution even in that harmless conversation. They all know something's up and they're not happy with it.

The next morning Muna, the man who went with Sciath, comes to fetch us. He leaves his horse at the inn's stables and we head out of the settlement on foot. Garbh and I are careful not to give any sign that we know the way up to the camp; we let Muna lead us. He's armed with a dagger and small knife. We both carry similar weapons, along with those we have concealed on our persons. It's not unreasonable when we're heading into a forest packed with Crow Folk, though it wasn't them I was thinking of when I got ready for the day. There's no sign of Sciath herself, and I don't ask.

Muna doesn't caution us to keep quiet on the way up, but

our training means we do anyway. At one point, while he stops to adjust his boot, I risk whistling the first notes of the jig called "Artagan's Leap." I'm almost certain Liobhan and the others will be keeping a covert watch on us. Or they may be close to the camp and watching Brocc. I don't expect Liobhan to whistle back. But if she heard that tune, she'll know it's me. We'll need to get a message to them, work out a plan of action. Maybe Garbh can make it to the safe house and back unobserved tonight.

Muna's chosen path goes close to the rock formation that looks like an old woman and on up the hill. There are no white stones on the track today, but he knows where he's going, at one point making a sharp turn to the right, then heading up a steep branching track over rocks. This is the way Seanan took, that day when we saw him. Up to the camp.

I see them before they see me. Sciath is in animated conversation with one of her men and has her back turned. And there beside her, listening with a scowl on his face, is my brother. It's like a punch in the gut. I can't go on. Muna is ahead of us and notices nothing. But I feel Garbh's big hand on my shoulder and I breathe again.

"You can do it," my comrade murmurs. "Hold your head up, friend."

We go forward, and Sciath, alerted, turns to greet me. Seanan is slower to turn. I seize the advantage. "Mistress Sciath, good morning to you!" I force a smile as I walk over to her. *Not too close,* says my inner voice. *He might have a knife.* There's open curiosity on the faces of the men around us, but no real surprise. Clearly she's told them the man she brought with her from Darkwater is the brother of one of their own. But it seems nobody has warned Seanan. Shock turns his face pasty white. There's something terrible in his eyes. Something that brings back the darkest of memories, the ones I hoped I had banished when I made him face justice.

"You! What are you doing here?" His voice shakes, not with fear but with fury.

Sciath regards him with eyes cold as a winter frost. "Master Dau is in Elderbrook as my honored guest, Sealbhach. He is here at the personal invitation of Lady Almha, chieftain of Darkwater. I see that is not to your liking. I remind you that when you joined my team, you chose to hold back the information that you were the son of our neighboring chieftain and that you had been banished from his territory. You gave a false name. But for that, I might have been able to spare you what has clearly been a nasty shock. Now, we have work to do. Let me not hear so much as an uncivil word toward Master Dau if you wish to retain your place in the brotherhood. Is that understood?"

Murmured comments pass between the gathered men. From the looks they turn on Seanan, it's clear more than a few of them would be happy to see him gone. As would I; but I am here as Master Dau of Oakhill, and must give Sciath no reason to doubt me. "My brother and I have never been the best of friends, Mistress Sciath, as you know. But in the interests of today's exercise, we will set aside our differences, of course." Garbh's stalwart presence by my side is reassuring. There's double danger here. Seanan might decide Mistress Sciath needs to know I work for Swan Island now. That would surely give her pause. And what about Brocc, whom I haven't seen yet? Seanan knows him. Brocc was the only independent witness to my brother's torture of Liobhan and his men's murder of a fine young innocent. Not to speak of Seanan's vile treatment of the imprisoned Crow Folk. It was Brocc's testimony that sealed his fate. If Seanan comes out with that story, both Brocc and I might be in deep trouble.

But as it casts my brother in a particularly bad light, I imagine he'll keep his mouth shut.

Sciath still has her cold gaze fixed on Seanan. She's waiting for him to speak. But he simply steps back and loses himself in the group of men. The Brotherhood of the Dobhar-chú. Each with his silver belt buckle. I had thought Seanan could sink no lower, but it seems he has done just that.

"Very well," Mistress Sciath says briskly. "Now that Master Dau is with us, I want another display, as we discussed yesterday. Where is Donal? Is he ready? Is all prepared?"

Various men move away, some to the hut, others down into the woods. Seanan is still here. I think I would be aware of his presence even if I could not see him, as a person senses danger in the dark. As a victim senses a circling predator. But I stood up against the man in a formal hearing and exposed his wrongdoing publicly. I am no longer a victim. He has no hold over me.

"Master Donal is here, Mistress Sciath." It's a very big man, as big as Garbh, with a surprisingly soft voice. And beside him is Brocc. No reaction at all from Seanan, whom I'm watching out of the corner of my eye. When Brocc came to our rescue at Oakhill, he was robust, healthy, his dark hair glossy, his eyes bright, his stance upright. He looked like the Swan Island man he was, and he looked like the gifted, good-hearted musician he is. What I see now is a shadow of that man—gaunt, hollowed out, his skin sallow, his hair lank. The striking leaf-green clothing in which he came forth from the Otherworld has been replaced by dull, shapeless garments that hang loose on his body. I'm too shocked to say a word. I don't think Seanan has recognized him; if he had, he would have said something. At the hearing Brocc did describe himself as a wandering storyteller. But Seanan didn't know he was a musician. And at Oakhill, Brocc used his real name.

"Master Dau, this is our remarkable bard, Donal. He has been working with the Crow Folk and has already achieved some interesting results. We hope for more, of course. A great deal more."

Brocc gives an awkward bow. He looks at me as he would at a complete stranger. "Master Dau. Mistress Sciath. We can give you a demonstration as you requested. But as I explained from the start, progress will be gradual. And we cannot perform thus every day; it will tire not only the creatures but me as well. To push things too hard would be to imperil the entire venture."

"Nonetheless," says Sciath, her tone sharp, "time is of the essence. The longer this preparatory work takes, the harder it will become to keep this from the outside world." She raises her voice, addressing all the men. "Your roles are vital in maintaining that secrecy. Let me remind you all of the rules you must follow. You will maintain silence on these matters when you are beyond the established boundaries. News of our work must not reach the ears of outsiders, be they the men you drink with at the inn or more powerful folk. Each and every one of you is answerable to me. You've had a recent reminder of what happens when you get things wrong. There will be no such errors made here. While Master Donal is working, those of you assisting him will follow his instructions in every particular. Those of you guarding the perimeter will be constantly alert, lest intruders attempt to enter this part of the forest. Should there be a confrontation, you will act swiftly and decisively. Is that understood?"

A general rumble of "Yes, Mistress Sciath."

"Good. Ruairi?" Another hulking man comes over to her.

Sciath lowers her tone to a murmur. "Find Sealbhach something to do. Make sure it's away from the area where Donal will be working. Keep him busy until the demonstration is over. Master Dau is a future ally in our endeavor and his welfare is important to our chieftain."

"Understood, Mistress Sciath."

I say not a word. Seanan stay away from me? Seanan miss the opportunity to see Brocc working with the Crow Folk? Not a hope of either. I'll have to watch out for him. I'll need to beware of the sudden knife in the ribs. Though unless he's changed a lot, he'll have someone to do his dirty work for him.

We move through the forest to a clearing, a spot easy to find thanks to the presence of one formidably tall pine that looms not far off. It's quite a big open area, and the ground is level and well-trodden. Clearly someone's been working here, though there's short grass—scythed, perhaps—rather than bare earth underfoot. The pine is a lone specimen of its kind; I see rowan, holly, and whitebeam, with oaks beyond. In all the larger trees perch Crow Folk. In the center of the open space several large flat stones surround a small pool.

"Stay well back, please," says Brocc, his tone quietly assured. He may look like a man tormented by devils, but he's in full control of this. Whatever it's going to be. "I need their full attention throughout. Do not call out, make no sudden movements, do nothing to break my concentration or to startle the Crow Folk. Mistress Sciath, I don't believe a presence of guards is necessary. By now I have your trust, surely."

Sciath glances quickly at me; I am careful not to meet her eye. She is embarrassed, perhaps, to have me hear that the guards are required as much to keep her bard in as to keep intruders out. "Two close at hand, but out of sight," she says to Brocc. "For your safety, Master Donal, and for ours. Others further away but ready to move if necessary. Not long ago we all feared the Crow Folk. That fear has not vanished so quickly."

"Remember what I told you, then. Any act of violence against the Crow Folk by one of ours will provoke retaliation. Once that occurs, I will lose control of them and the project will be over." Brocc speaks with quiet certainty. Sciath may not like what he says, but she does not challenge it.

The guards retreat to take up their positions. No sign of Seanan. I'm tempted to send Garbh to keep an eye on him, but I need my comrade here. Although we're playing the parts of nobleman and bodyguard, we're equal partners in the mission, and I want him to see this. I stand next to Mistress Sciath; Garbh is on my other side, one step back. Muna stands within view. I'm guessing Sciath has him as her personal protector should something go wrong, though that was not part of her orders.

I've heard Brocc sing before. But this is quite different. His voice seems to resonate within me, shutting off everything else. It seems too powerful, too large for one man to contain. He stands in the middle of the circle, his arms outstretched. The words are like an ancient poem, something a druid might chant.

> *Three pathways for the feet of a bard:*
> *The path to wisdom*
> *The path of discovery*
> *The homeward path.*
> *May I bathe in the wellspring of knowledge*
> *May I walk in peace under sun, moon, and stars*
> *May I set down strong roots and spread my branches*
>   *wide*
> *May I fly a straight path, strong and free.*

The chant comes to an end. Beside me, Sciath is strung tight; I need not touch her to feel it. Brocc's words were deep and beautiful. They were surely not the words a man would use when training others to attack. He stands very still out there, his hands by his sides again, and a powerful silence fills the open space. Then one of the Crow Folk flies down to settle on the stones beside him, and I hear again those three strange, deep notes, a greeting as lovely and as full of power as Brocc's. The two of them stay there, unmoving. Perhaps some silent communication is occurring between them. Sciath is intent, her eyes fixed on Brocc to the exclusion of all else. I allow my gaze to shift a little, and I think I see someone standing in the shadows on the far side of the clearing. Someone who is not one of Sciath's men, nor indeed a man at all, for all the practical trousers and tunic, the sturdy boots, the mud-brown felt hat pulled down hard to hide her bright hair. My heart leaps. I look quickly away, and when I return my gaze to that point, she's gone.

As we watch, first one, then another, then a whole group of Crow Folk glides down to join Brocc and that first creature. I lose count. Certainly more than twenty, and the creatures are far bigger than ordinary crows. I trust Brocc. All the same, I feel edgy.

"A volunteer, to stand with me in the center," Brocc says, looking over at us. "More than one, if you wish. All that is required is to stand still, no matter what happens. They will fly very close. Perhaps yourself, Master Dau?"

Morrigan's curse! Sciath is about to speak, perhaps to say no. I step forward, and Garbh comes after me. "Happy to oblige, Master Donal," I say, doing my best to look and sound perfectly calm. "What would you have us do?"

What we must do, it seems, is stand on those stones out in the middle while the Crow Folk fly over us. I don't ask what Brocc means by *very close*, or whether anything else is involved. If Swan Island has taught me anything, it's when to keep my mouth shut. We stand there, Garbh and I. Sciath sends a third man out to join us, a guard named Scoithín. All of us are tall men. Brocc suggests we face inward, which is something of a relief. This feels uncomfortably like that day in Oakhill when he released the captive Crow Folk and they flew out of their prison right over my head. The fact that I was blind at the time made it no less terrifying.

Garbh's lips are moving. He may be praying or counting. His gaze is on the stone at our feet. He has one hand on my shoulder and one on Scoithín's. The guard and I copy his stance, and from an unsettled group of possible victims we become, for now, a small band of brothers. *May I walk in peace under sun, moon, and stars.* I keep my eyes open; I make myself look up into the trees. I meet the baleful gaze of many Crow Folk and I stand steady.

If Brocc speaks again, I don't hear it. Perhaps he speaks in a way only they can hear. Then he steps up beside us and we make a place for him in our circle. He gives us a smile of thanks.

A moment later, the Crow Folk come. So many. The clearing is all beating wings and shifting shadows: a whirl of darkness. Our hands tighten on one another's shoulders. I struggle to draw breath; my chest hurts. And then it's over. They rise, up into the trees, up into the sky. We're left in our circle, dazed and blinking. We're alive. Brocc has kept control, and we are unharmed.

I bring my hands down, step off the stone, find myself without words. Brocc looks up at the Crow Folk, then bows his head. A gesture of gratitude, of thanks. There's a bird up there with terrible scars; it's the one that flew down first. That bird dips its head, returning Brocc's salute. I have not seen this creature before. At our last encounter, I was blind. But I know it for one of those tortured by my brother and later released by Brocc and Liobhan. There is some great story behind what's happening here, a tale for the ages.

"Master Donal! Come!" Mistress Sciath is beckoning.

I don't want to move. Not yet. I'm still caught in the magic of it, terrifying as it was. So, I think, is Scoithín. Surreptitiously, he wipes tears from his eyes. His expression has more in it of awe than of terror.

"Best go," murmurs Garbh, and we follow Brocc to the edge of the clearing.

"Good," Sciath says, but she's not looking overjoyed or even particularly impressed. Never mind that her bard just persuaded a few hundred Crow Folk to perform a maneuver that was incredibly difficult given their number and the limited space. "For tomorrow's display I require more than this. We've already seen that the creatures can be trained to move together, to fly in formation. We've observed that they can listen and respond to your . . . incantations. This is only a first step, Master Donal."

I want to interrupt, to tell her she's being ridiculous. Instead I stand beside her, a mute puppet.

"Mistress Sciath," Brocc says, still quietly courteous, though he sounds exhausted, "I have explained how long the training may take. If we try to rush it, the Crow Folk may rebel. They may cease to cooperate. Each step must be taken carefully, with respect."

"Master Donal." Her tone is chill now. "Interesting as this display may have been, I have yet to see any indication that these creatures can be trained to perform acts of aggression. We know they can inflict serious hurt; we know they can kill. It appears to me that your method, remarkable as it is, may be dampening that aggression rather than developing it into the required tool." Sciath turns to me. "What is your opinion, Master Dau?"

"I have no expertise at all in this field, Mistress Sciath." *Quick, Dau, weigh it up.* Comrades close at hand; Brocc in trouble. For the Crow Folk, a perilous turning point. But we can't act yet. Brocc needs time to finish whatever it is he's doing here. I must retain Sciath's trust. "What we saw just now deeply impressed me. Were I in your shoes, I would be inclined to give Master Donal whatever time he requires to complete this project. But I am here as an observer only. I am not yet party to the plan; nor is my father. The decision is all yours."

Sciath's smile is devoid of warmth. "We will not require a second demonstration today, Master Donal. In view of your comment, we will allow you time to rest and recover. Tomorrow, you will provide evidence of further progress toward our goal. I wish to see the creatures launch an attack. Not the practice maneuver we saw just now. A real attack."

I'm stunned. What can she mean? Are we to stand in a circle and allow the creatures to peck out our eyes?

Brocc clears his throat. He's turned white. But when he speaks, his voice is steady. "An attack on whom?"

Sciath's eye passes over those of her men who are in view: Scoithín, who stood strong with us; Muna, whom she seems to trust; a couple of others who have emerged from their semiconcealment under the trees. No sign of Seanan now. "Travelers," she says. "Strangers. You must make it seem like a random attack. In and out quickly. But no more of this feinting. I want to see blood drawn."

Morrigan's curse! The woman's crazy. What would Almha think of this? Brocc is gathering himself to respond, but I speak first. "Mistress Sciath, if you do not wish to draw outside attention to this place and its activities, surely that is not a wise move. If ordinary folk going about their business are hurt or even killed, the community will be deeply unsettled. I would even go so far as to say outraged."

Slowly, so slowly, she turns her head and fixes her eye on me. "It is for Master Donal to ensure that does not happen. The attack must take place in such a way as to divert attention from us. I imagine it would be easy. After doing their work, the creatures could be ordered to fly off somewhere else and wait until after dark to return here."

There is no point at all in speaking of good and evil, moral and grossly immoral. There is no point in raising an argument about deaths in battle being different from a random killing of the innocent. I say nothing. I watch Brocc.

"You understand, of course," he says carefully, "that this clearing would not be a suitable place for such a venture, since it allows no view of the valley and the road. I might send the Crow Folk off on such a mission and they might execute it perfectly, but that would be pointless if you were unable to observe them. Besides, I doubt I would be able to control them while they were out of sight. There is a suitable area east of the camp—a small lake, some open space around it, sheltering trees. And a view down to the valley, narrow but adequate. You can see a stretch of the road. The exact timing would depend on the appearance of an appropriate target. Ideally that would be a lone traveler, with nobody else in view. I lack the ability to divert attention if a crowd observes the attack, no matter where the Crow Folk fly afterward. And I would be inhuman if I cared nothing for how many souls perished for the sake of a mere demonstration."

Sciath takes him by the arm and walks him a short distance away from us. She lowers her voice to a murmur. But I am trained to listen, and I hear every word. "I sense a certain reluctance, Master Donal. The words of your incantation seemed to reflect that. I heard nothing in it of a rallying cry, a call to arms. Let me set this out clearly for you, since you appear slow to understand. You will provide the required demonstration tomorrow, without fail, or your daughter will suffer the consequences. My reach is long. I could end her life in a moment." A snap of the fingers. "Perhaps you do not believe I would do such a thing. Put it to the test if you will, and live with the consequences."

Gods. The woman is a monster. I look down at the ground, unable to guard my features. My mind is working fast. With his daughter's life in the balance, Brocc is sure to attempt this even though he believes it's too soon. If I'm right about what he's planning to do, we'll need to be here, all of us, and ready to get him safely away as soon as it's over. Whether or not he manages to do it, he'll be weakened by the effort. I can't count him among our fighters. That leaves six of us. Sciath's men number more than twice that. Our skills are superior. But Sciath's utterly ruthless. She's just made that clear. She'll draw every member of the brotherhood with her down that dark path until she reaches her goal.

Brocc's saying something. "I will show you the place now. Tomorrow, in the afternoon, we will attempt what you require."

"*Attempt* is not good enough, Master Donal."

"We will carry out the exercise. I'll need quiet in the camp for the remainder of today and overnight. The Crow Folk need rest and so do I. Leave a few men to watch over me if you think it necessary. Only a few. I am far too weary to run off anywhere, I assure you. And I must be at my strongest tomorrow."

For just a moment, while Sciath's attention is elsewhere, Brocc meets my gaze. I lift my brows a touch; he gives the very smallest of nods. Thus, under the very eye of our enemy, it is agreed. Tomorrow we act.

34

LIOBHAN

I'm short of sleep, but too wound up to feel it yet. Nobody expected this to come so soon. Today Brocc will attempt his near-impossible task. And we'll be there, ready to deal with the aftermath. Just about anything could happen.

Garbh came last night to warn us. For a moment I expected Dau to walk in behind him and my heart performed a little jig, but of course they wouldn't both come. It was risky enough for one of them to leave the inn and walk here with Mistress Sciath's crew in the neighborhood, not to speak of wretched Seanan.

We stayed up late trying to make a plan that covered all possibilities, or at least to draw up some basic rules of engagement. Galen hasn't come back, and that makes things more complicated. We know that if it comes to a fight we'll be outnumbered. But there's no way we'll leave Brocc in that woman's clutches. If we have to get him away in a hurry, we'll have no choice but to leave Galen where he is: in the Otherworld.

Garbh headed back to the inn while it was still dark. And now, in the faintest predawn light, Illann and I are taking a look at the place where this is going to happen—not the open space in the forest where I watched Brocc working before, but the spot where that waterfall spills into a small lake surrounded by elders. I wish it weren't so perilously close to the group's headquarters. Brocc's chosen it because there's a view across the fields to the Darkwater road. Sciath can watch as he sends the Crow Folk down there to attack some hapless traveler. At least, that's what she's asked for. There's no way he'll do it. He couldn't tell Dau that, not in so many words, but that was what both Dau and Garbh understood, and I know they're right. Brocc's chant was all about freedom and peace. Even Mistress Sciath thought it doubtful, despite the demonstration making it obvious what havoc the creatures could wreak, and the undeniable fact that Brocc already has remarkable control over them. She's pushed him too far. He has to defy her today, and knowing what I know now about the Crow Folk, I can guess what he'll do. It will leave him completely vulnerable.

In the early light there's something disturbing about this spot. The water shimmers as if fish or frogs are moving about beneath the surface, and though the air is still, the elder leaves tremble. I see no Crow Folk in these trees, though we spotted some roosting high in the oaks as we came up the hill. The only sound is the gentle splashing of the waterfall. Birds should be starting to call in the forest, sending out their greetings to the approaching dawn. But their voices are silent.

Although there are no guards around, Illann and I tread with caution as we take stock of the area, looking for quick exits, possible traps, places to hide. I wonder if Sciath will want all her men present to witness the feat, or whether she'll prefer to limit it to a select few so the news doesn't get out. She'd be deluding herself if she believed that possible. If Brocc did what she's ordered him to do, she'd have no hope of keeping it quiet.

Illann motions to me. It's getting lighter, and we must move. We retreat into the forest and back toward the safe house. I take him past the Hag of the Hill. This morning there is no white stone and no sign of an opening in the rock. I bow to the Hag anyway, whispering a *thank you* while Illann stands quiet beside me. The Otherworld being what it is, Galen might be anywhere: just on the other side of that spot where the portal opened, or in an uncanny place far, far away. He might emerge as a wizened old man, having lived many years in that realm while here only a day has passed. I want both my brothers back. I want them here in this world, safe and sound: Brocc with his child, Galen with his beloved Aolu. But each is on his own quest; each must endure his own trial and win through.

"All right?" murmurs Illann, glancing my way with concern.

"Mm. Just wishing I could fix everything right now. The feeling will pass. I hope."

"There might be some hard choices to make," says Illann as we head down toward the fields. "And not much time to make them in. You think Elka's up to this?"

"She'll be fine. She's quick, she's strong, she's unafraid. Just what we need."

Afternoon, and we're all in place. Getting in close was tricky with so much activity around the camp, but we know what we're doing, and we made sure we weren't spotted. The elder trees don't provide good enough cover, so we're a little further from the lake than is ideal, but we can see and we should be able to hear, unless people whisper. I'm in an oak tree, sharing my branch uneasily with two of the Crow Folk, while other birds perch above me. I'm next to the trunk, wearing clothing that blends, with my hat pulled down over my hair and a brown cloth over my nose and mouth. I wish I didn't need to be silent. I have my whistle stuck in my belt alongside my knife. A tune would be a good way to let these creatures know I'm a friend. But I can't make a sound. Can't even hum. Elka's concealed further up the hill, above the lake. Illann and Hrothgar are at ground level, not far from me.

Now we wait. I try not to do anything that might startle the Crow Folk beside me. I don't look either of them in the eye. But I notice something about the larger one, and suddenly I understand why they tolerate my presence so close. That creature has scars. One of those scars is the same shape as the burn that disfigures my own arm—a wound inflicted by Dau's brother Seanan, and based on their family emblem of a sword and dagger crossed. Here, not an arm's length from me, is one of the birds Brocc released from captivity while I sang a song of flight. This, I feel sure, is Brocc's friend and comrade in the work that's being done here. A survivor, like me. And he recognizes me; I don't need to roll up my sleeve and show him my own mark. He was there, caged and watching, when Seanan did it to me. My skin prickles with the strangeness of this. *You'll win through,* I tell him silently. *You'll fly home. I believe it.*

I watch as Sciath's men—the Brotherhood of the Dobharchú—come out and perform a quick patrol of the area, keeping well away from the water. Nobody makes an offering. I'm wishing I'd spoken words of greeting and thanks at the water's edge when Illann and I came here earlier. At least I showed respect to the Hag of the Hill. But this spot is different. Too late now. I speak the words in my mind as I look down toward the lake now gleaming in sunlight. *You are old. You are wise. I'm sorry we had to intrude on your home. I wish you nothing but good.*

The creature beside me ruffles his feathers and dips his head in my direction, almost as if he heard that silent greeting and approves of it. *I am the bard's sister,* I tell him, wondering if I am deluding myself about how much he understands. *I and my friends are here to help him, and to help you. I thank you for trusting him and for keeping him safe.* If not for this creature's courage, surely Brocc would long ago have fallen foul of the Crow Folk. There are hundreds of them in this forest. Without this comrade's support, he would not have survived.

An image comes to me uninvited. Brocc, looking harried and exhausted, out in the open somewhere, with rain pelting down. The infant in his arms, as in that vision we saw in the cavern on Swan Island. The two of them seeking shelter in the meager protection of a tumbledown outbuilding, and a bird, this bird, flying down to put something in Brocc's hand. Food. For just a moment I see the look on Brocc's face, and know that this was the difference between life and death for his child. As the image fades, tears roll down my cheeks. I look at the bird and bow my head. *Thank you. We owe you much.*

Then, below us, men come from the camp. Six take up stations where trees give way to lakeshore, one heads down the track that eventually leads to the settlement, and two move a short way further into the forest. That may or may not be good news for Hrothgar and Illann. We're trained to disable a man quickly without doing lasting damage. That's not so easy if he spots us before we get our hands around his neck, especially if he has time to draw a knife. Or shout for help. I note where they are in relation to my tree.

So that's nine men. And then it's twelve, because Mistress Sciath appears on the path from the settlement. She not only has Dau and Garbh with her as expected, but also three members of her brotherhood with their shiny belt buckles gleaming in the afternoon sun. Six of us, counting our two comrades out there, and twelve of them. At least none of them is Seanan. He may not be much of a fighter, but his presence would be less than helpful.

I glance over toward the rocks on the hillside, where Elka is hiding. I hope she can get away if things turn bad. If she has to act, she'll need to step right out into the open. She'll be vulnerable even with her leather chest-piece on.

Brocc enters the area without fuss. I recognize the guard who follows him. It's the big man who stood up with the others in the face of that mock attack yesterday. So that's thirteen of them. We can do this. We can and will.

My brother looks perfectly calm, though I bet his heart's going like a panicking horse, the same as mine. I make myself breathe slowly. Brocc inclines his head to Mistress Sciath in courteous greeting. She offers a tight nod in return, as if she wishes he would get on with things.

A hush descends. The guards stand in their positions, vigilant. Dau is an arm's length from Sciath, with Garbh behind him. That outfit Dau's wearing must be borrowed, like the one he had on for dancing. Back home, he'd never wear blue.

Brocc moves away from his observers. He has his back to the lake and his face to the trees. He lifts his arms, stretching them out as if he would encompass elders and oaks and Crow Folk in his embrace. A shiver runs through me. I've watched him perform this exercise before; heard the careful introductory greetings, waited through the silent communication that followed. Heard the song that called them all to move, to fly, to do what was asked of them.

But now, Brocc is silent. All eyes are on him. He does not move. He does not speak or sing. But . . . perhaps the Crow Folk can hear something. I sense my brother is gathering strength, gathering power from the land, from the ancient oaks, from the clear sky above us, and perhaps, too, from that oddly gleaming body of water behind him. I can feel it. I can hear it in my mind. *Wait, brothers and sisters. Wait just a little longer. Home is only a breath away.* Brocc's face is alight, as if some power from beyond the human world inspires him. Maybe it comes from the creature perched motionless beside me, for its eyes have turned bright as stars. I think of the seer in the cave on Swan Island. I think of Elka's tale. I think of marvels.

There's a moment, just a moment, when Sciath comes close to breaking the magic. She moves a hand, impatient; she mutters something, and such is the stillness that even up here in the tree I can hear the angry tone of it, though the words are unclear. My gut tightens. I can see from Dau's stance that he's ready to grab the woman if she tries to interfere. Garbh has his eye on the guards stationed close by. He'll be deciding which one to tackle first, and how he'll do it. But this mustn't come to a fight. Not yet. If Elka is right about the Crow Folk, the moment one of them commits an act of violence they are all condemned to remain in exile.

Brocc draws in a breath; waits a moment. Lifts his voice in song. It is not the formal greeting of last time. It is the voice he used once in Breifne when he warded off an attack: wordless, uncanny, full of power. When I first heard it, I thought it baleful and terrifying. It is even stronger today, ringing out across the forest, reaching skyward like the bright rallying call of a trumpet. He doesn't need words. The meaning is clear. *Rise! You are free! Spread your wings and fly homeward!*

"Safe journey, friend," I murmur to the dark-feathered being beside me, knowing my voice will be swallowed in the great music of Brocc's, but knowing, too, that this creature will hear it. "Lead your people home."

It blinks its shining eyes once, twice, three times, then opens its wings and, with one powerful beat, launches itself from the branch. A moment later my oak is empty of Crow Folk as they rise and follow, circling the lake, passing over Brocc in thanks and farewell. Tears glint on my brother's cheeks as he gazes up, still singing. One tree, then another releases its birds; each group in turn circles, then follows its scarred leader and his companions as they rise higher, then wing their way down toward the valley. Sciath has her head tipped back, one hand shading her eyes as she follows their progress. Thus far, they are doing exactly what she asked for.

A shifting shadow darkens the area. No sparkle on the lake water, no sunlight through the leaves, only the dense, moving cloud of birds passing overhead. So many. The movement of their wings makes a strange soft accompaniment to Brocc's song, which continues its wordless message of hope and freedom, courage and comradeship. Under cover of the temporary darkness I slip down from my perch and move to a position from which I can run forward.

The shadow lifts. They are gone. Sciath hurries to a spot that allows a view down to the Darkwater road, motioning to Dau that he should follow. Garbh lingers; he'll be preparing himself for a fight. Brocc falls silent.

It's never been so hard to keep still. My brother looks worn out, drained of life, barely able to keep to his feet. The urge to rush over and help him is almost overwhelming. But I don't move yet. Step in too soon and I'll turn the whole thing to disaster.

Sciath gazes down to the valley. She stands there a good while. I see her shoulders tighten, her hands clench into fists. Dau's stance is relaxed. He's good at this. I count to twenty.

I count to forty. Then, high above us, we see them returning. One leading; seven behind him. And then, the whole great flock of them, passing over us and away to the north, bound for their far-off island. It is a wondrous sight, the stuff of grand stories and epic songs. A tale for the ages.

Sciath turns. Dau is not watching her. He's looking across the water to the spot where men come in and out from the camp. His face is white. His mouth is a thin line. I follow his gaze, and there is Seanan.

Sciath walks with deliberate purpose around the lake's edge toward Brocc. "What is the meaning of this, Master Donal?" she demands. Her voice is deathly quiet and heavy with menace.

Brocc rocks slightly on his feet, as if he might faint. "Mistress Sciath?"

"You heard my orders! The creatures were to fly down to the road, execute an attack, then return here." She gestures up toward the oaks, where no bird of any kind at all is visible. "Instead, they are gone! Flown away! They could be anywhere! And there was no attack; all they did was fly past some travelers, who appeared completely unharmed!"

They did? I'm even more impressed. I wish I'd been able to see that. The tale of it will surely be told in this district for long years to come.

Brocc has nothing to say. He stands there, passive.

"Call them back! Make them obey!" When Brocc remains silent, Sciath's tone becomes menacing. My hands itch to throttle that woman. I'd do it without a second thought. "Have you forgotten the agreement, Master Donal? What of your child? Do you throw her life away so quickly?"

Brocc looks her straight in the eye. The strength of his spirit shines through the exhaustion of his body. "There is no point in your threats," he says. "The Crow Folk are gone.

Without them, there can be no army. I can no longer be of service to you."

A sound emerges from Sciath, something between a scream of frustration and a howl of rage. Then she calls sharply, "Sealbhach!"

Seanan steps forward. He's behind Brocc, who does not turn. "You heard what the man said," says Sciath. "He's outlived his usefulness. Deal with him. The child can wait."

Seanan has a knife in his hand. I'm too far away to act, and Dau can't see it. As Seanan advances, he raises the weapon. Garbh moves too late, shouting a warning, but someone else is there, a sturdy form leaping forward to throw himself between Seanan and his target. It's one of Sciath's brotherhood, the man who was guarding Brocc. He wrestles with Seanan for possession of the weapon. The big man must surely prevail—Seanan's not much of an opponent—but no. Seanan slashes about wildly as they roll on the ground, and it's the other man who's bleeding. A couple of the guards try to intervene, and Sciath orders them back sharply. But Dau is not one of her men, and it's Dau who moves in. My hand is on the hilt of my big knife. I'm ready to run forward but I can't see Hrothgar or Illann, so I wait.

The knife is on the ground; Dau picks it up. Seanan has his back to the lake. The man he wounded is advancing on him slowly, fists raised. There's a spreading crimson stain on his tunic, but he keeps on coming.

"You!" Seanan points at Dau, his face a mask of loathing. "Mistress Sciath, your fine friend here is a spy! He's here to undermine your plan, not to help you! You wonder why the bard let you down? They're in collusion, the two of them!"

"Shut your mouth, Sealbhach." The big man takes another step toward Seanan, and Seanan takes a step back. "You're no man to accuse others of treachery. I'll tell the tale now if the rest of you won't!" He's sheet-white, and the bloodstain is growing, but he looks around the other guards as he speaks, and not one of them moves to stop him. "He sent us in, on that woman's commands, to secure a target: the bard she was seeking to create her army. Sealbhach chose the wrong man, and because of that, four of our own lost their lives. Then, when Mistress Sciath demanded an accounting, Sealbhach blamed Finchán for the error. And who was it Mistress Sciath ordered to punish Finchán? To make an example of him? That man there. I saw it. I watched Sealbhach beat our comrade, I watched as Finchán was beheaded, and I didn't challenge it. I didn't speak up, and I'll regret that until my dying day. But I speak the truth now, and there are men among you who know it, men who witnessed it as I did. Sealbhach's a liar. He cares for nobody but himself. He's a betrayer of his own."

He takes another step forward. Now Seanan's feet are in the water. As for the brotherhood, they seem frozen. Not a single one of them has attempted to intervene. Seanan looks around wildly. The wounded man is still upright, and he's big enough to block Seanan from getting past.

"Help me!" Seanan gasps. The man he's looking at is Dau, who's standing back a little now, turning the knife over and over in his hands. "Don't just stand there, do something!"

I can't see Dau's face very well, but I think perhaps he smiles. Then, with graceful nonchalance, he tosses the knife out into the lake, where it sinks in a small burst of bubbles.

The big man lunges forward as if to attack. Seanan falls backward with a great splash. There's a collective gasp; I fail to keep silent, but nobody's paying attention to me. When I glance around I see figures moving quickly forward under the trees; my comrades are ready.

For a moment Seanan goes right under the water. Then he

bobs up, gasping, and struggles back toward the shore. The big man is faltering, his hand pressed hard to his ribs. Dau moves in on one side, Garbh on the other, to support him.

And then, oh, then . . . The force of Seanan's scream makes the leaves shiver; it makes my heart clench tight. I can't drag my eyes away from the water. The creature rises. Its body resembles neither dog nor otter. It is more like a serpent from an ancient tale of wonder and horror. Its gaping mouth is full of pointed teeth, its skin is all glistening scales, green and gray and moon-white, both beautiful and terrible to behold. Its eyes speak justice and vengeance and hunger. Its jaws fasten around the man in the water, and as they tighten the scream becomes a gasping squeal, and blood pours from Seanan's mouth to darken the sparkling waters with the stain of death. The creature curls its body and flicks its long tail as if to dismiss us, then both dobhar-chú and victim vanish beneath the water, leaving only ripples.

One of the men utters a shocked oath. Another spews up his breakfast in the long grass. Down by the water's edge, the big man has shaken off his helpers and is trying to unclasp his belt, but his hands are shaking. Dau reaches to do it for him. The big man bends to lay the belt, with its shining silver buckle, down on the lakeshore. He murmurs something, then rises to face Sciath, who appears both frozen and wordless. "My membership of the brotherhood is ended," he says simply.

Still she utters not a word. Shocked into silence, like the rest of us? Or something else? She stands watching as Dau strips off his tunic and shirt, wads the shirt up and presses it against the big man's side. Garbh casts about for something to strap it on with. In a moment when both are off guard Sciath moves, quick as a flash, too quick for me, and suddenly she's got a knife at Brocc's throat. "Move an inch, any

of you, and I'll kill your precious bard for you. Leave Scoithín, he's a useless great lump of flesh and not worth saving.
I said leave him! Get up, *Master* Dau, you devious piece of
scum! And your friend there! Let that wretch bleed!"

I can't reach her in time. Even Dau and Garbh can't; she's
a few strides away from them and she's pushed Brocc down
on his knees, weakened as he is. She's got the knife in one
hand, its blade trembling against his skin, and her other hand
is clasped tight in his curly hair. The moment any of us
moves, he'll be gone.

Dau rises very slowly, showing his open, empty hands.

"And you!"

Garbh releases his hand from the makeshift bandage he's
pressing against the big man's wound, and gets to his feet.
The injured man lets out a moaning sigh. If he doesn't get
help soon, his act of courage may cost him his life.

A sudden *whoosh* makes everyone start. Sciath's legs give
way and she collapses onto the shore. A terrible sound comes
from her. The sound a person makes when an arrow's just
gone through their neck. She lies sprawled on the ground,
her head curiously propped up by the arrow shaft, her eyes
wide and blank. Blood pools on the earth beneath her. Up by
the rocks, beyond the lake, Elka lowers her bow. Morrigan's
britches! I knew that woman was a good shot, but I didn't
realize quite how good.

The men of the brotherhood are slipping away. Nobody
wants to take charge. Nobody wants to help with the
wounded man, the dead woman, the whole situation. In particular, nobody wants to be any nearer to that lake. Those
few who remain size us up: Hrothgar, Illann, and me, all
well armed; Elka now concealed behind the rocks above the
lake, but doubtless ready to shoot again. Garbh and Dau,
standing by us. Dau looks shaken, as well he might; he just

saw a monster eat his brother. But that won't stop him from fighting. And Brocc, too, will play a part if he must. He's gone over to help the injured man, but he's taken Sciath's knife with him.

"You want a fight, you've got one!" shouts Garbh. "Come on, then, fools! Your leader's dead and that thing in the lake's just waiting for someone to get close enough! And half your men have already seen the wisdom of getting away, from the looks of it. Why not take yourselves off now, quietly? Head right out of Elderbrook, avoid the nasty sort of trouble that happens when the chieftain's right-hand woman is found dead next to your camp. We'll give you a head start. But not much of one. Best get moving."

They vanish like ghosts. Some back toward the camp, some into the forest by one path or another. Elka makes her way down the rocky hillside, her bow over her shoulder, and comes to join us.

"Expert shot," says Illann, giving her a sideways look. "Quick thinking."

"Well done," I add.

"Dau," says Brocc. "Scoithín here needs help. Fast. We need to get him down to the settlement."

His tone tells us the unspoken part: if we don't move right now, Scoithín's going to die. Brocc himself looks too exhausted to walk far.

"I'll carry him," says Garbh.

"Wait." Time for me to step in. "Let me have a look. I can at least bind it up properly before we try to get him down the hill." As the daughter of a healer, I have sufficient skill to keep this man alive for long enough. I hope I do. As I bandage the wound with various strips of cloth my companions find for me, I'm thinking of the tricky walk down. How likely is it that there will be a physician in a place like Elderbrook?

Besides, if we make an appearance in the settlement the whole thing will immediately become public knowledge. I glance over toward Sciath's body, still lying in its grotesque pose. Her men have left this area. That doesn't mean they won't decide to regroup and attack us on our way down. We might find ourselves accused of murder. All very well to say Sciath threatened Brocc's life and Elka saved him. Nobody will believe she could shoot so accurately from that distance. Besides, our rules say we don't draw attention to Swan Island. And we don't draw attention to a safe house or it can't perform that function any longer.

Scoithín's conscious. But the wound needs cleaning, it needs stitching, and he could do with a draft for the pain. There's a solution. A possible one.

"We have no choice but to move him," I tell the others. "Brocc and I will go ahead, looking out for trouble. Elka, you'll be the rear guard. The rest of you take turns carrying Scoithín. Two at a time would be best, we don't want any damaged backs. If the wound starts bleeding heavily again tell me straightaway. Illann, we should take him to the Hag of the Hill. We may be able to bypass the safe house. There's something we can try there." I glance at Brocc, who has moved to cover Sciath's body with someone's discarded cloak. Belatedly, I remember that I'm not in charge.

"Good plan," Illann says. "Garbh, you and I will take the first stretch. Lift him carefully. Scoithín, this may hurt. Tell us if it gets too bad and we'll let you rest a bit."

We're used to working as a team. As we make our way down the hill I tell Brocc about the portal and Galen's search for the prince. I don't ask questions about what just happened, or indeed about what drove him and his daughter out of Eirne's realm. He listens, but he seems distracted, glancing up toward the oak canopy from time to time as if he expects Crow Folk. There are none in sight. It seems they really have flown home.

It's slow going for Illann and the others, but they're Swan Island men, trained for such tasks. Where the path is steep, they handle the wounded man with extreme care, sometimes with all four of them helping support his weight as they maneuver down rocks or find a way over streams whose bridges are inadequate for their purpose. Dau looks grim; he understands that there's a life in the balance, though I tried to sound confident earlier, since Scoithín could hear me. If the portal won't open or is slow to open we'll have to go to the safe house, and it'll probably be up to me to look after him. I doubt my limited skills will be up to the task. Perhaps we should have sent someone ahead to ask for help. I curse under my breath.

Brocc keeps looking up. He's humming quietly. Is he still with us, or off in some trance? I need him alert. I need him ready at the portal.

"Brocc?"

He stumbles, then rights himself. Behind us, Garbh and Illann are transferring the wounded man to Hrothgar and Dau. We move on.

"Are you all right? What you just did . . . that was remarkable."

"Mm," murmurs Brocc. He walks on a while in silence, then says, "I don't think they're gone. Not all of them. Something's wrong."

Morrigan's curse. This, I hadn't expected. "The Crow Folk? But they flew away. Right away, Brocc. I can't see a single one of them."

"Something's wrong. I feel it."

I glance around, seeking shadows, attackers, enemies. Nothing. Sciath's gone. Seanan's gone. I don't see the Brotherhood of the Dobhar-chú girding their loins for a mass attack.

We come to the lower reaches of the forest, and at last we're on the path that leads past the Hag of the Hill. Now I hear voices: men's voices, distant yet but drawing closer. They're coming from down in the fields, and they sound agitated. Someone's taken the tale of Master Sealbhach's messy demise to the settlement. What they've said about us I have no idea, but the sounds I hear are not promising. We don't want to find ourselves fighting villagers armed with pitchforks. Our mission doesn't include killing the local populace.

"Along here," I say as the voices grow louder. "And trust me. This is it, Brocc. Right here, this is where Galen went through. We need to sing."

It's a measure of my comrades' trust that not one of them questions this, even though our voices will draw those folk straight to us. I glance at Brocc. What song will open this doorway for us? An old woman . . . a hill . . . an oak . . .

"There was an old woman with eyes so bright," I sing.

Brocc is quick to follow. *"Oh, the oak, the ash, and the yew!"*

> *Her hair shone silver by day and night.*
> *Oh, the holly and willow!*

Elka has an arrow to the bowstring; Hrothgar and Illann have knives at the ready. Garbh and Dau support Scoithín between them.

> *She was as wise as wise could be.*
> *Oh, the oak, the ash, and the yew.*
> *She dwelled within a sturdy tree*
> *Oh, the holly and willow!*
> *A song or rhyme would let them through*

Oh, the oak, the ash, and the yew.
Warrior, prince, or bard so true
Oh, the holly and willow!

We stand a moment in silence; Scoithín's labored breathing can be heard above the shouting from down in the fields. Then Brocc says, "Help us, please. A good man is in trouble. A whole clan is in peril. We come in peace. Will you open your door to us?"

And as figures appear below us at the edge of the woods, with an assortment of makeshift weapons over their shoulders, the Hag does just that. The entry is narrow; it's tricky getting Scoithín through. Dau directs the other men, who maneuver the injured man between them while Elka and I hold the villagers at bay. A few call out derisive comments—they are not used to seeing a pair of shapely women aiming weapons at them, I suppose—but we ignore that. With luck, we won't need to kill anyone.

"Liobhan!" comes Dau's voice from behind us somewhere. "We're in!"

We back toward the portal, Elka still with arrow to string, then before the villagers' shocked gaze we turn and slip quickly through. The doorway closes behind us, and we're in another world. Forest, still, and pathways under the trees, but . . . different. It's not so much the way it looks, but the prickling of my skin, the beating of my heart, the shifting shadows. Which way? We must find help before we lose Scoithín.

"This way," Brocc says, pointing down one of the three possible tracks. "Liobhan, you go first. Play your whistle." Because, of course, it's tucked into my belt, perfectly visible.

I play. Nothing sad. Nothing too quick and fancy, since I have to keep walking. But I know a lot of tunes, and I play them one after another as we make our way through this realm, which is both like and unlike the forest above Elderbrook. When he's not taking a turn to carry the wounded man, Dau walks beside me. Who would have thought something so simple could fill my heart with joy? Who would have believed that trace of a smile on his lips could make every part of me sing?

As we walk on, something remarkable happens. Whether it's the music, or whether it's the fact that Brocc is with us, it seems the folk of this place are helping us on our way. Wherever the path branches, a white stone has been placed on one track. We pass streams and pools shaded by water-loving elder trees. We climb hills clad in stands of stately pines. Mostly the way is easy, which is just as well, for Scoithín is barely conscious and he's a heavy load to carry, even for such a strong group.

At last we see a clearing ahead, and there seem to be figures there. Brocc stops walking so suddenly the men coming up behind nearly walk into us.

"Crow Folk," Brocc says, looking up into the pines. "Still here. Some didn't fly."

There they are, some at least, perched immobile above us. There's a terrible disappointment on my brother's face; I feel it myself, a heaviness in the belly. "There's still time, isn't there? Couldn't you sing again?"

"Shadow is gone. I can't do it without him."

"Move forward," says Illann from behind us. "There are folk ahead there, we can ask for help."

We approach with care. It's plain the folk we can see are not human folk, and I remember something. "Set your weapons aside," I tell my comrades. "All of them. Pile them up beside the track. These folk fear iron, and we need their trust."

They do as I ask, not without some muttered objections. And we go on. Near enough to get a good look at the strange assortment of small folk gathered in the clearing, watching our approach. They are very like Eirne's people, those among whom Brocc lived; that may be helpful.

And then—oh, then . . . there's a shout. "Liobhan! Brocc!" Galen's voice. And there he is, waving madly. He made it in, he sounds fine. Does that mean . . . ?

We advance, and the miracle is true. Galen comes striding to meet us, and behind him comes the unmistakable figure of Prince Aolu, looking somewhat unkempt and using a stick for support, but with a big smile on his face. Behind them walks a woman no taller than a child, whose necklace of tiny skulls and acorn cups and other things of the forest marks her out as exactly what we most need: a healer. She looks as the Hag of the Hill might look if she were made of flesh and blood rather than roots and leaves and stone.

Enough time later for explanations and plans. "We need help," I say, bowing respectfully to the being. "I am the daughter of a wisewoman and healer, in my own world. This man is hurt, bleeding. Will you tend to him?" I glance around at my companions, noting the pale faces, the tight jaws, the troubled eyes. Now that we've reached a place of safety, the enormity of what's happened is starting to sink in.

Aolu, prince of Dalriada, speaks. "This is Mother Ash. She mended my ankle, which was damaged when I first came here. Her people saved my life."

Mother Ash takes one look at Scoithín, then starts snapping out orders. "Set him down over there, in the shade. Hazel, Thorny, have folk lay out soft blankets. Fetch clean water and my bag." Small folk run to obey. "Robin!" she calls.

One of the beings comes forward. He is short but of upright stance, his large eyes alert.

"Stay with these human folk," she says. "Explain about

the . . ." Her gaze goes to the Crow Folk over there in the trees, immobile on the branches.

As Illann and Garbh carry Scoithín over to the shady spot indicated, and small folk scurry about doing the healer's bidding, Brocc crouches down to be nearer Robin's level. "Why did they not fly with the others?" he asks. "Why did they not follow the call?"

"Her," Robin says. "The one called the Storyteller. She held them back."

"Who is the Storyteller?" Brocc asks, but there's no need for anyone to answer, because we can see her on the far side of the clearing, and she's almost exactly like that creature in the cavern on Swan Island, save for a wisewoman's necklace and features that are undeniably female.

"A walking shadow," whispers Elka. "One of *them*."

"She wouldn't let them go," Galen murmurs. "She held them here by some sort of spell. We tried to convince her, but without success. And now they've missed their chance."

"We saw the others fly over," says Aolu. "So many. Remarkable."

"The Storyteller cannot speak as we do," puts in Robin. "She understands only the clickity-click tongue."

The Storyteller looks as if she would bolt at the slightest hint of trouble. "Maybe there's still hope," I say quietly. "But we shouldn't rush her." I think of the cavern, and say quietly, "Elka. You try. Go slowly."

"Healer's daughter!" Mother Ash calls out to me from where Scoithín is lying. "I need your assistance now!"

I go to help her, wishing I could see in both directions at once, but soon I'm busy passing cloths and sponges, and I only catch glimpses of what's going on behind me.

I see Elka kneeling down a couple of paces from the little

figure. Brocc does the same, moving with patient slowness.
The clickity-click tongue: that must be Galen with his stones.
And now Galen himself has joined that group. Next time I
look, the four of them are holding hands, forming a circle.
They don't seem to be talking. But maybe they are, in some
silent way. I want to keep watching, to wait for some moment of magic, but Mother Ash is keeping me busy. She doses
Scoithín with something that sends him into a half sleep,
then supervises as I clean up his nasty chest wound. She
readies needle and thread to stitch it up. Scoithín is conscious, and while he's trying to breathe slowly as instructed,
he's holding my hand so tightly I fear broken bones. What a
day for him.

As Mother Ash plies her needle, I sing to divert Scoithín's
attention. The warriors' marching song: *To arms, to arms, we're
ready for the fight.* A song I made up about a man with a crooked
leg who wants to marry the prettiest girl in the village, and
how he's helped by some Otherworld folk when they find him
weeping in their mushroom circle. Mother Ash asks me to
hold things and pass things and I do, singing all the while. The
song about the fisherman and the mermaid. *Ay-oh, way-oh,
waves of the sea!* From out there somewhere come the voices of
Dau, Garbh, and Hrothgar, joining in the chorus.

The stitching is done, the thread bitten off neatly, and a
bandage applied. Scoithín lies quiet. I have time to breathe,
while a bevy of small folk carry away the items the healer no
longer needs. Across the clearing, something's changed. The
four of them are on their feet, hands no longer linked. Brocc
steps away from the others. He looks at the Storyteller,
brows up in question, and she nods.

My brother starts to sing. It's not the powerful call he used
to send the birds on their great flight, and it's not the formal
greeting we heard up in the forest earlier. I can only describe

it as a wordless cry for help, though to whom I don't know. It makes my spine tingle. Such a call would surely wake the deepest sleeper, though on his makeshift bed Scoithín still lies somewhere between sleeping and waking. My comrades become still, all eyes on Brocc, save those of Mother Ash, who halts in her work to gaze out toward the pines. The small folk, too, seem frozen in place. A moment of change. A moment of magic.

As the song rings out, the Crow Folk in the trees begin to stir. It's as if they are awakening from a hundred years of sleep. They ruffle their feathers, stretch their necks, blink, shift their feet on the branches. A moment later, a dark form flies down into the open space, causing most of us to duck and shield our heads. Some of us reach for the weapons we no longer carry.

"Don't be afraid," says Brocc shakily, opening his eyes. "He's a friend."

It's that same bird, the one who perched beside me in an oak as I looked down on that extraordinary scene by the lake. Brocc has called him back, and here he is.

The small ones are making anxious noises now, chittering, squeaking, muttering. "Hush," says Mother Ash. "You are safe. The prince will keep you safe. Why else did you bring him here? Quiet, now."

The prince will keep you safe? I can't even begin to understand, but it doesn't matter, because Aolu himself comes to stand beside us, and the small ones gather around him, ceasing their noise. One wraps its arms around his leg, like an anxious child. Oh, there's a song in this. If Brocc doesn't write it, I surely will.

There's a cry from across the clearing. Not Brocc, who has fallen silent. Not the great dark bird that now stands there beside him. But the Storyteller, the sharp-clawed being in the feather garment, who opens her arms as if she would embrace the bird. Shadow, Brocc called him. The Storyteller is weeping. They are comrades, perhaps kinsfolk. The bond between them is plain. I think of the hundred years or more, and wonder how long it is since these two last met.

"She wouldn't let them fly," murmurs Mother Ash. "She held them back, kept them here, for she feared what this bard would make them do. Acts of violence. Terrible things. But they—the prince, the warrior—coaxed her out of her prison. They spoke to us all. And now, all depends on her."

The warrior she speaks of must be Galen, who speaks the clickity-click tongue. And the prince, it seems, has also played a role. It's plain he's much loved by Mother Ash's people. As for Shadow, he's only waiting for the Storyteller's word, I can see it.

She puts her arms around him; the two share an unlikely embrace, her face against his neck, his wings curved tenderly around her frail shoulders. Then both step away.

The Storyteller is not the only one weeping; Brocc has tears streaming down his cheeks. He looks over at Prince Aolu. "Will you speak words of forgiveness? For her, for me, for Shadow, and for all of them, for their acts of wrongdoing? She believes them unworthy to fly home. You are a prince. They respect that. Your words will be enough. Then they can move on."

Aolu rises superbly to the occasion. Unshaven and clad in ill-fitting garments, he is nonetheless every inch a prince. He spreads out his arms as if to gather in everyone present; nods to the Storyteller and to Shadow, and reaches up toward the Crow Folk in the trees. "I am Aolu, prince of Dalriada!" His voice is resonant as a bell, his manner like that of a druid or priest conducting a solemn ceremony. "You are forgiven for all wrongdoing! You are forgiven for all acts of violence! You have served your long penalty, and now you are free to go! No more guilt, no more suffering. Go forward on paths of peace!"

The Storyteller shifts awkwardly from one foot to the other, as if uncertain of what may come next. But Brocc is not uncertain. "Fly true, Shadow," he says. "We will meet you by the sea."

Shadow responds with the three deep notes we heard earlier. Recognition. Acceptance. He spreads his great wings and rises, flying high, circling once above us, then making a course to the north. And across the clearing, from every tree, they rise to follow him. It's quick, so quick. The sky is darkened by their passing, then bright again as they vanish into the distance. The trees are empty, the Crow Folk winging home at last. Or are they?

"We will meet you by the sea?" I echo, looking at Dau. "What does that mean?" There's something in the back of my mind, something I'm suddenly too tired to remember.

"Sit down, healer's daughter," commands Mother Ash. "You've come a long way and worked hard. You were an excellent helper. I like an assistant who doesn't need everything explained. Go on, sit down before you fall down. Hazel! Thorny! Some provisions and some mead! These big folk are weary, and they have a journey ahead of them."

I do as I'm told, because she's right; my knees are feeling quite wobbly and sitting down sounds like a good idea. Scoithín is coming back to himself, asking Dau to help him sit up. Garbh moves over to assist them. The Storyteller is now seated on the ground further across the clearing, with long-legged Galen sprawled beside her. They have some of Galen's stones out, and seem to be making a pattern together. Elka watches, offering suggestions. Brocc and Prince Aolu are deep in discussion; so are Hrothgar and Illann.

More of the small folk emerge from the bushes, and I get

a closer look at them. Each is a curious blend of human and animal. Some wear clothing, some have pelts of fur or wool, some are feathered. They're just like something Father spoke of seeing long ago. However many times he told that tale, his voice would go soft with wonder when he described their neat little forms, their red caps or green scarves or pointed boots, their bright, sweet faces. They helped him then and he never forgot it. And now they're helping again. When we planned this mission, we didn't ever consider that the fey folk of this land might play such a part in it. It sounds as if they brought Aolu here to protect him, then realized he might be able to help them, though exactly how all of that came about is a story for another time, I think. They all seem to be friends now, Galen included.

Someone spreads a blanket on the grass, and gradually our comrades make their way to join us. The small ones bring provisions.

"Safe to eat," says Robin, setting down a platter of little cakes shaped like birds and beetles and flowers.

"Thank you." I'm so tired I probably would have eaten Otherworld food without a second thought, never mind all those tales about it being a dangerous thing to do. I eat, I drink. Scoithín makes a wobbly progress over to the blanket, with Garbh and Dau supporting him, then sits, leaning heavily on Garbh. Brocc is still out there with Elka and the Storyteller, and Illann has joined them. They're gazing up at the sky. I should go and find out what's happening. I start to get up, but Dau shifts over until he's right beside me, and says, "Stay here a bit longer. Just sit by me for a while." Then his arms are around me, rather awkwardly, and he kisses me on the mouth, never mind the audience. We hold on to each other for a few heart-stopping, precious moments, then sit side by side, hands clasped. It's enough, for now.

Illann's been talking to Robin and the small ones. After a while he returns to us. "We can't leave without letting the folk at the safe house know what's happened. And our horses are there. Hrothgar and I will go back and retrieve them. He and I will ride home through Hunter's Glen and on past Winterfalls. We'll wait until Sciath's men are out of the area before leaving, and we'll ask Colm and Morna to send a message to King Oran straightaway, letting him know Aolu is safe. The rest of you will head straight for the coast."

"Straight for the coast . . . why?" I don't understand this. "And how, if we're not taking the horses?"

"Brocc's ally among the Crow Folk has told him they'll need us there. Brocc doesn't know why, but he says we must go. And after that, he must find his daughter. This woman, Mistress Sciath, has her held hostage somewhere in the south."

"Somewhere in the south? No more than that?" Gods, we could spend our whole lives searching. Sciath is dead, her men are scattered and unlikely to be cooperative even if we do track them down. Oh, poor Brocc. He must be desperate. How in the name of the gods has he managed to do what he has today, with that weighing on him?

"I know where she is." It's Scoithín, his voice dulled by the draft. "I can go and fetch her. Or take Donal—Brocc—to the place."

"No, you can't," says Mother Ash. She narrows her eyes at me. "Don't even think of letting that man get on a horse until he's healed."

"You could help us make a map, Scoithín," Dau suggests. "We have plenty of folk who could go. How far away is this place? You know Mistress Sciath threatened the child's life?"

"Dau," I say. "Shh. Scoithín, is the place in Dalriada?"

"In Breifne, near the border. They wouldn't hurt the little girl. They're good folk. Idle threats, that's all it was."

"Maybe you're right. But Brocc won't be satisfied until his daughter's safely in his arms again."

"You wouldn't be wanting me to do it." The big man's face, his tone, bring tears to my eyes. "Of course not. I was with her when she sent the little girl away. I did her bidding when I knew it was wrong."

There's a silence. Then Illann says, "That's a discussion for later. But none of us will be staying here. While we could take you back to Elderbrook, I don't think that would be wise, with the brotherhood still in the area. And we won't leave you with these folk, helpful as they've been. Best go on with Liobhan's team." Before I can ask the obvious question, he adds, "In my absence, you're team leader, Liobhan, assisted by Dau. And no, I'm not expecting you to walk all the way back to Winterfalls. Talk to Brocc and the others. There are possibilities. Hrothgar and I will head down to the safe house now; the day's advancing."

"Be careful," I say. He's a comrade and a friend, one of the most balanced and reliable folk in the Swan Island community. If he thinks I can lead this team after everything that's happened, perhaps I can. Or maybe it's a test.

We gather together, all of us who are left. Mother Ash and the small folk; the Storyteller, less nervous now, though I note she stays close to Brocc and Elka; Scoithín making a brave effort to remain sitting up, though he's pale as chalk. The Swan Island team, minus Illann and Hrothgar. I hope our comrades don't have any unexpected encounters with the remnants of Mistress Sciath's brotherhood. Aolu and Galen, now sitting close together. Those two seem the calmest of all, as if their happiness is such that nothing can dent it.

"Shadow believes the Crow Folk will wait on the shore," Brocc says. "Something further is needed before they make the last part of the flight, over water. Exactly what, I'm not sure, but it relates to the curse or spell that sent them into exile. A final step."

"Scared," Elka says. "Last time they fly, old ones, young ones drop from the sky into the waves. Too tired to go on. A long flight, very long. They fear the same will happen again."

"You believe these are the same beings from your grandmother's story?" I ask. "They would be very old."

"A hundred years. Two hundred. Who knows?" says Brocc. "A long, long exile. It would drive the sanest creature half-mad."

There's a question I must ask, though it's awkward. "Mother Ash. Robin. Will we be allowed back through the portal?"

Mother Ash smiles enigmatically. Robin shakes his head. "Not that portal. Another, maybe."

"The Storyteller will lead us out," says Galen. "Her folk, too, will be waiting to fly on. It needs to be today." He glances up at the sky; the day is already well advanced. "I think the way back may be shorter. Quicker."

This is what I hoped might happen when I brought my comrades to the Hag of the Hill. Not only that we could shelter in the Otherworld, but that there might be just such a way back. But I'd thought we might emerge in the woods above Winterfalls, where Aolu was brought in. I'd imagined him and Galen going back home and Brocc heading south to find his daughter. I'd thought I might have a little more time with my parents before the rest of us went on to Swan Island.

"Elka," I say, "what's missing? The Storyteller's folk accepted the prince's pardon. Once they catch up with the others, why shouldn't they all fly on?"

"Earth, sky, and ocean," says Elka. "Aake, the spirit, torn in three. Cast away. She must return. Lead them home. You think?" She's talking to me, but she's looking at the Story-teller, that little person who, it seems, has been hiding in a cave in this forest and holding her people close while setting fear in the hearts of Mother Ash's clan. Though now she sits near them, and they don't shrink away. Her Crow Folk are gone, and she will be gone, and things will return to what they were in this peaceful place. She's a creature of earth, and Shadow, whom she embraced, is a creature of sky. And . . .

"Elka. The being in the cavern by the sea, with its visions of violence and despair . . . Can you ask the Storyteller if that is another like her? A . . . a seer, a prophet, a . . . leader?"

Elka's eyes light up with sudden understanding. "The third part." She barely breathes. "The sea. Cast away, lost, forgotten . . . I cannot do alone. Brocc? Galen? Please?"

They form their small circle again, she and the Story-teller, Galen, and Brocc. A hush falls on the clearing, though in the woodland I hear the calls of linnet and lark. Already, so soon, they are returning.

After some time the circle breaks apart. The Storyteller puts her hands over her face, as if this latest revelation is too much to bear. Elka rises to her feet. "She says yes. The one in the cavern, not lost as she feared. Waiting. We can go."

Right, Liobhan. Time to be a leader. I look around my team. "It's getting late," I tell them. "We must move. Be ready for whatever may come. We'll have to leave our weapons be-hind." I glance at the Storyteller; we can't carry iron while she is with us. "Gather what other belongings you have and say your farewells. Mother Ash, we are deeply grateful for your help. Robin, I think we owe you and your people our lives."

"Ah well," says the healer, grinning, "you've rid us of those wretched birds. That's worth a favor or two."

The small folk are crowding around the prince, some of

them weeping, some offering gifts. Under cover of this activity, Garbh comes over to me. "What about Scoithín?" he asks.

"We do as Illann said. We take him with us. He'll need a lot of support on the way; we don't want to undo Mother Ash's good work. I don't know if he has family, or where he would go in the longer term. But he can't return to Elderbrook." The big man performed the bravest of deeds today on our behalf, and spoke truth at great personal risk. But we know nothing of his life before the brotherhood.

"There's a place for him in my household if he wants it," says Aolu, who has heard this interchange. "Baodán's always looking for men of courage and strength to add to his team."

"Or Swan Island, yes?" Elka suggests. "Where bad past is forgotten. Where you move into a new life."

I blink back sudden tears. "Good, Elka. You could talk to Scoithín on the way. Explain to him how things work on the island."

35

BROCC

I feel Shadow's presence, though he has flown ahead. The need is urgent. The longer the Crow Folk stay on this shore in one great assembly, the higher the risk. If they are close to the dwellings of humankind, they are close to trouble. I see it in my mind: a farmer with a pitchfork thinking to defend his sheep, another with a flaming brand, fearing for his family. One of the Crow Folk killed, as Watcher was, and another diving in retribution, all rending talons and tearing beak. As soon as one of them is driven to violence, the pathway forward closes for all. Considering what happened the day Niamh and I left Eirne's realm, it seems miraculous that this chance has come so soon.

I'm weary to the bone. My head aches. I'm drained of music. If ever I had the smallest spark of magic in me, it is gone. But I am not alone. There is a good fellowship around me. My sister and my brother, brave souls both. My old comrades from Swan Island, with some new additions. The prince of Dalriada. Perhaps I need only walk on with them, and bear witness at the end.

Up there by the lake I nearly died. Scoithín saved me. An act of pure courage. I can hardly take it in. And Sciath . . . oh, gods, that moment. Sciath is gone. And if Scoithín was right, my daughter is safe. But I cannot fetch Niamh until this work is done, this task achieved. Shadow's voice is loud in my mind. Somewhere, the Crow Folk are waiting.

Liobhan gives orders; the team follows them with precision and speed. The little ones are distressed that the prince and Galen are leaving them. These gentle beings are no relatives of the Crow Folk or of the Storyteller. They are folk of Erin's earth, like Eirne's clan. They help us out of pure kindness.

I am not hungry, but Liobhan tells me I must eat before we leave, so I do. I think of my comrades in the Otherworld, my brothers of the heart, True and Rowan. I think of Moon-Fleet and Nimble-Swift and the others. How are they faring? Will I ever see them again? I cannot go back there. Not after what Eirne said. Not after what she did. I could never trust her with Niamh. What the future holds for my daughter, what path I might possibly follow, is a blank. Niamh is a child of two worlds. I would not have her torn between them. But how can it be otherwise?

I watch as the team prepares to depart. The Norsewoman, Elka, is a striking figure, her golden hair spilling out of its neat combat style, wheaten-fair in the sunlight. She shared a story with us, with me and Galen and the Storyteller. No words were needed, no gestures or miming or symbols. It seems the gifts of each of us combined to create something truly powerful, a sharing of images akin to what I can do with Shadow. So, the tale: The clan on the remote island, the offense against natural law that saw them banished by their own goddess. That guardian spirit breaking into parts that were split between earth, ocean, and sky. It was the same story I had from Shadow. This is their true tale.

The Storyteller showed us her doubt; she had not believed her people could keep a promise of peace. She had been sure that I, the bard working his mistress's evil will, would lead them to vile deeds if she let them go. More than that; one among them had performed an act of violence in recent times, and she believed that barred them all from moving on. When she showed us this, it was startling, for Galen was in it, fighting and falling under attack by both Crow Folk and men. The Storyteller conveyed that this attack was made in error; that the man the Crow Folk sought was one who had tormented their people, subjecting them to unspeakable acts of cruelty. She meant Dau's brother, Seanan, I am certain of it, he who burned his brand on Shadow and Watcher; he who met his end in the jaws of a monster. Was he not part of that strange band of men, the Brotherhood of the Dobhar-chú?

It was not until Shadow came that the Storyteller knew she had been wrong to hold her folk back. She knew him. They were of the same blood, and she trusted him. So she accepted the prince's pardon, released her own folk, and let them follow.

There is another part to this. Another step to take. Earth, ocean, and sky. I must find the strength to finish this. If Scoithín can move on, sorely wounded as he is, then so can I. *Oh, Niamh. Be safe, little one. Be among kind people. I'm coming for you. I'm coming soon, I promise.*

In my mind, Shadow lingers. With what little strength I can summon, I make an image for him: our oddly assorted party walking out of this place, passing through a portal, emerging somewhere within sight of the sea. I picture myself, with Liobhan and the Storyteller, looking up, and in the sky Shadow with his group of seven hovering, ready to depart. I show the pathway home. *All can rise, brave friend. All can rise.*

36

DAU

These portals can take many forms. I have seen only two: the high stone wall that guards Eirne's realm, and the rock and root formation called the Hag of the Hill. The Storyteller leads us now to a meadow bright with wildflowers, within which stands a grove of white-trunked, silver-leaved birch trees. This is not the Elderbrook forest with its ancient oaks, its tall pines, its rocky hillsides and shadowy pathways. We walk forward in wonder. Tiny birds dart about, snatching up insects that dance between the flowers. It is brighter here; surely the sun was lower in the sky when we bade the small folk farewell and thanked the healer for her help. Is time playing tricks?

Galen and Garbh support Scoithín, though the injured man insists he is well enough to make his own way. We take no chances with him; he lost a lot of blood, and we don't know how far we have to walk. The Storyteller does not speak aloud. For now, her beckoning and pointing are sufficient to keep us on the track.

In truth, it's not Scoithín I am most concerned for, but Brocc. The man looks shattered. He looks too tired to walk a few steps, let alone make any kind of journey. Not long ago he was a hair's breadth from having his throat cut. He's worked tirelessly with the Crow Folk to achieve today's victory, if victory it is. And all with the threat to his daughter hanging over his head. That would be enough to break the strongest man. Liobhan's given Elka the job of walking beside him and keeping an eye on him. I'm the rear guard, which means, I imagine, that I'm the one in most peril of getting left behind if the portal decides to shut before we're all out. Liobhan walks at the front with the Storyteller.

I'm trying to unsee Seanan's expression as he staggered backward into the lake, and the way it changed as the dobhar-chú opened its gaping maw to take him. My brother was vile, he was cruel, he did great harm in this world. He fed our father poison. He came close to destroying me. But I would not wish such a death on my worst enemy. Perhaps it was natural justice. The dobhar-chú must eat, and there happened to be a fine meal within its grasp. Perhaps it is immaterial whether the man who furnished that meal was good or bad, kind or cruel. Seanan is gone, and foremost among the many feelings that war in me is a deep and profound relief. As for the need to inform other folk of his death and of Mistress Sciath's demise, that can wait. How it can be done without implicating Swan Island is something of a challenge. Perhaps I will write to Brother Íobhar.

"Look," says Aolu quietly, pointing ahead.

The grove of birches becomes an avenue. As we walk on, the trees seem to reach out to one another, high above the path, so we're walking through a shimmering silver-green tunnel. There's a constant rustling, a soft music complementing the rhythm of our steps, and—oh, yes!—now Liobhan is singing.

From one world into another
Move with courage, move with care

Comrade, Guardian, Sister, Brother
Folk of land and folk of air.
On this earth may we walk softly
In this sky may we fly free
May our hearts echo the music
Of the ever-changing sea.

As she sings this last word, everything does indeed change. A sudden wind from the north tosses Liobhan's fiery hair out round her head, snatches at our clothing, sets the birches swaying. A moment later the trees vanish away, and we are under an open sky full of scudding clouds. The air is full of the salt smell of the ocean. We're standing on a cliff path. Far below us, waves crash onto a rocky shore. Not far to our west lie the sheltered settlement, the pebbly beach, the jetty where boats rock gently at their moorings. Across the water rises the familiar shape of Swan Island. We're home.

"Careful!" warns Garbh. "Watch your step!" For the path is narrow, and must be trodden with care even by those of us who know it well.

"Wait!" calls Liobhan from the head of the line, and we pause. Brocc goes forward to speak with her and the Storyteller.

"Dagda's britches," observes Galen. "From there to here in the blink of an eye. Takes some getting used to."

"The stuff of a fine epic poem," says Prince Aolu. "Nobody would believe it was true."

"Look!" Elka has been watching the sky, and now she points to a lone bird flying toward us: one of *them*. It circles us, then flies ahead, and at a word from Liobhan, we follow. Not to the settlement; only as far as a spot on the clifftop where there is enough level ground for all of us to retreat from the edge and sit down safely on the rocks.

"Rest," Liobhan says. "Drink. Gather yourselves."

We hardly need rest. We've traveled many miles in very few steps. But the experience was odd, and no doubt there's more strangeness to come. Where are the rest of the Crow Folk? The solitary bird has come down to settle near Brocc. Not speaking; not cawing; simply looking at him. It's Shadow. The survivor.

The Storyteller reaches out a long-fingered hand to touch the creature's plumage gently. She bows her head, and the bird returns the gesture of respect. Then, before our eyes, the Storyteller changes. The feather cloak or robe rustles and shifts to wrap her body, becoming one with it. Her arms become wings, her legs and feet reshape themselves, and within a count of ten she is a bird. Elka murmurs under her breath, in her own tongue; her face is alight with wonder.

"She, too, will fly," says Aolu.

"But where are the others?" Garbh speaks the question that must be on all our minds.

And I hear Brocc say, "Not far away. But I can't do it. I have no strength left."

Then, for a while, there is only the wash of the waves and the cries of gulls overhead. We're visible from the mainland settlement. I see Haki down there, and Brigid and the boatbuilders, standing on the road watching us.

"Liobhan," says Elka. "Earth, sky, and sea, yes? We do it?"

Liobhan's intense features are transformed by a smile of sheer joy. This moment will be in my heart forever. As I look at her I make a decision. I will take a risk. Not now, but soon, when all this is over.

The two women stand side by side, looking out to sea. Elka raises her voice in a high, pure chant. A moment later, Liobhan's deeper, richer voice joins in. The power of their call makes my spine tingle. It rings out over the water. My skin prickles as a sudden shaft of sunlight breaks through cloud, illuminating the western point of Swan Island, where that cavern lies. Elka sings words in her own tongue; Liobhan sings of flight and freedom. And from the island a bird rises, dark wings against the sky. It spirals upward, then circles as if waiting.

The scarred creature by Brocc's side lifts his own wings and flies out from the clifftop. In his wake comes the Storyteller, at first a little unsteady in her bird form, but soon soaring high with the other two. Liobhan and Elka keep on chanting, each covering for the other's snatched breaths. The sound is otherworldly: the deepest of magic. The power of it thrums through my body. The three birds dance in air, turning and twisting around one another in an intricate series of moves. The sunlight brightens. I close my eyes for a moment, and hear a gasp from my companions. When I look again there are no longer three birds, but only one. She is a great golden creature something like an eagle. She moves with power and grace, her plumage shining bright as she passes over the glittering ocean. A being born of story, of prayer, of hope. A being returned to life by her people's courage. This is truly a tale of wonder.

"Farewell, Shadow!" calls Brocc. "I will never forget you!" He gestures to the women, and they all turn to face inland. There is a band of trees, a woodland, that stretches southward behind the settlement, forming a shield between Swan Island's domain and the world beyond. It's the place where Deirdre and Liobhan go to gather wild herbs. Now those trees are darkened by Crow Folk. Perched on every available branch, they move restlessly, lifting their feet, ruffling their feathers, full of the longing to depart.

Brocc finds his voice. As the women's song grows quieter, he joins them with his own chant.

> *Three blessings from the lips of a bard:*
> *In times of trouble, courage*
> *In times of sorrow, hope*
> *From exile, a safe journey home.*

He raises his arms, spreading them wide.

"Fly free!" he calls. "Fly true! She will lead you home!"

They rise, a great feather cloak that shifts and moves in a swirling pattern. They circle once, as if in recognition. Then Aake beats her powerful wings and makes a course northward, leading them, and the flock crosses over Swan Island and away. As they vanish from sight, the chant comes to an end. Liobhan and Elka have an arm around each other as they recover their breath. Brocc dashes away tears. I am without words. What can a man say about something so remarkable?

Scoithín, too, is weeping. "Gods, that I saw such a sight! After all the wrong I've done, that I was blessed by this . . ."

"I'm no great believer in gods," I tell him quietly, putting a hand on his shoulder. "But your acts of courage make you entirely worthy, brother. You saved a life at risk of your own. You set aside your own safety to speak truth. Now sit down, will you? I see friends on the way up the hill. They'll find you a place to rest. It's been a long day."

He sits, which is just as well, because racing up the path from the settlement comes a solid, brindled form with his mouth open and his tongue hanging out. Justice barrels into our group, almost toppling the prince of Dalriada. The dog turns on the spot a few times, then plants his front feet on my chest as I fondle his ears in the special way he likes. "Good boy, Justice. My best boy! Oh, I'm so glad to see you!"

I don't care if my comrades see me crying. "Down, Justice. Good boy." He obeys, though he can't keep still. Every part of him is wriggling with delight.

Then Haki is here, and Brigid, and the boatbuilders, Cairenn and Odar. After them comes Deirdre, who gives Liobhan a big hug, then after a brief conversation goes over to crouch down beside Scoithín and talk to him. He'll be well looked after here. Fergus, who lives on the island, is an expert physician. I know it from personal experience, though I failed to show proper appreciation at the time. Between him and Deirdre, Scoithín will have the best of care. That's if the elders are prepared to let him stay. We've already brought him far closer to the island than outsiders are generally permitted. I'll need to talk to Brigid as soon as we get to the Barn. But perhaps I don't need to. Illann passed the leadership over to Liobhan, and it's Liobhan who now greets our welcoming party, not with any formality, but by stepping over to Brigid and putting her arms around our hard-bitten combat veteran.

"As you see, we're home," Liobhan says. "And we've brought Prince Aolu. We have a long and strange story to tell. Illann and Hrothgar are safe; they're coming later. And we have a wounded man with us, a friend seeking safe haven. A fighter. A good man. He needs to stay here, at least for a while. Perhaps longer. His name is Scoithín."

"Morrigan's britches," says Brigid, her thin lips twisting into a smile. "Welcome, my lord. I'm delighted to see you safe and well." A nod to Aolu. "Anything else I need to know?" Her gaze moves to Brocc.

"Only that we'd love a bath, some food, and time to breathe before we tell you the tale," Liobhan says. "A message should go to the island, asking Fergus if he'll come over and look at Scoithín's injury. I can't think past that right now."

"You'll be wanting your cottage for the night," Brigid says, with a quick glance my way. "We'll find room for the rest of you at the Barn. As for Fergus, he's over here already. One of the children sprained an ankle." She looks out to sea, where the sun still touches the water in points of bright light, like moving lamps. "They're gone," she says. "They're really gone. I've never seen anything like it." And as we move down the hill toward the settlement, she turns to me. "I'll be glad to have my bed to myself tonight," she says, grinning. "That dog of yours is an expert blanket thief."

To which I can think of absolutely nothing to say.

37

LIOBHAN

I have something for you."

Dau's sounding unusually hesitant. We're in the cottage at last, and despite our party of eight arriving unexpectedly in the settlement, Brigid has arranged things so it's just the two of us. And, of course, Justice, who's refusing to let Dau out of his sight. I've resigned myself to the fact that the dog will be sleeping on the bed tonight. We've bathed, we've been fed, we've told our tale as well as we could. Tomorrow, Brigid wants Dau and me to go over to the island and give our account to Cionnaola directly. Nobody's said I'm in trouble. Yet. Tomorrow, Galen and Aolu will ride back to Winterfalls. Brocc's eager to head south and look for his daughter; he doesn't want anyone else to do it. I've persuaded him that he needs one night's rest at least.

"Don't laugh," Dau says. He's taking something out of the pouch he had on his belt when we went up into the forest this morning. Morrigan's britches, only this morning! I'm still wondering if there was one of those quirks of time when we came through the birch portal. Dau hands me a neat small package, wrapped in cloth and secured with a cord. "A gift. I made it for you, with some help."

I'm too surprised to say a word, let alone laugh. I unwrap

the protective wrapping with care. It's a book, beautifully
bound, and small enough to be held in the hands while reading. "A Book of Strange Tales," I read aloud. On the title page
there's a tiny ink drawing of a dragon breathing forth a mi-
nuscule puff of smoke. I turn the page.

"A scribe did the binding and the pictures," Dau says with
diffidence. "But I wrote the stories."

Oh, he's so hesitant! Does he really imagine I would mock
such a perfect gift? The first tale is called "Under the Moon"
and it's about a dobhar-chú. Dau's script is neat and even; he's
taken time and care over this. The tale is charming and
funny, and contains nothing at all of blood and gore. The
scribe has done a picture of a dobhar-chú and his mate curled
up on the riverbank together, so closely entwined that I can
hardly tell where one ends and the other begins.

I think I might be crying, just a bit. "When did you have
time to make this?" I ask him.

"During my very awkward stay in the household of Lady
Almha of Darkwater. I'll tell you that story later. Let's just
say escaping to the scribe's workroom for a few hours at a
time was quite a blessing. I told the lady I had a sweetheart
back home who loved strange old tales, especially ones about
monsters, and that I was gathering lore to make a book for
her. Good excuse for asking questions locally about the
dobhar-chú and visiting unusual places."

I feel curiously disappointed by this explanation. To cover
this, I turn more pages, finding a tale about clurichauns and
one about selkies.

"Only," Dau says, sounding as if he, too, might shed tears,
"it turned into something different. I missed you so much,
Liobhan. Like a bit of my heart had been ripped out. All the
time I was playing a part in Darkwater, I was thinking of
you. Seeing you that evening, hearing you sing . . . it was all

I could manage not to leap up and make an exhibition of myself. Every single night, lying in bed, I wanted you there beside me, in my arms . . . your touch, your voice, your warmth. So the book of tales for the imaginary sweetheart turned into a . . . a gift of the heart. I made it for you, only for you."

And he made sure it was on his person when we went up into the forest ready for a fight, just in case he couldn't get back to the safe house to retrieve it. "As you can see," I say somewhat indistinctly, "you're making me cry. I missed you, too, Dau. I worried about you all the time, even though I know how capable you are."

He clears his throat. "I have something to ask you. I know what you think about this, and I respect that. But I want to ask it anyway."

"Go on, then." I imagine him asking solemnly whether Justice can sleep on the bed, and suppress a smile.

"Would you consider . . . would you think about . . . I don't know if . . ."

"May I say something?" When he nods, looking entirely miserable, I say, "Consider that we've just returned from an astonishingly successful mission, the two of us. Remember how reluctant they were to send us out together? So that didn't happen, but when it came to the hardest part we ended up in the same team, and look what a success it's been. I'd say we've proven we can work together, even though we're sharing this cottage and this bed and everyone on Swan Island knows it. Though I may still get thrown off the island for disobeying orders. You need to remember that." A long pause. "You can go on now. If you want."

"I love you," Dau says simply, reaching across to take both my hands in his. "I'd like us to be handfasted. I don't expect you to turn into the sort of person who's content to stay at home and raise a brood of children and warm her husband's bed. The woman I want to share my future with is not that woman. She's this fearless and wonderful person here." He's looking straight at me now; he's found his courage. "Will you marry me, Liobhan? Before you answer, note that you've just provided the perfect argument to support my case."

I lean over and kiss him gently. "You can take that as a yes. Though you can be the one to explain to the elders that we expect to be sent out on missions together just as if we weren't wed. And I'll expect you to take a turn looking after any children that might happen along, since even the best precautions aren't entirely foolproof. As for the handfasting itself, I'd like us to wait until Archu gets back, and Hrothgar and Illann. Just a quiet celebration."

"What, no singing and dancing, no ale and roast meats, no flower garlands and friends making silly speeches?"

"Maybe just a little of all that." I can't wipe the grin off my face. "I doubt we'll have much say in the matter."

38

BROCC

We're here at last. A farm somewhere in Breifne, a place I'd never have found on my own. Last time I was in this area, I was cold and hungry and deep in despair. My sanity was hanging by a thread. Today I am well prepared. And I have good company. I had thought to come alone on this rescue mission, but common sense prevailed. It will be a long ride home for Niamh. And despite Scoithín's assurances I cannot be certain these folk will give up my daughter without protest. I do not let myself dwell on the possibility that she may not be here; the long arm of Mistress Sciath surely does not reach out after death to exact vengeance. Nonetheless my heart is beating fast as we ride up to the house: Elka, Garbh, and me.

Many of the Swan Island team wanted to come. Refusing Liobhan the opportunity was the only penalty Cionnaola placed on her for breaking rules. I don't believe they would ever banish her from the island. She's far too valuable. No penalty was meted out to Elka, and she rides with me because of her gift with children, along with her various other skills. Garbh is stalwart, strong, and reliable. Both of them understand my situation as well as any relative stranger could. I might wish for Liobhan or Dau to be with me, but these companions suit me well.

"Ready?" I ask them when we've tied up our horses, and both nod. We're armed, but only to the extent that any wise traveler should be. When we stopped at wayfarers' inns for a night, all folk could talk about was the disappearance of the Crow Folk. A blessing. A wonder. Magic. Or maybe some kind of bird plague, though no corpses were found. Certainly, a cause for the drinking of much ale and the telling of wild tales. I listened quietly and drank a single cup of mead with my companions. I offered neither tales nor songs. Perhaps that part of my life is over.

The door opens. If I hoped to be greeted by a friendly farmer holding a beaming Niamh, I thought wrong.

"Who are you and what do you want?" asks a boy of about twelve, using the back of his hand to brush lanky hair out of his eyes, and leaving a streak of what looks like blood. Both his hands are ruddy with it.

"Master Donal of Winterfalls, here to collect my daughter, Niamh." I speak calmly. "I believe she was placed in the custody of this family some while ago."

The lad looks at me rather blankly. "Niamh," he echoes. My heart sinks. He's never heard of her. The directions were wrong. She's not here.

"Mam!" the boy yells, making all of us start. "Where's Niamh?"

"We come in, please?" Elka speaks sweetly, all good manners.

The boy steps aside as a woman comes bustling from the back of the house, wiping her hands on her apron. "No need to shout the house down, son." She sees me and halts. "Oh. You'll be here for the little one." A pause as she takes a good look at us; she seems less than pleased with the situation, but she summons up a smile in response to Elka's, and invites us in. "Master Donal. Yes, we wondered, when we heard nothing for so long. We'll be sad to say good-bye to Niamh; she's part of the family now. Son, go and fetch her, will you? Wash your hands first, there's a good boy. He's been plucking chickens," she adds as an aside.

I find myself suddenly unable to speak. My throat is tight; my body is tense; I can hardly breathe. Fortunately, Garbh and Elka do the necessary talking. We are taken through to a big kitchen at the back of the house, where the aforementioned chickens are hanging in a row and a girl is continuing the plucking process. Feathers everywhere, and a smell of blood. The boy sluices his hands in a bucket and goes outside.

"Sit down, please," the woman says. "We didn't know you were coming. It's something of a shock, Master Donal. I'll need time to get Niamh's things together, and . . . Do you have a cart? How will she be traveling? She does like a nap in the middle of the day."

I hold back the words. *She's my daughter. Who better than I to understand what she needs?* "We're well equipped, Mistress Dáire." Scoithín has given me her name. He wanted so badly to come with us, but he needs time to recover not only from his wound but from all that's happened. At Swan Island, he's the newest of the new. Still, he was welcomed there, an unlikely hero, without whose courage things might have been very different indeed. "We have a basket in which she can ride, and we'll make frequent stops."

And now, here she is, carried on a hip by the boy. She's wearing a little gray tunic and warm leggings, and offering a dazzling smile. When she sees me, it fades. Danu's mercy, have I been gone long enough for my beloved daughter to forget me altogether? What cruelty is this?

"Here," says Elka, stepping forward with confidence to

take the child bodily from the boy's arms. She moves to the far end of the room, away from the chickens, and sits down on the floor with Niamh between her legs. Both of them look entirely at home. Elka fishes in her pouch, brings out a woolen ball, plays at hiding it and making it reappear. Niamh reaches for it, grabs, reaches again and captures it. She gurgles with laughter.

I realize I am shedding tears. I wipe my cheeks. I must be Master Donal for a little longer. "She looks very well, Mistress Dáire. Thank you for your good care of her. Might we prevail on you for a bite to eat and something to drink before we move on? Perhaps my man could help pack up Niamh's things."

Garbh moves the purse of coins in his pouch, producing a faint jingling sound.

"And of course, we will pay you further for your services," I say. There was some arrangement with Mistress Sciath, I hate to think what. I hope these folk will not demand a fortune for what they've done, though I would pay anything to ride away from here with my daughter safe.

"We've been well paid already, Master Donal. And it's been a joy to have little Niamh here. She took a while to settle, but she's been happy playing with the bigger ones. Charmed every one of us, didn't you, sweetheart?"

While Mistress Dáire puts the kettle on and slices bread, I get down to Niamh's level. At first I only watch while my daughter plays with Elka, though when the ball strays into my territory I hide it, then find it again, and Niamh takes it from my hand without hesitation. After a while, I begin to sing quietly: the counting song about the frogs and bees and dragonflies, which my daughter knows well. Niamh's gray eyes go wide. She stares and stares, the ball forgotten. It seems the song is a startling revelation, whether good or bad

I cannot tell. I sing the lullaby about the birds falling asleep one by one, until only the owl is left to talk to the moon; Elka hums along in the refrain. When I am done, and Mistress Dáire is setting out platters and foodstuffs on the table with her son's help, Niamh starts to cry, not loudly as she might if she were hungry or wet or hurt, but a soft sobbing that breaks my heart. Does my own daughter not know me, even after that? Tears sting my eyes.

"Look," says Elka quietly. My daughter is stretching out her arms toward me. I gather her close and hold her against my shoulder, patting her back, humming "Flight of the Fair One." I rise to my feet, somewhat awkwardly lest I drop my precious burden. I carry my daughter to the window and look out over the farm, where walled fields hold healthy-looking sheep, and closer at hand, chickens roam freely. A man whistles as he walks across the yard, a dangerous-looking farm implement carried with confidence over his shoulder. Two black-and-white dogs go with him, one on each side. Scoithín was right. This is a good place. We've been so lucky.

Niamh is quiet now, but for the occasional sniff. Her little hands grasp my tunic firmly. Her body is warm, relaxed against me. Today will be another parting for her. Another farewell. When she is grown, how much will she remember?

Words of congratulation. Words of support. Words of welcome, words of love and concern from my parents. They flow past me half-heard and vanish into nothing. I walk in a different world, a world where there are no clear pathways. A world in which the only true constant is my daughter. Here at Winterfalls she is surrounded by folk who can tend to her every need, wipe away her every tear, ensure she is safe and warm and happy. Her grandmother and grandfather. Her newly found Uncle Galen, and the equally besotted Uncle Aolu. Every person in the prince's household loves this child, half-fey though she is. And I love her. She is sun, moon, and stars to me. But I am adrift. There seems no place for me in this world, nor in the world from which my wife banished me and my daughter. I will not say *her* daughter. On that terrible day, Eirne forfeited any claim to Niamh.

My parents would welcome us home, of course, whether to live with them in their cottage or to stay here in Prince Aolu's residence, where he has offered us safe haven. Is that not what I wanted, that Niamh should have as happy a childhood as I did, surrounded by family and friends? It seems like a simple choice. But if she grows up as I did, knowing little of her fey heritage, she, too, may face the same impossible choices, make the same errors, feel as miserable and untethered as I do now. And if we stay here, what am I to do? Pretend to be a courtier? Ask my father to teach me thatching, or learn my mother's craft? In truth, I have little inclination for either. I am a musician. That life is spent on the road, traveling from one settlement to the next, playing for festivals and weddings and in the halls of nobility, earning enough to pay for a night's shelter, a bite to eat. No life for a man with a child.

And there is no life for me in the Otherworld, though I found magic there, and friendship, and work I could do well—making music to keep the clan happy; setting up the patrols with Rowan and True; offering the best advice I could when things got hard. Though Eirne always listened to Nightshade before anyone. Oh, that terrible day! The memory still pierces my heart. Perhaps my whole life will be one of farewells.

Niamh makes a burbling sound, and I look up. My mother has entered the walled garden where my daughter and I are sitting on the ground. Niamh has been examining a clump of grass with great interest.

"Brocc," says Mother. "You have a visitor."

I look around, not sure whom to expect. It's only a matter of days since we arrived back here. Garbh and Elka, their duty done, returned to Swan Island. Fine folk, both of them, as is Scoithín. He will be pleased to know his trust in Niamh's carers was justified. I am glad he is staying on the island. The man deserves what he has found there: a home, respect, true friends.

"Not here." Mother crouches down to greet Niamh. "Over at Dreamer's Wood. Your father sent a message. Come with me, we'll walk there. Bring Niamh."

I don't ask questions. In truth, I don't much care who this visitor is. This is most likely a strategy of Mother's to get me moving, in hopes of jolting me out of my despondent state. I pick Niamh up, settle her on my hip, and follow Mother out past the gate guards and across the fields toward my childhood home, the cottage nestled under the fringe of Dreamer's Wood. Smoke rises from the chimney; Father has the fire going. I see no horse tethered outside.

We pass grazing sheep, cows placid in their field, ducks by a small pond, a shepherd with a dog at heel. Niamh is captivated by all, waving her arms and letting out excited squeals. I wish I could sing to her. I wish I could sing songs of joy and laughter and purpose. But I have lost the heart for it.

At the front door of the cottage Mother pauses. "Go around the back, Brocc. Pass Niamh to me, here." And when I look blank, she adds, "I'll bring her out soon. Go on."

I walk around the path to the patch of greensward that lies between our garden and the edge of the woodland, an area Father keeps neatly scythed. And there is the visitor, a tall, pale man clad in a dark cloak that moves around him with a life of its own. That cloak may be Conmael's only self-indulgence. My mother's fey friend, the man who may or may not be my true father, is both wise and generous. The last time I saw him was at my own request, when my Other-world comrade, True, was in desperate straits. Has Mother summoned this powerful person to give me a good talking-to? Surely not. I know he and she have been friends since they were children. Conmael has never forgotten the favor young Blackthorn did him then, though according to Mother he has more than repaid it.

"Conmael," I say. "Welcome." My voice sounds flat and sorry to my ears.

"Greetings, Brocc. Come, walk with me a little."

We follow the path around the edge of the wood, then in under the trees. A good place to talk privately; few local folk venture close to Dreamer's Pool, which holds a particularly perilous kind of magic.

"So, the Crow Folk have flown home," he says. "You achieved what nobody else could. Thanks to your persistence and presence of mind, not to speak of your bardic talents, they are free at last. And your daughter is safe. Yet you are full of sorrow. You seem surprised that I know this. The story has come to me from many voices."

"I don't belong in either world." The words come spilling out, the ones I have been unable to say to anyone else, even my parents. "I'm neither one thing nor the other. I'm no hero, Conmael. If I had never gone to Eirne's realm, if I had not walked away from my human family and my work on Swan Island . . ."

"Then the Crow Folk would still be here, in exile and suffering, and there would have been even more losses. And your daughter would not have existed. Brocc, the world is full of hard choices. Sometimes we get them wrong. Sometimes we lose our way. But you are brave and wise, my boy, however helpless you may feel at this moment. You have your parents' strength and goodness, not to speak of the special talent that comes from another source. You have done great things already. And that is only the start."

"The start of what? My first responsibility must be to Niamh. She is a child of both worlds, like me."

"And like me," says Conmael quietly. "A dilemma, yes. Will she grow up here at Winterfalls, in the love and security of her human family? In doing so, will she never return to the world in which she was born, the world of magic and wonder and mystery? Will she grow to be a woman with those earliest memories still nagging at her mind? Will she always be seen as somewhat different? Are these the questions that set confusion in your eyes, Brocc, and silence your singing voice?"

We stand awhile under a graceful willow. The sweet voices of birds come to my ears, a chorus full of the joy of the coming summer. And I blurt out a question that perhaps I should not ask. "Is that why you brought me here as an infant? Because the same questions troubled you?" It's as good as asking him if he is my father.

"My childhood was not a happy one. I wished to ensure yours would build you strong and wise and good. I chose a family I knew would do just that. Brocc"—his tone changes—"you are a child of both worlds, as I am. Would you wish you had not grown up in the human world with this mother and father? Would you then have been content?"

"You didn't answer the question."

Conmael is silent for a while. His high-boned features are somber. "It is in our nature to question," he says eventually. "To be forever restless, torn as we are between two worlds. I am no different from you in this, son. We strive and we serve. We do not work to better our own condition, but that of others. I think it unlikely that your daughter will be any different. But you can ensure she grows up strong. Knows kindness, courage, wisdom, security, before she sets out on that journey to knowledge."

"How? How can I be a good father to her if part of me yearns to go back to the Otherworld and make sure my friends there are safe? How can I be the bard who sings and plays and makes magic, and the loving son and father and brother, and also a man of courage and resolve, a fighter for justice and fairness? I will not abandon my daughter to the care of others, even if they are my closest kin and beloved to me."

He looks away. My words were ill-chosen, perhaps. I've hurt him. But it's the truth.

"You're a fine man," Conmael says, and there is a fragility in his tone that jolts my heart. "A son any father would be proud of. A comrade any leader would welcome to his team. A bard of rare skill. And you will make as good a father as Master Grim, which, believe me, is a very fine father indeed. Brocc, I have a proposition for you."

I cannot imagine what he's going to say. There surely cannot be any solution to my dilemma.

"I have not spoken to you of my own vocation," Conmael says. "It could be described as fighting for justice and fairness—precisely the words you used. It is work that requires both courage and resolve, as well as quick wits and flexibility. A talent for music would not go amiss on occasion; sadly, I lack that gift myself. Folk call on me in need, and I try to be there. Indeed, I am something akin to the warriors of Swan Island, save that my work lies in the Otherworld. Or mostly so; I once aided your mother with a task that brought me into this realm."

I am full of wonder, not so much that he has chosen to tell

me this, as that I never asked my mother exactly what Conmael did. "And you aided me when True and I were lost on
the Long Path," I say. "Doing good. Standing up for what is
right. Helping folk heal."

"You might join me," he says with a certain diffidence.
"We would work well together, I think."

I can see it. A way forward. A great work for good. "You
forget one thing," I say.

"Your child? She is young, yes, and needs her father. That
I understand. But she is well loved here; Master Grim spoke
to me of this. If you were sometimes away, others would tend
to her and love her and teach her. I would ensure you had
plenty of time with her, Brocc. I am not without compassion.
I am capable of learning from my own errors. Your brother
lives just over the fields; that house, too, could provide
Niamh with loving care."

Oh, gods, I love this idea more than I can say. Perhaps
more than I should. "And the Otherworld? The clan into
which she was born? I cannot go back to Eirne; what happened between us was too bitter for that. But I miss my comrades, Conmael. I am concerned for their welfare. True and
Rowan are like brothers to me."

I had thought Conmael too dignified to grin, but it seems
I was wrong. "Who do you think called me here, Brocc? Not
your mother. Not this time. How those two knew you were
in trouble, they did not make clear. But they asked me to
check if you and Niamh were safe and well. A vision, perhaps? Or maybe the disappearance of the Crow Folk from
that area alerted them to a shift in the fabric of things. I cannot make a promise. But I think it likely you will see more of
Rowan and True in the future. I do not know your queen's
state of mind. It seems likely that with the Crow Folk gone,
she and her people will be more at peace. They will miss

their bard. They will miss Niamh. It is always possible to send messengers, subtly. To pass on good news."

A tear rolls down my cheek. "Thank you," I say, with a welter of emotions in my heart.

"You could have called on me," he says quietly. "When you were in deepest trouble. When your wife banished you, with the child. When you were cold and hungry and exhausted. When that woman held Niamh's safety over your head. You could have asked me for help. You can always ask, Brocc."

My smile feels shaky. "The idea did occur to me. But that felt wrong. Selfish. Calling you to help True when he was at death's door—that was different. Remember what you told me, when we met on the Long Path? You said solving the problem of the Crow Folk might be my mission. I tried to help them when I lived in Eirne's realm, and my efforts brought down disaster. I promised myself I would try again, on my own. And my daughter became a pawn in the game of power. In the end, of course, I did have help, from all sorts of folk. Folk of both worlds. Shadow, the brave survivor, a true leader and a true friend. My brother and sister, my old comrades. The fey folk of Elderbrook. A young woman with some remarkable gifts. And a man who was once an enemy, and who risked his own life to save mine. I needed help even with parts of it that should have been easy for me. Others raised their voices in song, at the end."

"Ah, that call," Conmael says. "It was heard even in the Otherworld. A moment of great power. Three singers, three birds, one guiding spirit. The high song of flight, and your chant beneath—*From exile, a safe journey home*. And, speaking of home, may I meet your daughter before I take my leave?"

We walk back, our steps peaceful. Mother emerges from the cottage with Niamh. My father, a giant of a man, comes out behind her, smiling broadly, though I sense he is a little nervous in Conmael's presence. The old dog, Trusty, stands in the doorway, reluctant to leave the warmth of the hearth fire. Mother sits on the steps with Niamh on her knee, and Conmael kneels beside them. I wait for Niamh to protest, as she well might when confronted by a stranger at such close quarters. But she babbles as if telling Conmael a story, then reaches out a small hand to pat his face. There's no doubt he has her approval.

"She's beautiful," Conmael says, and the look in his eyes is something to behold. Is she his granddaughter? They gaze at each other in fascination. "I see a singer, a dancer, a spirit rich in generosity, a being full to the brim with the joy of life."

"She loves music." And I haven't played for her, or sung to her, since that day in Mistress Dáire's farmhouse. "I wish I had my harp. When we . . . when we left, I could not carry both it and Niamh."

"Your harp is here, Brocc." Father's deep voice is all gentleness. "Conmael brought it."

I walk inside our modest dwelling as if drawn by magic. There, in the middle of the main room, stands the beloved instrument I have played since I first set finger to string as a boy eight years old. It's a little out of tune, as one might expect after a journey, even if that journey may have been shortened by magic. My hands move almost despite me to pluck a string, tighten a peg, check another. When the tuning is to my satisfaction, I sit on a bench, set the harp on my knee, and play. My fingers are hesitant at first, but as the melody I made for Niamh rings out they gain both strength and confidence, and the music flows. I am aware that my audience has moved to stand in the doorway: Mother in front with a delighted, wriggling Niamh, Father and Conmael behind, while Trusty, apparently content with the state of affairs, has returned to his spot by the fire. I play "Flight of the Fair One" from start to end. I play "Artagan's Leap," the jig I always associate with Liobhan, though without the voice of the whistle it is less exciting. Perhaps I may play and sing with my sister again, if a celebration comes up that allows her to visit Winterfalls, or me to go to Swan Island. They might let me into the mainland settlement, as they did on the momentous day when the Crow Folk flew away. I was once a Swan Island warrior, after all. And now it seems I will be warrior and bard both, and in two worlds.

Mother comes in and sets Niamh on the floor beside me. I put the harp down. My daughter stretches out to touch the strings. I pluck a single note, making a string vibrate against her fingers, and Niamh shouts with surprise and delight. I look up at Conmael. There's no need to say yes. There's no need to say thank you. Joy must be written all over my face. Not to speak of tears. Even he is shedding them.

"I'll make a brew, shall I?" says Mother briskly. "Grim, will you fetch out some cups? Let's see . . . chamomile, lavender, a bit of this and that . . ." She busies herself finding jars of dried herbs, stirring up the fire, making sure the kettle's full. "And we have honey cakes. A celebration. Am I right in thinking that's in order?" Her shrewd gaze moves from me to Conmael, who has taken a few steps inside the house. I think this may be a first for him.

"A celebration of life," I say as I help Niamh pluck another string. "Of music. Of hope. Of purpose." As the pure tone rings out, I think of Shadow and his people. My mind conjures an image: a wild northern reach of ocean, an island, steep and stark, the sun lighting the water, and in the air above, Aake, the great golden bird, leading her tribe to safe haven. And I know deep in my heart that now, in this moment, all have come home.

ACKNOWLEDGMENTS

Thanks to all who have helped bring this book, and this series, to fruition. *A Song of Flight* is dedicated to Aiki Flinthart, whose expert assistance with combat scenes was invaluable. Aiki faced her terminal illness with courage, humor, and grace, and maintained her generous spirit right to the end.

I greatly appreciate the support and professionalism of my Australian publisher, Claire Craig, and my long-term editor, Brianne Collins, as well as the excellent work of the team at Pan Macmillan. The US team at Penguin Random House did a great job of guiding this project to fruition despite the challenges of 2020—a big thank-you to editor Anne Sowards and all who assisted her.

My agent, Russell Galen, provided his usual sound insights. The team at Baror International have continued to seek out new opportunities for the series. Their work is greatly appreciated.

My beta reader, Annette McQuarrie, deserves a special mention for applying her keen eye to both the initial completed manuscript and the revised (and greatly altered) version within an uncomfortably tight timeframe.

Photo by Mike Beltrametti Photography

Juliet Marillier was born and educated in Dunedin, New Zealand, a town with strong Scottish roots. She is a graduate of the University of Otago and has had a varied career, which included teaching and performing music.

Juliet now lives in a historic cottage in Perth, Western Australia, where she writes full-time. She is a member of the druid order OBOD. When not writing, she looks after a small crew of rescue dogs.

Juliet's historical fantasy novels and short stories are published internationally and have won numerous awards.

CONNECT ONLINE

JulietMarillier.com
 Juliet.Marillier

Ready to find
your next great read?

Let us help.

Visit prh.com/nextread

Random
House